PANACEA

THE RUINED GODS BOOK ONE

ALEX ROBINS

Cover Illustration by Félix Ortiz
Cover Layout by stk-kreations
Maps and Interior Design by Alex Robins

ISBN 978-2-9576580-9-1 (paperback)
ISBN 978-2-9585811-0-7 (ebook)

Published by Bradypus Publishing
49380 Bellevigne en Layon
Dépôt Légal : décembre 2022

www.warofthetwelve.com

For Dad, who gave me my love of Ancient Greece

&

For Mum, who encouraged me to write about it

THE CITY-STATES OF TYRRIS

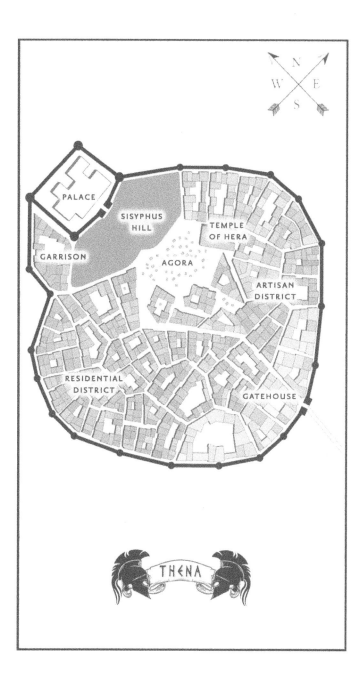

GLOSSARY

Agora: a marketplace, or more generally an assembly area, located in the middle of the city.

Amphora (pl. Amphorae): a tall jar with two handles and a narrow neck.

Andron: a room in the household reserved for meetings and entertainment. Primarily used by men, although there is some evidence of it being used occasionally for mixed-gender events.

Arche: the tip of the spear, the first rank of the phalanx.

Ariston: the midmorning meal, the first of the two meals a Tyrrean would have during the day.

Aspis (pl. Aspides): a large wooden shield coated with bronze and carried by the hoplites.

Basileus: a baron or lord. The leader of a city-state.

Chiton: a linen or wool tunic worn by men and women, fastened at the shoulder and belted at the waist.

Drachma: a silver coin. Each city-state mints its own. One drachma is roughly the daily salary of a skilled worker and the equivalent of six obols.

Ennea: the mobilisation of nine able-bodied citizens out of ten.

Ephebe: a young man serving a two-year military apprenticeship. After the first year, he receives his own spear and shield. After completing his service, he assumes the full rights of a citizen.

Hera Herkeios: the aspect of Hera known as the protector of the hearth.

Hiereiai: the priesthood. In Tyrris, there are only female priestesses, and their position is either inherited or granted by appointment.

Himation: a cape or shawl worn over a chiton.

Hoplite: a citizen soldier of the Tyrrean city-states, armed with a spear and shield.

Katasterismoi: the constellations, mythological figures placed among the stars.

Kopis (pl. Kopides): a forward-curving, one-handed blade with a single edge.

Kosmetes: a teacher supervising the athletic and military training of the ephebes.

Kottabos: an ancient drinking game that consists of throwing the dregs of wine from one's glass at a disc positioned on top of a metal stand.

Kylix (pl. Kylikes): a broad, shallow wine-drinking cup with two symmetrical handles.

Linothorax: a breastplate made from sheets of hardened linen.

Lochagos: a captain. A man who fights in the first rank of the phalanx, the foremost of a file.

Malaka: a curse word meaning idiot or fool.

Misthios: a mercenary, a soldier for hire.

Obol: the smallest form of currency. Six obols make up one drachma.

Panoply: a complete suit of armour. For a hoplite, most likely a helm, a cuirass, and greaves.

Parthenos: a virgin, used disparagingly towards unmarried women.

Phalanx: a square or rectangular military formation using a combination of shield wall and spear hedge tactics.

Polis (pl. Poleis): a city-state i.e. a city that has governance over the contiguous territory. In Tyrris, the city-states are ruled by a basileus.

Sophistes: a teacher supervising the rhetoric, historical, and geographical aspects of an ephebe's education.

Strategos: a military general, commander of a city-state's armed forces.

Strigil: a small curved blade used to scrape sweat and dirt from the skin.

Symposium (pl. Symposia): a primarily male social gathering where discussion and light debate are helped along by large amounts of wine and other forms of entertainment.

Taverna: an establishment serving wine.

Tavli: an early version of backgammon.

Telos: the file-closers, the last rank of the phalanx.

Thorakes: a bronze breastplate. The most common are the 'bell' and 'muscle' varieties.

Xiphos (pl. Xiphe): a double-edged short stabbing sword, traditionally made of iron

PART ONE

FOREBODING

INSTRUCTION

"A shrewd enemy does not attack in the midst of battle. He waits until bloody swords are sheathed and fallen bodies start to rot. Until the victors return home, tired and complacent. Then, with strength born from vengeful wrath, he strikes."

CERBRIONES, 'ALALAGMOE'

I T WAS A blisteringly hot summer's day, and the merciless sun beat down on the two figures sparring across the hard earth of the enclosed courtyard, the harsh cracks of their wooden practice swords resonating off the marble columns.

Dexios grunted as he parried a flurry of cuts aimed at his left flank, each blow sending a throb rippling from wrist to shoulder.

"Pause," he barked, stepping back and lowering his weapon. His chiton was soaked with sweat, the moist linen sticking uncomfortably to his back and thighs. Dust from the courtyard covered his leather sandals, and tiny grains of dirt had found their way between his toes, making them itch. Dexios transferred his weapon to his free hand, stretching his fingers to loosen the cramped tendons. The rough hilt of the practice sword had rubbed against his palm, and he could see a tell-tale oval shape forming there. He shook his head ruefully.

"Blisters from a training sword. I must be growing old. Or soft."

The distant screech of a hawk made him look up, idly scratching his grey beard as he scanned the cloudless sky. A dark smudge circled high overhead, buffeted by the thermals, waiting for the perfect moment to swoop down on its prey.

Dexios tried to imagine what his manor house must look like from such a height, its limewashed walls a splash of white among the neat green rows of vines and the darker clumps of oak woodlands. The grapes were ripening nicely, slowly swelling and changing colour as they soaked up the sun's rays. If the good weather continued, the harvest this year would be exceptional. And, for once, he would be here to see it.

"Father!" his opponent called irritably.

The hawk dived suddenly, flashing across the sun and down behind the walls of the courtyard, out of sight. Dexios lowered his gaze.

"Ready." The word had barely left his lips when his son lunged at him, sword arm extended in a forward thrust. Dexios dodged easily, stepping to the side and tapping his son lightly on the shoulder with the flat of his blade as he stumbled past.

"You are too hasty, Keres," he said with a tut of disapproval. "A duel is not a race, nor is it won on strength alone. You must use your wits as well as your sword. Your kosmetes has been lacking in his instruction. I will have words with him before the ceremony of the spear and shield."

Dexios's son glared back at him, breathing hard, the dark, crescent-shaped locks of his hair plastered to his forehead. His grip tightened almost imperceptibly around the haft of his weapon. There was an anger there, simmering just below the surface, drawn forth by the relentless heat and his father's admonishment.

"It is not Galleas's fault," Keres replied, each word spoken slowly and with effort. "Ephebes like myself are no longer drilled in the art of single combat, as you would know if you had bothered to visit the garrison at least once during my term there."

Dexios sighed. A part of him wanted to tell his son why he had not been able to bring himself to return to the place that had trained him in the art of war. That simply standing before the great double gates would trigger a hundred painful memories.

But Keres wouldn't understand. The ceremony of the spear and shield was a celebration of his passage into manhood. The culmination of all he had strived for. On that day, he would stand proudly beside his friends. His comrades. His brothers in arms. He would stand beside them and listen to the crowd chant their names. He would think himself invincible.

Dexios remembered the day of his own ceremony well. It had been the last time he had seen all his ephebic companions alive. For Charon, ever impatient, had soon come for them, one by one. Some had died in the very first year, pierced by an arrow or javelin, crushed by the unyielding shield wall of an enemy phalanx, or drowned in the icy waters of the Sea of Scales. Others taken by injury, sickness, or disease. For every season that passed, another

brother was lost. Their decline was as inevitable as the grape-
vine losing its leaves in winter. Slow yet inescapable.

Of the score of eager young boys who had earned their
spear and shield that day, only a handful remained, haunted
by the shades of those who had fallen before.

Loss was a terrible ordeal to endure. After rising to the
rank of strategos, Dexios had begun leading the funeral rites
himself, placing Charon's toll in the mouths of the dead
before ordering their burial or cremation. It was he who had
taken upon himself the burden of returning the shields of
the deceased to their next of kin, watching as their children
sobbed inconsolably, and their women tore at their hair in
grief.

No, his son wouldn't understand. Not yet. Maybe, in
a couple of years, when he had faced more than bales of
hay and wild animals. When he had stood in the sweat and
blood and piss of a shield wall and held his own against a real
enemy. When he had killed for the first time.

But not now. Dexios couldn't tell him now.

"Kosmetes Galleas is wrong to abandon the pyrrhic
dance," he said instead. "The spear is a powerful weapon, but
what if the phalanx collapses, or the enemy breaks through
the front ranks? If you are ambushed whilst out of formation? If your spear is shattered on your opponent's shield?
Knowing how to wield a xiphos has saved my life more than
once, boy, and if your teachers will not educate you in its
proper use, then, by Hera, I will do so myself!"

Keres dabbed at his face with his chiton. "It's not fair,"
he began. "Tychos has been—"

"Tychos is the son of a stonemason," Dexios interrupted

sharply. "*You* are the son of a strategos. People will expect more from you as a result. As will I. Now, prepare yourself."

Keres opened his mouth to reply, then closed it again when he saw the storm clouds swirling in his father's eyes. Biting his lower lip, he settled into an offensive stance, his right leg anchored behind him, his practice sword held perpendicular to his body, ready for an underhand thrust.

Dexios came at him in a cloud of dust, batting his son's blade aside and delivering two swift jabs to the ribs.

"You're dead," he growled. "Stop using your sword like a spear. That will work in the shield wall, but not in the chaotic melee that happens afterwards. Remember what I told you. The xiphos is versatile; it can stab, it can slash, it can cut. By combining these styles, you can catch your enemy off guard. Once more, then we break for water."

They traded blows, moving back and forth across the courtyard, their wooden blades enabling a speed and fluidity not possible with their iron counterparts. Dexios found himself caught up in the rhythm of thrust and counter-thrust, parry and riposte; the ebb and flow of the dance of war. Keres was finally learning to vary his attacks, forcing Dexios to give his son his full attention.

He not only absorbs knowledge like a sponge, Dexios thought, dodging a cut to the face. *He has the skill to apply what he has learnt almost immediately. He is worthy of receiving the spear and shield. Although still in need, perhaps, of one final lesson.*

He parried an overhead swing with a crack of wood and punched Keres hard in the stomach. His son gave a surprised *oomph* as the air left his body, dropping his practice sword and bending over double.

"Your second year of ephebic training will be harder than the first," Dexios said, watching his son cough and splutter. "You will leave the comforting haven of the garrison to patrol our borders. The basileus will have the right to call upon you in times of war or civil unrest. The spear and shield you are so eager to receive will be used to kill other men."

Keres knelt to retrieve his fallen weapon. "My kosmetes has prepared me, Father. I am ready."

"You cannot know that. I too thought myself ready. But the field of battle is not the training ground, Son. Your opponent will not wait for you to adjust formation. He will not allow you to regroup or retreat. He will try to end your life by any means necessary. If he cannot best you with his spear, he will use his fists, his elbows, his feet. He will knock you down and gouge out your eyes with his nails. And if you turn your back on him, he will not hesitate to cut you apart as you flee. Do you understand?"

Keres was silent. His parched tongue darted over chafed lips. He nodded.

"Very well." Dexios raised his hand over his eyes to protect them from the glare of the sun and squinted towards the corner of the courtyard where Nambe, his oldest and most trusted slave, waited patiently. The big man was leaning against one of the marble columns, his dusky skin making him one with the shadows.

"Water!" Dexios called. "And strigils before we bathe!"

Nambe disappeared into the cool interior of the manor, seemingly untroubled by the heat. Dexios had bought the slave during his first military campaign as strategos: a hard-fought series of skirmishes against the men of the south, culminating in a great victory for the Thenean phalanx on the sun-scorched drylands bordering the desert.

That was close to eighteen years ago, and since then Nambe had followed his master across the battlefields of Tyrris, maintaining Dexios's armour and weapons, pitching his tent, and washing his clothes. In time, his role had evolved from that of a simple servant to a full-time camp administrator, assisting Dexios in deciphering the never-ending stream of reports, letters, and receipts that were an inescapable part of his duties.

At the end of each campaign season, Dexios returned to his vineyards, and Nambe faithfully accompanied him, transitioning smoothly from running a war camp to managing the day-to-day business operations of a thriving winery. It was Nambe who supervised the harvesting, crushing, and fermentation of the grapes, marshalling the household slaves as easily as he did the soldiers under Dexios's command. An ephemeral respite from the atrocities of war … lasting only until the basileus called them away once more.

And so, it had always been, year after year after year. But this time it would be different. The basileus had finally bled Dexios dry. He could no longer find the will to return. Could no longer stomach any more death. For the first time since receiving his spear and shield, Dexios would refuse the summons and relinquish his officer's plume. He had already warned Letho that next season Thena would need a new strategos.

And Nambe? Dexios knew that the man had saved almost enough drachmae to purchase his freedom, along with that of his wife and daughter. If the weather held, and the harvest was as bountiful as Dexios hoped, Nambe would be a slave no longer, at liberty to go wherever he pleased. With a bit of luck, he would choose to carry on managing the estate, tempted by the added incentive of being able to own a stake in the business.

The big southerner reappeared with a set of strigils and two pewter cups filled with water. Dexios accepted one gratefully and took a welcome sip, relishing the sensation of the cool liquid in his mouth.

"My thanks."

"Fresh from the northern spring, Master. The heat has reduced the stream to a trickle but it is sufficient for our meagre needs. I have sent Lyne back there to fill a couple of amphorae so that you may bathe. Would you like me to apply the strigil while we wait?"

Dexios shot him a look. "I'm quite capable of doing that myself, as you well know. Why don't you go and help Lyne instead? Those amphorae will be heavy when filled with water."

"Yes, Master," Nambe replied with a bow of his shaved head.

"Still trying to pamper me after nigh on twenty years," grumbled Dexios, throwing one of the bronze strigils under-arm to Keres who caught it deftly. "Right. Let's get out of this Gods-forsaken sun."

The two men escaped the oppressive heat of the court-yard, entering the cool respite of the andron. Keres collapsed onto one of the couches lining the walls with a contented sigh. Dexios sat down next to him and began drawing the strigil across his lightly-tanned skin, scraping off the dirt and perspiration.

"So …" Keres began carefully. "About the ceremony …"

"Yes?"

"The kosmetes is looking for veterans to speak to the ephebes. To advise them, I think, on how best to prepare for the second year. I was wondering if maybe you would consider …"

Dexios frowned. Lifting his right leg, he ran the strigil along his thigh. "And what makes you think they'll listen to me?"

"Really? Are you so self-absorbed that you are not aware of the weight your name carries? Many believe you to be one of the greatest military leaders Tyrris has ever known, Father! Perhaps even greater than Cerbriones! Your … your offensive strategies are used by our trainers to illustrate just how effective a phalanx can be in the right hands."

"We have already discussed this, Keres. It is … difficult for me to talk about what happened on those distant battle-fields. I would rather keep such memories hidden deep, far from the light."

"Yes, yes, I know … but there must be so many inspiring stories you could tell! Tales of glory and triumph!"

Keres was sitting up straight, his eyes wide and yearning. Dexios turned to him, and for a moment his son's face was replaced by another, pale and lifeless, one cheek torn open by the spiked barbs of an enemy arrow, blood and saliva dribbling from the ragged hole.

"I have nothing to say," he said softly. "Nothing any of you would want to hear."

"But, Father—"

"Master!" Nambe's deep voice carried a tone of urgency.

Dexios dropped his strigil and ran to the vestibule. Lyne lay propped against the altar of Hera Herkeios, his face and arms covered in ugly scratches. The young house slave had a deep gash in his midriff, and blood was seeping from the wound, turning the marble altar red. His eyes were rolled so far into the back of their sockets that only the white sclerae were visible. Nambe hovered over him, his chiton spattered with crimson droplets.

"Nambe, are you hurt?"

"Hmm?" The slave seemed to notice the stains on his tunic for the first time. "No, Master. That's not mine. I found Lyne not far from the stream and carried him here. Something attacked him. Something big. There were marks in the mud around his body." He paused. "I … have seen those types of tracks before. Although never this far south. Hoofprints."

Dexios squatted down next to the injured house slave and gently lifted the torn chiton with the tips of his fingers. The jagged wound underneath was two inches wide and shaped like a comma with a deep, circular indentation over the belly that arced upwards as far as the thorax. Dexios let out a tired breath. There was no mistaking the creature responsible for such a gruesome injury.

"Nambe," he said, feeling the joints in his knees crack as he stood. "Carry Lyne to the andron and fetch some wine to clean the wound, then round up a half-dozen slaves and meet me in the courtyard. Keres? Please ask your mother to join us. We will have need of her sewing skills. Oh, and send someone on a fast horse to Thena. The physician there will know what to do."

Keres hesitated. "Forgive me, Father, but I don't understand. What sort of beast would do this?"

"Horns and hooves, Son. That can only mean one thing. Tauros."

2

TAUROS

"Happiness is the most fragile of emotions. Its conception is fuelled by a thousand positive decisions, a thousand threads woven together in perfect harmony. Yet, it takes only a single mistake to lose that feeling of contentment forever."

THE TEACHINGS OF HERA, VERSE 12.1

DEXIOS SAT ON one of the benches that lined the courtyard of his manor, cursing as he attempted for the third time to clip on his old greaves. The supple bronze sheaths had been made to fit the form of his calf muscles many years ago and relied on the natural springiness of the metal to hold them securely in place. Dexios's lifestyle and diet had improved considerably since then, his body becoming decidedly softer around the edges.

Not just growing old but fat, too, he thought to himself as the left greave finally clicked into place. A slave approached with his burnished bronze thorakes, and Dexios could see his own reflection in the polished metal. A man closer to fifty than forty, his close-cropped hair and beard silvery-grey, his dark green eyes flecked with gold. A face weathered and tanned by days spent in the sun, making him look older than he really was.

Dexios knew that his wife, Melia, hated the shorn

hair. Tyrrean men were supposed to wear their hair long, as a symbol of power and health. Short hair was reserved for slaves and ephebes. But, as was so often the case, those who established ridiculous societal traditions were not those who crawled on their bellies through the muck of the battle-ground or stood at the prow of a trireme, showered with icy brine. A year of hard campaigning and two itchy infestations of head lice had been enough to convince Dexios that the practicality of short hair far outweighed the sideways glances and poorly-hidden smirks he had grown accustomed to on his rare trips to Thena.

He took the muscled cuirass and placed it over his tunic, using the lateral pins to lock it in place. It was strangely reassuring to feel the weight of the body armour on his shoulders once more, like being reunited with a long-lost friend. Another slave held out Dexios's plumed helm, but he waved the young boy away. The tight-fitting helmet, with its wide cheek guards and narrow elliptical eye slits, would only muffle his hearing and reduce his vision. Besides, the thin bronze would offer little protection from a tauros's fists.

On the far side of the courtyard, Nambe was helping five burly slaves lace up their linen breastplates. They were the strongest of Dexios's team of labourers, trained in the use of spear and sling in addition to their duties in the vineyard. Two of them had killed a wild boar last autumn, luring it into a dead end before peppering it with stone pellets until it fell. They were good men. Hardy men. But they were not soldiers.

"Shall I fetch your shield, Master?"

It was the slave boy who had spoken. The words hit Dexios like a punch to the gut.

"Is that supposed to be some sort of joke?" he growled, his face burning with anger.

"I'm sorry, Master?"

"Did one of the other slaves put you up to it? A dare, perhaps?"

"I … No … I"

"OUT WITH IT, BOY!"

Dexios hadn't meant to shout. His voice echoed around the columned courtyard, causing Nambe and his men to stop what they were doing and stare at him in astonishment.

"It was no jest, Master." The boy was in tears, his hands shaking so hard he nearly dropped the helmet he was holding. "I am sorry! Whatever I have done to anger you, I am sorry!"

Dexios drew in a lungful of air and exhaled slowly in an attempt to calm his pounding heart. "You are new here, are you not? I have not seen you before."

"Yes, Master. I had the honour of joining your household two months ago."

My wife purchased you at the slave market, you mean, Dexios thought. *And without consulting me first. Again.*

"Then, it seems there has been an unfortunate omission in your instruction. I no longer carry my shield. It hangs in its cover on the wall above my bed. And there it shall stay. You are not to go near it — for any reason. Nor are you to speak to me of it. Is that understood?"

"Y … Yes, Master."

"Excellent. Now, go and fetch my son. Tell him to hurry up or we leave without him."

Keres soon appeared, the pure white fabric of his linothorax glaring brightly as it caught the rays of the sun.

Dexios winced. The linen breastplate was too flawless, too pristine. Armour like that had obviously never been within a hundred feet of battle. After the ceremony of the spear and shield, the ephebes would spend their second year away from the city. If Keres was sent to patrol the borders looking like he had just stepped off the parade ground, he would be mocked mercilessly. Dexios made a mental note to tell his son to smear some mud and scratch a few cuts into the fabric as soon as possible.

Nambe was handing out spears; ash wood topped with a leaf-shaped iron tip. Keres moved to take one for himself, but Dexios intercepted smoothly.

"No."

"Father, I can't fight without a weapon."

"I will not risk Hera's wrath by placing a spear in your hand before the ceremony. You will carry a sling, and you will follow my orders to the letter, or I will leave you here." Dexios turned to address the others. "We move now. I have never fought a tauros after dark, and I never want to. Nambe and I will take the centre. Two more spears behind us then slingers on our flanks. Keres, your place is at the rear. Loose formation. The tauros will be strong but slow. Our speed is our greatest advantage."

His gaze went to the sundial. They still had a few hours of daylight left.

"Husband?"

He turned to see his wife, Melia, emerge from the manor's interior, cleaning her hands with a towel. Her thin, angular face was drained of colour, her long hair drawn up into a tight bun.

"I have washed the wound with wine and sewn it shut,"

she said curtly, the tone of her voice as hard as her eyes. "Lyne did not wake. I fear he will never do so, but the physician will be the one to judge that."

"Thank you, I—"

"This would not have happened if you had correctly secured the vineyard's perimeter, as I recall having suggested to you on several occasions."

Dexios bit back a snide retort. Melia was the daughter of the region's basileus, Letho, one of the most powerful men in all of Tyrris. At the time of its conception, the arranged marriage between the two households had been seen as a shrewd power play that would enable Letho to strengthen his military might and Dexios to further his social standing.

Melia and Dexios were about as different as two people could be. Eleven years separated them — Melia had only been fourteen when the couple wed — and both held very divergent views on the world and their place in it. Dexios, a pragmatic, restrained, militaristic man like his own father, was completely disinterested in the hustle and bustle of Thena, preferring the open fields of battle and the rolling hills of his vineyards to the stifling city streets.

Melia, on the other hand, was unabashedly a socialite, revelling in the reputation and influence that resulted from her position as the basileus's daughter. She was the centre of attention at all of her father's gatherings; sycophants buzzing around her like bees to a flower, showering her with syrupy compliments and saccharine smiles. All in the hope of being chosen for a place in her coveted inner circle, with access to the ear of her doting father.

It should never have worked … yet, strangely, against all odds, it had. They had found strength in each other's differences, and for a time, Dexios had known happiness he had never believed possible.

Until the Gods had contrived to take it all away.

"Well, Dexios?" Melia was waiting expectantly for him to answer, her lips pursed.

"Tauran males are rarely found this far south," he said. "He must have been driven here by something. As for securing the perimeter … I have fences set up along our borders, but, admittedly, they are primarily to dissuade thieves and keep out wild animals. A tauros is another problem entirely."

"Another problem you failed to account for. And do you think it wise to let our son accompany you?"

"I'm standing right here, Mother—" Keres began hotly.

"Indeed, you are. In your squeaky-clean uniform. Your kosmetes has yet to declare you fit for battle. Remember that."

"I will take care of him," Dexios replied, struggling to keep his anger from returning. "As I always have."

Melia looked at him, and he recoiled slightly at the contempt in her eyes. "Yes. You have been consistently clear that you are solely responsible for our son's upbringing. Go then, and may Persephone keep you from Charon's embrace."

She stalked from the courtyard without another word, leaving Dexios to wonder when his wife's feelings for him had devolved from passive indifference to outright hatred.

The hunting party moved swiftly through the vines and into the edge of the forest that bordered the northern part of the estate. The tauros's tracks were easy to follow; he made no attempt to disguise his trail, cutting a chaotic swathe through the undergrowth, ripping the bark and smaller branches from the trees as he passed. Dexios found clumps of coarse black hair torn from the creature's pelt.

"Looks like he's heading away from us," Nambe said, trying to spy the sun through the thick canopy. "Although we'll need to find a clearing with an unobstructed view of the sky to be sure. Do you still want to pursue?"

"We can't leave him to settle here," Dexios said. "Tauros are fiercely territorial; the vineyard will be under constant threat while he stays."

Nambe nodded once and pushed forwards, motioning for the spearmen to cover him. Dexios glanced back at his son. The young ephebe looked as pale as his breastplate, his right hand gripping the braided cords of his sling tightly, his eyes darting furtively from left to right as if he expected the tauros to spring out from behind one of the ancient oaks.

"Keres."

His son flinched at hearing his own name.

"Calm yourself. The hooves of a tauros pound the earth like a beating drum. You will hear him well before you see him."

Keres smiled weakly and relaxed a little.

The beast's tracks petered out at the entrance to a narrow cave. Flies circled a half-eaten boar carcass, the stench of its slowly rotting flesh permeating the air. More animals, in various stages of decomposition, dotted the path leading into the cave itself, a grisly trail of malformed shapes soon lost to the shadows.

"Spread out," ordered Dexios, hefting his spear as he pondered his next move. He had encountered tauros only

twice before and knew them to be arrogant, aggressive creatures. They were generally found roaming the great plains far
to the north, forming nomadic herds that fought each other
for land or other spoils. This continual infighting, and the
natural barrier of the snow-capped Dorias Mountains, were
what had so far spared the human cities of Tyrris. The tauran
herds did not often try to brave the treacherous passes, and
the occasional raiding parties that made it into Ruxia or
Lendes were swiftly met by a cohort of hoplites.

Lone tauros were rare, but not unheard of. Herds followed the same pack-like mentality as wolves, with one
undisputed alpha male ruling over the others. Occasionally,
subservient males challenged the alpha for dominance, with
the loser being ostracised. The mountains offered a way
for the exiled tauros to escape persecution by his former
herd-mates.

So, the beast will be desperate, Dexios thought, warily
approaching the mouth of the cave. *Filled with resentment
and wounded pride.*

Most tauros spoke a smattering of human language.
Entering the pitch-black lair would be suicide. He had to
find a way to draw him out.

"TAUROS!" he shouted into the blackness. "I am
Dexios, alpha of these lands. You are not welcome here."

There was a snuffling, snorting sound from beyond his
sight.

"LEAVE."

The voice was deep and guttural, amplified by the acous-
tics of the cave. It was loud enough to rouse a murder of
crows from their nests in one of the nearby trees, sending

them spiralling into the air in a cacophony of angry squawks and fluttering wings.

Hawks and now crows. Not the best of omens. Both were enemies of the owl of Athena.

"You have wounded one of my pack," Dexios continued. "You must—"

An enormous shape barrelled out of the darkness, a nightmarish abomination of scraggly black hair and hard muscle. Dexios's warrior reflexes kicked in, and he dived out of the charging beast's path. A clawed hand clipped his right greave, and he fell heavily, his spear tumbling from his grasp. A scream sounded from somewhere behind him followed by the unmistakable crack of breaking bone.

Dexios picked himself up with a curse. The tauran male had his back to the tree line, hemmed in on all sides by Nambe's spearmen. He was over seven feet high, from his vicious-looking hooves to the tips of the curling, ridged horns that protruded from his skull. His jet-black hide was covered in scars and open sores that wept clear pus. Red-tinged eyes glared menacingly from under an overhanging brow.

The beast is sick, realised Dexios. *Maybe that's what drove him here.*

Of his seven companions, only six were still standing. One of the slingers lay close by in a pool of his own blood, his ribcage caved in by a cloven hoof. Dead eyes stared at Dexios accusingly.

There was a high-pitched whistle as Keres released his sling. The stone flashed across the clearing with the speed of an arrow and caught the tauros on the shoulder. He stumbled but did not fall, retaliating with a roar that made Dexios's ears ring. The second slinger let loose, but he misjudged his throw, his missile scraping the creature's arm before disappearing futilely into the undergrowth.

"Keep your distance!" Dexios cried, retrieving his fallen spear. Nambe sprang at the tauros, carving a red line across the thing's belly before leaping back out of range. A projectile ricocheted off a bony horn with enough strength to jerk the tauros's head back. Dexios used the distraction to attack, thrusting his weapon at one of the muscular thighs. There was a moment of resistance as the spear tip encountered the leathery skin before punching through into the flesh beyond. Dexios twisted the blade as he withdrew, further widening the wound.

The tauros bellowed in pain, bright-red blood pumping from his leg. A slave moved in to finish the job but underestimated the creature's reach. One huge clawed hand clamped down on the man's shoulder and pulled him close. A second hand wrapped around the slave's tibia, and he was hoisted bodily into the air. The tauros snorted victoriously and pulled.

With a sickening tear, the struggling man was torn in two, showering the tauros in blood and viscera. Ropy intestines uncoiled from the lower half, the sandalled feet still kicking and spasming reflexively. The dying slave whimpered once, then was still.

The tauros threw the mutilated corpse aside and raised his bovine head, his jaw opening wide for another deafening roar.

Then his left eye exploded.

It happened so fast that Dexios didn't understand at first until the stone pellet exited through the back of the beast's skull and lodged in the bark of an oak tree. The tauros grunted in surprise and raised a blood-soaked claw to his face, prodding at the hole. He tried to take a tentative step forward, but his injured leg could not hold his weight, and he toppled over, hitting the earth with a sodden thud.

Keres lowered his sling, his eyes bulging from their sockets. Dexios marched over triumphantly and grasped him by the shoulder. "A fine shot! Your kosmetes taught you well! Your first victory in battle! How do you feel?"

Keres turned his head to one side and retched.

BLASPHEMER

"An evil thought must be drawn forth and excised before it can take root, just as a splinter must be removed as soon as it pierces the skin. If left untended, it will only burrow deeper into the flesh. Festering. And corrupting."

THE TEACHINGS OF HERA, VERSE 1.2

D AWN CAME RELUCTANTLY to the city of Thena, seeping slowly through the early morning mist to warm the tiled roofs and cobbled streets. Soft light streamed along narrow alleyways, slipping under closed doors and half-open shutters. It lit up the colourful shops and stalls of the agora before climbing the winding road that led to the city's garrison, perched like an eagle on the side of a hill overlooking the residential and trade quarters.

The garrison was a sprawling complex of columned buildings housing the barracks, gymnasium, school, and armoury. A huge training field ran the entire length of one wall, scattered with bales of hay and encircled by an elliptical dirt track six lanes wide.

The sun's rays crept unhurriedly up the side of the structure to the second floor, filtering through an open window to alight on the sleeping face of a blonde-haired woman. Her eyelids flickered once, twice, then blinked open.

"Hera's tits, already?" Elena groaned, stifling a yawn. She sat up groggily and stretched, feeling something pop in her lower back. A golden lock fell across her face, and she blew it away irritably. Her room was a mess. Last night's dark blue chiton sat in a crumpled heap on the floor next to one lonely leather sandal. Its companion was a few paces away, dangling by its straps from the small wooden stool by her writing table.

She swung her feet off the end of the bed, inadvertently knocking over an empty amphora. It rolled erratically across the room, leaving purple wine dregs in its wake, before hitting the far wall with a clunk that made Elena wince.

She padded barefoot to her chiton and gave it a tentative sniff. It smelt of sweat and old perfume, but it was the only decent one she had left. Shrugging, she wrapped it tightly around her waist and over one shoulder, pinning the fabric in place with a couple of bronze pins.

"Belt. Belt. Belt," she muttered, tired eyes scanning her tiny bedroom. She eventually spied the offending strip of leather hiding under a pile of yellowed parchment and ink-stained reed pens. Elena pulled on the belt and knotted it twice begrudgingly. The second knot indicated that she was still unmarried and would be symbolically untied by her future husband on their wedding night. A simple thing but enough to draw sympathetic stares and the occasional raised eyebrow whenever she roamed the crowded streets of the agora.

But what all those curious passers-by didn't know — and wouldn't understand — was that Elena didn't *want* to get married. She never had. Financial security and social conformity were just not enough to justify all loss of independence.

And so, while most young Tyrrean women spent their adolescence chasing after suitable husbands, Elena had spent hers running in the other direction, fending off potential suitors with a mixture of lies, feigned ignorance, and, when all else failed, bad manners.

Over the years, the stream of bachelors had slowed to a trickle as the frustrated youths of Thena moved on to easier prey. Once Elena had turned thirty-five, the trickle had dried up entirely, which suited her just fine.

She rubbed her eyes with her knuckles and peered out of the window down into the town below. The agora was just beneath her, a patchwork of multicoloured awnings and stalls where merchants plied their wares from sunrise to sunset. It was said that whatever you were looking for, no matter how rare or bizarre, you could find it in the agora. Caramelised dates from across the Straits, honey and cheese from Lendes, wine in amphorae or decorated pots, woven wool rugs, exquisitely-crafted jewellery, tools, and weapons of iron.

The entire eastern quarter was home to slave traders who could offer men and women of all sizes, races, and colours. Elena could hear the muffled shouts of merchants opening their businesses for the day, their strident cries almost drowning out the clinking of chains and the crack of the slave traders' whips.

Beyond the agora, several hundred white-washed houses filled the space between the marketplace and the outer walls, packed so closely together that it was difficult to discern where one building ended and the next began.

Like pebbles on a beach, thought Elena, her gaze wandering over the defensive walls to the arid plains, the once verdant grass scorched to a dirty brown by the summer heat. A solitary horseman was riding away from the city, crouched low in the saddle, a thick cloud of dust in his wake. Elena watched him enviously. One day that would be her in the stirrups, feeling the powerful muscles of her steed contract and release, the pounding of its hooves, and the roar of the wind.

One day. But not today.

She tore her eyes away from the window and reunited her leather sandals, slipping them on and tightening the straps. Her satchel hung from a peg by the door. She scooped an armful of scrolls from the desk, thrust them hurriedly into the bag, and bent her neck to loop it over her shoulder. Taking a deep breath, she stepped out into the corridor, pausing only to upright the fallen amphora.

She reached the top of the stairs leading down to the common area before realising that she had forgotten her hairnet. Whispering another frustrated expletive, she rushed back to her room and fished the cap out from under her bed, securing her shoulder-length blonde hair with the tips of her fingers.

By the time she made it down to the common area, she was no longer alone. Galleas, the flinty-eyed kosmetes, lounged on one of the couches, dipping a slice of barley bread into his cup of watered wine.

"Elena!" he exclaimed, taking in her rumpled chiton and puffy face. "You look terrible. What time did you get in last night?"

She stuck her tongue out at him. "That's none of your business, Galleas, you're not my father. Even though you're obviously old enough to be."

The kosmetes raised his wine cup in salute and smiled amiably. "A good point. But something tells me that if you can't answer the question, it's because you can't remember."

Elena shot him a dark look and collapsed onto one of the other couches. A slave entered with an amphora and a plate of sliced bread. "Breakfast, Sophistes?"

The strong smell of fermented grapes assaulted her nostrils. Her hand reached out reflexively, ready to accept a cup, before her stomach heaved in protest. "Just water, please," she managed to say, waving the boy away. He bowed and retreated.

"Too much wine?" Galleas was studying her curiously, the slight furrow of his brow adding more lines to his wrinkled face.

"I've already told you, you're not—"

"Fine! Fine! But you'll never get away from here if you spend all your wages at the taverna. I thought you wanted to move out of your apartment and find your own place. How can you do that if you drink your drachmae away?"

Elena sighed. "You just can't help yourself, can you? I'm not one of your ephebes, you know."

"Aye, and I am not one of yours. I'm your friend. Friends give advice to each other, that's how friendship works."

The slave returned with a large cup of water, and Elena drank deeply, feeling the liquid calm her agitated stomach. Galleas was right. He was her friend. One of her only friends, if she really thought about it. The rowdy bunch of men and women she met with in the taverna were glorified drinking partners, nothing more. In fact, she could barely remember most of their names.

"Perhaps I have been … overindulging in my nightly

activities of late," she conceded. "I will try to find something else to do with my time in the coming weeks."

Galleas leant back, apparently satisfied. "That would be for the best. How about I take you out hunting? I doubt we'll find anything — game is scarce over the summer months — but it'll be an escape from the city."

Elena's eyes lit up. "Really? You'd do that for me? What will people say when they see us leaving together?"

He smirked. "That I'm a very lucky man."

She made a face at him.

"People will talk," he continued with a shrug. "They always do. Doesn't bother me. So, what do you say?"

"I'd love to. When?"

"End of the week? It's the ceremony of the spear and shield tomorrow, and I need to get the ephebes looking somewhat presentable."

"Is it? Already? It feels like they arrived here yesterday!"

"Hah! It's been a year, Elena. A long, hard year. The basileus will be sending most of them to our northern outposts. There have been reports of increased activity in Ruxia over the last few months. Probably nothing, but Letho is a prudent man."

"End of the week, then." She took one last swig of water and placed the empty cup on the floor. "I suppose I had better go and see what my students have in store for me today."

"A good education is the foundation upon which all else is built," quoted Galleas through a mouthful of bread.

She sighed. "I know that. And you know that. But I'm not sure *they* know that."

♋

The classroom was the newest addition to the garrison, commissioned by the basileus a decade ago, officially in an attempt to keep the city culturally relevant. Elena secretly believed it was more likely that Letho needed to draw attention to his populist ideologies from time to time to keep his citizens sufficiently docile. Thena was principally a city of merchants and middle-class workers who traditionally could not afford the prohibitive costs of private tuition. Expanding the typical physical training of the ephebes to include a smattering of history, geography, and literature suddenly made education more attainable — and the basileus more likeable.

Elena tramped her way across the training field and pushed open the door of the long, rectangular structure where she would be spending the rest of the day. The interior was already warm. It would become hot and stifling in the summer and dreadfully cold in the winter. Narrow openings allowed bored students to gaze out over the hay bales and race track. Elena shrugged off her satchel and took her place on a wooden stool at the front of the room as her students began to arrive in small groups of two or three, slowly filling the rows of benches.

She spotted Keres, the strategos's son, hands gesticulating wildly as he chatted with his friend, Tychos. On the row behind him, surrounded by his cronies, sat Helydices, the guard captain's eldest. He was a good head taller than all the others, with massive arms and legs that hung from his muscled body like tree trunks. Strong as an ox. Brains of an ox, too. Anything she tried to teach him rolled right through his skull and out the other side without stopping. Elena had managed to get him to recognise and write his name, which was already a miracle in itself. That would have to do.

She clapped her hands for silence. "Quieten down, all of you. I know the ceremony is tomorrow and that you are all eager to wrap your grubby little hands around your ash wood spear, but you're with me this morning, and we have plenty to get through." Her eyes fell on an empty spot in the front row.

"Where's Makar?"

The door banged open, and a gangly youth careened breathlessly into the room as if summoned by his name. He had short jet-black hair and pale skin; his frail body was so wafer-thin that Elena often worried that a strong gust of wind would be enough to knock him off his feet. Makar stumbled and almost fell, then righted himself with a strange half-pirouette that would have made a dancer proud. He stood there panting, a flush of red on his lean cheeks.

"Sorry, Mistress," he gasped. "Got caught up in the workshop again."

Makar's father was a one-armed jeweller named Desha, among the best metal-workers in Thena despite his handicap. Elena had met him once or twice, and he seemed pleasant enough, although definitely far more interested in his gold and silver than in people. Makar spent an hour or so every morning helping his father work and a couple more when he left the garrison in the evening.

"Where's your tablet?" Elena asked the boy.

Makar looked down at his feet as if expecting to find his wax tablet and stylus nestled between his sandals. "Ummm ... left it at the workshop, Mistress."

"Of course you did. There's a spare in my satchel that you can borrow."

She waited patiently while he rifled through her bag, found the tablet, and shuffled to his seat.

"Right, can we finally get started?"

The murmur of hushed conversations faded to silence. A score of heads swivelled in her direction. Elena took a deep breath. This was the moment she loved; the quiet apprehension before she began to impart her knowledge. The calm before the storm.

"YOU SHUT YOUR LYING MOUTH, YOU SON OF A WHORE!"

Elena's gaze snapped to Helydices, who had risen from his seat and was towering over Keres, his face an ugly shade of purple.

"Helydices, you forget yourself," Elena said sharply. "You're not on the training field. Sit down."

The brawny ephebe stared at her. "But he's lying, Mistress. I overheard him talking with Tychos. Making up stupid stories about hunting down a wild tauros."

"I'm telling the truth," Keres retorted. "Three of my father's slaves died. Why would I lie about something like that?"

"To be the centre of attention. Again. As if being the son of a strategos wasn't already enough to curry the kosmetes's favour. That old man—"

"Quiet!" Elena's voice cracked like a whip. "Do not speak of Galleas in this manner. You must calm yourself, Helydices. Now, Keres. Are you sure it was a tauros you saw? You might recall from your studies that they are rarely found this far south."

Helydices's mouth split into an ugly smile. "That's just what I was saying, Mistress. Keres must have—"

Makar cleared his throat. "I ... I have, um, I mean, they have been seen in the area before ... "

"Oh yeah, by whom?" Helydices shot back.

"My ... my father lost his arm to a tauros."

"What? Ridiculous! More lies. You planned this together, didn't you? Trying to make me look bad?" The big youth whirled on Keres, bunching his fists. "You scum! You self-righteous, low-life scum! Bastard of Zeus! I should—" He stopped suddenly, eyes widening as he realised his mistake. His cronies scattered, scrambling over each other in their effort to get away, leaving him alone in an empty circle.

Elena shuddered despite the warmth of the classroom. Prickly goosebumps appeared along her bare arms. The door swung open, pushed inwards by a chill breeze that swirled around her feet and rustled the crinkly sheets of parchment poking out of her satchel.

"How dare you utter his name," she whispered. "He is the Betrayer. The Despoiler. Chief among the Ruined. Never, ever say his true name out loud."

Helydices gave a quivering nod. Beads of sweat had formed on his large forehead. "I'm sorry, Sophistes, I was caught up in the moment. It was an honest mistake."

"Out."

"But—"

"Out, blasphemer, and let us hope that you will be spared Hera's wrath."

Helydices scanned the faces of his companions. None would meet his gaze. He would find no support there.

"Fine," he said. The others stood aside to let him pass.

He stopped in front of Makar and bent to murmur something in the ephebe's ear. Then he was gone, slamming the door shut behind him.

Elena felt the tension slowly drain from the room. She instinctively made the sign of Hera, crossing her arms and pressing her palms flat against her chest. Several of the other students were doing the same. The inside of her mouth was parched and dry. She thought back to the amphora of wine she had turned down that very morning. Imagined what it would be like to feel the fruity tang of fermented grapes on her tongue. Her right hand began to tremble ever so slightly. Elena looked down with a frown and covered it with her left.

One more trip to the taverna this evening. Then I'll stop.

"Back to your seats," she ordered. "We still have a lot to get through."

The students returned to the benches, apart from Makar who was still staring vacantly at the classroom door. Keres went to him and touched his arm gently. The boy flinched as if stung.

"What did he say to you?"

"That this was all my fault," Makar said softly. "And that he is going to find a way to make me pay."

TRIALS

"The trials should not be seen as only entertainment or a way for us to honour the Gods. They are, above all, a test of our city's strength. For the boys you see participating here today will become the men who patrol our borders and guard our walls tomorrow."

BASILEUS LETHO, 'RUMINATIONS'

THE CEREMONY OF the spear and shield was one of the most important Tyrrean festivals, a day-long celebration of feats of strength and skill culminating in the ceremony itself when the basileus of the polis presented a plain bronze-sheeted shield and ash wood spear to all of the city's ephebes who had successfully passed the first-year review.

The shield was known as the aspis. At just under three feet in diameter, it was the most vital piece of equipment a soldier could own, indispensable for forming the impressive shield walls of the phalanx and protecting its bearer from neck to knee. Once bequeathed, each shield would be decorated by its owner, with either his personal heraldry or some other image that held great significance.

Keres had been waiting for this moment for nearly a year and could barely contain his excitement. He strode out onto the garrison training field with a joyful spring in his step, his white chiton shining, his dark curls tamed by a leather headband.

"Tychos!" he called, seeing his sandy-haired friend exercising a few paces away, warming up his arm and leg muscles with a series of lunging stretches.

The stonemason's son flashed him a smile. "Keres! Today's the day! I can almost feel the weight of that shield on my arm!"

"Unless Hera strikes us down."

Tychos punched him playfully in the ribs. "Don't even joke about it! We're forbidden from pronouncing the names of the Ruined for a reason. I was half-expecting Helydices to be found floating in the river or hanging from the city walls."

"Me too. He's still alive and well, then?"

"Definitely." Tychos jerked his head over his shoulder, and Keres spied Helydices on the far side of the training field, pummelling a bay of hale into oblivion, bits of straw falling around him like snow.

"Ouch ..." Keres said. "I do *not* want to be on the receiving end of one of those ham-sized fists."

"Not going to happen," came a loud voice from somewhere behind his right ear. Keres nearly jumped out of his skin. Turning, he saw Galleas, the aged kosmetes. He was wearing his bronze thorakes and greaves, both polished to a fine sheen. A xiphos was sheathed at his belt, and his plumed helm was tucked under his arm.

How in Tartarus did I not hear him creep up on me? Keres wondered.

"Practice," Galleas said, sensing the other man's thoughts. "Practice, and the patience to wait until you were distracted." He gestured to Helydices, who had destroyed one hay bale and was moving on to another. "If you let your mind wander like that when on guard duty, you'll end up with a spear in the gut or an arrow in your throat. Stay focused."

"Yes, Kosmetes," Keres replied respectfully.

"Hmm. Your father here yet?"

"No. I'm not sure he'll be coming at all. The vineyard has been severely understaffed since the tauros attack. He's been helping Nambe prepare the grapes for harvest."

Galleas scratched at a spot on his balding scalp. "Aye, I heard about what happened. Elena tells me that it was you who felled the beast?"

"A … a lucky shot, Kosmetes."

"Defeating a tauros always takes a bit of luck, boy. If you ask me, Dexios was unwise to take you along. Putting his only heir at risk like that. Then again, he always did have a bit of a reckless streak in him."

Keres thought of his father, with his calm demeanour and austere eyes. Reckless was definitely not one of the words he would use to describe his character.

"I'm not sure …" he ventured.

"Oh, he's got better at hiding it, but it's still there. Especially when he gets angry. Gods, I remember him taking on ephebes twice his size during the trials. Beat them most of the time, too."

"Wait … you trained my father?"

"Aye. Young whippersnapper caused me no end of problems. He never told you?"

Keres shook his head. He could count the number of times his father had spoken of his ephebic training on the fingers of one hand. Persuading Dexios to talk about his past was like pulling teeth.

"It's no matter. He must have his reasons. Tell me, is there any truth in the rumour that he is stepping away from his strategos duties?"

"He is."

"A pity. He was a great tactician, Dexios. Whoever replaces him has some big shoes to fill."

Another trait of my father Galleas knows more about than I do, thought Keres glumly.

"Did you ever fight under him?"

Galleas smiled proudly. "Many times. Even fought some tauros once. A raiding incursion into Lendes. They burnt a couple of villages before we sent them packing." His eyes glazed over. "Never been so scared in all my life. The shield wall collapsed on the third charge. It was only thanks to the tenacity of our arche that we didn't scatter. By Hera, we lost some good men that day."

The sycophantic cheers of Helydices's faithful admirers brought Galleas back to the present. He tapped Keres on the shoulder and marched to the middle of the training field where a life-sized marble statue of Cerbriones surveyed the grounds from atop its pedestal.

"Gather round!" Galleas bellowed, his well-honed voice carrying easily to all four corners of the field. He was soon surrounded by twenty sweating men garbed in a mixture of chitons and loincloths. Makar was, as usual, the last to arrive, positioning himself as far away from Helydices as possible.

"Sun's high in the sky, lads," the kosmetes said. "Which means that the fine men and women of Thena will soon arrive, to be awestruck by the greatest display of human athleticism they have ever seen!"

There were some quiet chuckles and muted smiles.

Galleas whistled sharply. "I'm not joking! If any one of you fails to perform to my expectations, I'll have you all back here tomorrow running laps in the heat until your tongues fall out and your balls drop off. Understood?"

A chorus of "Yes, Kosmetes."

"Good. Now, unless you've been living under a rock for the past six months, you know what the basileus wants to see this year. Javelins, wrestling, and the foot race. In that order. The winner of each trial will receive a wreath from Letho himself. The loser will receive my boot up his backside. Questions? No? Excellent. It appears you are finally capable of following simple instructions. Now, pair up, strip off those tunics, and find some oil!"

Keres pulled his chiton off over his head and followed Tychos into the shade of a large oak tree where a group of slaves were waiting with amphorae of olive oil. Keres motioned for his friend to turn around and began lathering the thick liquid all over his back. The oil was used primarily to protect the skin from the harsh rays of the sun and the itchy dust of the training field. Galleas swore that it helped loosen the muscles, too. Ephebes were taught how to anoint themselves and their fellow soldiers efficiently — there would be no slaves at the outposts to do the job for them.

"This stuff smells amazing," Tychos said as he rubbed the oil over Keres's shoulders.

"It's not the ordinary watered-down slop we're used to, that's why. The basileus provides the oil for the trials himself.

It's probably as close to pure as we'll ever get. My father calls it liquid gold."

"Nice and slippery," Tychos agreed. "If we're lucky, Helydices will trip over his own feet, and we won't have to face him in the wrestling ring."

Keres laughed. His terrible encounter with the tauros was already fading from his mind. He could still remember certain details: the blood of the house slave drenching the soil, the whistling of his stone pellet as he released it from his sling … but they were blurred and distorted, almost as if they were the memories of someone else. Is this what his father felt after twenty years of campaigning? A kaleidoscope of half-forgotten images, far too many to count, all running together like honey mixed with wine?

Thinking of Dexios made him look towards the benches slowly filling with eager spectators as the start of the first trial drew near. His heart sank as he spied Melia alone with Nambe; his father was conspicuously absent. There were others he recognised: Elena, in her dark blue tunic and wide-brimmed straw hat, and Tychos's father, the stonemason, his bald pate already covered in sweat. Sitting next to him was the massive shape of Crenate, captain of the city guard and Helydices's father. He was wearing a linothorax embroidered with the stylised 'theta' symbol of Thena.

There was a commotion near the outer gates as the basileus arrived, flanked by his honour guard. Keres's grandfather was a short, rotund man, his ample belly barely contained by the thin fabric of his purple chiton. A circlet of burnished silver rested easily on his thinning white hair, and a variety of jewelled rings covered his pudgy fingers.

Keres watched as those present bowed respectfully. He

had never understood how Letho still managed to hold Thena under his sway. He was neither physically imposing like Crenate, nor self-assured and authoritative like Dexios. In fact, from what little Keres had seen of him, the basileus came across as meek and conciliatory. But he must be doing something right, as he had held the title of basileus for thirty years and even now, at close to sixty, showed no signs of slowing down.

Letho walked serenely to a raised dais set up in the middle of the stands, nodding and smiling to his citizens as he passed. Two slaves followed in his footsteps, struggling under the weight of a huge parasol that they moved in line with the sun's trajectory to keep their master in the shade. Pale skin was seen as an ostentatious sign of wealth in Tyrris: only the richest of men could afford to spend their days completely shielded from the sun.

Another piercing whistle from Galleas drew the ephebes to his side. The kosmetes had donned his crested helmet, its sloping cheek plates covering almost the entirety of his face and upper neck, leaving only his eyes and mouth visible. Bronze-tipped javelins had been stacked neatly next to him, the wooden poles as tall as a man and as thick as two fingers.

"Looks like the basileus is here," he said. "Let's not disappoint him, shall we? You'll get only one throw each, so make it count." He made a line in the earth with a sandalled foot.

Keres formed up behind the others, waiting patiently for his turn. He knew he was an average thrower at best, nowhere nearly as proficient as he was with a sling. There would be no wreath to be won here; he just needed to avoid ridiculing himself in front of his mother. The foot race though … that would be another matter entirely.

Whenever Dexios returned to his estate on leave, he had the habit of running a mile or two every morning to keep in shape. In recent years, Keres had slowly managed to integrate himself into his father's daily routine, initially only capable of matching the military man's long strides for a few hundred yards, then five hundred, then a thousand, until finally, he could hold his own for the entire distance. Keres allowed himself a secretive smile. He could outrun the other ephebes without even breaking a sweat. The olive wreath was as good as his.

"Stop daydreaming," said Galleas in a harsh whisper. Keres blinked. He was at the front of the line. He chose a javelin from the pile and took seven steps back from the point of release. His eyes found his mother in the crowd of onlookers. Melia gave him an encouraging nod.

Keres raised the shaft above his shoulder and ran. As soon as he felt his foot hit the throwing line, he snapped his right arm forwards with a grunt of effort, hurling his javelin skywards. His missile curved gracefully through the air and landed tip-first in the hard soil of the training field.

"Not bad," Galleas muttered, his voice distorted by his helm. "Bend your right leg a bit more and twist your body as you throw and you'll gain at least five feet."

Helydices won the javelin trial to the surprise of none present. His technique was deplorable, but what he lacked in skill he more than made up for in strength. He threw his javelin without a run-up, grinning as it sailed past its competitors to net him the olive wreath under the admirative eyes of his father.

Galleas allowed them a short break for water. The sun was now high in the sky as midday approached, and Keres could feel it beating down on his naked back. Tychos came and squatted next to him, scooping some loose dirt into his hands to help with his grip. A slave approached with a large pitcher filled with twenty numbered pebbles. Keres rummaged around inside and drew a stone marked with a two. Tychos did the same, smiling when he saw what he had ended up with.

"Well?" asked Keres impatiently.

Tychos flicked his pebble round. Another two. Keres groaned. "We will face each other in the first round? But I've never even come close to beating you! By Tartarus, what have I done to anger the Gods so?"

"Look on the bright side," Tychos replied, still smiling. "You could be facing Helydices!"

The first match pitted Makar against one of Helydices's dim-witted sidekicks. It was over in a matter of minutes. Galleas called Keres and Tychos to the circular sandpit in the middle of the training field and reminded them of the rules.

"No biting, no gouging, and no grasping of the genitals, understood? Three points to win. Take up your positions."

Keres rolled his shoulders and moved to stand a foot away from his friend. He gauged his options. A point could be won in three different ways: by forcing his opponent onto his back, pushing him out of the ring, or making him concede through a submission-hold. He was heavier than Tychos and slower. He needed to use his weight to his advantage.

Galleas gave a shrill whistle, and Keres lunged forwards with his head low, wrapping his arms around his opponent's shoulders and pulling him to the ground. Tychos squirmed in his grasp, landing on his stomach instead of his back. His elbow whipped round and thumped into Keres's ribs, who let out a surprised gasp and relaxed the tension in his arms enough for Tychos to flip him onto his back.

"One point," stated Galleas solemnly.

Keres attacked again, feinting a jab to the stomach then aiming a straight punch to the face. Tychos dodged under the extended fist, lashing out with a leg sweep as he did so, which sent Keres tumbling onto his back again.

"Two points."

"It's like you've got … worse, somehow," said Tychos, helping Keres to his feet. "Are you even trying?"

Keres growled in annoyance. His hands were slippery from the oil, and he cursed himself for not coating them with dirt as Tychos had done. He tried another lunge, but this time Tychos was expecting it and sidestepped smoothly before hammering his foot into Keres's rear and sending him careening out of the ring.

"Three points. Victory to Tychos."

"Well fought," said Keres grudgingly, holding out his hand for Tychos to shake. "And good luck."

Tychos inclined his head in thanks. They moved back into the shade as the next contestants stepped into the ring. The wrestling trial was a single-elimination tournament, with the winner of each bout moving on to the next round. Keres watched happily as Tychos sailed through the quarter- and semi-finals, dispatching his opponents with a varied combination of throws, locks, and chokeholds. He moved with a fluidity that made him appear to be dancing, never staying in one place for long, but constantly dodging and weaving like a reed in the wind.

Keres gave a whoop of joy as Tychos skilfully twisted his rival's arm behind his back and forced him to submit, securing his place in the final. The crowd burst into thunderous applause, several rising from their seats to show their admiration. Even Letho looked up from the bowl of sticky dates he was devouring and raised a jewelled hand in salute.

"Final match," boomed Galleas, his parade ground voice cutting through the noise. "Ephebe Tychos against … ephebe Helydices."

The applause faded away, to be replaced by an excited buzz of conversation as Helydices strode into the ring, his hairy chest slick with oil and speckled with droplets of blood. Tychos licked his lips nervously. Keres knew his friend well enough to recognise his fear. Helydices was a bruiser who eschewed the traditional grapples of wrestling, transforming the sport into something more akin to a boxing match.

The two finalists moved into their starting positions. Tychos had to crane his neck back to look into Helydices's eyes. Oily sweat from the larger man trickled down his beard and dripped onto Tychos's face.

"No biting, no gouging—"

"We know the rules," Helydices interrupted.

Galleas frowned. "Very well. Then, begin."

Helydices threw a heavy punch. Tychos brought his guard up and deflected the blow with his forearms. His riposte slammed into the bigger man's thigh, soliciting an angry growl. The two circled, fists raised, each searching for a crack in the other's defence. The stalls were silent, the entire crowd's attention focused on the combatants.

Suddenly, Tychos saw an opening. He dived under Helydices's guard and hit him with a devastating uppercut to the gut. Keres heard the sound of the blow from where he was standing a few feet away, like a mallet hitting a slab of meat. Helydices doubled over in pain. All Tychos had to do was knock him down. He flicked out a low kick, aiming for his opponent's tibia.

Helydices *dodged*.

Tychos was so surprised that he stumbled forwards, arms flailing. An enormous hand caught his left arm just below the shoulder.

"Submit," Helydices wheezed, still recovering from the punch to the abdomen.

"No."

The large ephebe twisted, and Tychos grimaced in pain. He dropped to his knees.

"Submit."

"Ne … never." There was a commotion in the stands. Both of the men's fathers had sprung from their seats and were running towards the wrestling ring.

"So be it," said Helydices. He looked over to where Keres was standing, his beady eyes boiling with undisguised hatred. "I told you that you'd pay for what you did to me," he said softly. "You will *all* pay."

And with a jerk of his wrist, he broke his opponent's arm.

Tychos's screams were loud enough to wake the dead.

HAWK

"Fear is not something to be avoided. It is to be faced, fought, and conquered. It is to be embraced as part of who we are. For without fear, there can be no courage. And without courage, there can be no victory."

CERBRIONES, 'ALALAGMOE'

KERES RAN AT Helydices without thinking, the screams of his fallen friend ringing in his ears. A bronze figure blocked his way.

"Careful, lad," Galleas said calmly, his thorakes flashing in the sun.

"Let me pass!"

"So that you can do what? End up like Tychos? Helydices followed the three rules. And we all heard him order his adversary to submit. Twice."

"It was revenge, Kosmetes! He let slip the name of one of the Ruined yesterday and holds us responsible." He peered around Galleas's shoulder and saw Tychos's father leading his injured son towards the school building where the physician would be waiting. Helydices stood in the middle of the ring, both arms raised in triumph, and cheered on by his peons.

"Elena told me of the altercation," Galleas said. "But it changes nothing. If you attack him now, unprovoked and with half the population of Thena as witnesses, you'll be excluded from the ceremony of the spear and shield."

Those last words cut through Keres's anger like a knife. He slumped, defeated, and gave a resigned nod. Galleas squeezed his shoulder briefly and spun back to face the stands.

"As ephebe Tychos has declared forfeit, the wreath of victory is once again awarded to ephebe Helydices!"

There was a scattering of polite applause and more than a few angry murmurs. It seemed that Keres was not alone in thinking that the olive wreath was not entirely deserved. The crown itself was a worthless amalgamation of branches and leaves. But what it represented was priceless. The name of the victor would be recorded in the archives of the polis so that future generations would know of his accomplishments. Better still, anyone who earned a wreath could incorporate the design into his personal heraldry so that all would be reminded of his status every time he raised his shield.

Helydices received his prize from the basileus with aplomb, winking at Keres as he lowered it onto his head.

Savour it, you feckless malaka. The next wreath will be mine.

"And so, we come to the final trial," Galleas said. "The footrace! A harrowing contest of speed and skill! Our valorous ephebes must run from the starting point here by the garrison gates to the distant city walls and back again. No competitor may attack or harm his rivals or they will be disqualified."

Keres was only half-listening. Tychos had still not re-emerged from the makeshift infirmary, and would in any case not be able to partake in the trial with a broken arm.

He felt his anger return, burning like a fire in his belly. He stoked the flames, using his rage to give strength to his limbs.

The only thing Helydices will see are the soles of my sandals as I leave him in the dust.

He joined the others, jostling for a space near the front of the group. Galleas drew his xiphos.

"Ephebes! This is your last chance for glory! Seize it!" He brought his sword down in a chopping motion, and nineteen young men hurtled through the garrison gates and down the slope of Sisyphus Hill towards the lower part of Thena.

Keres soon took the lead, settling into an easy, loping stride that he had perfected during his many morning runs with his father. He reached the bottom of the hill and cut right into the maze of tents and stalls that made up the city's agora. Most of the shops were closed due to the festivities, but a few tenacious traders remained, eyes widening in astonishment as he whisked past. He bounded over a rug strewn with dried medicinal herbs, skirted around the edge of a potter's stall, and accelerated past an old woman haggling the price of a statue of Athena, passing through the outer edges of the market and into the residential area.

Here he hesitated. The most direct route was through the back streets, a tentacular labyrinth of narrow alleys. The main road was longer but much wider, built to allow cartloads of goods easy access to the agora. The irate cry of a merchant told him his rivals were not far behind. He needed to decide quickly.

He chose the main road, arms pumping rhythmically, sandals tap-tapping on the paving. The city gates were in sight, its reinforced doors thrown open. Two bored-looking guards in dirty linothoraxes stood on either side leaning on their spears, their aspides resting against their knees.

Keres skidded to a halt in front of them, pausing for a moment to catch his breath.

"Take a baton from the basket," one of the guards said to him, picking at something stuck in his teeth. He gave the near-naked form of Keres an appraising look, his eyes roaming over the lightly-tanned, oiled muscles. "How about you run back down here when you're done, eh? We could find somewhere nice to have a little chat?"

"Um, would love to, but no time," Keres replied a little too hastily. He grabbed a stick from the basket. The top half had been painted blue and was etched with the theta sign of Thena. He wiped a trickle of sweat from his brow. There was still no sign of his pursuers. He tapped the baton against his cheek thoughtfully. Most of the ephebes were likely to choose the main road, as he had done. Going back that way would be risky.

He flashed what he hoped was a grateful smile at the two guards and plunged into the network of alleyways. The air was cooler here, the sun's rays thwarted by tiled, sloping roofs that covered the cobbles in shadow. Keres would have to be careful. Without the sun to guide him, and with the familiar shape of Sisyphus Hill hidden from sight, he could only rely on his own sense of direction to lead him back to the finish line.

There was a shrill cry from somewhere ahead. Keres frowned. One of the ephebes? No, it was too high-pitched. A girl or young woman, perhaps. He continued down the street, his eyes searching. Another cry, closer this time. He came to a crossroads and angled left into a cramped alleyway, barely wide enough for two men to walk abreast. A dark green blur flashed across the edge of his vision.

"He … hello?" he called tentatively, slowing his pace to a jog. Broken glass tinkled in the gloom. "Hello?"

A whimper. A green shape huddled on the ground. Chestnut-brown curls poking out from under a woollen shawl. Keres stopped and dropped to one knee.

"Are you all right?" he asked, reaching out to touch the woman's head. She moaned and rolled over onto her back.

"I … I don't know. I think so." Her fingers went to her neck. "My necklace! They took it! It's the most important thing I own. My … mother gave it to me. It's all I have left to remember her by."

A tear escaped the corner of one eye. Keres hopped from one foot to the other, wracked by indecision. He'd already wasted precious minutes; the other ephebes couldn't be far behind. Gods, those who had decided to take the main road back may even be overtaking him while he dallied here!

Guilt crept into his mind. He imagined explaining to his father how he had abandoned a crying, defenceless woman alone in the alleys of Thena in exchange for a wreath of olive leaves. Leaves that would desiccate and crumble to nothingness within days. And every time he saw his shield, he would remember the choice he had made.

What was it his father had said to him once? It is not the victory itself that counts, but how it was achieved.

The woman was sitting up, drying her eyes with the corner of her chiton. Keres glanced at the blue-coated baton. It looked so small and insignificant in his hand.

It was a game. Just a game.

He sighed and dropped it onto the cobbles.

"I'll escort you to the watchmen by the main gate, Lady. They'll look after you and send a patrol out to catch whoever did this to you." He held out his hand to help her up. She took it in her own, her fingers cool against his oiled skin.

"Damn you," she said softly, her voice tinged with sorrow. "Damn your kindness, and damn your gallantry. You should have just walked away."

Keres saw a flicker of movement reflected in her eyes as she focused on something behind his shoulder. He tore free of her grasp with a desperate cry and turned just in time to catch the wooden cudgel on the right side of his forehead. Pain exploded in his skull. His teeth clashed together causing him to bite down on his tongue. Blood filled his mouth. A shadowy figure materialised on the edge of his blurred vision, smelling of sweat and old wine.

"Helydices sends his regards," the man said before the cudgel came down once more, and Keres knew only darkness.

♋

An unending field of battle. Decaying corpses stretching as far as the eye could see, packed so tightly together they hid the grass beneath. There was no way of knowing who they were or why they had fought. The company standards were torn to unrecognisable shreds. Shield heraldry defaced by grime and blood. Bodies of friends and foes merged, left to rot where they had fallen. United. At peace. Death had brought them the solace that war never could.

Keres lay atop a pile of dead hoplites, looking up at the sky. He couldn't move, his legs crushed under the weight of something heavy that he could not see. He was surrounded by an unnatural silence. The cries and pitiful moans of the mortally wounded were eerily absent. A morbid tranquillity.

Although … he was not entirely alone. A tiny black spot marred the slate-grey skies. A bird of prey, circling.

A hawk.

In a flash, the raptor dived, tucking its wings in close to its body to gain momentum. Keres watched helplessly as it drew closer. Close enough for him to see its hooked beak and powerful talons.

The hawk screeched, shattering the stillness. Keres let out a cry of his own as the bird landed on his cheek, sharp claws lacerating the flesh. Two huge wings unfurled majestically, shrouding his face in shadow.

Move, he commanded his paralysed body. *By all the Gods, move!*

An avian head bent down, and Keres heard the sickening pop as the tip of the bird's beak skewered his eyeball like a ripe olive. Searing agony exploded on the right side of his face. He opened his mouth to scream.

The hawk ripped out his tongue.

Keres jerked awake with a start, his scream still forming on his lips. The dream had been more vivid than anything he had ever known; the pain he had felt was both horrifying and visceral. Something hard was pressed against his cheek. A curved cobblestone. He was lying on his side in the alleyway, face in the dirt. He grimaced and spat a mouthful of blood. The right side of his forehead throbbed terribly as if he had drunk too much unwatered wine.

He sat up groggily, pausing as the world span around him. His wavering finger probed his skull and found a large bruise already forming, pulling the skin tight.

"Helydices," he growled. How long had he been unconscious? Minutes? Hours? The sun was still hidden by the sloping roofs of the alley. He stood, fighting down a wave of nausea. His foot trod on something, and he looked down to see the blue baton, covered in muck.

"Helydices," he repeated. The name helped rekindle the smouldering fires of anger in his gut. He bent to pick up the baton, gripping the wood so hard it hurt.

"Helydices." He set off at a jog, ignoring the vibrating ache in his skull every time his sandalled feet hit the cobbles. He emerged from the backstreets, his heart sinking as he realised how far the sun had moved. He had lost too much time. There was no hope. He was last.

Beaten but not broken, he thought, spitting out more red-coloured saliva. *I will see this through to the end. I will not give up. I will not give Helydices the satisfaction.*

He weaved in between the market stalls and started up the slope of Sisyphus Hill, digging deep into the reserves of hidden strength he didn't even know he had.

"Helydices," he muttered, his legs burning, his head throbbing like the charging hooves of a tauros. He passed through the gates of the garrison and onto the training field. The finishing line was two hundred feet away, partially obscured by two men in armoured bronze, arguing. To the left, hands on his hips, stood Galleas, his plumed helm masking his features. Opposite him was a tall, gaunt man with short, silvery-grey hair. He wore a magnificent panoply; the greaves and breastplate sculpted to mimic the forms of the muscles beneath. A skirt of leather strips protected his groin and upper thighs, and a crimson cloak hung from his shoulders. The cloak of an officer. The cloak of a strategos.

Father!

He had come. Despite all he had said to Keres back at the vineyard, Dexios had made the effort to come. Keres was overwhelmed with emotion. He jogged onwards, shouting hoarsely at the top of his voice. The noise of the crowd swelled as more and more people caught sight of him. A whisper then a murmur then a chatter then a roar. A symphony of stamping feet and exuberant cheers. His father turned and, for once, appeared to be actually smiling.

Keres hit a loose patch of earth and went sprawling. Dexios rushed to help him, his expression changing to one of concern. "Son!" he gasped, taking in the egg-sized bruise on Keres's forehead and the blood still seeping from his mouth "Gods, boy! You look like you've crawled out of Tartarus itself. What happened?"

"Spite," Keres replied. "Spite and wounded pride." He waved away his father's hand and hauled himself wearily to his feet. "Stand back. I must do this on my own."

Dexios handed him his baton. Keres no longer had the strength to run, so he walked. Inch by inch. One foot after the other. Basking in the encouraging shouts of the crowd, feeling the eyes of the basileus on him. The eyes of his fellow ephebes. The eyes of this father. It did not matter who had finished first. *This* is what the people of Thena would remember. And it was far better than any victory.

He crossed the finish line with a triumphant yell, then

the last of this strength gave out, and he pitched over backwards. Dexios caught him before he hit the ground. "Well done, Son," he said thickly. "You have brought great honour to your household … and to me. You are worthy of the spear and shield. You will make a fine hoplite. Your aspis may not bear the olive wreath, but you will find another suitable emblem, I am sure."

Keres looked up into his father's careworn features, the cries of the crowd ringing in his ears.

"I have already found one," he said.

A hawk.

6

OATHS

"Most promises are made without a thought, easily spoken, and easily broken without consequence. A sincere apology is often enough to warrant forgiveness. An oath is different. It changes who we are. Oaths make us husbands, soldiers, or leaders. To breach an oath is not only to incur the wrath of the Gods, but it is also to renounce our new identity. It is to refuse who we have become."

BASILEUS LETHO, 'RUMINATIONS'

DEXIOS STOOD BESIDE Letho on the raised dais, close enough to smell the basileus's extravagant perfume that failed to mask completely the underlying odour of red wine. His father-in-law was sucking honey off his ringed fingers, sticking each one into his mouth with a popping sound. He appeared relaxed, affable, and harmless.

Dexios knew it was all a lie. He had seen what those same hands could do to anyone who threatened the basileus's reign. Under all that pale, scented skin was a heart of cold iron.

"An obol for your thoughts?" Letho asked playfully. He was poking at the inside of his mouth with his tongue, attempting to dislodge a particularly sticky piece of date.

"I was wondering if you ever get tired of this ridiculous

pantomime whenever you appear in public. Are you not bothered by how people judge you?"

"It is a weak man indeed whose decisions are weighted by how he is perceived by others, and an even weaker one who is so lacking in self-assurance that he cannot withstand a little ridicule."

"Yes, but—"

"Your hair, like mine, is not styled according to social convention. Some will see it as a sign of weakness or mock you for not conforming to what they believe to be normal. Does that not worry you?"

"No," admitted Dexios.

"Exactly. My father was a tyrant. He used his power oppressively, and Thena was almost ruined by his authoritarian policies. He was universally reviled ... his death at the hands of his palace guard probably saved this city from annihilation. And now, forty years later, we are one of the greatest poleis in Tyrris. Conciliation and kindness *work*."

"Except for those who displease you."

Letho made a tutting sound. "And we were getting along so well, Dexios. Let us not talk of such sensitive subjects. Your marriage to my daughter has bought you a fair amount of leeway, but please be careful not to overstep."

He held out the empty bowl of dates, and a slave rushed forwards to take it away. Below him, the ephebes were beginning to congregate in anticipation of the ceremony of the spear and shield.

"I was surprised to see you here," the basileus continued. "You've always avoided this place like the plague."

"I have come for my son," Dexios replied. It had been hard, tragically hard, to walk through those gates. In the end, his desire to see Keres receive his shield had outweighed old pains. He would make new memories here today that would hopefully smother those of the past.

"My grandson was quite courageous, finishing the race after that nasty fall he had. Following in his old man's footsteps, eh?"

"Yes … the fall. I am very proud." Keres had become quite adept at hiding things from his father, but Dexios had spotted the tell-tale leftward flicker in the boy's eyes as he was telling his story. A lie. Besides, Dexios had seen enough cudgel wounds in his time to know that the large bruise on his son's forehead was not the result of him hitting the cobbles. He was protecting someone. But why? Dexios had no idea, but, by Hera, he was going to find out.

"Ahem." Letho cleared his throat. Despite his overbearing stature, his voice was high-pitched and wavery; he had to shout to be heard.

"Ephebes," he warbled. "Your basileus congratulates you. We will soon proceed with the recital of the oath. But first, a word from the man who will be your commanding officer for the following year: Strategos Dexios."

Dexios inclined his head in recognition and stepped forwards, fixing each of the ephebes in turn. The brutish Helydices. The wafer-thin Makar. Tychos, his left arm wrapped tightly in bandages. Keres, chest and loincloth covered in muck from the city streets. All of them watching him, expectantly.

And behind them, the statue of Cerbriones, his xiphos raised high as if challenging the stars.

Dexios took a moment to gather his thoughts. For him, the trials had been a formality. As the son of a strategos, he had been training for that very moment for as long as he could remember. His mother had often jokingly told him that he had been born with a spear in his hand and greaves on his shins. She was probably not far from the truth. His earliest memory of his father was the grim-faced old man instructing him on how to polish a shield correctly, a lesson beaten into his brain by the stinging pain of the birch stick whenever he got it wrong.

A childhood dominated by his father's unwavering desire to shape his only son in his image. Dexios's sole respite was during the campaign season when the strategos was called away to settle border disputes or help repel raiders on the western coasts.

It was not until Dexios had started his ephebic instruction that it had finally dawned on him how well his father had prepared him. He was so far ahead of the other students that it was laughable; he won all three ephebic trials unopposed and served for seven years as lochagos until his father's untimely death overseas. There was never any hesitation over who should take his place. At the age of twenty-five, he had become the youngest strategos in Thenean history.

He could tell them of the many battles he had won. The brave men who had fought beside him in desert sands and mountain snows. Glory-filled, awe-inspiring stories. It would be what they wanted to hear.

But it would not be what they *needed* to hear.

"There was once a soldier called to war," he began. "The very thought filled him with euphoria. He kissed his wife and son goodbye and joined the city phalanx, proud to serve beside his fellow citizens; the bakers, the merchants, the butchers, and the craftsmen. They marched to the music of the pipes, singing the praises of the Gods. Soon, they came across the enemy host, and a great battle was waged. A hard-pressed, bloody battle. The soldier fought bravely, slaying many with his sword and spear.

"He was victorious and returned to his city in triumph, his head wreathed in olive leaves. After the celebration, he returned to his farm, sacrificing an ox to Hera in thanks. And yet ... the following year, the harvest was poor. Fields lay unsown, their owners slain in distant lands. Trade faltered. Slaves deserted. The soldier grew thin from lack of food. When his wife and son fell sick, there was no physician to keep them from the welcoming arms of Charon. That summer, the soldier died on the steps of his home, too weak to stop a band of looters from taking his grain."

Dexios put a hand on the stack of twenty plain bronze shields by his side. "When you take up this aspis, when you feel its weight on your arm, remember what it represents. War is not a game. It is a penance. A price to pay for failure. The last possible solution when there are no other options. Do not wish for it. Do not strive for it. Victory is ephemeral. Death is eternal."

He felt their confused stares. They didn't understand. Just as he had not. Right up until the first scream of pain. The first splash of bright red blood.

"Look at the ephebe to your left," he continued doggedly. "And to your right. These are the faces of the men you may one day have to bury or burn. Your duty is not to win or to conquer. Your duty is to stop these deaths from happening. Your duty is to keep those around you alive."

He stepped back without another word, clasping his hands in front of him, and bowing his head to show that he had finished. There was no applause. It did not matter. He owed it to himself to try and warn them of the dangers they would face. Whether they took his advice to heart or not was now up to them.

"Thank you, Strategos," said Letho. He looked like he was going to say something more, then stopped himself.

"Ahem. Wise words, indeed. Our city has grown and prospered not by stealing what we did not have from others but by finding a means to make it ourselves. By inviting great craftsmen to ply their wares here. By allying with our neighbours. By surrounding ourselves with those we trust and respect. But sometimes, despite our efforts, we are forced to protect what is ours."

Dexios was silent, knowing that the last comment was aimed at him and their earlier conversation. What exactly had the basileus done over the years in the name of Thena? To … protect what was his?

"Let us take the oath," Letho said, raising one hand to point to the sky. "Before your basileus. Before the Gods of Olympus. Before Hera herself. Swear your fealty."

This is the moment, Dexios thought, past and present merging in his mind. *This is the moment when everything changes*. He looked down at his son. Keres stood tall, tears glistening in his eyes, his proud voice joining those of his fellow ephebes.

"We will never bring disgrace on this, our city, by any act of dishonesty or cowardice, nor ever desert our suffering comrades in the ranks. We will fight for the ideals and sacred beliefs of the city, both alone and with many. We will revere and obey the city's laws and do our best to incite a like respect and reverence in those above us who are prone to annul them or set them at naught. We will strive unceasingly to quicken the public sense of civic duty. Thus, in all these ways, the city that we will transmit will be even greater and more beautiful than it was when transmitted to us."

While they were speaking, a priestess of Hera appeared before them, the hair shorn from the left side of her head as was the custom. She was clothed in an ankle-length chiton and leading a majestic white bull. The beast had obviously been drugged; its black pupils were dilated, its tongue lolled from its mouth. Woman and beast halted before a wide pewter bowl that had been placed on the dirt before the dais. The priestess tugged the unresisting animal to its knees and swiftly drew a curved dagger across its throat.

"Hera. Our Protector. Heed our words. See our gift," she intoned as blood spurted from the wound, cascading into the bowl below. Plunging her hands into the red liquid, she beckoned the first of the ephebes forwards. Helydices advanced, his victor's wreath planted firmly on his head. The priestess pressed her palms against his chest leaving two bloody prints. The sign of Hera, Queen of the Pantheon.

Helydices bowed reverently and climbed the steps to the dais where Letho handed him the plain bronze-covered shield and ash wood spear. "Your polis and your basileus thank you, ephebe."

The big youth grunted, gave Dexios a reluctant nod, and clumped back down into the stalls to receive the congratulations of his father. More ephebes followed. Keres waited patiently for Tychos, helping his wounded friend awkwardly grasp his spear with his bandaged arm.

The bull gave a final shudder and was still, its bowels releasing their contents as the muscles lost their strength.

Dexios's gaze was drawn to the half-empty bowl of crimson fluid. He had always found the blood sacrifice ominous, a foreshadowing of things to come. He watched as the priestess tipped the bowl over, spilling its contents onto the ground.

Blood on earth.

Just as when the infected tauros had torn his house slave in half.

"Dexios?"

He felt a tug on his cloak.

"You haven't been listening to a word I've been saying, have you, Strategos?" asked Letho.

"I … apologise, Lord."

"News from the palace. A Ruxian seeks an audience. On today of all days."

"A messenger? Not a carrier pigeon?"

"No. It's serious, Dexios. Problems at the border. I would like you with me on this."

"I am no longer your strategos, Lord."

"Then, consider it a favour to a friend."

Dexios sighed, knowing he could not refuse. He readjusted his officer's cloak, feeling more than ever its heavy weight on his shoulders. A few dozen feet away, Keres was showing his spear and shield to Melia and Nambe, grinning happily. The house slave caught his master looking at them and raised an inquisitive eyebrow, but Dexios shook his head.

Letho clapped his hands, and his honour guard formed up around them. Galleas marched over and saluted smartly. He was accompanied by a blonde-haired woman with tired-looking eyes and a wide-brimmed straw hat.

"Apologies for the delay, Lord," he said, as they fell in

step with the others. "I thought it best to ask Sophistes Elena to join us; her knowledge of Ruxia could be a great help."

Dexios stared at her.

"*You* are Keres's sophistes?"

"Yes."

"But … you are a woman!" he blurted out before he was able to stop himself.

"How perceptive of you, Strategos. I can see how your razor-sharp tactical mind is such an important asset on the battlefield."

"Elena …" warned Galleas.

"Your uncanny knowledge of the feminine anatomy must have helped you lead the brave men of Thena to uncountable victories."

"Elena!"

Dexios raised an apologetic hand. "She's right," he said. "It was stupid. Forgive me, Sophistes. Keres has spoken of you many times; I just wasn't listening hard enough. In my time, your position was only available to men, so I just thought …"

"Perhaps if you had come to visit your son once or twice over the last year, you would feel less confused?"

"Gods, you too? Is there any other advice you would like to give me as to how I should raise my son?"

"Well, now that you mention it—"

"Stop your bickering, both of you," Letho snapped. "We're here."

The basileus's palace had been built at the very top of Sisyphus Hill, the highest location in all of Thena and the closest to the Gods. Purple banners embroidered with the theta symbol hung on either side of tall gates of iron and gold, another example of Letho's substantial fortune. The gates swung ponderously open to reveal an armoured figure pacing back and forth across the courtyard beyond. He wore a plumed helm of dyed horsehair and the red officer's cloak of a strategos.

"Polydius?" Dexios exclaimed incredulously.

The general removed his helm. Two bloodshot eyes stared out at Dexios through a mane of long black hair. "Aye, brother," the man said with a tired smile. "It's me. You look terrible."

Dexios strode forwards with a smile of his own and grasped his friend's wrist. "Gods, man, you think *I* look terrible? What happened to you? I'd wager you haven't slept in a week!"

Polydius rubbed at the thick layer of stubble on his lower jaw. "That sounds about right. Sleep is a luxury I cannot afford at the moment. I see you're still allowing old Galleas to wander around without a minder."

"Careful, boy," the balding veteran replied. "I remember taking the birch stick to your pretty little back a few times during your training. I'd be quite happy to do so again."

"Why are you here?" Dexios asked. "What brings Ruxia's strategos to Thena?"

Polydius fixed him with his haggard eyes. "The same thing that has always drawn us together ever since we were ephebes."

"War."

RELUCTANCE

"I SEE YOU HAVE not lost your sense of exaggeration, Strategos," said Letho drily, waving away his honour guard. His voice was subtly different from the wavering treble he used in public. Deeper and richer. Dexios saw Elena raise an inquisitive eyebrow. She had never heard the basileus's real voice before.

"I'm not—" Polydius began.

"In the andron, I think," interrupted Letho. He brushed past the Ruxian strategos and heaved his large frame up the three marble steps leading into the palace.

A slave was waiting for them in the cool of the vestibule with towels and a bowl of water. Dexios wiped the sweat from his face and neck, admiring the statue of Hera Herkeios as he did so. This particular aspect represented the goddess as a guardian of hearth and home, and consequently, nearly all Tyrrean dwellings had altars or effigies dedicated to her worship.

"Not quite infallible, though, are you?" Dexios muttered. Lyne's lifeblood had run so deep into the curves and grooves of his own statue that no amount of scrubbing would ever remove it all.

"Still talking to yourself, I see," said Polydius, handing his plumed helm to the slave in exchange for a towel soaked in fresh water.

Dexios dabbed at his damp beard. "Only when there's no one nearby worth talking to."

"Hah! Gods, I've missed having someone around who dares to talk to me like that! Most of my lochagos would rather eat their own excrement than disagree with me. Stupid malakas."

Dexios grunted noncommittally. He had known Polydius for over twenty years now, one of the last survivors of his group of ephebes, a veteran of uncountable battles. He was brave, loyal, and steadfast. Unfortunately, these fine qualities were offset by his atrocious temper: wild mood swings and fits of rage that had led to several awkward situations between the two friends, including a trio of duels that had luckily all ended with both of them bloodied but still alive.

The contentious subject was always the same: Dexios believed he had been chosen for the position of strategos on merit alone. Polydius did not. To him, it was pure nepotism on the part of the basileus and, to a lesser extent, Dexios's father.

Their frayed relationship might have degenerated further if Xenokrates, the basileus of Ruxia, had not offered Polydius the title he had always craved, albeit in a city that was not his own.

"Onwards!" boomed Polydius, throwing his towel at the startled slave and striding confidently out of the vestibule.

The andron was small and sparsely decorated: five couches grouped around a central mosaic depicting Artemis during one of the Great Hunts. The goddess sat astride a beautiful white gelding, her countenance fierce, her long hair flowing behind her as if tousled by some imaginary wind. One hand held a curved bow nocked with a silver arrow whose tip was aimed at a tusked boar fleeing before her majesty.

Dexios got the impression that this was not a place men came to relax and socialise; Letho must have other androns for that. This was his unofficial council chamber, somewhere to discuss matters of import unheard and unseen.

The basileus had already installed himself on one of the couches and was cleaning his nails with a dagger. He motioned impatiently for the others to take their seats.

"Come, Polydius, tell us of this war that endangers us all."

"Lord." The strategos tapped a finger against the arm of the couch, pondering how to begin.

"Our lands have always been threatened. Pirates raid the coasts. Our eastern neighbours covert our proliferous silver mines while to the north, the Dorias Mountains cast an ominous shadow."

Polydius grabbed a cup of watered wine and took a long sip, swilling the liquid around the inside of his mouth before swallowing. Dexios frowned. He had never seen his friend look so nervous.

"It is no secret that the tauros roam the plains beyond the mountains. Our borders are protected accordingly:

ten outposts placed strategically at the head of the widest passes, each manned by fifty hoplites. Signal fires and carrier pigeons to warn Ruxia of an impending assault. Our heavy cavalry is the best in all of Tyrris. Any infringement into our territory by those bovine monstrosities is met by a host of iron hooves."

Another long, clumsy sip. Excess wine dribbled from the corners of his mouth into his stubble.

"A couple of weeks ago, we lost contact with one of the outposts. Xenokrates charged me with leading a scouting party there myself. The place was … deserted."

"Any signs of a struggle?" asked Galleas. The old man was perched on the end of a couch, elbows resting on his bony knees.

"No … at least, nothing inside the outpost. The pigeons were still in their coop. The kindling for the signal fires was dry and unused. But one of my riders picked up traces of fresh blood on the trail leading into the mountains."

"An experienced lochagos would not have abandoned a superior defensive position without good reason," mused Dexios. "Something or someone must have been dangerous enough to draw those fifty men out from behind the protection of those walls."

"Agreed," Polydius said. "I set up camp and sent a half-dozen men into the pass to track the missing hoplites. They didn't find them. But they found something else."

"Tauros, I'd wager," spat Galleas. "One of the herds must have mustered enough courage to cross the mountains. I've fought against an entire herd before. Eighteen of the beasts. It was not an easy encounter."

Polydius gave an incredulous laugh. "A herd? We can

handle a single herd, Kosmetes. No, it was far worse than that. My men counted *ten* different tribal markings. Ten herds … close to two hundred tauros."

His words were greeted with stunned silence.

Dexios felt the familiar tendrils of fear snaking up his arms and legs, curling around his intestines, slithering across his rapidly-beating heart. He tasted the vile tang of bile at the back of his mouth.

"Two … hundred," he murmured, still unwilling to believe what he had heard. That was not a herd.

That was an *army*.

Polydius drained his cup of wine and wiped his mouth with the back of his hand. "More or less. Heifers and calves too. Moving slowly southwards. Ruxia doesn't have the men to stand against such a horde. My basileus sent me here to ask you to honour the age-old alliance between our two cities. Hera willing, our combined strength will be enough to push them back."

"What does the Oracle think of all this?" asked Letho, speaking for the first time. He did not seem as troubled as the others, or if he was, he was hiding it well.

"I have sent envoys to her temple but did not want to delay coming here any longer," answered Polydius dismissively, brushing the question aside with a wave of his hand. "Besides, our decision should not be based on the enigmatic prophecies of an old woman."

"An old woman who speaks for Hera," Letho countered. "You would be wise to remember that."

"Of course," Polydius replied hurriedly. "I meant no disrespect. I'm sure Xenokrates will analyse all available options … but time, as always, is against us. The tauros are moving at a leisurely pace, often pausing for days in the same location. Nevertheless, they will reach Ruxia before the end of the month, of that, I am sure. And when they do, we need to be ready."

"We?" Letho repeated. "I have not yet decided on the best course of action for Thena."

Polydius scowled and looked down at his empty cup. His bleary eyes scanned the room, searching for the house slave, but the young boy had mysteriously vanished.

"I … don't understand, Lord," he said. "The alliance between our two poleis goes back decades. We have always—"

"Not always," Elena interrupted, finishing off her own wine with practised ease. "There are numerous documented cases of Ruxia leaving Thena to face its enemies alone."

Polydius seemed to see her for the first time.

"And you are?"

"A historian. One with a good memory. I believe we asked Ruxia for aid before embarking on our long and costly campaign against the men of the south. Is that not right, Strategos?"

Dexios squirmed in his seat. "It is."

"Ridiculous," growled Polydius, his cheeks mottled an angry shade of red. "You are comparing a … a foolhardy crusade instigated by pride and avarice to the defence of our *homeland*. The protection of our *people*. We must stand together or fall divided."

"You insult the Oracle, and now you insult me," said Letho calmly, examining the rings on his left hand. "I was the one who approved the so-called foolhardy crusade of which you speak. Does that make me a fool, Strategos?"

"No, I …" Polydius let out a frustrated sigh. "Charon's balls, why did Xenokrates pick me to come here? I have the diplomatic skills of a blind pig!"

Letho smiled thinly. "He sent you because you were born a Thenean, Strategos. And because you are known to Dexios and Galleas. It is easier to be swayed by the words of a man you trust than by those of a stranger, no matter how eloquent he may be." He rose from the couch with a grunt of effort. "How many men do you have?"

"Two hundred cavalry. Close to three hundred hoplites but only if we empty the entirety of our northern outposts and city garrisons. We would be leaving our borders completely defenceless."

"What else?"

"We've sent riders east to Lendes and put out a call for misthios. We have the silver to hire maybe a hundred archers."

Letho nodded. "Then, there is only one question left to ask." He turned to Dexios. "Will it be enough?"

"It will not," the strategos replied with a shake of his head. "If we do not help them, they will fail. And we will be next."

"In that case, we will help them. Galleas! Assemble the hoplites. All able-bodied citizens and ephebes. An ennean muster. Those not chosen will remain here to defend Thena under Crenate. Dexios—"

"Lord … I have relinquished my commission."

"You have. And I have accepted your resignation. But the Thenean phalanx cannot march without a strategos, and there is none better than you. Will you serve your polis one last time? Will you lead them?"

The answer was simple, but Dexios could not bring himself to say it. He was so close. So close to that wonderful moment when he would hang his spear up next to his shield and pass his panoply on to his son. There would be no more soldiers for him to bury. No more evenings spent washing the blood from his hair and beneath his fingernails. Just the rustling of the vine leaves caressed by the wind, bathed in the light of the setting sun.

He could almost smell it. The toiled earth. The sweet aroma of fermenting grapes.

Why should he help Ruxia? What did he owe them? Nothing.

He should just let them die. Let them all die.

"Dexios?"

The idyllic sunset he had pictured so many times faded away.

"I will lead them, Lord."

"Excellent. Then, you leave tomorrow at dawn. Hera protects."

"Hera protects," answered Dexios dismally.

The harvest would have to wait.

"You'll have to tell them," said Galleas to Elena as they stepped through the imposing gates of the palace and out into the chill of early evening. "I need to go and help Captain Crenate with the conscription lists. The man can barely read, let alone handle the register."

Elena looked at him inquisitively from under the brim of her hat. "Tell them? Tell who?"

"The ephebes. They'll still be at the garrison, and they should stay there."

"The … Hera's tits, Galleas, you're not seriously considering sending them to Ruxia?"

The old kosmetes's face was hidden by his helm, but Elena could still see his eyes; hard and unflinching. "They've taken up their spear and shield," he said. "They've sworn the oath. They are obligated to serve in the phalanx just like any other citizen of Thena."

"Today. They swore the oath *today*. They are probably celebrating as we speak! I'd wager half of them are drunk, and the other half are working hard at getting there."

"Good. Let them make the most of the time they have."

"Kosmetes—"

"Enough, Elena! Our laws are clear. The oath was sworn before the Gods. Will you risk their anger by breaking that bond?"

She shook her head unhappily. "It's just … they are so young."

Galleas slowed his pace and put a hand on Elena's arm. She looked down at the dozens of tiny scars that dotted the veteran's wrinkled skin made by the splintered wood of broken spears and shields or the kiss of an enemy's xiphos. Every soldier bore such scars, and soon the ephebes would have them too.

"I will do what I can to protect them," Galleas said. "Make sure they're placed in the middle of the phalanx: third or fourth rank. Surrounded by my best men. If Hera wills it, they will never even see the tauros, let alone fight them. Besides, they will not necessarily be any safer here. If we fail to stall the beasts' advance, Thena could be next."

They reached the garrison. Someone had lit the torches set into the stone walls, and the dancing flames cast long, rippling shadows as the last of the colour bled from the sky. Muffled cries of laughter could be heard from within, buoyed by the sound of a badly-tuned lute.

"It is here that I leave you," Galleas said, making the sign of Hera. "Send a slave to the gatehouse if you have any … issues. Oh, I almost forgot. You'll have to tell Makar and Tychos that they are staying here. Makar was last in the trials — excluding Keres's mishap, of course. In any case, the poor lad can barely hold an aspis; he'd be a danger not only to himself but to the entire shield wall. And the physician tells me that Tychos's arm is broken. Two will stay, eighteen will go. That will satisfy the basileus's ennea. You'll find scrolls of passage for Makar and Tychos in my office. They should carry them at all times."

His words were clipped, his sentences short and precise. Gone was the affable colleague and friend who had offered to take her hunting, buried under the return of Galleas's second persona, the uncompromising, stern-faced drill instructor. Elena shivered. Most people believed that war was the worst of humanity's sins, for it could never create, only destroy. But Elena knew that wasn't quite true. War excelled in creating many things: poverty and famine. Sickness and disease. Orphans and widows.

She removed her hat and asked Galleas the question that had been bouncing around in her head ever since meeting Polydius.

"Can we win, Galleas? If Ruxia, Thena, and Lendes stand together, can we win?"

There was a long pause before the kosmetes replied.

"I cannot lie to you, Elena. I … I'm not … I'm not sure we can. But I hope to Hera I am wrong."

And turning on his heel, he left her alone before the entrance to the garrison, the shadows leaping and spinning above her head like the pyrrhic dance of the damned.

8

PARTHENOS

"For many, virginity is synonymous with fragility. I believe it to be quite the opposite. It is a sign of independence and strength. A woman not subjected to the will of man. When we gaze upon the godly countenance of Athena, we do not see a virgin; we see a warrior. A scholar. A poet. We see a goddess of creation."

GRAYCEA, PRIESTESS OF HERA

ELENA STOOD A few feet away from the andron, gathering her thoughts. In one hand, she held the scrolls of passage that she had found at the bottom of a chest in Galleas's office. The paper was brittle and yellowing around the edges but bore the unmistakable imprint of the kosmetes's seal. He must have written them an aeon ago and buried them under a mound of paperwork, like a squirrel hoarding its nuts for the winter.

So organised. So dependable. Elena felt a pang of envy. She could name all the rivers and tributaries of Tyrris, or discuss in great detail the various treaties signed between Thena and the other poleis over the last decade, but was still living in that minuscule apartment, knocking over empty amphorae and searching for her lost sandals. Or her next kylix of wine.

What was it that she feared? Was it change? Or the

unexpected? One of the reasons she loved teaching history and geography was the comforting reassurance of their near immutability. There were small variances, of course, but the majority was undisputed. She couldn't have an invalid opinion as there were no opinions to be had … no waves to rock the proverbial boat.

She knew Galleas disapproved of her complacency. In fact, she suspected he confused her lack of ambition with laziness, which was far from the truth. She was simply … content. Why strive for more when what you have is enough? She thought back to the lone horseman she had spied that morning on the plains before the city.

Well, nearly enough.

She straightened her chiton, fixed what she hoped would be an authoritative frown on her face, and strode confidently into the andron … only to be promptly hit on the shoulder by something wet and sticky. Dark purple liquid trickled down her arm.

Right.

"WHAT IN TARTARUS IS GOING ON HERE?" she yelled.

There was the twang of a lute string snapping. Her eyes widened as she took in the scene of unrestrained chaos. The andron looked like it had been attacked by a rampaging tauros. A half-dozen bodies lay in various states of consciousness on the tiled floor, one of them resting peacefully in what appeared to be its own vomit. At the far end of the room, Makar and another ephebe had been playing a ditty on the lute and pipes. Couches had been pushed against the walls to make space for an impromptu dance floor.

Closer to the doorway, a group of ephebes had arranged

their own couches in a circle around a disc balanced precariously on the end of a metal stand. Kottabos. They were playing kottabos. Elena knew the game well and had even tried it once or twice herself, towards the tail-end of her wine-infused soirees. The goal was surprisingly simple: players would drink from their cups until they reached the dregs, then fling the last drop of wine at the stand in the hope of knocking off the disc. Those who failed refilled their cup and tried again. Those who succeeded … often did the same.

Keres hurried forwards with a towel, his face flushed with a combination of embarrassment and too much wine. "Apologies, Mistress," he stammered. "We didn't see you there. It's Tychos. He's playing even worse than usual."

The stonemason's son gave her a friendly wave from his spot opposite the door. "It's not my fault, Mistress. I have to play right-handed on account of someone breaking my arm!" He gestured to a large shape on the floor that turned out to be Helydices.

Elena dabbed ineffectively at her wine-spattered chiton. "You shouldn't even be here in your condition, Tychos, and you should most definitely not be drinking."

"It's for medicinal purposes, Mistress!"

"Then, you should be bathing your wound in it, not tipping it down your throat." She raised her voice again. "All of you, on your feet!" There was a screeching of wood on marble followed by a scuffling of sandals.

"Gods, half of you can barely stand! How did you manage to drink so much in so little time? You're lucky it's me who found you and not the kosmetes."

Keres tried to process this information. "But Galleas said we could celeb—"

"Not by drinking all of the garrison's reserves of wine! On any other night, I'd have you out running laps around the training field until the cold sobered you up a bit ... but something's come up. Something important."

"That's why my father left with Letho," Keres said. "They must have decided to muster the hoplites. How many?"

Elena was slightly taken aback by the young ephebe's perspicacity, at odds with his red face and crumpled chiton.

"Ennea. Nine in ten. Two will be staying behind."

She held up the scrolls of passage before setting them down on one of the couches. "Makar, one of these is for you."

The wiry youth bobbed his head as if expecting this. Putting down his lute, he threaded his way carefully through the drunken ephebes.

"Makar," Elena said quietly to him as he picked up his scroll. "This is not a punishment, nor does it make you any less worthy of the spear and shield. Remember that."

"Yes, Mistress. I should be heading home, anyway. My father will be wanting me up bright and early tomorrow to rekindle the fires at the workshop."

He shoved the scroll into his belt and walked away with his head bowed. Elena wondered what the young man must be feeling. Even after a year in his company, she still didn't really know him. Makar was solitary and introverted, rarely mingling with the other ephebes unless absolutely necessary. He was an excellent student — bright-minded and attentive — he just lacked that all-important spark, preferring instead to keep his emotions bottled up inside his scrawny chest. Maybe he feared that if he let them out, he wouldn't be able to shut them back in again.

Elena sighed and turned her attention back to the others. "The second scroll—"

"It's for me, Mistress, isn't it?" asked Tychos.

And speaking of emotion … the stonemason's son was Makar's complete opposite. If the quiet-spoken young man was as pale and lonely as the moon, then Tychos was as warm and striking as the sun, his bronze skin and fair hair complementing his charismatic smile. The sort of person who wore his heart on his sleeve, for better or worse. Elena watched a tear trickle down the man's face, his right hand clenching and unclenching in frustration.

"It is, Tychos. I'm sorry."

"By Hera, Mistress, you must tell Galleas he is wrong! Only the sick and the infirm should be excluded from the muster. I can fight! Keres will strap my aspis to my left arm, and I will wield my weapon with my right. My place is in the spear wall with my ephebes. With my brothers! Do not take this away from me! Please!"

Elena moved closer and locked her eyes with his. He stared back at her defiantly.

"What is the most important part of a hoplite's equipment, Tychos?" she asked.

He faltered. "The … the shield, Mistress."

"Yes. Do you remember why?"

"In the shield wall, it protects both myself and the brother to my left."

"Correct once again. I do not doubt you can hold a shield, Tychos, but what will you do when the enemy charges at the phalanx? When they crash into that wall of bronze? Pressing against it like this." She laid a hand on his broken arm and pushed gently. Tychos remained stoically silent, but fresh tears brimmed in his eyes.

"And the battle line is an ever-moving, ever-changing thing," Elena continued, pressing harder. "Like the ebb and flow of the tide. A commander, sensing a weakness, could order his men to put pressure on the opposing force, to crash into the shields again and again and again." She punctuated each word with a squeeze. Tychos, no longer able to contain himself, cried out in pain.

"Stop it!" Keres shouted. "You're hurting him!"

Elena let go. "I have studied enough battles to know how most of them end," she said sadly. "Once the phalanx is broken, it is as good as finished. You have to understand, Tychos. This is about more than your own needs and ambitions. It is about the difference between victory and defeat."

Tychos, cradling his left arm with his right, pushed past her, grabbed the remaining scroll, and fled the andron.

They're still children, she thought. *No matter what Galleas says. This is all just a game to them.*

Well, to most of them.

"Keres?"

"Sophistes?"

"You are the only one here who has seen a tauros. Do you believe Tychos should be sent north with a broken arm?"

Keres shook his head.

"Go after him. Try and make him see reason. He trusts you. And as for the rest of you … if you think the garrison slaves are going to clean up this mess, you are sorely mistaken. The quartermaster will need every available set of hands to prepare the food and supplies for tomorrow. You'd better start now if you want to get a few hours' sleep before Galleas returns."

There was a chorus of half-drunken groans. Elena smiled inwardly. The ephebes had probably been thinking that tonight would be a night to remember … and it would, just not quite in the way they had hoped. She reached for one of the half-empty amphorae and tucked it under one arm. That was her evening settled. Just a couple of cups to soothe her nerves. As she turned to leave, her foot bumped against something on the floor, sending it rolling under a couch. Setting down the wine with a frown, she dropped to her knees and peered into the shadows. A roll of paper. One of the scrolls of passage.

"Hera's tits!" she muttered, stretching out her hand to retrieve it. If either Tychos or Makar was stopped and couldn't prove that they were exempt from conscription, they would be imprisoned or worse. Desertion was punishable by death. But who did the scroll belong to? She blinked in an attempt to disperse the soft veil of tiredness dulling her senses. The wine would have to wait. She'd have to check on them both. Tychos had his arm in a sling, and most likely Keres by his side, whereas Makar was alone. Makar first, then.

She left the garrison at a slow jog, ignoring the warning throbs in her thighs. *What are you doing?* they seemed to be saying indignantly. *We don't run! We never run!*

"Shut up," she said aloud, reaching the agora. The market was eerily quiet, the silence only broken by the soft rustling of awnings and the creaking of wooden posts. Makar would be heading northeast, back to his father's jewellery shop and the cramped living quarters above. Elena had been there once before, three or four years ago, when her trips to the taverna weren't quite as frequent, and she still had money left for clothes and trinkets.

She coughed; the sound of her own voice uncomfortably loud. The night sky was covered in thick grey cloud, and what little moonlight escaped the ashen shroud twisted her surroundings into strange shapes: an abandoned amphora became the bloated body of an enormous spider; the diagonal supporting poles of a tent the pronged horns of a tauros.

Elena pressed onwards, more slowly now, acutely aware that, thanks to her impetuousness, she now found herself alone in the middle of a deserted marketplace. She should have asked one of the ephebes to accompany her. Her eyes flicked left and right. Every corner was a potential hiding place. Every crossroads an ambush waiting to happen.

Two yellow lights appeared, bobbing like fireflies. Elena breathed a sigh of relief. Torches. A shopkeeper working late, perhaps. Or a duo of nightwatchmen on patrol.

"Hello?" she croaked.

Gods. Clearing her throat, she tried again.

"Hello?"

She rounded the side of a large perfume stall, the lingering mixture of floral smells the only clue to the myriad of concoctions that must have lined its shelves during the day. Three figures stood illuminated in the faint glow of the torches beyond. The man closest to her was big and flabby, his protuberant pot-belly pressing against the fabric of his dirty green chiton. His companion was shorter, his hair so covered in grease it looked like he had doused himself with an amphora of olive oil. A spindly finger was stuck in one ear, rooting around for some unknown treasure.

The two torchbearers loomed over a third man sprawled

in the dirt, a chaotic jigsaw of long limbs, jutting elbows and bony knees. Makar. A splash of red darkened his pale upper lip.

Elena ducked behind an empty set of shelves, as yet unnoticed. What in the name of Hera was she supposed to do now? Whatever was going on here, it wasn't any of her business. She was a teacher, not a bodyguard. Besides, any duty she had towards the ephebes started when they walked through the garrison gates and ended when they left. She should turn around, find an open taverna, and bring some relief to her parched throat. One of the slaves could take the scroll of passage to Desha's workshop tomorrow.

Another voice pushed its way to the forefront of her mind, tramping unperturbed through the wine-scented self-pity of her psyche to make itself heard. "That won't work," the voice said. It sounded suspiciously like Galleas. "Drink half an amphora and you'll forget about what you saw here for a while, but it will come wriggling back. Bad memories are like weeds in a garden. You can cut them, break them, tear them out by their roots, but the bastards always find a way to regrow. And don't talk to me about a lack of courage or fear of reprisal. That second knot on your belt is proof enough. You've survived years of scrutiny and criticism. You can survive this."

Elena sighed, checked her hair was still more or less in place, then strode confidently out from behind the market stall.

"Makar, there you are!" she said loudly. "The whole garrison has been looking for you! You forgot your scroll of passage."

The greasy-haired man removed his finger and flicked

a piece of earwax from the tip. His eyes roamed her body, lingering slightly on her belt.

"Who in Tartarus are you then, parthenos?"

Parthenos. Virgin. A word too often wrongly associated with unmarried women. Elena felt a surge of anger.

"Sophistes Elena, from the Thenean garrison and aide to Kosmetes Galleas. The young man you are … conversing with is one of our ephebes."

"We know that," the bigger man replied with a smirk. "That's why we're 'ere. Got paid to have a little chat wiv' 'im."

Elena heard once more the crack of Tychos's arm breaking. Remembered the ugly welt on Keres's forehead.

Helydices. What have you done?

"Your chat will have to wait," she said. "Makar is expected back home. His father is waiting."

Pot-belly laughed, making his torch jiggle. "Don't think that'll work. We don't get paid if we don't finish the job." He thumped over to her, and she felt a clammy hand land on her bare shoulder. "Best if you take a quick stroll and come back in a few minutes."

Elena could feel the roughness of his skin against hers. Smell the stench of wine on his breath. The anger washed the last of her fear away. "Please take your hand off me."

"Nah, don't think I—"

Elena smiled sweetly and brought her knee up between the man's legs as hard as she could. He yelped in surprise and collapsed, dropping his torch so he could clutch at his crotch with both hands. Elena kicked him twice in the stomach, then stepped over his writhing form to help Makar to his feet.

The second man still hadn't moved, staring at her with a mixture of fear and admiration.

"What's your name?" she asked him.

"T … Tobias."

"Well, Tobias, there are a half-dozen ephebes combing the agora for their friend. What do you think we should tell them when they find us?"

She felt his eyes on her once more, probing, searching for hidden cracks in her facade. She clasped her hands behind her back and kept them there so he wouldn't see them shaking.

"Leave 'em be, Tobias," came a pain-filled voice. "My balls are burning like the fires of Tartarus. Stupid little *parthenos* must've broken something. You need to get me to a physician."

Tobias cursed and went to help his partner, somehow managing to pull the groaning man upright despite his considerable girth. In a final act of defiance, he hawked and spat at Elena's feet before retreating into the maze of stalls, the light of his torch quickly fading from sight.

"That … was … amazing!" panted Makar, his eyes gleaming in the gloom. "I've never seen a man go down so fast."

Elena's heart was pounding like a galloping horse, but she decided against revealing to her student how close she had come to running away and abandoning him to his fate. She tried a nonchalant shrug instead. "He made the same mistakes as a lot of men: he was overconfident, and he underestimated his opponent because she was a woman."

"Yes, Mistress. Although, if I may ask, why didn't you wait for the other ephebes?"

She stared back at him impassively until she saw understanding bloom on his chalk-white face. "There aren't any
other ephebes, are there, Mistress?"

"No, Makar. There are not. Which is why I suggest we
don't linger here any longer. I'll come with you as far as your
father's workshop, if you don't mind. For your own safety."

And for mine.

RESPONSIBILITIES

"Hear tired sandalled foot on stone.

The silent soldier bows his head.

Hear the woman's anguished groan.

The harbinger.

Her son

Is dead."

OLD TYRREAN MARCHING SONG

KERES READJUSTED HIS aspis for the tenth time that morning, wincing as the bronze rim dug into his shoulder. They had been marching northwards non-stop since dawn, and everything was starting to hurt.

The standard issue clip-on greaves that Galleas had issued to the ephebes pinched Keres's skin when he moved. His linothorax rubbed everywhere that wasn't protected by his chiton. And his xiphos, hanging from a knotted baldric under his left armpit, banged constantly against his ribs. To make matters worse, the foul-smelling salve that the physician had slathered onto the bruise on his forehead was melting in the mid-morning heat, escaping from under the bandage and dribbling down his nose.

Normally, he would complain about all of this to Tychos, but his friend was now miles away in Thena. Keres had done his best to comfort him the night before, promising him that the campaign would be over in a matter of weeks, and that once Tychos's arm was healed, there would be many more opportunities for glory.

That, of course, was before Galleas had revealed the nature of the enemy.

Tauros. A horde of tauros.

He remembered Helydices roaring excitedly at the news, beating his chest and thanking the Gods. He already saw himself as the hero. They had no idea. None of them did.

Dexios thundered past on a chestnut stallion, his officer's cloak billowing out behind him. "Break for ariston," he shouted, heading to the front of the line.

Ariston was the first meal the hoplites would eat during the day, a late breakfast or early lunch. Keres gave a sigh of relief and stumbled over to one of the olive trees bordering the road. He leant his spear against the twisted trunk and set his shield down next to it. The image of the diving hawk gleamed; the black paint not quite dry. Keres had sent for one of Thena's most prominent artists — at great cost — and the wizened little man had worked hard through the night, sketching, outlining, and finally painting the majestic bird of prey. The bronze of the shield's surface made it look as if the hawk was swooping down from the sun itself.

"Watered wine, Master?" Nambe stood basking in the midday heat, soaking up the rays like a lizard. He seemed to have appeared out of nowhere.

Keres accepted a cup, along with a hunk of dry bread. He took a seat on a large rock in the shade of the olive tree and stretched out his legs. "Thank you, Nambe. Should you not be attending to my father?"

Nambe made a puffing sound. "Dexios can look after himself. This is not his first campaign. If he wants a cup of wine, he can go and get one."

Keres let the liquid trickle down his throat. It was much weaker than he was used to. More water than wine.

"Nambe?"

"Hmmm?"

"Father told you to check on me, didn't he?"

Nambe joined him on the rock. "Do not take it as a slight, young Master. Your father has been doing this for a long time. Buried a lot of good men. And now he must prepare himself to bury even more. I reckon he doesn't want you to be one of them."

"By sending his slave instead of coming himself."

The southerner shrugged. "Most of the men here do not know you are the strategos's heir. You do not bear the family heraldry or wear his panoply. It's a long road to Ruxia, and an officer's son is the perfect scapegoat for a bunch of bored hoplites. He's only trying to protect you."

"Then, he should tell me that," Keres groused. "He's always keeping things from me. My sophistes has taught me more about Thena's military campaigns than he ever did."

"What makes you believe he was doing it for you? It's just as likely he avoided the subject to block out unwelcome memories."

"And what about you, Nambe? Still haunted by the past?"

The big slave ran a hand over his shaved scalp. "I helped him place the obols on the tongues of the fallen. Return their shields to their next of kin. Some of them were younger than you are now. Their shades were sent to the shores of Tartarus unmarried and with no descendants. After a time, just the sight of him approaching a soldier's home was enough to fill its occupants with dread. People started calling him the herald of Charon. The harbinger of grief." His gaze wandered further up the road where Dexios was deep in conversation with Polydius, Galleas, and the other lochagos. "It … It takes its toll."

"Then, why take on the responsibility? He is a strategos, not a pallbearer. Why not share the load? There are others in the phalanx that can dig holes and make pyres."

Nambe tutted. "Don't ask questions you know the answer to, young Master. Your father taught you better than that."

Keres thought for a moment. "He believes it to be his penance, doesn't he? That as strategos, he is somehow responsible for their deaths." He leant back with a sigh. "Gods … that's ludicrous! He cannot protect his men from every loosed arrow. Every spear thrust. No one would expect that of him. One of the first things Galleas told us is that there is a random moment in every battle that can tip the scales. A drop of rain falling into the enemy's eye. A gust of wind that deflects an arrow's trajectory. A patch of loose earth that causes a man to stumble … does my father not see this?"

"He did. Once. But time is a treacherous companion, young Master, whispering falsehoods into our minds, slowly eroding those stalwart pillars of truth, hoping to raise others in their place."

Dexios had finished talking to his captains, and the

high-pitched trill of the pipes signalled to the hoplites that the ariston was over.

Nambe stood. "I never saw your father happier than when Letho agreed to accept his resignation. And now that honey-tongued man has taken advantage of my master's sense of duty and honour to trick him into serving Thena once more." The dark-skinned slave scowled. "Dexios should have refused. We should be harvesting the vines and signing the contract that will finally give me my freedom. Mine and that of my family. Instead, we are marching to defend a polis that has never lifted a finger to help our own …" he trailed off, realising he had said too much.

Keres smiled sadly. "I am sorry, Nambe. For all those times I've whinged and moaned. Complaining to you about trivialities while you worked tirelessly to set yourself free. I must have sounded like a spoilt little brat."

Nambe grinned back. "Do not concern yourself with that, young Master. Dexios has always treated me with kindness and respect. He extricated me from a very uncomfortable situation. My former master was … not a good man. No, I am content with the life I have. There is one thing you can do for me, however."

"Yes, Nambe?"

"Next time we stop, how about it's *you* who gets *me* some food and a nice cup of wine?"

The day wore ponderously on. Keres began to mark the passage of time by the amount of dust that caked his sandals as the leather straps slowly disappeared from view under layers of dirt. His left shoulder grew numb from the weight of the aspis. He lost his bandage at some point, and the wound on his forehead started to ache.

He was surrounded by strangers, men older than himself who were taking up their spear and shield for the seventh or eighth time. Their mismatched armour was covered in furrows and scratches, the bronze crinkled in places where it had been beaten back into shape by a craftsman's hammer. Helmets were missing cheek guards. Linen breastplates were rife with unravelling threads. One veteran only had half a cuirass tied around his torso with a length of rope. The decorated shields, however, were pristine.

There appeared to be no common theme to the various depictions of heraldic imagery. The simpler designs incorporated the 'theta' symbol of Thena, the open-palmed blessing of Hera, or the long bow of Artemis. Less common were the animals: lions, wolves, dogs, horses, and ravens. There were even a couple of bulls, which seemed ironic considering the enemy the hoplites were marching to face.

While stopping to empty his bladder, Keres found himself next to a ruddy-faced butcher who bore a shield decorated with a nine-headed hydra. Upon seeing Keres's admiring stare, he turned his aspis round so that the young ephebe could see it in all its glory.

"Hydra's unkillable, ain't it?" he added proudly. "Cut off a head and it just grows right back. That's me, that is. Unkillable."

The butcher squinted at Keres's own heraldry. "A crow? Not very unique, is it? We've got plenty of crows."

"Um, no. A hawk."

"Ah, yeah, didn't see the talons. Masterful work. Why the hawk?"

Because the Gods gifted me with a vision, Keres thought. Probably information best not shared, for now at least. The last thing he needed was to be stuck with some stupid epithet like 'zealot' or 'fanatic'.

"A powerful bird of prey," he said carefully.

"Hah! Indeed! Brain the size of an olive, though!" The butcher gave Keres a hearty clap on the shoulder, adjusted his chiton, and returned to the column of hoplites.

Keres followed reluctantly, scanning the line in the hope of spotting a friendly face. There was none to be found. During his first year of ephebic training, he had rarely ventured forth into the labyrinthian streets of Thena, preferring to spend what little free time he had back at the vineyard. Aside from his fellow ephebes and their teachers, he knew barely anyone. It was a depressing thought.

After a time, he gave up and traipsed back to his spot next to the loud-mouthed butcher who was regaling a group of younger hoplites with his account of a previous military campaign, his arms miming battle lines and formations, his booming voice accompanied by copious amounts of spittle.

"Ah! Little hawk!" he grinned. "I was just explaining to these ignorant fools how the Thenean phalanx flew to the aid of Atlis four years ago. Beset on all sides by pirates, they were. Crumbling under their ferocious attacks. We stood on the shore, sixteen men wide and sixteen deep, our spears stuck in the sand, the waves lapping around our feet. Opposite us, five thousand raiders sought to land their boats. We would stand firm. We would deny them victory even if every last one of us was sent to Charon's embrace."

"You faced two thousand, not five," Keres said grumpily, heaving his aspis back onto his shoulder as the column began to move. "And you weren't on the beach, you were positioned at the top of an incline just beyond, using the higher ground to your advantage."

The butcher's cheeks turned a darker shade of red. "What you talking about, boy? I was there, I remember it well. One of the bastards nicked my ear with a xiphos, you can still see the scar. Who's been filling your head with all this offal?"

"My father."

"Well, unless he was there too, he should shut—"

"My father, Strategos Dexios."

There was a clang and a muttered curse as the butcher dropped his aspis in surprise, the bronze rim catching the top of his left foot. He recovered gracefully.

"Ah, so you're the Harbinger's son. There were rumours you would be marching with us. The ... the hawk, it threw me off. Why don't you wear your family heraldry on your shield?"

Keres shrugged. "I do not know what emblem my father chose. His shield hangs in its cover over my parents' bed. He has never shown it to me, and I have never asked."

The butcher looked at him strangely. "Fair enough. If he hasn't seen fit to tell you, then it's not for me to say. A good man, your father. I fought with him several times. When you next see him, please tell him Syphos sends his regards." He tapped the tip of his spear to his forehead and dropped back a few paces, leaving Keres alone with the two hoplites. They were both only a few years older than him, most likely ending their second year of ephebic training, sporting near-identical wispy beards.

"So … your father," one of them began hesitantly. "He crossed the Straits? He fought the men of the south?"

Keres allowed himself an all-knowing smile. "He did. He always told me it was the hardest campaign he had ever fought. Thena nearly lost, you know."

"What? No, that can't be right. I heard our phalanx slaughtered a thousand men a day."

"Whoever said that was spending too much time at the taverna. This is what my father told me …"

Of course, Keres didn't have much of a clue about what had really happened, but he gamely filled any gaps in his scant knowledge with a mixture of guesswork … and action-packed tales born from his vivid imagination. He soon found himself swept up in his own narrative. His shield felt lighter, and the throbbing of his forehead faded to a dull itch. Time's languid stream became a fast-flowing river, carrying him through the rest of the day and into the evening with the speed of a loosed arrow.

His crowd of eager listeners had grown exponentially over the afternoon, and there was a collection of disappointed groans when the pipes sounded the order to make camp. Keres set down his spear and shield and raised his hands placatingly, promising more stories the following morning.

He wandered over to the nearest supply wagon to pick up a bedroll, tripod, and cloak. The summer nights were warm and dry so there would be no need to pitch tents; every hoplite could sleep under the stars with nothing in between him and the Gods. In fact, arguably the most important piece of equipment was the tripod. It would allow his aspis to remain upright and keep his heraldry out of the mud. An overturned shield was seen as an egregious omen, a reminder of how the wounded and dead were carried from the battlefield. Any hoplite found with his shield lying face down would be whipped.

Keres accepted his bundle from one of the camp slaves and turned, nearly bumping into Helydices. The guard captain's son was wearing an opulent helm that only added to his already impressive physique.

"How's the head?" Helydices asked innocently. "Heard you took a nasty tumble. I was surprised old Galleas let you join us, to be honest. I expect your father forced him to, you know, to avoid the dishonour."

Keres bit down on the flesh of his tongue to keep himself from lashing out.

"Perhaps," he replied with forced cheerfulness. "I was equally surprised Galleas made you part of the phalanx after your blasphemy the other day." Keres leant closer. "Some say Hera can take days to punish those who utter the names of the Ruined. Striking when they least expect it. In their sleep, for example. How have you been sleeping recently, Helydices? Tossing and turning in your bed, jumping at shadows …"

Helydices uttered an angry growl, his hand straying to his xiphos hanging under his left armpit. The two ephebes suddenly found themselves in the middle of a circle as those around them backed away.

"What is going on here?" a deep voice rumbled. The ebony head of Nambe appeared over the crowd of onlookers, bobbing up and down as he pushed his way closer.

"Here comes your slave to save you," mocked Helydices. "But you won't be able to hide behind him forever. It's a long march to Ruxia, and all I need is one tiny minute alone with you."

"Like during the trials."

"Exactly."

Keres smiled triumphantly. "I thought you said I fell."

Helydices opened his mouth to reply, but then Nambe was there, hands on his hips.

"Ephebe! Explain yourself!"

"I don't have to answer to you, slave. Get out of my sight, or I will have you whipped."

Nambe nodded calmly. "That is your right. For that is what I am. Property. Strategos Dexios's property. I wonder what he will do to the man who unjustly damages his slave?"

Helydices said nothing, his eyes boring into Nambe, who stared back. Finally, with a wry smile, the guard captain's son grabbed a bedroll from the back of the cart and stomped away, the crowd parting silently to let him through.

"I didn't need your help," Keres said testily. "Helydices may be an ox-brained idiot, but he was right about one thing. You can't keep fighting my battles for me."

Nambe gave a look of mock surprise. "Why, whatever are you talking about, young Master? Your father sent me to procure a bedroll, nothing more." He pressed a finger to his lips thoughtfully. "But that reminds me, did we not agree you would bring me a cup of wine the next time we met? A large cup, two-thirds water, if you would. They are offloading the amphorae over there somewhere." He gestured vaguely.

"Fine," huffed Keres. "You can watch my spear and shield for me while I'm gone."

The food wagon was easy to find, under heavy assault by a large group of thirsty hoplites. Keres waited patiently for his turn. The wine was being handed out by a lightly-tanned slave clad in a long green cloak, his hair shorn to lumpy stubble. He was reaching into the cart with one hand, the other hidden in the folds of his cloak.

Oh no, thought Keres.

Pale blue eyes met his, and there was a flash of recognition.

It was Tychos.

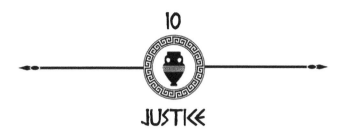

10

JUSTICE

"*Paradoxically, a wounded lion is far more dangerous than a healthy one. An injured animal has been confronted with its own mortality, its own vulnerability. It no longer fights to quell its hunger; it fights to prove its existence. It fights to prove its strength.*"

CERBRIONES, 'ALALAGMOE'

MAKAR WALKED SWIFTLY through the deserted marketplace, his long, bouncing strides forcing Elena into a brisk walk to keep up.

"It's funny," the ephebe said. "The agora is always patrolled at night. Not everything here can be carted away in the evening. So where were the city guard? The merchants will be furious if they find out their wares have been left unprotected."

"The agora is large and sprawling. Maybe they were on the far side, out of sight and sound."

Makar was silent for a moment. "Those men … they were sent by Helydices."

"Yes, I thought that was probably the case."

"Helydices … the guard captain's son."

Elena mulled it over. "From what I've heard, Crenate is a stubborn and bullish man. But to imply he played some part in his son's petty vengeance … it's a big leap, Makar."

"I'm sure you're right, but maybe … maybe it would be best not to involve the night watch, Mistress? Until we know more, at least?"

Elena nodded. Makar had spoken more in the last few minutes than he had over the last few months. He seemed different away from the harsh stares of the other ephebes, more in control. As if to prove her wrong, Makar chose that exact moment to catch the lip of his sandal on a cracked cobblestone. He stumbled and almost fell, pinwheeling his arms desperately to remain upright. After a short battle between boy and gravity, he regained his balance with a shrug and a bashful grin. The grin was infectious, and Elena found herself responding with one of her own.

Desha's workshop was situated about ten minutes' walk away from the agora, running the entire length of one of the many small squares that dotted the dense network of alleyways like clearings in a forest. The square had seen better days: prickly weeds forced their way through cracked paving stones in their quest for sunlight. In a refuse-filled corner, two faded and forgotten amphorae leant against one another like a pair of half-drunk lovers. And positioned at its very centre, a dry, empty fountain topped with a weathered statue of Persephone completed the depressing vista.

Makar banged on the wooden gate of the workshop, which creaked open to reveal a bleary-eyed house slave. "Master? Back so soon?"

"The basileus is forming the city phalanx," Makar replied. "All ephebes are eligible since the ceremony. They march at dawn."

"*They* march, Master?"

"I … have been chosen by the kosmetes to stay and

defend the city in their absence." The words were said without any conviction. The slave's eyes widened ever so slightly. He pulled the gate all the way open and motioned them both inside. "Master Desha is still working. Please wait here for a few minutes, I'll go and fetch him."

The vestibule beyond was well-lit, its marble statue of Hera gazing haughtily down at them from atop her pedestal. An intricately wrought necklace of polished bronze hung from the goddess's neck and her arms were adorned with spiralling jewelled bracelets.

"I helped make that one," Makar said proudly, pointing to the statue's right arm. "Some of our best work, on display for all to see."

"It's … beautiful," Elena agreed, admiring the way the bronze curled up the statue's bare arms like a snake. "I didn't know you were so talented, Makar."

"Oh, it's my father, mostly," the young ephebe replied, blushing furiously. "I only—"

"My son does not give himself enough credit," interrupted a gruff voice. Desha was standing in the opening that led deeper inside the house, clad in a dirty leather apron. His long salt-and-pepper hair stopped abruptly halfway up his head, giving way to his bald pate and making it look like he was wearing a skin-covered skull cap.

White burn marks covered his face and left arm like tiny snowflakes, the unfortunate consequence of long years working with molten metal. His right arm ended just above the elbow with a lump of puckered skin that reminded Elena of a large wrinkled fig. The old man caught her staring and gave a slight frown.

"Who are you?" he asked irritably.

"Sophistes Elena. I'm the—"

"Ah, the boy's teacher. I remember now. Sold you a brooch."

"Um. I don't think so? We've met a few times but—"

"Oval-shaped with a cobalt centre." He sniffed. "I'm poor at remembering faces, but I never forget a piece of jewellery."

Elena paused, wondering whether she had just been insulted or not. Desha turned to his son. "And what about you, boy? Did you bring honour to our house at the trials? Where are your spear and shield?"

"Still at the garrison, Father," Makar replied, pointedly ignoring the first question. "Letho has called up the phalanx. Trouble in the north."

Desha's eyes glittered. "Ah, excellent. A chance for you to prove your worth, at last. I'll have rations and clean clothes prepared for your departure, and that old rat Clovis owes me a few favours, he can fill in for you at the workshop while you are away."

Makar looked down at his sandalled feet. "I … I won't—"

"Speak up, boy! How many times have I told you not to mumble? You're an ephebe, not a house slave!"

"Yes, Father," Makar replied, slowly raising his gaze. "I was saying I have not been chosen. Letho has called for the ennea. Nine in ten. I am among those picked to defend the city."

Desha sniffed again, the gesture sending wrinkles rippling up his bald head like a stone dropped in a pond. "Of course you are. Picked to defend the city. The city of Thena, with its protective walls, surrounded by allies, and miles away from the front lines. Just where you always wanted to be."

Makar bristled. "I am no coward."

"No. But you are no hero either. Go and clean the workshop. We will talk more of this tomorrow."

The young ephebe's shoulders slumped in resignation. He wandered away, his head bowed so low that his chin almost touched his chest.

"Um." Elena wracked her tired brain for something interesting to say. "Makar is a bit clumsy sometimes, but he has a sharp mind. One of the sharpest."

"Wars are not won with sharp minds. They are won with sharp spears."

"Well, I'm not sure that's true. A competent strategos—"

"Won't be able to change the tide of battle if his soldiers don't know their shield from their arse. Before moving here, we lived in Lendes for a while. There was a tauros incursion, and I was conscripted."

His eyes took on the glazed look of someone dredging up ancient memories. "The strategos was a bright lad. He chose the terrain well, gave a few rousing speeches, and made sure we were well prepared. Thing is, that didn't change who we were. I was surrounded by a bunch of craftsmen and traders. We pissed ourselves silly as soon as the first tauros came over the hill. Our pitiful shield wall shattered almost immediately."

His left hand went to the stump of his right arm, probing the flesh. "They rolled over us like … well, like a herd of stampeding cattle. Luckily, I only lost my arm. I still don't know why they didn't finish me off."

Elena imagined a tauran axe hammering into the old

man's side. The spurt of blood. The crunch of shattered bone. "I'm sorry for what happened to you," she said softly. "Look, I shouldn't be telling you this, and the other ephebes don't know, but they won't be facing bandits or mercenaries. A herd of tauros has been spotted coming over the mountains. Several herds, in fact."

Desha's eyebrows shot up in surprise. "Balls, girl! Are you sure?"

"I was there to hear Ruxia's plea for aid."

The old man deflated slightly. "Then ... perhaps I spoke too hastily. I will admit that my son is not quite prepared for such a ... challenging adversary. I will apologise. I suppose that means I won't need Clovis after all. A small blessing, at least. The man stinks so bad I can still smell him a week after he leaves. What about you, girl? Heading back to the garrison?"

"Yes, if you can spare someone to accompany me. The streets are not the safest place to be at the moment." Elena briefly explained the events of the last few days and their run-in with Helydices's thugs.

"Spoilt brat," spat Desha when she had finished. "Sounds like he needs to spend some time in the stocks to rethink his priorities. I'll take the matter to the basileus himself."

"I think you'll find that Letho is currently a bit busy."

"He'll listen to me. He owes me. In the meantime, you'll have to stay here. You saw my slave, he can barely stand on his own two feet, let alone serve as an escort. And I shudder to think what would happen if I gave him a weapon. He'd be just as likely to stab you as he would the enemy. You are welcome to my andron. It doesn't see much use nowadays anyway. My slave will bring you anything you need."

He bowed curtly and disappeared back inside, leaving Elena alone under the withering gaze of the jewelled statue of Hera.

♋

Tobias was pissed off.

It was supposed to be an easy job. Find the kid, rough him up a bit, and report back. Easy.

His partner, Endikes, gave a small groan. Tobias knew why. He had taken a look at the damage wrought by the blonde-haired parthenos, and it wasn't pretty. It wasn't pretty at all.

"This the place?" the big man growled, one hand massaging his crotch, the other holding a vicious-looking cudgel. Three more men stood behind him. The kind of men you would find slouched against the bar of a taverna or lying in the gutter outside.

"Aye," Tobias replied, glancing up at the high walls of the jeweller's workshop. "Looks impressive, but the place is 'alf-empty from what I've 'eard. Just the old man, 'is son, and a doddering 'ouse slave. Shouldn't prove much of a challenge."

Endikes tapped his cudgel against his thigh. "Careful, now! You said the same thing last time, and look 'ow that turned out. We're not gonna let that 'appen again." His sunken eyes took on a dark look. "I can imagine 'em, all nice and cosy inside. Probably laughin' at me. The stupid man who was bested by a woman. Let's see 'ow loud they laugh without their teeth."

Tobias licked his lips. He'd worked with Endikes a few

times before, collecting debts, recovering certain ... items for interested parties, that sort of thing. The pay was good, but it was always just a job, the bruised faces fading from thought as soon as he had washed the blood from his knuckles. Endikes was different. Endikes *enjoyed* it.

"No need to go that far, eh?" he said. "Helydices is paying us to slap 'em about a bit like you did to that other one during the trials."

The cudgel was waved under his nose. "Not doin' this for Helydices anymore," Endikes said in a low voice. "Or 'is money. I'm doin' it for *me*. You got that?"

"Ye ... yeah, sure. It's just ... 'e's only a boy, you know?"

"Not since today. Got 'is spear and shield, didn' 'e? 'Is shade'll go to Tartarus a man."

"Go to Tar... you wanna kill 'im?"

"Deserves it. Laughin' at me. Laughin' at us all. You gonna sit there and let 'im do that?"

"I ..."

"'Cause if you ain't with us, you're against us. No skin off my back. Easier to split the drachmae four ways than five."

Tobias became keenly aware of his current situation, his back literally against the wall, facing four men of questionable reputation. His eyes scanned the empty square. There would be no help there. The city guard wouldn't patrol the area for another hour at least; he knew this because he had bribed them himself. He'd have to play along. For now.

"You're right, Endikes," he said. "They deserve to pay. What's the plan?"

"One of us goes in to scout out the place. If it's safe, 'e

unbolts the main gate. We slip inside, find that chalky-faced brat, and 'ave a little chat."

Endikes motioned one of his men forwards, a small, wiry individual with prominent buck teeth and a scar across his nose. Tobias thought he looked like an annoyed hare.

"Over 'ere, Syrec. I'll give ya a leg up." Endikes shuffled over to the side of the warehouse, bent his knees, and interlaced his massive hands together to make a step. The scar-faced man clambered on and, with a grunt of effort from Endikes, was propelled upwards. One flailing hand found the edge of the warehouse roof and hung on tight.

"Now, we wait," muttered Tobias as Syrec disappeared into the shadows. The words had barely left his lips when he heard the *thunk* of a bolt being drawn back. The gate opened with a groan of rusty hinges, revealing the darkness of the vestibule beyond.

Endikes eyed the door warily. "That was fast, even for Syrec."

"Too fast," Tobias agreed. "Somethin's not right. I feel it in my gut. Maybe we should 'old off for tonight. Retribution can wait."

"Charon's balls, Tobias," snarled Endikes. "I barely recognise you anymore. Five years ago, if someone had done ya wrong, you wouldn't 'ave rested until you'd pummelled his head into the cobbles. An eye for an eye. We're not turning back. Get inside."

"I just don't think—"

Endikes had his cudgel out again. "Get. In. Side."

Tobias swallowed. He'd seen what Endikes could do with that cudgel and had no desire to be on the receiving end of it. Gathering his courage, he pushed the door open as far as it would go and stepped into the vestibule.

"Take one of the men and search the workshop," Endikes said softly. "We'll take the house. Remember, all quiet and dark like. No noise. No torches."

Tobias entered the gloomy interior and turned right, creeping past an empty kitchen and well-stocked larder before entering the workshop proper. There was some light here, a pale golden glow emanating from the smouldering embers of the forge. The jeweller's tools were hung neatly on hooks along one of the walls while stacks of wood and coal were piled up against the other. Everything was perfectly organised … except for a crumpled tarpaulin that had been left in the middle of the room.

For the second time that evening, Tobias felt that tingling sensation, warning him that something wasn't right.

"Hera give me strength."

He drew his dagger and inched closer, eyes darting left and right as he scanned for signs of danger.

He was so focused on the dark corners of the room that he missed the puddle on the floor. His feet went out from under him, and he hit the dirt with a crunch, much to the amusement of the thug following him.

Scowling, he picked himself up. He could feel whatever he had slipped in between his toes, thick and sticky. He put his hand in the puddle and rubbed some of the liquid between his thumb and forefinger. Touched his finger to the tip of his tongue. Blood.

He turned reluctantly back to the tarpaulin. The human-shaped tarpaulin. The tip of a scarred nose poked out from under one corner. Tobias knew that if he pulled the fabric aside, he would find himself face-to-face with the buck-toothed Syrec.

"It's a trap!" he cried, just as an agonising cry pierced the night.

Hera's tits, he cursed. *I should never have come here.* "Back to the house!" he ordered, pushing past his stunned escort. A dark shape flittered across the edge of his vision, and there was a sound like a xiphos slicing into a ripe orange. Something heavy hit him in the back. He wheeled around just in time to see the decapitated body of his companion topple over backwards, bright red blood fountaining from the jagged hole in its neck. He glanced down. The severed head that had hit him stared back at him, eyes open wide in surprise.

Tobias fled, running from the workshop back into the house. He saw the ravaged body of Endikes too late, tripping over the gory remains of a mangled torso and crashing to the ground for the second time.

"GODS!" he screamed, wiping his face clean of his friend's blood. Endikes had been torn apart, his limbs scattered haphazardly across the floor, his viscera spattering the stone walls. There was a hole in the middle of his chest the size of a pomegranate. His heart was gone, leaving behind a messy crevasse of shattered ribs and dark grey lung matter. Endikes bore an expression of pure terror, his lips drawn tight into a terrible rictus, his tiny eyes bulging from their sockets.

Tobias could taste blood in his mouth, and it wasn't his. His stomach heaved. He had to get out. Vengeance. Money. Neither was worth this.

"I'm leaving!" he cried shrilly into the empty corridor.

He ran back to the vestibule, but there would be no escape. The mutilated corpse of the last of Endikes's men had been shoved violently into the doorway, the bones twisted at impossible angles so as to block it completely. The marble statue of Hera glared down at him. It appeared to be gloating.

"GODS!" Tobias yelled once more. There had to be another way out. Through the courtyard, perhaps. He headed back inside, turning left this time, pointedly avoiding the gory remains of Endikes's mutilated body. Another opening. The andron. He risked a peek inside. A woman lay on one of the couches, snoring softly. An empty amphora lay on its side at her feet. The woman from the agora. What was her name? Elena? It was her fault they were here. Her fault the others had died. He fingered the tip of his dagger. It would only take a moment to slit her throat.

"Leeeaaaavvve hhhheerrrr."

It was a hiss. A whisper. Yet, the voice still buzzed around Tobias's skull like a swarm of bees. He dropped his weapon with a clang.

The creature standing at the end of the corridor was of average height, its face hidden in darkness. Unnaturally long arms covered with pulsating veins ended in razor-sharp claws.

"Leeeeeaaave."

Blood dripped from the extremities of its talons. Endikes's blood.

Tobias whimpered as his bladder gave way. Warm urine cascaded down his thighs and pooled at his feet.

"You … you killed my friend."

The figure cocked its head, and Tobias saw a flash of ivory as the creature smiled.

"Jusssssstice."

Tobias gave a mad chuckle. "Justice? For who? That parthenos assaulted us! She 'as to pay." He took a hesitant step towards the woman, repeating his words in the hope of making them real. "She 'as to pay."

His death, when it came, didn't really hurt at all. One moment he was turning towards Elena, next the creature's talons burst through his chest, punching through his back and out through his ribcage in an explosion of blood and bone.

How in Tartarus did it move so fast, he thought, his failing eyes focusing with difficulty on the four claws protruding from his torso. His killer bent closer, and he heard a sibilant voice whisper in his ear.

"Sheeee is ours. You will not touch her."

The creature withdrew its hands from Tobias's chest, and he sank to his knees. Elena turned in her sleep, murmuring something incomprehensible. But she did not wake.

"Shhhhheee is ouuuurs," the voice repeated.

Tobias didn't understand. He tried to speak, but his mouth refused to comply. He coughed instead, showering the andron with a spray of crimson droplets.

His strength began to fade. His shade was bound for a distant shore, far beneath the earth. He would enter Tartarus and be judged. And considering the life he had led, Elysium's doors would remain closed. Only pain and torture awaited him now.

Colour fled his vision, rendering everything a depressing hue of grey. Tobias focused on Elena, her bosom rising and falling as she slept peacefully, unaware of the violence that surrounded her.

"I'm …"

Sorry.

But it didn't matter. Nothing mattered. No one could hear him. No one could save him. There was only one thing left to do.

Prepare for Charon's embrace.

ARRIVAL

"Tyche is a goddess of overwhelming contradictions. She has no temples, yet her believers number almost as many as those of Hera herself. A farmer mutters a hopeful prayer before sowing his crops. A woman screams her name as she gives birth. A soldier seeks her blessing before an enemy charge. She is as ubiquitous as she is fickle, and, perhaps worst of all, she destroys just as many lives as she saves."

BASILEUS LETHO, 'RUMINATIONS'

I T WAS TWO more days before Keres managed to find a moment to speak to Tychos alone. His friend had a gruelling daily routine preparing and serving the hundreds of men who made up the Thenean phalanx. Countless sacks of grain needed to be milled into flour or mixed into porridge. Scouting parties had to venture far from camp to search for kindling and water to dilute the stock of concentrated wine.

The officers and richer citizens could afford to bring their personal house slaves with them on campaign, but the greater part of the hoplite army relied on the polis slaves provided by the basileus for everything from cooking the evening meal to digging the latrines.

At dawn on the third morning, Keres spied the stone-mason's son leaving the camp in the direction of a grove of olive trees, an earthenware amphora balanced precariously on one shoulder. The pipes had not yet roused the hoplites from their slumber, and Keres was wedged in the midst of snoring cloak-covered lumps. He slipped on his sandals and crept silently towards the olive grove, doing his best to avoid the shields and pieces of armour that littered his path.

Tychos was standing knee-deep in a pool of water, filling his amphora, unaware that he was no longer alone. Keres grinned to himself and padded closer.

"TYCHOS!"

His friend gave a startled yelp, tried to turn around, caught his foot on the amphora, and pitched head-first into the ice-cold pool with a splash.

"Keres!" he spluttered angrily, his eyes blazing. "Hera's tits, I nearly soiled myself! And this is my only chiton!"

Keres took one look at Tychos's bedraggled face and burst out laughing.

"Serves you right for being a stubborn fool. What were you thinking, following us out here? And what have you done to your hair?"

"I'll explain," grumbled Tychos. "But only if you come and help me up. I'm a wounded man, remember?" He held out his hand.

Keres shrugged off his sandals and stepped into the pool. "Gods, that's cold! Must be spring water, bubbling up from underground." He gritted his teeth and waded further in to grasp his friend's hand. "No hard feelings?"

"None at all," answered Tychos with a sly grin. One hard tug was all it took to pull Keres off balance and plunge him underwater.

"COLD!" he shrieked as he re-emerged, his dark hair plastered to his scalp.

"No hard feelings?" asked Tychos sarcastically.

"Stupid malaka."

"You started it. And you got my bandage wet. The physician will not be pleased."

"Let's just ... can we just find a place in the sun? I'm starting to lose all feeling in my legs."

They left the amphora by the pool and stretched out on a patch of scraggly grass warmed by the early morning light.

"Your hair looks terrible, by the way," Keres said, rubbing some heat back into his arms.

Tychos shrugged. "It was the only thing I could think of on the spur of the moment. I wasn't going to let you fight a horde of tauros by yourself. You can barely strap your sandals on without me around."

"Very funny. And you're deflecting. You know that if you're caught, you'll be whipped, right? Or worse? You disobeyed a direct order from a superior officer. You ... you abandoned your post on the walls of Thena. That's ... desertion. Punishable by death."

Tychos turned onto his side, propping himself up on his one good elbow. "I don't care. You can't expect me to sit on my arse while the rest of you are gaining all the glory. I'd rather die a soldier than live a coward." He leant forwards, his gaze penetrating. "Honestly, what would you have done if Galleas had picked you to stay? Would you have waved us off with a smile on your lips and returned to your peaceful vineyard to harvest your grapes?"

Keres remembered the look of admiration on his father's face as he stumbled over the finishing line. The look of pride when he received his spear and shield. "No," he said reluctantly. "I suppose I would have thought up some hair-brained plan to tag along unnoticed."

"Exactly! And, as luck would have it, hair-brained plans are my forte. Everyone knew the polis slaves would be part of the muster. And who notices a slave? Helydices passed within two feet of me yesterday and didn't spare me a second glance. They're invisible, like pieces of furniture, hiding in plain sight."

"I suppose, but the other slaves …"

"Have neither reason nor inclination to rat on me. Most of them are pleased to have an extra pair of hands … well, an extra hand."

"And your father?"

Tychos gave a slight frown. "Yes, he's probably the only one apart from you who would recognise me anywhere. Fortunately for me — and for him — he's been promoted to lochagos. Eats and sleeps with the officers. He's even allowed his own tent; can you believe it? I've had a few close shaves, but for the most part, he hasn't stooped to mingling with the rank-and-file."

Keres laid back, enjoying the sun on his face. "I don't like it, Tychos. What you've done is stupid and reckless …"

"… But you'll help protect my secret and find me a xiphos or a spear so I can defend myself when the time comes?" his friend finished hopefully.

"Gods, I don't know. Honestly, I don't know. I've just realised something. It was Nambe who sent me to fetch him a cup of wine. He's as sly as a fox, that one. It can't have been a coincidence; he must have recognised you too."

"That's unfortunate. But hey, he can't have told your

father, or instead of having this conversation you would be standing weeping over my funeral pyre."

Keres became serious. "Don't even joke about that, Tychos. If anything ever happened to you, I would—"

He was interrupted by the familiar sound of the pipes, filtering through the olive trees like a bird call from the heavens.

Keres sighed and gave Tychos's shaved head an affectionate rub. "Time to get back. I'll help you carry the amphora."

"And my weapon?"

"Let's wait and see. Perhaps Polydius was wrong. Perhaps we won't be needed after all."

Another two days' hard march brought the Thenean phalanx within sight of the snow-capped Dorias Mountains. To Keres, they looked like a row of misshapen grey teeth, as if the ground itself was snarling up at the constellations. He found it hard to tear his eyes away from the horizon, watching as the massive shapes drew closer and closer until they towered over him.

He felt strangely humbled in their presence … and slightly unnerved. The mountains were proof that, after days of agonising anticipation, they were nearing their goal. The reality of the situation hit him almost as hard as the blow from the wooden cudgel. In a few short days, he would be facing a tauros once again. And not just a single tauros either, but a whole horde of them, several herds combined, each as monstrous and as terrifying as the diseased beast he had killed in the forest what seemed like aeons ago.

He forced himself to remember. His hand trembling as he raised the leather sling and sent it whirring round above his head. The soft *whumph-whumph* sound as it accelerated. The twitch of his wrist as the pellet was catapulted forth from its sheath. He had been aiming for the centre of the beast's torso, but that last little movement, that last fear-induced jitter, had sent the missile arching away from his planned trajectory. There had been no skill involved. No courage. Only blind luck, an ephemeral blessing from the goddess Tyche.

And he had told no one. Not Dexios, Nambe, or even Tychos. He was a fraud as well as a coward. Fickle Tyche may have guided his hand once, but she would not do so again. Whatever happened next, he was on his own.

Cries from further up the line pulled him from his melancholy thoughts. A plume of smoke had been spotted on one of the nearby hills: the allied forward camp and their base of operations for the foreseeable future. An eight-foot-high wooden palisade ringed the butte, further strengthened by a deep trench peppered with sharp stakes. The Ruxians and their mercenaries had not been idle.

Keres passed through two sets of double gates and into the hectic bedlam beyond. Hoplites milled uncertainly near the entrance, unsure of where to go, blocking the heavily-laden polis slaves who were trying to push their way through the throng without drawing the ire of their masters. A riderless horse cantered past, nearly braining a distracted Thenean. It was swiftly followed by a portly Ruxian dressed in the military garb of a cavalry officer, hurling profanities at whoever would listen as he chased after his steed.

A strong hand banged loudly on Keres's aspis. "Ephebe,"

barked Galleas. "You're billeted in the north-western corner. Strip off your panoply and get some food. No wine. Hera has blessed us with another crushing heat wave, it seems. We'll begin training mid-afternoon."

"Mid-afternoon? There are no sundials, how do I—"

"Gods, lad! Listen for the pipes! Did you actually learn anything during your first-year training, or were you just pretending to pay attention?"

"Apologies, Kosmetes."

"I'm not your kosmetes anymore, I'm your captain. Your lochagos."

"Yes, Lochagos. What will you be teaching us?"

Galleas gave a humourless laugh. "Me? Nothing. But your father is going to remind you all what it's like to fight in a phalanx."

♋

Dexios removed his horsehair-plumed helm with a contented sigh. His short-cropped hair underneath was wet with sweat.

"Gods, Letho, there's a reason you don't send men to fight in the summer," he grumbled, placing the helm down carefully atop his breastplate, officer's cloak, and greaves. His thighs ached from the long hours spent in the saddle. He could only imagine what the hoplites must have endured on their frenetic march north, forced to contend with the relentless heat. Normally, a trip like this would have taken twice as long, but they were racing the tauros to the pass, and it was imperative that they got there first.

Melia had not been pleased to see him go. Unsurprisingly.

Not because she would miss him, of course, but because he was leaving just before the harvest and taking Nambe with him. He knew she thought him a coward for not standing up to Letho; she had never understood the responsibility he felt for the men of the phalanx. Even more so now that Keres marched with them …

Keres … The last thing Dexios had done before leaving was the same thing he had done before every single campaign since the birth of his son. He had stood before the covered shield hanging above his bed. His fingers had brushed against the leather. Handled the drawstrings holding the cover closed. One tug was all it would take to see his aspis again.

And then, as always, his hand had dropped to his side, and he had left the shield untouched.

His eyes wandered to the four bulging money pouches that sat on top of his traveller's chest, filled to the brim with obols, small coins worth one-sixth of a drachma. They would be placed in the mouths of the dead after the impending battle so that their shades could pay Charon's toll and cross into Tartarus, where they would be judged. The pouches had grown steadily larger over the years as Dexios commanded larger and larger contingents of men. One of his many worries was not having enough: those who could not pay for their passage would be forced to wander the shores of Tartarus for all eternity.

A hasty knock on one of the poles of his tent made him jump. Polydius stormed in, his muscled cuirass covered in dust. He was accompanied by a small, weasely man with an enormous hooked nose and equally prominent chin. Long muddy-brown hair was pulled into a tight ponytail.

The man appeared to have eschewed the traditional Tyrrean beard, preferring instead to grace his upper lip with a fine charcoal line of a moustache.

"Dexios," Polydius greeted him with a nod. "This is Krinne, leader of the misthios archers. They've been scouting the pass for us."

"Strategos." The mercenary smiled, making his moustache wriggle like a capricious earthworm. "We've met once before, I think, during the Lendes incursion. My men held the right flank."

"I … Yes, you're right. Apologies, it's been a long week."

"Killed a lot of the buggers on that rainy afternoon. The pelts and animal skins they were wearing weren't much good against our arrows."

"It was a … decisive victory."

"And you were most prompt with your payment. Can't fault a man who pays on time. You should've come with me and the lads to the whorehouse after, though. There was a southerner who could do things with her legs you wouldn't believe. Makes me shiver just thinking of it. She had breasts like—"

"A story for another time, misthios," interrupted Polydius impatiently. "Might I remind you that Ruxia is being invaded? Tell the strategos what you told me."

"Fair enough," Krinne said, with a churlish pout. "Only wanted to lighten the mood."

"And you can do so, once every last one of those flea-infested beasts has been sent screaming into the arms of Charon."

"Don't think they believe in Cha—"

Polydius slammed his fist against one of the tent poles,

making the entire structure wobble dangerously. "Your report."

"Right, right. Been sending men into the mountains since we first arrived. Horde is still moving south at a steady pace."

"The initial sightings spoke of families," Dexios prompted.

"Yeah, calves and heifers. It … doesn't look like a warband, you know? More like an exodus. Could be they're running from something."

"That's irrelevant," Polydius said tersely. "It doesn't matter why they are heading to Ruxia, only when they will arrive. How close are they?"

Krinne rubbed his pointed chin. "Close. Very close. If they keep up the pace, they'll be out of the pass by tomorrow."

"Charon's balls," swore Dexios. "So soon? We've only just arrived."

"I told you we should have got here faster," said Polydius, the frustration clear in his voice. "If you had done as I had suggested and increased the marching hours from—"

"If I had increased the marching hours, we'd have lost half the phalanx to exhaustion and the other half to dehydration. Don't question my decisions, Polydius. You are strategos of Ruxia, not of Thena."

His words were met with a strained silence. Polydius's eyes flickered, but his jaw remained firmly clamped shut. After a moment's indecision, he snapped his heels together, made the sign of Hera, and left the command tent as brusquely as he had come.

"Got some fire in him, that one," said Krinne conversationally.

"He always did," Dexios replied, lost in his memories once more. "But he used to be better at holding that temper in check. He's changed. Though I suppose time changes us all."

"Not me it hasn't. I've always been a money-loving son of a whore." The mercenary had produced a small toothpick from somewhere and was poking at his gums, the movement making his leather armour creak. Dexios spied two gold molars in the upper left side of his mouth.

"Best place to keep your fortune," Krinne explained when he saw the strategos studying him. "Hidden away for a rainy day." The toothpick disappeared again. "What now? Polydius has told me I'm under your command. Want me to set up a few ambushes? Harry the bovines' flanks? Might slow them down a bit."

Dexios shook his head. "No, you wouldn't do much damage, and we'd lose the element of surprise. Pull your men back. I'll need every last one of your archers tomorrow."

"You're the one with the silver, Strategos. It'll be as you command. Do you have a plan?"

"An inkling of one. I'll need to see the terrain myself to be sure."

"As you wish. Just send that big old southerner a-hollering when you need me. Unless you want to join me for a glass of watered wine? I've got plenty more interesting stories to tell."

Dexios reached reluctantly for his cuirass. "Another time, perhaps. My phalanx awaits me." He settled the bronze breastplate onto his shoulders and snapped the hinges closed.

"Let's see if they remember how to fight."

12

ORCHESTRATION

"I am often asked what makes a competent phalanx. The tactical acumen of its strategos? The grit and determination of its lochagos? I would argue that it is neither. It is the kosmetes who shapes and moulds the formless clay of youth. It is the kosmetes who takes that fragile kindling and sets it alight with the spark of his knowledge. It is the kosmetes who nurtures that tiny flame into a blazing fire."

CERBRIONES, 'ALALAGMOE'

THE GROUND BEFORE the forward camp was packed with Theneans. Some wore the coveted bronze cuirass, helm, and greaves; others the layered linen body armour known as a linothorax. The less fortunate hoplites could only afford simple breastplates of boiled leather, which left their backs and shoulders vulnerable.

It was every citizen's duty to provide and maintain his own panoply; an age-old tradition that had the unfortunate consequence of making every mobilisation an unofficial display of a man's financial and social status. There was a saying in Tyrris: if one wishes to know the wealth of a man, seek him out in the ranks of the phalanx.

The diversity of the hoplites' armour was in stark contrast to the uniformity of their spears and shields. Each man held in his right hand the same eight-foot-long spear of ash and iron, crafted in the workshops of Thena and paid for by the basileus himself. Row upon row of triangular-tipped shafts stabbing up at the sky like a forest of nails.

The other hand grasped the enormous bronze-coated heavy shield, the aspis, another gift from the basileus. When positioned correctly, it could be used to protect the hoplite's entire body, leaving only his face and lower legs open to attack. The aspis was sometimes jokingly referred to as the social equaliser, for it hid not only the man but also the armour he wore. When the shields were raised, all hoplites looked the same.

Dexios nudged his horse down the dirt track that led from the camp to the mustering field, his aching legs unhappy at having to spend more time in the saddle. He knew the horse was a source of envy among the rank-and-file, regarded as a frivolous luxury, one of the many benefits of being the strategos. A sentiment in all likelihood further exacerbated by the forced march north.

There was some truth to this, but the horse was far more than just a status symbol. It enabled Dexios to see and to be seen. A lochagos fought on the front line, inspiring those around him, pushing the phalanx towards the enemy, and striving to keep the hoplites in formation. He was the glue that held the phalanx together, the stubborn ox that pulled the plough. A competent lochagos could win battles … if he was positioned in the right place at the right time.

However, an ox, if not guided by the hand of its master, will trudge placidly forwards in a straight line. A chair, if not glued together in the right places, will collapse the first time it is sat upon. Having obtained the rank of strategos, the warrior becomes the tactician, no longer focused solely on the enemy pushing against his shield wall but on the entire battlefield. And for that, the strategos must have sufficient elevation. For that, he must have a horse.

Although being able to ride everywhere is an added bonus, thought Dexios as his chestnut stallion reached the mustering field. Galleas was the first to lay eyes on him, bellowing at his men to form ranks. The grizzled veteran snapped to attention, his back ramrod straight, the palms of his hands perfectly placed on his torso as he made the sign of Hera.

"Strategos."

"Lochagos. It has been a while since I called you that, Galleas."

"Aye. 'Needs must', as they say."

"Only Letho says that, Galleas. And take that spear out of your arse, we've known each other for twenty years. Loosen up before you break something."

Galleas grunted. "I'd rather not, Strategos, if it's all the same to you. The men are watching. Unless it's a direct order."

"A direct … Gods, you haven't changed. I thought becoming a kosmetes would … I don't know … help you unwind."

"I was starting to, Strategos, but the tauros had other plans. Would you like to address the men?"

"Yes, but not here."

"Sir?"

"Follow me." And Dexios led his horse past the surprised captain, leaving the relative safety of the forward camp's perimeter in the direction of the jagged mountains. He smiled to himself as he heard Galleas hastily bark a series of orders to the other lochagos, followed by the sound of innumerable leather soles pounding the sun-baked earth and the trill of the pipes.

He led them along a winding path through the hills, crossing a dry stream bed and passing a colourful orchard of clementine trees before reaching their final destination: the entrance to the mountain pass, half-hidden in the shadows of two colossal peaks that were leaning towards each other like a couple of lovers beginning to embrace.

The pass itself was unremarkable. A dry, desolate stretch of land roughly two hundred feet wide, bordered on either side by steep cliffs. Dexios slowed his steed with a gentle tug of the reins.

"Galleas, form the men into a single phalanx. Fifty men wide, twelve ranks deep."

The lochagos's eyes, visible through the slits of his helm, flickered with incomprehension.

That's twice I've managed to catch you off-guard today, thought Dexios smugly.

"Are ... are you certain, Strategos?"

Concentrating the entire military strength into a single unbroken phalanx was extremely rare. Traditionally, hoplites would form rectangles up to sixteen files wide and eight or sixteen ranks deep. Splitting the force into smaller units sacrificed cohesion for greater manoeuvrability.

"Just get it done, Galleas."

"I ... It will take a moment, Strategos. I have not yet chosen the arche and the telos. If you had told me earlier, perhaps ..."

"Apologies, Galleas. I needed to evaluate the terrain first. Discuss the matter with your fellow lochagos. I can wait."

A phalanx was like a spear. The men of the first rank,

the arche, were the tip, strong and hard as iron. Their shields would be the first to bear the brunt of the enemy's assault, their blades the first to taste the enemy's blood. The arche were the elite. The ambitious. The wealthy. Men in the prime of their lives, their shields depicting the wreaths of olive leaves won during their ephebic training. All wore a full bronze panoply and a plumed helm.

The telos were the file-closers, the last rank of the phalanx. They were the veterans: calm, sturdy, and unyielding. The final bulwark, the last obstacle that the enemy must overcome before the phalanx was routed. If the arche was the tip of the spear, the telos was the grip, the all-important leather-wrapping that the hoplite used to thrust his weapon forwards and to stop it from slipping.

Between the arche and the telos were the 'fillers', the rank-and-file, the shaft of the spear. They were the struts that would strengthen the shield wall, using their own shields to anchor the first rank in place. If one of the arche was wounded or killed, the man behind him would be forced to move up and take his place. As such, the second and third ranks fought just as hard as the first, driven by a mixture of comradeship, fear, and self-preservation. It was here that the considerable length and reach of the ash wood spear proved its worth, allowing the hoplites to jab through the spear wall by passing over the shoulders of the men in front of them.

It took less than a half-hour for Galleas to organise the phalanx. Dexios rode up and down the line, pleased with the result. He searched for Keres and found him in the fifth rank, surrounded by his fellow ephebes. He breathed a sigh of relief. Galleas had placed them all in the very centre of the phalanx. The safest place they could be.

"Theneans," Dexios cried. "I look upon you and my heart swells with pride. I see farmers, craftsmen, merchants. Fathers, sons, brothers. Citizens all. Theneans all. Comrades all."

It was the same speech he always gave, barely changed from the one he had written when first accepting the title of strategos all those years ago. And yet, it still had the same effect. Men stood a little taller. Shoulders and backs straightened, chests expanded, heads were held higher.

"Tomorrow, we will face a monstrous foe. They are bigger than us. Stronger than us. But we have something they do not. We stand united."

Galleas and a half-dozen other veterans banged the shaft of their spears against their shields in approval.

Dexios moved slowly up the line, fixing all those that looked upon him with his steel-flecked gaze.

"We stand united," Dexios repeated. "We stand as one. We stand in the glow of Hera's holy light. The tauros will arrive here at the end of a long, tiring journey. They will have spent time and energy navigating the narrow mountain paths. They will emerge, weakened, from the shadows of these twin peaks and what will they see? A host of six hundred proud Tyrreans waiting to greet them!"

Spears crashed against shields.

"They will have no other choice but to advance, to brave our thicket of deadly thorns. They will be desperate. They will be reckless. They will not think to look to their flanks."

Dexios smiled broadly. "And so, they will die." He swept one arm theatrically to his right. "While they grunt and claw ineffectively at our shield wall, Polydius and two hundred heavy Ruxian cavalry will hit them from one side."

Another sweeping gesture. "Our allies from Lendes will hit them from the other. They will be trapped. There will be no escape. And we will reap such a slaughter that even the Gods themselves will take notice."

Every man was hammering at his shield now, swept up in the glory of the moment, their exhaustion and fear replaced by a new sense of purpose.

"Friends!" Dexios held up his hands for silence. He swallowed; his throat raw from the effort of projecting his voice. "We can win this. We can put an end to the tauran threat and return home to our loved ones before the harvest ends. But only if we fulfil our role. We must be the rock that breaks the tide. The stout oak tree that resists the storm. We must stand firm. We must stand together. Look to the man on your left. Your shield will cover him. You are his protector. You are his guardian. Now, look to your right. This is the man whom you must trust with your life. This is the man who will keep you from Charon's embrace. These men are your brothers. They are your family. Will you help them? Will you help them stand firm?"

A great roar exploded from six hundred mouths, drowning out the rhythmic banging. Hoplites turned to their comrades, exchanging names and touching spear tips.

"ARE YOU READY?" Dexios shouted, caught up in the moment. "THEN, SHOW ME! SHOW ME OUR STRENGTH!" He paused, then yelled. "SHIELD WALL!"

With a thunderous crack that echoed off the cliffs of the mountain pass, six hundred aspides locked together. Dexios stretched his hand out to Galleas who tossed him his spear. He wheeled his stallion round and galloped along the front line, thrusting the butt of the spear against the row of raised shields as hard as he could, aiming high, then low, left then right. Searching for a weak link. A hole in the wall.

There was none.

Again and again and again, until the muscles in his arm burned from wrist to shoulder. At last, with a final exultant cry, he slammed the spear tip-first into the dry, cracked earth.

"This is as far as we will let them come," he said. "This is the line they shall not cross. They will test us with axe and sword. With hoof and horn. We will not waver. We will hold. And then, with the support of the good men of Ruxia and Lendes, we will crush them. For Thena!"

"FOR THENA!" came the tumultuous reply. Dexios looked once more towards Keres and saw that his son was screaming the name of his city, his cheeks wet with tears.

Galleas approached cautiously, wary of the way that Dexios's stallion was pawing at the ground. The beast was used to the noise and chaos of battle but was nonetheless skittish, its ears twitching nervously. Dexios slid from the saddle and placed a calming hand on its neck.

"A good speech," Galleas said, raising his voice to be heard over the excited hoplites. "Just as it was when you gave it before the walls of Kalendar seven years ago."

Dexios smiled. "One of my favourites. Besides, it inspired them then, and it will inspire them now. Your spear will have to stay there, I'm afraid, I need the symbolism. The weapons cart can issue you another."

Galleas removed his helm and patted down his thinning hair. "It's not their inspiration I'm worried about. It's your plan. A single phalanx. Putting all your eggs in one basket."

"You would do things differently?"

"Aye. Two units, maybe three. Keep one in reserve to counter any flanking manoeuvres."

Dexios considered it for a moment. "We can't risk not committing all our forces. You are treating the tauros like men, Galleas. They are not. They are beasts. They will not try to flank us or outmanoeuvre us. They will try to overwhelm us. The plan stands. What is your assessment of the men?"

"The arche and the telos are as reliable as always. As for the shaft … I honestly don't know."

"You still drill them once a month?"

"During spring and summer, yes. Once every two months during winter. It's not a question of skill, but of size. Half the hoplites have never fought in a formation this big. Any attempt made to advance or retreat will shatter the phalanx. And if the tauros pierce the shield wall … it will be a massacre."

"Five minutes, Galleas. Just give me five short minutes. Enough to sound the pipes and bring our allies to our side. Then we can all go home."

The kosmetes exhaled slowly. "You have never steered us wrong before, Strategos. You will have your five minutes. Permission to drill the men for another hour or so? The shield-lock was not quite as fast as I would have liked."

"Granted." Dexios placed his right foot in the stirrups and hauled himself back into the saddle. He turned to look back at the man who had taught him how to throw a javelin. How to hold a spear. The man who had helped him curb his arrogance and insolence through a few kind words … and many tiring laps around the training field. Who was responsible for transforming inexperienced young boys into men. His role was just as important as that of strategos, yet he never received any of the glory. Or the gratitude. A kos-metes's job is done when he has made himself unnecessary.

"Galleas?" Dexios asked.

"Yes, Strategos?"

"Thank you for keeping my son safe. And thank you for … everything else."

The older man nodded and turned away.

Dexios would never speak to him again.

RECOLLECTION

"Towards the end of my father's reign, Thena was riddled with corruption, rotting from the inside out like a worm-infested apple. I excised what I could with little remorse: their insatiable greed was killing my city, one bribe at a time. Only a few were spared. Not through mercy, but necessity. There is always a use for a man willing to do anything for a handful of drachmae."

BASILEUS LETHO, 'RUMINATIONS'

FOR THE SECOND time that week, Elena awoke with a throbbing headache. She spat out a strand of blonde hair that had somehow worked its way into her mouth while she was sleeping and opened one bloodshot eye.

Then closed it again.

There appeared to be a dead body in the middle of the andron.

Too much wine, she thought groggily. She must have downed two-thirds of an amphora last night to dull the stress of her close encounter in the agora. She waited for a few minutes then lifted her eyelid a fraction. The corpse was still there, its head lolling towards her couch, its glassy stare fixing her through a curtain of glistening, greasy hair.

She knew that face. It belonged to one of the thugs who had harassed Makar. What was his name? Tobias.

Gods.

She sat up, fear and adrenaline hitting her like an ice-cold bucket of water. She was suddenly very awake and very sober.

"Um … Desha?" she called out in a wavering voice. What if the other thug was still here? The one with the belly like a beer barrel? What then?

"Desha?"

She swung her feet off the couch and strapped on her sandals. A glint of something metallic near the corpse caught her eye. A dagger.

"That could be useful," she mumbled, creeping cautiously closer. Tobias stank of blood, urine, and excrement. A particularly foul concoction that was unfortunately eerily similar to the awful stench that permeated the air close to her favourite taverna, especially around closing time.

Pinching her nose with her thumb and forefinger, she picked up the dagger and stuck it into her belt. Curiosity made her linger, her gaze drawn to the gore-spattered tunic. Four circular holes were evenly spaced across the corpse's ribcage, each the width of a finger. Elena frowned. The wounds were too round to have been made by a xiphos or a dagger. Too clean for a spear or a sling. An arrow, perhaps?

"How did you die?" She leant closer, searching for any sort of clue, studying the neck, the jaw, the—

"Elena?"

She let out a startled shriek. Desha was standing in the andron's entrance, his face pale. He breathed a sigh of relief. "You are safe."

"As are you. And Makar?"

"He's fine. I told him to stay upstairs. Don't want him to see this … whatever this is. There are more bodies; two in the workshop, one in the hallway, and another in the vestibule. The one in the corridor …" He looked down, and Elena saw that his sandals were covered in blood. "… I've never seen anything like it. Insides spread out left and right like he had been caught in the middle of a tornado. And the one in the doorway." He shuddered. "Had to pry him out with a hammer and a crowbar. He'd been stuck into the frame."

Elena felt the room start to spin. The familiar acid tang of bile tickled the back of her throat. She sat down on one of the andron's couches before she fell. "What now?"

"Once the door was cleared, I sent my slave to summon the city guard. They'll need to see this."

"Why?"

Desha pointed to the lifeless form of Tobias. "Because I know who that one is."

The corners of his mouth twitched.

"He's a guardsman."

♋

It didn't take long for the city guard to arrive, personified not just by any old ranker, but Captain Crenate himself, one of the most influential men in all of Thena.

And Helydices's father, thought Elena as the burly man squeezed into the andron wearing the 'theta'-embroidered linothorax of his function. Crenate looked like he had been carved from a block of granite, his chiselled jaw and flat, squashed nose further heightening the squareness of his head. He was chewing loudly on some sort of herbal mixture. Rumour had it that Crenate loved his salvia leaves, some even going as far as to say he was addicted to the stuff.

"My … Lady," he said, leaving just enough of a pause so that Elena would know exactly what he was thinking. His silence was more effective than a thousand words. *Parthenos*.

"Captain," she replied calmly, refusing to take the bait. "A pleasure to see you again, although I would have preferred under better circumstances."

"Hmmph." Crenate looked past her to the mass of flesh and bone that had once been Tobias. "What happened here, then?"

Desha clicked his tongue in disapproval. "What happened here, *Captain*, is that five armed men broke into my home and workshop, probably under the misguided notion that they would find gold and jewels stashed away somewhere. Then it appears they all … died."

"Murdered, you mean," Crenate replied, his jaw working furiously.

"A just punishment for all those who seek to rape, steal, and kill. Who knows what might have happened if this mysterious vigilante had not intervened? What they would have done to my son or Sophistes Elena?"

A brown dribble escaped Crenate's lips. He wiped it away with the back of his hand. "I very much doubt that this is the work of one man. At least two of the victims were well-trained and—"

"Knew them well, did you?" interrupted Elena innocently, twisting one finger around a lock of hair.

Crenate scowled, lines appearing on his craggy face like

cracks on a block of stone. "I did. The one behind you and the big man whose viscera were used to repaint the hallway are members of the guard. *Off-duty* members. Once they finish their shift, they are no longer my responsibility. Nothing I could have done to prevent this."

"You could have paid them a decent salary."

"What did you say?"

"Nothing. The two you describe accosted Makar and me in the agora earlier that evening. We were there for some time and never caught so much as a whiff of one of your patrols. And I have a feeling that Desha's workshop was surreptitiously removed from their usual route as well."

"You have no proof of—"

Elena pressed her fingers to her temples. "No need to raise your voice. You're right, it's pure conjecture. But a body was squeezed into the entranceway last night, and it was still there this morning so either your men walked by, saw it, and did nothing, or they didn't come this way at all."

Crenate glared at her. For a moment, there was only the sound of mastication. "That is a fair assessment," he conceded eventually. "I will speak to the guardsmen assigned to this district, and if it turns out they have been shirking their duties, I can promise you they will be appropriately punished. That does not, however, mean they were in any way involved with what happened here."

He is extremely apt at deflecting blame from himself, Elena thought. The tell-tale dryness in her mouth had returned, gently reminding her pounding head that it had been several hours since her last drink.

"So, what now?" asked Desha.

"Bodies will go to the physician, and I'll have one of the

slaves transcribe the details. Then that scroll will go on my desk with all the others, to be dealt with when the military action to the north has been resolved."

"That's it?"

Crenate turned his head and spat a wad of half-chewed leaves onto the tiled floor of the andron. It sat there glistening, slowly congealing into a mound of dark green sludge.

"You may have been spared the muster, old man," he said. "But, unless your brain was damaged along with your arm, you will recall that in times of strife the Captain of the Polis Guard is responsible for the defence of the city. I've got conscripts to train, supplies to check, and walls to reinforce. All of those things are exponentially more important than chasing down some frankly questionable leads in the hope of finding who killed these poor bastards. Now, if you'll excuse me." He inclined his head sharply towards Elena, made the sign of Hera, and marched away.

"Gods, that man becomes more and more insufferable each time I speak with him," Elena complained. "Did you hear how he called them poor bastards? It's as if he pitied them. Aren't we supposed to be the victims here?"

Desha shrugged. "All that extra responsibility must be getting to him. He's right about it not being a top priority, though."

"Oh, come on, Thena's in no danger. That battle is happening miles away."

"I'm not worried about the tauros. Thena is vulnerable without its phalanx. A risky yet tempting target."

"For whom? Boena? Atlis? They wouldn't dare. We shouldn't give in to paranoia."

"Hmmph. I'm old enough to know the difference

between paranoia and caution, young Sophistes. You'll see when you've lived as long as I have. When you've seen the things I've seen." Desha scratched the nub of flesh at the end of his right arm. "Doesn't matter anyway. In ten days' time, we'll be either celebrating the return of our victorious phalanx or singing a lamentation for the dead."

Ten days, thought Elena with a slight flutter of panic. The ephebes were gone. Galleas was gone. There was nothing and no one to keep her mind occupied. To stop her from heeding the call of the taverna. She would become another drink-addled regular, a permanent fixture propping up the bar … a part of the furniture.

She needed something to keep her busy. Anything. Perhaps Desha would let her help in the workshop? Her eyes roamed the andron, alighting on the gory mess that had once been Tobias. The four strange holes in his chest …

"Thena will triumph," she announced. "And if Crenate refuses to help us, I'm going to do some digging myself and see if any of those 'questionable leads' take me anywhere."

"You're welcome to try. But you don't seem to have much to go on. I've already told you, I've never come across any tool or weapon that makes such a distinctive mark."

"I have," came a voice from the andron's entrance. Makar stood there, his gaze fixed on the dead body.

"I thought I told you to stay upstairs, lad," growled Desha.

"You did, but I got bored. Besides, they're making a good effort at cleaning the corridor, although they'll never get the blood out of the cracks. Maybe we should just paint the entire thing red." He pointed at Tobias. "How did this one die?"

"We're not sure," Elena said. "Are you certain you've seen this sort of injury before?"

Makar took a step closer, drawn by the same morbid curiosity as Elena had felt earlier. He crouched down next to the corpse and stretched out his hand, his middle finger inches away from the four circular wounds. For a moment, it seemed he was going to touch them, then he stopped and pulled away.

"I have."

Desha cuffed him soundly on the back of the head. "What are you prattling about, lad? I've already warned you about mistaking your ridiculous daydreams for reality. This is not a game."

"I swear it," Makar insisted, standing up. "May Hera strike me down if I lie."

Desha's eyes flickered to the heavens as if he expected his son to be executed on the spot, but nothing happened. He frowned.

"What have you been hiding, lad?"

"Nothing! I mean … nothing important."

"Well then? Spit it out!"

"Remember a couple of winters ago we got that series of orders from a daughter of Aphrodite? Rings, bangles, necklaces, and the like?"

Elena said nothing, but her mind was racing. A daughter of Aphrodite? The self-styled 'daughters' were in reality well-paid, highly qualified courtesans. Or, as Galleas would have rudely put it, whores.

Desha rubbed his bearded chin with his hand. "Of course I do. I told you, I never forget a piece of jewellery. That woman was one of the best-paying customers we've ever had. I probably made more off her that year than all the others combined."

"Right. And you had me make most of the deliveries. Didn't trust the slaves. Well, one night, I got there early. Way too early. The shutters were drawn, and I could see candle-light through the slats. I thought the … lady was probably entertaining, so I found a nice spot in the shadows to wait until the agreed-upon time. Someone left moments later, someone I recognised. It was the basileus, Letho."

"Ridiculous!" Desha said loudly, raising his hand again. Makar cringed. "It's not, Father, I swear! I was just as unbe-lieving as you at first. I thought my eyes were playing tricks on me. So … I decided that the next time she ordered some-thing, I would make sure I arrived early again."

"You did what?"

"I had to know! It was *him*. Cloaked and without an escort but it was definitely him. Each time we received a new order, he was there."

"It was payment," said Elena in disgust. "The orders weren't really from her. They were from him."

"How the basileus chooses to spend his free time is none of our concern," Desha said sharply. "Nor do I see how it pertains to our current situation."

"I'm getting to that. It was the very last time you sent me there, her very last order. When I arrived, the whole place was shrouded in darkness. And the door was ajar." Makar's hand gave a slight tremble. "Something was wrong."

"You should have left," Desha said.

"I had a necklace worth three hundred drachmae in my pocket, Father! What would you have said if I had returned empty-handed?"

"Nothing, if you had trusted me enough to explain it to me."

"I … You … You are so *tired* at the moment, Father. Your workshop is wearing you down to the bone. I wanted to tell you, it's just that in your current state of mind you have been … difficult to talk to."

Elena began to feel uncomfortable, like she was an intruder, listening in on a private conversation. She coughed politely. "Please go on, Makar."

"Yes, thank you. So, not wanting to disappoint my father, I pushed the half-open door wide. The lady's quarters were surprisingly small. No vestibule, no andron, just a single room that served all her personal and professional needs. And in the centre of the room, I found Letho, covered in blood, standing over three dead bodies. The first was the lady, her throat cut. The other two were mercenaries from the looks of them, or assassins, clad in close-fitting black leather and turbans."

"Men of the south?" Elena asked.

"I don't know. Maybe. They were masked and gloved; I couldn't see the colour of their skin. Whoever they were, they had been torn apart. One was covered in claw marks, the other's arms had been pulled from their sockets and laid across his chest … just under a strange-looking wound similar to that on the man on the floor of our andron. Four circles."

"And Letho?"

"Dazed but unharmed. He obviously had no idea who I was and mistook me for a slave. He asked for water and a towel to clean his face and hands, and not really knowing what else to do, I obliged. It was while I was scrubbing the blood from his skin that he told me he had arrived to find his … um … companion already dead, surrounded by her attackers."

Elena frowned. "And you believed him?"

"I had no reason not to, Mistress. He sent me to fetch the polis guard shortly after."

"Crenate?"

"Maybe."

"Hera's tits!" Elena cursed. "That lying snake! I was sure he knew more than he was letting on. We need to talk to him again."

"That won't work," Desha countered. "He's already made it clear that he's not going to help us. Unless we can find some damning evidence, he'll just stonewall you."

"Then, we don't have any choice," Elena said decisively, already moving for the door. "We'll have to interrogate the only other person who can help."

"Where are you going?"

"To the palace. It's time to request an audience with the basileus."

14

PANACEA

"Hera teaches us that with luck and perseverance all our dreams will come true. Fine words. But she would do well to remember that not all dreams are good. There are dark images that haunt that terrible limbo between sleep and wakefulness, where we are not yet sure what is real and what is fantasy."

GRAYCEA, PRIESTESS OF HERA

KERES SAT STARING at the fire, a bowl of gruel held loosely in one hand, still untouched. His aspis was propped up next to him, the shadows cast by the flames making it seem as if the hawk was beating its powerful wings. He had had no more visions since the ephebic trials, but when he closed his eyes, he could still feel the grip of the bird's talons on his cheeks.

"Falling asleep already?"

Helydices loomed, his face twisted into an ugly smile as he laughed at his own joke.

Keres looked up at him fearlessly. "Gods, Helydices, just leave me alone, would you? It's been a long day."

The ephebe bent closer. "Yeah." His lips moved soundlessly as if he was working out what to say next. "About that." Two bristly eyebrows crunched together over his jutting brow.

"I hate you, Keres. Everything you have, you owe to your father. Never had a day of hardship in your life, have you? Never felt the sting of the whip across your back or the lash of your father's belt. And d'you know what? It's made you weak."

Keres opened his mouth to reply, but Helydices cut him off.

"Wait ... wait. I'm not done. I will never like you, Keres. And I know you don't like me. Thing is ... Galleas came to see me. At first, I reckoned he was going to haul me over the coals for breaking your boyfriend's arm, but he didn't. Just wanted to let me know he's putting me next to you in the shield wall tomorrow ... on your left. And what with your old man spouting all that stuff about standing together ... got me thinking ... maybe try and put our differences aside for a time? Until the cows are routed?"

Keres sighed. The kosmetes had purposefully placed Helydices in a situation where he would depend on Keres to protect his right flank. Wily bastard. If Keres wanted to, he could have his revenge. A slip of the shield. A gap in the wall. That was all it would take.

He glanced at his aspis. The hawk glowered back.

"You paid a man to beat me."

Helydices shuffled his feet. "Aye."

Keres shook his head. There would be no forgiveness. No redemption. Not even the so-called unity of the phalanx could change that. But there would be no revenge either. That was not who he was. And it was not part of the values that his father had taught him.

He thought of Tychos. The desperate longing he had seen in his friend's eyes. His despair at being turned away.

Keres had promised, had sworn to the Gods themselves, that he would do everything in his power to …

Everything. And anything.

"I would consider a truce," he said to Helydices. "On one condition." The man's beady little eyes narrowed, flattening the pupils to the size of olive pits.

"Tychos is here," Keres continued, feeling a sharp jolt of satisfaction as the secret he had been holding on to was released. "And he wants to stand in the phalanx. I need you to help me make that happen."

"Hera's tits, Keres! How in Tartarus am I supposed to do that?"

"You can start by getting him a spear and a shield. The man in charge of the weapons cart is from the polis guard. That means he knows your father. And probably owes him a few favours."

"Hmmph. So, let's say I succeed. Then what?"

"We get him to the front lines without Galleas noticing. Should be easy enough, he's been walking among us disguised as a slave for a week, and no one's batted an eyelid."

"A slave, huh?" Helydices smirked. "Shaved his golden locks, did he? That would be something worth seeing."

"Shut up. We get him there, we help him fight, and we bring him back. Oh, and make sure none of your idiotic friends goes and rats us out to Galleas either. What do you say?"

Helydices looked past Keres, out into the night.

"I won't have him on my right," he said firmly. "I won't have him protecting me, or any of the other ephebes. His shield will fall at the first blow. If I agree to this, the only place he can be is next to you."

Keres smiled grimly and held out his hand. "Agreed."

Helydices took it and yanked Keres effortlessly to his feet.

"Very well. You can go and tell him the good news."

"Thank you."

"After we've had a drink."

Officially, the hoplites were forbidden any sort of alcohol on the eve of battle, but veteran lochagos knew the value of a cup of wine: how it could ease tensions and calm nerves. This inevitably led to the odd amphora being purloined from the supply wagon.

Helydices and Keres found the other sixteen ephebes sitting apart from the rest of the phalanx, exchanging increasingly ludicrous tales of that afternoon's drill. No longer boys but not quite men. They had built up their own fire and were passing around two amphorae and a large piece of crumbling goat's cheese.

Keres found an empty spot, carefully positioning his aspis with the decorated side facing upwards so as to avoid the wrath of the Gods. Looking around, he saw all of his fellow ephebes had done likewise, exhibiting the menagerie of painted animals to the stars. A trio of ravens, the owl of Athena, a stag, two boars … Keres was unsurprised to discover that Helydices's shield bore the snarling face of a maned lion. *Big, impressive, dumb, and lazy,* he thought. *Just like its owner.*

An amphora was pressed into his hands, and he brought it to his lips. The wine hit the back of his mouth with a

burning tang that made his eyes water. It was unwatered …
and very strong.

"Gods," he croaked as the fire travelled down his throat
and set up camp in his belly.

"What in Tartarus is going on here?"

The sound made Keres jump. Wine sloshed from the
amphora and dribbled down the long neck.

Hera's tits, I know that voice.

He cranked his head round reluctantly to see his father
clad in a simple chiton, his hands clasped behind his back.
Nambe hovered protectively nearby like a hound guarding
its master.

"Um." Keres blinked. It felt like the wine was burning a
hole in his stomach lining.

"You should know better, Son. It is customary for the
men of the phalanx to offer their commanding officer a
drink before facing the enemy, and yet I have been standing
here for at least two minutes and not one of you has given
me a cup. I expect this terrible affront to my sensibilities to
be remedied within the next few seconds."

"Of … of course, Father," Keres babbled, his head
spinning. His father was being … nice? He proffered the
amphora and watched as Dexios took a quick swig.

"Make some room, would you? The men Polydius sent
to seek the Oracle's counsel have returned. He's speaking to
them now, and here is as good a place as any to wait for him
to come and report to me."

Nambe bent and whispered something in his ear.

"What? Oh, yes, I almost forgot. We come bearing
gifts!"

The brawny southerner dug into one of the pouches on

his belt and drew forth a handful of rectangular linen strips roughly an inch wide and ten inches long.

"Garters!" Dexios exclaimed with a smile.

Keres struggled to understand.

"I hated my first set of greaves," the strategos said with another swig. "They were so tight it felt like a dog was sinking its canines into my shins every time I bent my knee." He hiked up his chiton and moved closer to the fire, pointing to two thin white scars on his lower legs. "Turned out that wasn't far from the truth. Bloody things were chafing the skin raw. It was my lochagos who told me about the garters. Just tie them on where the metal pinches the skin."

Nambe moved around the fire, handing each ephebe four strips of fabric.

"The phalanx won a great victory later that day," Dexios continued. "My fa— the strategos rewarded us all generously with a share of the spoils. I can't have been much older than you are now. My comrades-in-arms drank and whored most of it away the very same evening. And guess what I did? I found myself a metalworker and had him beat my greaves into shape. Added a leather lining, too. Best thing I ever did."

"What ... of what battle do you speak, Sir?" Helydices asked, using a respectful tone that Keres had never heard before. The big ephebe looked infinitely more interested than he had during the sophistes's classes, his huge arms wrapped around his raised knees.

Dexios nodded as if expecting this and launched into a detailed retelling of his first campaign. It was new to Keres, but it was obvious what his father was doing: attempting to bond with the men under his command. Once he'd finished here, he would probably excuse himself politely, move to another bonfire, and tell the entire story again to another group of hoplites.

But it's working nevertheless, Keres thought, scanning the line of firelit faces hanging on his father's every word. *And tomorrow, when they tie on those garters, they'll remember the man who gifted them.*

Dexios was halfway through his second story when Polydius joined them, a strange half-smile on his face.

"Strategos!" Dexios called loudly. "What news? What riddle has the Oracle saddled us with this time?"

"No riddle," Polydius replied, pushing his long hair back behind his ears. "That's the strangest thing about it. According to my men, she spoke quite plainly."

"And?"

"She told me I would win."

"You are telling me we have been favoured by the Gods themselves? That is most auspicious news, Polydius. Why are you not shouting it to the heavens?"

The Ruxian strategos sighed. "Something doesn't feel right. You've consulted the Oracle before, Dexios. Have you ever heard her answer in so few words? 'You will win.' There must be a hidden meaning. Remember Panacea."

Dexios scoffed. "A legend, my friend, an old wives' tale dreamt up to scare little children. Probably invented by the Oracle herself!"

Polydius looked unsettled. "All legends start off as truth," he said ominously. "A truth that is reshaped by the swirling currents of time."

"What is Panacea?" Keres asked curiously.

"A cautionary tale," Polydius answered. "The moral of

which is to be careful what you wish for." He glanced at Dexios who gave a nod of encouragement.

"It starts, as most stories do, with a man and a woman, bound by a love so great that the radiance of their happiness could be seen from the heavens. They were always together, as inseparable as flesh and bone. One day, the man received word that his mother, who lived in Carenos, was gravely ill and close to death. He rushed to her side, promising his wife that he would take her in his arms once more before the month had passed.

"On the return trip across the Straits, his trireme was caught in the grip of a terrible storm. It sank, sending all its passengers to a watery grave on the ocean floor.

"The woman was inconsolable. She would not eat. She would not sleep. She wailed and pulled at her hair every time the name of her husband reached her ears. She refused to believe that death was the end. The Gods were immortal, she argued, so why could man not aspire to the same level of greatness?"

There was a smattering of uneasy murmurs among the listening ephebes. To compare oneself to a God was an unpardonable heresy.

"Her friends and family tried to dissuade her from embarking on such a blasphemous path, but she was either too mad or too overwrought with grief to care. She travelled to Eldenstar Lake to consult with the Oracle, who told her of Panacea, a mythical item with the power to heal any wound, to cure any disease, even death itself. The Oracle then warned the woman not to search any further, for such a road would only lead to pain and suffering."

Polydius's voice took on a darker tone. "The woman

would not listen. For how could being reunited with her loved one bring her a pain worse than the agony she already felt? She begged the Oracle to reveal all she knew and, armed with that knowledge, set out to scour the land of Tyrris, from its highest peaks to its lowliest ravines …"

"And she failed," finished Keres.

"What? No … she succeeded. She found Panacea and spoke the incantations the Oracle had taught her. But nothing happened. For months, she tried everything she could think of until, at last, she was forced to admit defeat. Abandoning the artefact, she returned, heartbroken, to her village. Time passed, and her grief faded. She struck up a friendship with the dead man's brother, a friendship that bloomed and grew into love. Not a lustful, overwhelming, soul-crushing love, but a calm and serene one, built on mutual respect and trust.

"A year later she gave birth to her first child, a baby boy. When he looked at her, her heart swelled with so much love she thought it would burst. Then, as the last days of summer gave way to winter, it happened. A knock at the door, late at night. Her husband calling out, asking who was there. But she already knew. She could smell the stench of rotten seaweed. Of brine. Of bloated flesh.

"Too late, she understood. Too late, she realised her awful mistake: Panacea had worked. It had brought her lover back to life, deep, deep under the waves. Brought him back and made him impervious to harm. He must have clawed and crawled and slithered his way to shore, inch by gut-wrenching inch, then dragged himself as far as the village. Back to his house. To be with her. Forever."

Polydius had spoken those last few words softly. Sadly. Keres shuddered despite the heat from the fire.

"What … what happened next? What did he do to her husband? Her child?"

Dexios leapt hastily to his feet. "A story for another time, eh, Strategos? Congratulations on draining all the good humour from the immediate vicinity. I think it's time for Nambe and me to move on. Coming, Polydius?"

"I … I should see to my men and the Lendians."

"Very well. Then, I will see you all on the field of battle. Hera protects."

"May Persephone keep you from Charon's embrace."

Keres waited until his father was firmly out of sight, then excused himself from the circle of ephebes and went to look for Tychos.

He found his friend resting with his back against one of the spoked wagon wheels, staring up at the stars.

"Well?" he asked hopefully.

"I've found a way. Tomorrow, you stand in the phalanx."

Tychos gave an ebullient laugh and pulled Keres close for a one-armed hug.

"I don't know how you did it, you beautiful bastard, and I don't care. You have no idea what this means to me. I have prayed for it every day since we left Thena. My greatest wish, granted!"

Keres thought of Panacea and the mounting terror the woman must have felt at hearing that knock on the door.

Be careful what you wish for.

15

PHALANX

"Sacrifice before battle is an unfortunate necessity. The beast is chosen by one of the lochagos and purified by his hand. The throat must be pierced, not slit, to maximise the force of the arterial spray. For it is the flow of blood that will reveal the outcome of the impending conflict. If the signs are not favourable, the strategos would be wise to delay his attack."

CERBRIONES, 'ALALAGMOE'

ERES AWOKE TO the undignified sound of Tychos's snores. He extricated himself from under his friend's arm and staggered over to the latrine pit to relieve his full bladder. Helydices was already there with the scruffy hair and puffy eyes of a man who had not had much sleep.

"Got the weapons you wanted," he grumbled. "Had to share an entire amphora of wine with the guards, though. My head feels like it's been stomped on by a tauros's hooves."

"Or hit with a wooden cudgel," retorted Keres.

Helydices cursed as a splash of hot urine hit his sandals. "Gods! That's your fault, Keres! You're the reason I've only had three hours' sleep. I've left everything on your bedroll. Now, go away and leave me to piss in peace."

The aspis was undecorated and in poor condition: the

normally smooth rim marred by a series of triangular cuts made by sword or spear. Keres flipped it over and checked the shield's interior. The leather lining was still firmly stuck to the wooden frame, the central arm-hole and handle were intact. He strapped on his linothorax and was about to clip on his greaves when he remembered his father's gift of garters.

He was thinking of him, just like Dexios wanted.

Keres tied the strips around his shins then snapped the greaves into place. His father was right. It felt infinitely better.

I may get killed by a tauros today, but at least my greaves won't be pinching my skin while it rips my head off.

Tychos came into view wearing a conical felt cap pulled down almost as far as his eyebrows. "One of the misthios lent it to me," he explained with a yawn. "I figured it would draw less attention to my shaved skull."

"It makes you look like you have half a lemon on your head."

"As long as it doesn't make me look like a slave, I don't really care … What in the name of Charon's hairy balls is that piece of battlefield scrap?"

"It's your aspis. Best we could do at such short notice."

"Best Helydices could do, you mean. That rat. If he thinks this is going to make me forgive him, he'll be sorely disappointed."

"I've checked it, and it seems sturdy enough … if you can handle the weight."

Rather than answering, Tychos removed his left arm from the sling. Keres helped his friend thread his forearm through the central hook and position the upper part of the inner rim on his shoulder.

"Can you grasp the handle?"

Tychos was grinning. "There's barely any pain, Keres! My shoulder is taking the weight. Elena was wrong! She was wrong!"

"You won't be able to hold it like that in the shield wall …"

"I know. I know. I'll manage five minutes. Trust me."

"I always have. And always will."

Helydices brushed past them at a jog, his face red. "Stop blathering, both of you. The scouts are back. The tauros are close to exiting the pass. Didn't you hear the pipes?"

The two ephebes joined the stream of men leaving the forward camp. A group of Ruxian riders cantered by, the pennants attached to the end of their spears flapping in the wind. Further along the narrow trail, a priestess of Hera, the hair on the left side of her head crudely shaved down to bloody fluff, blessed the passing hoplites in a shrill voice.

"May Hera's light guide you."

"My thanks, Lady," Keres mumbled. Only the most devout of Hera's worshippers chose to sacrifice their hair in this way, imitating the wounds received by the goddess herself when fighting the Ruined. It always made Keres feel uncomfortable. All Tyrreans were taught from a young age never to mention the names of those who had stood against the Queen of the Pantheon. Every single polis made constant efforts to scrub that unfortunate event from the annals of history. Yet, paradoxically, by mutilating themselves in this way, the women of the temple were keeping the memory of that war alive.

The priestess saw Keres looking at her, and her mouth jerked.

"We will win a great victory here today, brave one. I have seen it. A great victory in *Her* name."

Keres, swept along by the tide of marching soldiers, could only nod.

They reached the wide, open stretch of muddy-brown earth where so much would be decided. It seemed strange that the fate of the entire polis of Ruxia hinged on holding a tiny area of land smaller than his father's vineyard. The spear Dexios had planted was still there, marking an invisible line; a boundary that must not be crossed.

The Ruxian riders whom Keres had seen earlier were cresting the western rise to rejoin Polydius and the heavy cavalry who were mustering on the other side, out of sight. His gaze swivelled to the low hills on the opposite flank. Squinting, he could see the occasional flash of Lendian yellow and the twinkle of polished bronze.

The pincers of the crab. And we are to be its shell.

He guided Tychos to their place in the centre of the phalanx, four ranks behind the arche. Keres spied the familiar plumed helm of Galleas through a forest of raised spears. Beyond the defensive line of hoplites, the misthios archers were deployed in a loose skirmish formation, each man standing twenty paces apart. All held curved composite bows of horn and sinew, their arrows either carried in goatskin quivers or thrust into the ground in front of them, within easy reach. There were a few light leather breastplates and a smattering of domed caps, but for the most part, the archers wore no armour at all.

What courage it must take, thought Keres, *to stand alone*

and unprotected against such a monstrous foe. And they do so
for a pouch of silver coins.

An aspis banged against his back, followed by a muttered apology. The ranks were tightening as the latecomers
jostled and pushed their way into place. The heavy stench
of sweat and unwashed bodies permeated the air. Spear tips
waved and dipped as hoplites shifted position. The anticipation led to silence; each man lost in his own thoughts. For
once, even Tychos was still, his eyes closed.

Keres remembered asking his father what was the worst
part of battle. The waiting, Dexios had replied. The time
before the chaos when every soldier was forced to face his
own conscience. When there was nothing to stop the worms
of fear from burrowing deep into heart and mind. And so,
another battle must be fought, not one of flesh and iron
but of determination and grit. Of fortitude and courage.
The strength to stand and fight despite those earnest, sibilant
whispers urging one to throw down spear and shield. The
quiet promise that to flee will not be seen as cowardice but
as self-preservation. Lies upon lies.

Keres could hear them now. The voices, interspaced
with flashing images of the diseased tauros ripping a man in
twain. His mouth felt unnaturally parched and cracked like
the ground beneath his feet. His tongue became a swollen
hunk of flesh pressed against his left cheek.

Gods, he thought. *Gods help me.*

There was a distant rumble of thunder.

His bladder was full to bursting. His grip on his spear
slipped. Tychos's shield bumped against his linen breastplate.
He staggered. Helydices's foot caught him on the ankle.

I'm trapped, he thought, his breath quickening. *Hemmed*

in on all sides. The spears were no longer a forest; they were the bars of a cage.

He had to get out. He had to get out.

"Hera protects," a voice said calmly, pulling Keres out of his downward spiral. He raised his head. Galleas had left the ranks and was standing facing the men of the phalanx with his hands on his hips, much as he used to when he was only a kosmetes imparting words of wisdom to his ephebes. The familiarity of it was reassuring somehow, and Keres felt his pounding heart slow to a more reasonable rate.

"Glory to Hera!" another voice agreed. It was the priestess, her long robes trailing in the dirt as she dragged a sacrificial goat behind her on a leash. The animal bleated pitifully, its rectangular pupils dull and empty. The woman handed the leash to Galleas who accepted it with a cross-armed sign of Hera.

"Athena, bless us with your wisdom!" he cried in his parade-ground voice, drawing his xiphos with his free hand.

"Artemis, guide our hand!" He grasped the hind legs of the goat between his knees and pulled back the beast's neck. The animal, sensing something was wrong, struggled weakly.

"Persephone, keep us from Charon's embrace!" The xiphos arced down, stabbing through the thick skin and the carotid beneath. A crimson fountain gushed forth, drenching Galleas's greaves and sandals with blood. The goat spasmed, but the lochagos held it fast, tipping its head forwards slightly so that the red fluid poured from the pierced throat and splashed onto the thirsty earth.

"Hera, see this gift we offer you. See this sacrifice we make in your name. Hera … GRANT US YOUR STRENGTH!" Galleas yelled, punching the gory xiphos into the air. His zeal was infectious, rippling through the phalanx from arche to telos. Spears clanged against shields as the hoplites voiced their approval. Galleas released his hold on the dead goat. It was dragged away, leaving a wet, bloody smear.

Thunder again, a deep, rolling grumble that made the ground vibrate. Keres looked up at the clear blue sky with a frown. Then he recalled what his father had said.

Not thunder … hooves.

Hooves pounding the earth like a beating drum.

The tauros emerged from the shadows of the mountain peaks as if spewing forth from the depths of Tartarus itself. Over a hundred monstrous, twisted beasts, an unnatural fusion of animal and man. Their bodies were covered in coarse, grimy hair and daubed with a multitude of vibrant markings that came alive with every rise and fall of their muscular torsos. Horns of varying lengths protruded from their skulls; some straight and dagger-like, others curved and majestic, curling skywards as if searching to pierce the heavens.

They wore little in the way of armour: rotting rags wrapped around the groin and upper thighs, the occasional bulbous shoulder guard, mouldy leather cuirass, or vambraces of rusting iron. The weapons they carried, however, more than made up for this lack of protection: huge double-handed axes, hammers, clubs, and mauls fashioned from chunks of raw metal and stone. Crude but effective tools of death, built to crush, pummel, maim, and kill.

The bestial horde came to a shambling halt. A lone figure took a single step forwards, its double-axe raised high. A male, colossal in size, close to eight feet tall, his broad shoulders brushing against the heads of his brethren. His pelt was charcoal black, his tattoos the colour of fermented wine. One intricate marking snaked up his neck and cheek to coil around his right eye. He was missing most of one horn, the bone reduced to an ichor-encrusted stump. Somehow, the injury made him seem even more dangerous.

The beast's bovine muzzle twitched, then he began to speak in a low, resonant growl. "Humans. I am K'vath. Alpha of this herd. Who are you to bar my passage?"

There was a moment's silence, then Galleas broke ranks once more. He had not sheathed his sword since the sacrifice, and crimson droplets dripped from the tip.

"I am Lochagos Galleas. Of Thena. There is nothing for you here, Alpha K'vath. You must turn back."

The tauros snorted loudly. "Foolish human. We have come with calf and heifer. We have braved the mountain peaks. Lost many to the winds and snow. A poor way to die. Unworthy for a warrior. No, there is no turning back."

"Then, we are at an impasse," said Galleas coldly. "For the way forward is blocked."

K'vath bared his teeth. "Then, we will break you." He tilted his head back and bellowed. The other tauros answered with roars and bellows of their own, a titanic wave of sound that reverberated off the mountains and returned magnified tenfold.

A lone arrow flashed across the space between the two forces and punched into the leader's shoulder. K'vath tore the metal point from his flesh with an angry howl. More of the deadly shafts buzzed through the air as Krinne's mercenaries loosed their bows as fast as they could draw them. A tauros took an arrow in the eye, lodged so deep that the goose-feathered fletching touched his cheek. Another drilled through a beast's palm, making him drop his hefty club.

With a barking cry from K'vath, the horde advanced into the storm of iron, their weapons raised to protect their faces.

"SHIELD WALL!" Galleas yelled, his order echoing down the line as it was relayed by the other lochagos. Six hundred shields locked together with an explosive boom so loud that it drowned out the sound of the approaching tauros.

The enemy drew closer. The rain of arrows slowed to a trickle. The misthios archers slung their bows onto their backs and raced away. Nothing now stood between the phalanx and their enemy.

"SPEARS!" The arche pushed their weapons through the gaps in the shield wall, the second and third ranks lowering their own eight-foot ash shafts to rest on the sturdy bronze rims. One hundred and fifty spear tips gleamed in the sun, row upon row of deadly barbs.

"BRACE!" Galleas screamed. This was the crucial moment when twelve individual walls became a cohesive whole. The arche anchored themselves firmly against the shields pushing into their backs, forcing the second rank to support their weight. The second rank in turn were supported by the third and so on until each row was fortified by the men behind, all save for the telos, the veterans, the grip of the spear, the hardiest and most experienced hoplites who would bear the weight of their comrades alone.

The tauros were two hundred feet away. They began to accelerate with long, bounding strides that tore up the earth.

"ATHENA, GRANT US YOUR WISDOM!" Galleas chanted.

Keres clenched his spear so tightly he could see the whites of his knuckles. To his right, Tychos was already trembling with the effort of keeping his shield upright, his face twisted in a grimace of pain.

A hundred feet.

"ARTEMIS, GUIDE OUR HAND!"

There was a whimper from somewhere to Keres's left. The man in front of him vomited, spewing hot bile down his breastplate and greaves. "I want to go home," he pleaded pitifully to anyone who would listen. "I just want to go home."

Fifty feet.

"PERSEPHONE, KEEP US FROM CHARON'S EMBRACE!"

The psalm was muffled by the bovine grunts of the tauros and the hammering of hooves. They were so close that Keres could clearly see their snarling muzzles, flecked with spittle. Their tribal markings. Their necklaces of wood and human bone.

"I'm sorry, Keres." It was Helydices, his face ashen. "I'm sorry for what I did." He looked at Keres with fear in his eyes. "Will you forgive me? Please?"

"HERA, GIVE US—"

The tauros crashed into the phalanx with the force of a tidal wave. Spear shafts shattered like twigs, sending splinters spiralling in all directions. The arche were thrown backwards, slamming into the shields of the second rank. The shockwave rippled onwards and outwards. Tychos screamed as the man in front of him pressed against his aspis, putting further strain on his injured arm.

But miraculously, the shield wall held. The high-pitched sound of the bone pipes reached Keres's ears over the harsh screech of metal on metal.

Father is calling in the pincers of the crab, he thought. *We just need to hold on a little longer. Five more minutes.*

He could see the tauros battering the front line with their primitive two-handed weapons; strong overhead blows rising and falling like a miner excavating a rich vein of ore. The arche were defending well, hunkering down behind the limited protection offered by their aspides and jabbing at the tauros with their spears and xiphe.

One of the hoplites took a jaw-rattling blow to the head and lowered his shield a fraction. A sideways slice from a cleaver ripped out the front of his breastplate and most of the ribcage beneath. He toppled forwards with a gurgle. The soldier to his rear stepped up to plug the gap, locking shields before the enemy could attempt to push through.

We're doing it! Keres thought, sharing a brief smile with Tychos. He craned his neck to the left, searching for the tell-tale flutter of the Ruxian banners.

Nothing.

Two more arche fell, unable to withstand the constant pummelling. Keres and Tychos were drawn forwards as hoplites moved to fill the gaps in the shield wall.

The pipes spoke once more, shrill and urgent. To Keres, it seemed like they were screaming.

Where in Hera were the Ruxian and Lendian reinforcements?

Something was wrong.

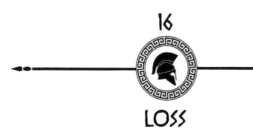

16

LOSS

"I have held many titles. Ephebe. Lochagos. Strategos. Harbinger. But there is one title that I cherish above all others. The only one that fills my heart with joy ... Father."

DEXIOS, STRATEGOS OF THENA

"SOUND THEM AGAIN!" Dexios ordered in exasperation, watching with slowly mounting horror as the shield wall swayed like a branch buffeted by the wind. The phalanx was on the verge of breaking.

"NAMBE!" he yelled, twisting in the saddle. The big house slave ran to the top of the grassy slope where Dexios had set up his command post, the individual bronze scales of his mail coat jingling. Two short swords were sheathed in a cross-like scabbard on his back; not the traditional straight blades used by the Tyrreans, but shorter, single-edged recurved weapons known as kopides.

"Master?"

"Take one of the horses. Polydius isn't responding to the pipes or flags. The phalanx is teetering on a knife edge. If he doesn't act now, it'll be a massacre."

"Yes, Master. I—" Nambe stopped, his face splitting into a wide grin. "He's here."

Two hundred Ruxian cavalry crested the rise on the

western flank with Polydius at their fore, easily recognisable by his majestic lavender-coloured plume. The riders paused; spears raised.

Dexios breathed a sigh of relief. "Malaka had me worried for a moment. He was always first on the training field during our ephebic training. Old age has made him less punctual. Now, where in Tartarus are the Lendians?"

Excited shouts cut through the frenetic melee below as the hoplites on the left flank of the phalanx glimpsed the distant figures who were the sign of their salvation.

Polydius turned his stallion towards the command post and Dexios. His spear dropped, the tip now aimed at his fellow strategos. Despite the distance that separated the two men, Dexios could feel his old comrade's gaze upon him, that same feral, wolf-like stare that couldn't quite disguise the deep-rooted envy slowly growing. Spreading … festering.

I have been blind, Dexios thought. *The warning signs had all been there. The eagerness. The pleading. The subtle smile as he approved the strategy — my strategy. And now I have sent six hundred Theneans to their deaths.*

The traitor's spear fell, and the Ruxians retreated, wheeling their horses away from the crumbling phalanx.

Dexios had fought a hundred wars on a hundred different battlefields. He had stood before the so-called impregnable fortresses of the men of the south, and he had taken them. He had led a daring night assault on a moored fleet of corsairs, killing dozens while they slept and setting fire to their triremes. The bodies of the countless men he and his armies had murdered over the years would form a mountain to rival the size of the peaks under which he now stood.

His hands were stained with two decades of blood. He

knew the theatre of slaughter, knew instinctively how to adapt. How to win.

He had always believed that no battle was unwinnable, no matter the odds.

Until now.

He bit down on his tongue, the pain chasing the fear from his mind.

"Sound the retreat!" he ordered the trio of pipers, who were gaping at the Ruxians in shock.

"Nambe! Mount up! I need you to race back to the forward camp and get everyone there moving. No wagons, the bare essentials only. Then ride as hard as you dare for Thena. Send a pigeon too. Letho must be warned as soon as possible."

Nambe unhitched one of the nearby courier horses, an ochre-coloured gelding. He was about to pull himself into the saddle when it hit him. "Would it not be better for you to inform the basileus yourself, Master?" he asked carefully.

Dexios rammed his helm onto his head. "It's my fault, Nambe. My men. My *son*. They are dying because of my misguided trust. My stupidity. I can't leave them."

The phalanx was close to collapse. The front line bowed inwards as the tauros concentrated their efforts on the centre, the arche unable to withstand the relentless battering.

"You … I strongly advise you to reconsider, Master," Nambe said. "The field is lost. If you go down there now, you will not survive."

Dexios smiled grimly. "It shall be as the Gods will it. And I would rather go to Charon with my head held high and my heart free of guilt than be dragged before him in shame."

"Then, let me come with you."

"No. Your time of serving me is done, friend. The papers are already signed, on the desk in my office. Take them. They are yours. You and your family are free. May your life be long and full of joy. When you see Melia, tell her … tell her I am sorry, but I have failed her twice. And I wish things could have been different."

His stallion reared, its nostrils flaring as it picked up the battlefield stench of blood, sweat, and death. Dexios drew his xiphos, touched it to his helm in a final salute, then sent his steed galloping down the hill into the chaos, his crimson cloak streaming out behind him like an unquenchable flame.

Keres turned his shield to let the wounded hoplite through. The second-ranker had lost his own aspis and was covered in so much blood it was impossible to tell who he was. He pushed on towards the rear of the phalanx, and the ranks closed up tightly behind him.

Coward, Keres thought bitterly.

The men guarding both flanks had confirmed what Keres already suspected. There would be no pincers. No salvation. The men of Thena were on their own.

An anguished cry from ahead, followed by a scream. Something hit Keres on the shoulder and rolled off into the muck. A severed finger. The tauros were exploiting every weakness in the faltering shield wall, punishing each mistake.

"Move up!" ordered Galleas from somewhere ahead, and Keres found himself in the third rank. Tychos was already there, his face creased with pain and effort, his shield arm wobbling dangerously as he fought to keep it upright. Less than eight feet away, the tauros howled and roared, consumed by a terrible carnage and bloodlust that made them appear even more like beasts.

Keres was close enough to smell them; the dank, unwashed odour of their hairy hides, the putrescent stench of their breath. He fought back the urge to vomit and readied his spear. A gap opened briefly, and he thrust into it with all the strength he could muster, hitting something soft and eliciting a pain-filled roar.

He pulled his weapon back and tried again, but his foot slipped on the muddy terrain and he would have fallen if not for the support of the shield at his back. The once bone-dry stretch of land was rapidly becoming a quagmire, soaking up the blood, vomit, and urine of six hundred men.

A soft fluttering overhead made Keres look up to see a score of arrows arch over the phalanx and patter down among the attackers. The misthios, at least, had not abandoned them. Not yet. But their volleys were proving to be mostly ineffective at longer range, failing to penetrate the tauros' thick hides.

Keres returned his focus to the front line just in time to see the hoplite two rows ahead have his skull crushed by an enormous maul. The tauros responsible raised his weapon triumphantly, blood and brain matter still dripping from the tip. A xiphos snaked forwards, lightning-fast, and stabbed into the exposed armpit. The beast cried out in surprise. He wheeled in fury, bovine eyes seeking out his attacker. A duo of spears slammed into his stomach and kidney, forcing him to his knees.

Galleas withdrew his xiphos and thrust again, ramming the blade deep into the thing's skull.

They can be killed, Keres reminded himself. *They are terrifying, but not immortal.*

"HERA IS WITH US!" Galleas screamed over the creature's death-throes. The lochagos had lost his helm and was bleeding from a dozen cuts, but his eyes were sharp and clear. He turned, and Keres saw the old man's aspis for the first time. A trio of laurel wreaths surrounding a nesting dove.

Galleas's eyes widened as he spied Keres in the third rank. He opened his mouth to say something, but before he could speak, a boulder-like fist slammed into the side of his head. His cheekbone broke with a crack, and he collapsed. The arche to his left turned to help him, only to take an axe blow to the neck, the blade slipping through the tiny crack between shield rim and helmet.

K'vath, the colossal tauros alpha, pushed the dying hoplite aside and careened into the soldier just behind.

"The shield wall is broken!" Keres tried to yell, but it came out as a croak. "Tychos!" he spluttered. "With me! The line! We must reform the line!"

He forced his trembling legs to move. One grime-covered sandal bumped against something soft. He looked down into the pale face of Helydices, already half-submerged in the mud, his left arm mauled by a tauros's hooves.

Gods. Gods. Gods.

The first line had collapsed, and there was nothing to stop tauros bursting through the shield wall, running amok among the less-experienced lower ranks beyond. Horrific screams filled Keres's ears. A crimson spray blinded him momentarily. He shook his head to clear the red film from his eyes. This is what his father was trying to protect him from. This ... nightmare of mindless slaughter.

A hoplite pushed past him gibbering madly, his left arm hanging by a sliver of tendon and flesh.

I can't stay here, Keres thought, turning to follow him. His apsis banged against his shins, and he looked down at the diving hawk, half-hidden by mud. His fears. He had to face his fears. What was it Tychos had said? Better to die a soldier than live a coward.

Hera give me strength.

He stepped over Helydices's corpse and found himself standing alone before the blood-spattered form of K'vath. The tauros had a spear shaft protruding from one shoulder and a jagged wound running from torso to navel.

"Flee, little hawk," the monster growled. An injured hoplite whimpered softly in the dirt close by, legs twitching. K'vath brought a hoof down hard on the man's back, crushing his spine. "Flee," he repeated menacingly.

"St ... stay back." Tychos moved protectively in front of Keres. He had lost his cap and was shaking with uncontrollable terror, his old, beat-up aspis scored with fresh claw marks.

K'vath cocked his shaggy head, bemused. "Why do you continue to fight when all is lost? There is no honour in such a death. You shame your ancestors."

Tychos answered with a desperate scream, jabbing his spear at the tauros alpha. K'vath caught the weapon just below the tip, yanked it from Tychos's hand, spun it round, and impaled him with it, punching effortlessly through the young ephebe's unprotected chest.

Blood poured from Tychos's open mouth. His hands

scrabbled at his throat. Keres looked on in horror. *He's drowning,* he thought. *Drowning in his own blood. This can't be happening.*

He threw down his spear and shield and rushed to his friend's side. "Tychos!" he cried in anguish, pulling the shaft free. "I'm here. I've got you."

Tychos fell against him, and Keres could only hold him close as he thrashed and spasmed, suffocating.

"Don't leave me," Keres pleaded. "I need you, Tychos. Fight it. Please, fight it."

Tychos tried to reply, but his lungs filled with fluid. His dying words were lost in a choking gurgle.

"I will find you," Keres murmured in his friend's ear. "I will look for you on the shores of Tartarus. Wait for me there. We will enter the afterlife together."

Tychos's body jerked one final time, then was still. Keres lowered his friend gently into the dirt and covered him with his aspis. His head was pounding. He blinked away the tears forming in the corners of his eyes. Everything was blurry and indistinct as if he was under water. He thought he heard the faint sound of the pipes ordering the retreat, but that couldn't be right. The phalanx had to hold. Dexios had told them to hold.

Whatever cohesion remained in the phalanx disintegrated. A fleeing hoplite slammed into Keres as he passed, catching him on his aching shoulder. All around him, exhausted soldiers abandoned their posts; the risk of exposing their backs to the enemy far outweighed by their almost primal desire to flee.

Keres heard a guttural bark. He had almost forgotten K'vath. The tauros was making no move to pursue, his man-sized axe planted upright in the muck with his hands resting calmly on the haft.

"Little hawk," he muttered when he saw Keres. "You are still here. Your alpha calls you home. Begone."

Run! Keres's brain screamed at his unmoving legs. He had done all he could. It was time to go back to Thena. Back to his old life.

Alone.

He remembered standing before the basileus, his body bruised and bloodied by the trials. Reciting the ephebic oath.

"We will never bring disgrace on this, our city, by any act of dishonesty or cowardice," he said softly, bending to pick up his shield.

"Do not do this," K'vath warned.

"Nor ever desert our suffering comrades in the ranks."

Keres hammered his spear into the tauros's side, feeling it pierce the skin. K'vath grunted and ripped the weapon free, tossing it aside. It landed next to the spear that Dexios had thrust into the ground the day before. The symbolic line that would not be crossed. They had failed to halt the tide.

They had lost.

"I did not wish this," K'vath said. "I was told you would flee. I was told you would not resist."

Keres felt two huge hands close around his neck. He lifted his head and stared defiantly into the eyes of his killer.

"We will fight for the ideals and sacred beliefs of the city, both alone and with many." He smiled. "You will never win."

The awful stench of battle receded for a moment, replaced by the sweet smell of grapes ripening on the vine.

Keres was running, his father by his side. The early dawn light made the leaves sparkle like emeralds.

"Foolish hawk," the tauros growled, and twisted.

The last thing Keres heard was the crack of bone as K'vath broke his neck.

♋

The wind shrieked in Dexios's ears as his stallion galloped down the hill, the fissured earth and tufts of scraggly grass a blur under its hooves. An insufferable rage overwhelmed him, stoked by his own guilt.

I will burn in the fires of Tartarus for this, he thought angrily, digging his heels into his steed's flanks. *Persephone herself will set me ablaze.*

The phalanx had devolved into a tangled mess of broken men and howling beasts. Dexios searched for the horsehair-plumed helm of Galleas, but everything was covered in muck and blood. Cursing, he swung left around the melee. He would hit the tauros from behind. One stood taller than the rest, his black hide covered in a mass of scars. The alpha. And before him ... the lifeless body of Keres.

"No ..."

His son. His only reason to live. Gone.

A half-dozen tauros stood between Dexios and the alpha. He charged into them like an avenging god, screaming his son's name. The first beast was caught unawares, his focus on the fleeing hoplites. Dexios hacked into the back of his neck with his xiphos hard enough to sever the spinal cord. He collapsed, no longer in control of his limbs.

With a flick of the reins, Dexios avoided two more of

the creatures, then dodged under the slicing cut of a third. The two remaining tauros rushed him. The stallion reared, and two powerful hooves lashed out, knocking the attackers down.

"VENGEANCE!" Dexios yelled, lost to grief and anger. Nothing else mattered now. Only revenge. Revenge on the bastard who had taken his son from him. He saw the alpha through a buzzing red haze and singled him out with the tip of his blade. "TAUROS! FACE ME! YOUR DEATH AWAITS!"

"Then, come," the tauros replied, hefting his enormous axe.

Dexios's mount leapt over the fallen enemy and ploughed forwards. The one-horned tauros stood his ground, axe held high, then, at the very last moment, he stepped to the side and hammered his blade into the stallion's chest.

The animal screamed in pain, throwing Dexios from the saddle. The strategos instinctively tucked in his knees and lowered his head to break his fall. His shoulder hit the ground first, and he rolled twice through the mud before bumping against the body of a dead hoplite.

The tauros ripped his axe free from the dying horse. "I am K'vath," he said in a voice like churning gravel. "You must be the alpha of this human herd. You have come to surrender?"

Dexios spat out a mouthful of muck. "No. I have come to end you." His knee and back ached terribly as old war wounds awakened. He gritted his teeth and fought through the pain.

"Ah." K'vath surveyed the battlefield. The last of the surviving hoplites were vanishing into the hills. The tauros did not pursue them. The cacophony of war was ending, replaced by the quieter aftermath, the weak cries for help, and the dismal weeping of the dying. Charon would be making many trips to the Halls of Judgement tonight.

"Which one was your son? I have killed so many."

"And you will kill no more," Dexios vowed. Three feet from where he stood, a black and bronze aspis lay askew, taunting him with the image of a diving hawk. He picked up his son's shield and slipped his hand through the hook. It fit his arm perfectly.

"I do not understand vengeance," K'vath said. He pulled the spear tip from his shoulder with a grunt and threw it aside. "In our herd, the calf does not take up the yoke of the bull." He snorted derisively. "You are tired, and your mind is clouded by anger. It would not be a fair fight. I offer you this. Make me bleed and I will allow you to carry your dead from the field for an honourable burial. Fail, and I will build a pyramid of skulls from the severed heads of your herd, denying their shades entrance to the afterlife."

He's goading me, Dexios thought, his mind buffeted by the crimson seas of rage. *Trying to use my anger against me. I need to focus. Hera help me.*

He looked down at his shaking hands. At the dark blood dripping from his xiphos. At the aspis with its diving hawk. This was the only thing left he could do for his son now. He had failed him in life. He would not fail him in death. He concentrated on his hands. The grains of dirt stuck under the fingernails. The wrinkled skin forming pits and furrows over the knuckles. The blue veins that writhed like worms.

The shaking slowed, then stopped.

Keres.

Dexios attacked.

He came in low, his blade held underarm, hoping to catch his opponent unawares. He feinted a short stab left, then cut right, aiming for the beast's calf. K'vath jerked his leg out of the way, and Dexios's blade hit the tip of the hoof instead, screeching across the bone. He scrambled backwards with a curse, narrowly avoiding K'vath's counter.

The alpha tauros squared his shoulders and gave an appreciative grunt.

Dexios powered forwards again, sword held high. K'vath deflected the overhead blow with a clang that made Dexios's ears ring. The beast replied with a heavy punch that knocked the strategos's plumed helm from his head. He blinked to shake his blurred vision.

K'vath's second punch broke Dexios's nose.

He screamed in pain and dropped his shield, blood pouring down his face. K'vath reached out with his hand. "You fought well, human alpha. I will take no pleasure in crushing your skull."

Dexios fixed his bleary gaze on the tauros's massive fingers. Something came unbidden to the forefront of his mind. Something he had said to Keres back at the vineyard.

… If he cannot best you with his spear, he will use his fists, his elbows, his feet. He will knock you down and gouge out your eyes with his nails.

Dexios grinned manically, a flash of ivory on crimson, then opened his mouth and bit down hard. He felt a moment's resistance as the tough, leathery skin grated against his incisors, then he was through, crunching through meat and bone, ripping off the beast's forefinger.

K'vath gave a surprised bellow and tore his hand away as a thick red liquid began to pump sluggishly from the wound.

Dexios turned his head and spat the morsel of flesh into the muck. "That looks like blood," he said.

One of the watching tauros started forwards, but K'vath stopped him with a rasping bark.

"I underestimated you, human alpha," he said, bovine nostrils flaring. "You may bury your men. Now, listen well. When you are done, do not return to Thena. You will find only death there."

K'vath made a chopping gesture with his hand, and the surviving tauros moved away, leaving Dexios alone. With the last of his remaining strength, he stumbled over to the hawk-painted shield and sank to his knees before the body of his son.

"I'm sorry," he murmured, the words sounding weak and hollow.

He brushed a lock of dark hair from one pale cheek.

The flash of a distant memory. Holding Keres for the first time. Cutting the cord that linked him to his mother. Filled with an indescribable joy, stronger and purer than anything he had felt before.

Watching as those tiny lungs filled with life. That first, unforgettable intake of air. That first breath.

Then … another scream. Another voice.

Another life.

Keres and Oneiros.

Two miracles. And he had lost them both.

"I'm sorry," he repeated, not knowing what else to say.

Tears dripped from his face onto the corpse of his son.

Then the pain overwhelmed him, and he surrendered himself to the darkness.

PART TWO

DENIAL

17

PERCEPTION

"A farmer came across a fox dying in the middle of the road. Unwilling to let the poor beast perish, he brought it to his farm and, with the help of his three daughters, nurtured the animal back to health. A week later, he was awoken by terrible screeches. He rushed outside to find the fox covered in feathers and blood, a dead fowl clenched in its jaws. 'What have you done?' the farmer exclaimed in horror. 'I helped you. I healed you. Why are you doing this?'. The fox looked at him strangely. 'You know why. Because I am a fox.'"

TYRREAN FABLE

THE GATES TO the palace were shut. *Again*. Elena had been trying to gain access to the basileus for over a week now and had been thwarted at each and every turn. The obstacle wasn't so much the gates, but the man who stood vigil on the other side: Derka, the head of Letho's house slaves. Derka was a pasty-faced northerner with ferret-like eyes and a crooked nose; as unflappable as he was unlikeable.

Elena had attempted flattery, indignation, brazen duplicity, and, when all that had failed, a modicum of reluctant flirting. Everything had been met with the same monotonous excuse: the basileus was focusing on the defence of the city and was not to be disturbed.

This time it would be different. This time she came armed with a secret weapon.

"Good morning, Lady," one of the guards said respectfully as she approached. His bronze helm was pushed up his head as far as it would go, revealing a kind, careworn face.

Elena flashed what she hoped was a friendly smile. She had spent a portion of her meagre funds on a trip to the bathhouse, and a slave had washed her blue chiton while she bathed, pounding the fabric vigorously under a stream of cold water until the odours of old perfume and wine had been scoured away. Strangely enough, she found herself missing the smell now as if she was wearing something that didn't belong to her. And it itched. Terribly.

"Hera bless you," she replied, resisting the urge to scratch at her back and chest. "Is the basileus holding court today?"

"Aye, Lady, but Derka is here also, and you're as likely to get past him as you are to fly into the palace on wings of flame. Best leave it."

"I think I'll try anyway," Elena said, holding up the wicker basket she was carrying. "I came across some new information that might just tip the scales in my favour."

The guard shot a furtive look at his companion. "I suppose there's no reason to stop you, Lady." He rapped on the gate with the butt of his spear, and Elena walked into the vestibule where Derka awaited her. The northerner was perched on a stool behind a tiny table upon which sat a marble counting board and a wax tablet. Bony fingers were flicking metal discs up and down the carved grooves to keep track of his calculations.

Elena coughed politely. Derka stopped with a frown, making a small note on the tablet with his stylus.

"Oh, it's you again, is it?" he said with a sigh. "The basileus is very busy. Very busy indeed. The city must be prepared. I'm sure you understand."

The tone of his voice inferred that he didn't care in the slightest whether Elena understood or not.

"Of course, of course," she replied in mock regret. "Heavy lies the crown. It's a pity. I have a couple of amphorae of red that I was hoping to gift him. A fine variety imported straight from Boena. Expensive, naturally, but our Lord deserves only the best."

Derka's nose twitched ever so slightly. His fingers hovered over the counting board, moving in the empty air as if still doing some invisible sum or subtraction. "Perhaps ... an exception can be made. Just this once. The basileus would certainly appreciate such a generous offering. Although ..."

I have him! Elena thought.

"One amphora should suffice. You may leave the second here with me."

"As you wish." She set the wine down on the rickety table and hurried past the dour house slave before he could change his mind. Or taste the wine, which was no Boenian red. In fact, it was one of the cheaper varieties; an abrasive, vinegary mixture she knew all too well as she had filled her own kylix with it on many a trip to the taverna. The only expensive thing about it was the fake seal burnt into the cork, a forgery that had cost her close to a month's salary.

It was one of the other palace slaves whom she had managed to persuade to let slip Derka's one vice: his collection of fine wines. Somehow, despite being indentured, he had succeeded in amassing several dozen amphorae. He had no intention of ever drinking them but was using them as an investment that he would eventually sell in order to buy his freedom.

Everyone has their weakness, she thought, exiting the vestibule. *Even those who believe themselves incorruptible.*

The inner courtyard was the basileus's pride and joy; a botanical paradise of colourful flowers and sculpted bushes. Palm trees arched overhead, offering some shade to the multitude of plants artfully arranged in vibrant groups of light blue, orange, burgundy, rose, and violet. A gravel path led to a circular pool in the courtyard's centre, its mirror-like surface almost a perfect reflection of the cloudless sky.

Letho sat by the pool dressed in a crimson chiton, his silver circlet glinting in the sunlight. He seemed lost in thought, the bowl of caramelised dates next to him untouched. He turned as Elena crunched up the gravel towards him.

"Sophistes Elena," he said in his reedy voice. "You made it past my own personal Cerberus, I see. To what do I owe the pleasure?"

"Lord," she replied, making the sign of Hera. "Thank you for receiving me. It has been … difficult to reach you these last few days."

"Hmmm? Ah, yes. Apologies. Affairs of state and the like. You know how it is."

"Not really, Lord."

"No, I suppose not." He snapped his pudgy fingers, and a slave materialised from behind a palm tree. "Can I offer you anything? Some watered wine, perhaps? These scorching summer days are becoming quite uncomfortable, are they not? It almost makes one wish for winter."

Gods, a glass of wine would be perfect, Elena thought before the more rational side of her brain took over.

"No, thank you, Lord. I am fine."

"Really? I'm surprised. I was informed you had acquired a certain taste for the stuff. Are you sure?"

His eyes twinkled mischievously.

Everyone has their weakness.

"Yes … th … thank you, Lord."

"As you wish. Now, tell me why you are here. Trying to find something to keep you busy while the ephebes are away?"

"Yes … I mean no, Lord," Elena replied hurriedly. She was beginning to feel flustered. How did he know so much? She put down the basket and scratched at a particularly itchy patch of skin on her left arm while trying to regain her composure. "It's actually quite a serious matter. A crime has been committed. A murder."

Letho smiled thinly. "I think you'll find in a city this size that such misdeeds happen on a regular basis. I'm sorry you waited for a week to tell me this, but I can't personally oversee the investigation of every act of misconduct. That is what the polis guard is for. Crenate is not a particularly diplomatic man, but he is extremely good at his job."

Elena took a deep breath. "You misunderstand, Lord. I've come to ask for your help not as the basileus, but as a potential witness."

Letho was in the process of putting a date into his mouth. He paused, jaws open, then removed the piece of fruit and flicked it away into the bushes. "Explain."

Elena launched into her well-rehearsed summary of last week's events, beginning with the trials and ending with

Crenate's visit the following morning. Letho watched her impassively, his round face expressionless.

"I see," he said in a strange voice. "It always baffles me how intelligent, well-cultivated people like yourself still manage to do things that are so catastrophically stupid."

"Lord?"

"Follow me, please." He heaved himself out of his seat and made for the opposite side of the courtyard garden. Elena stayed rooted to the spot, alarm bells ringing in her skull.

"Um, I think—"

"It wasn't a request," the basileus said sharply without turning round. There was a slight movement from behind one of the fig trees. The top of a plumed helmet belonging to Letho's honour guard. Elena bit her lower lip in frustration. Things were not going according to plan.

The basileus led her along a series of long corridors, across a smaller, tiled courtyard, and down a flight of stairs into what appeared to be a storeroom. Amphorae lined the walls, and haunches of cured meat hung from the support beams. A half-dozen large goat cheeses were stacked in a row under a well-stocked spice rack. At the far end, Elena could see the raised dome of a grain silo protruding from the floor. Letho pushed the cover aside. The interior of the container was empty save for a wooden ladder descending all the way to the bottom.

"All our grain is kept above ground in granaries now," Letho said by way of explanation. "Has been for years. This old silo is a vestige of the past. I had once thought of filling it in but have since found it … useful." He gestured at the ladder.

Elena glanced behind her. The honour guard who had been shadowing them had disappeared. She was alone with the basileus.

"Surely you have better things to do than give me a tour of the palace, Lord," she said nervously. Her heart felt like it was doing a pyrrhic dance on her ribcage. "I would not want to detain you further."

"Down."

She gripped the rungs of the ladder with sweaty hands and descended to the bottom of the silo. The air was cooler here, hidden from the sun and chilled by the surrounding earth. With a creak of wood, Letho joined her.

"What now?" she asked.

The basileus readjusted his circlet and pointed into the gloom behind the ladder. She squinted. There was a door there, strong and thick, built into the wall of the silo itself.

"As I said, I have since found it useful," Letho murmured, drawing a key from a chain around his neck. He unlocked the door and ushered Elena inside. She found herself in a room even smaller than her tiny apartment at the garrison. There were shapes pressed up against the far wall, but it was dark, darker than the silo, and despite straining her eyes, she could not make out what they were.

"Some light, perhaps?" There was the crackle of a torch catching fire, and the room was suddenly illuminated in a warm glow, revealing all.

Elena let out a horrified shriek and backed away, bumping into the portly yet solid body of Letho who was completely blocking the way out.

"Look," he said, his eyes cold. He thrust the torch towards the far wall. "Look and understand."

The prisoner was on his knees with his arms outstretched, hanging from two manacles bolted into the hard stone. His once-black leather armour was in tatters, his turban torn and dirty. The man's emaciated face was covered in cuts and bruises, but he was unmistakably a southerner. What had made Elena cry out, however, was the damage done to the prisoner's eyes and lips. Both had been stitched crudely shut with black thread, rendering him blind and mute.

Letho drew closer. The southerner, sensing the torch-light on his skin, raised his face and moaned.

"Perception," the basileus said softly. His voice had changed. It was deeper. Stronger. "Perception is key. And I am fully aware of how people perceive me, with my expansive girth, my jewelled fingers, and my extravagant lifestyle. They mock me behind my back. Share a laugh at my expense. Even the most prominent of Thena's political figures tend to forget that they are talking to their Lord. I am seen as weak. Obedient. And, above all, I am not considered a threat."

Elena listened silently, her eyes riveted on the mutilated face of the prisoner. Letho's words hit closer to home than she would have liked. She knew only too well how it felt to constantly suffer the superficial judgement of others, reduced to a single defining characteristic with one dismissive glance: a middle-aged, unmarried woman.

"They never stop to think," Letho continued in the same quiet monotone, "how this pudgy, gaudily-dressed aristocrat has succeeded in ruling over thousands of Theneans for over thirty years. How he has kept them safe. Protected their interests. Built and shaped this city from the cesspool it was to the flourishing epicentre of trade and culture it is today. They are surprised when charismatic leaders like

Strategos Dexios follow my orders without hesitation or contradiction."

"He … knows who you really are," Elena stammered.

"He does. As does Galleas. Crenate. A handful of others. Which brings us to you." He turned to her, his eyes flashing, and she wilted under his gaze.

"You had the audacity to come to the palace with the imbecilic idea of dredging up my past indiscretions? In broad daylight? Surrounded by slaves? My *wife's* slaves?" His voice grew louder, startling the prisoner who gave a frightened whimper. Letho put a calming hand on the broken man's shoulder.

Stupid woman! Elena's mind screamed at her. *What have you done?*

"I … I'm sorry."

"I did the stitching myself," Letho said as if nothing had happened, moving his hand from the man's shoulder and running his thick fingers over the closed eyelids. "I take no enjoyment in it, but I find it helps create a certain rapport. I have several cells like this scattered throughout the palace. Occupied by people who have threatened me. Threatened all I have accomplished. I visit them often, as a reminder of the price that must be paid for our continued peace and prosperity."

Elena didn't answer, thoughts whirling around her brain. If she was fast enough, she could make it around the basileus and up the ladder. But what then? The only way out of the palace was back past Derka and the guards at the gate. Still, anything was better than staying here. She tensed her muscles, waiting for the right time to move.

"I'm sure you have surmised who this particular guest

is," Letho continued. "Makar was correct, there were two assassins. Only one was dead, however. This fellow was badly wounded but very much alive. Crenate helped me bring him here. There are tunnels underground that allow me to enter and leave the palace discreetly. After some unfortunate unpleasantness, he became very eager to share all he knew. Which, as it turned out, wasn't very much. He had been hired by a southern noble, someone who had lost a son fighting Dexios's hoplites. Or was it a brother? I can't recall. In any case, they eventually found out about the daughter of Aphrodite. Poor woman. I had grown quite fond of her."

He slapped the prisoner's face, ever so lightly. "A despicable tactic, using the blood of innocents as a means to attaining one's goal. This man's companion is surely languishing in the fires of Tartarus as we speak — or whatever name these foreigners give to their afterlife. Anyway, the manner of his death did confuse me somewhat at the time. Crenate's investigation led us to an elderly priestess of Hera, a supposed expert in the mystical and the mythological. Turned out she is a charlatan. Graycea, her name is. Go and see her for yourself if you don't believe me."

Elena felt her muscles unclench.

Go and see her …

"I am free to leave?"

"What?" Letho gave a surprised chuckle. "Of course! You didn't think I brought you here to join this poor man on the wall, did you? Gods, woman, I'm not a monster. If I had considered you a threat, you would have already been dealt with. No, it's quite the opposite in fact. I have been monitoring you for some time, Elena. Galleas always spoke highly of you, and your knowledge of Thena and its history is quite extensive. I had always planned on bringing you into our inner circle, and with many of my advisors up north or otherwise indisposed, it seems like the right time. I need more allies. People I can count on."

"And so, you reveal to me your most closely-guarded secret."

"Yes. I find it serves a dual purpose: it proves to you I am ready to give you my trust …"

"And at the same time warns me of the consequences incurred by breaking that trust."

"Exactly," Letho said with a half-smile. "Trust and fear. Both so very different, yet both equally viable ways to obtain compliance. What do you say?"

Elena tried and failed to meet his gaze. It was an innocent question, and everything about the basileus's demeanour seemed to indicate she could refuse … But, as Letho had so rightly said, she was far from stupid. There was no choice here. No choice at all.

"I would be honoured to serve," she said, bowing her head in defeat.

"Excellent! I knew you would. Shall we return to the garden? I abhor the heat, but I'm beginning to miss the sunlight."

He plunged the torch into a bucket of water, extinguishing it in a cloud of steam.

The mutilated prisoner, once more confined to solitude, let out a whispering sigh of despair.

18

BURIAL

"When the pipes of victory sound. When the exuberant cries of triumph echo from arche to telos, then begins the final hardship. The entombment of the dead. For there is no greater affront to the Gods than leaving an empty husk of flesh uncovered and visible to their celestial eyes. Some believe it is because they do not understand death. I believe it is because they fear it."

CERBRIONES, 'ALALAGMOE'

I T WAS NAMBE who found him. Hunched over the cold body of his dead son as if the closeness would somehow make him live again.

"Dexios," the slave called softly.

"I told you to leave," the other man replied, his voice cracking. "Go away."

"You did." Nambe knelt next to the strategos. "Unfortunately for you, I no longer have to follow your orders. You made me a free man. Free to choose my own destiny. Free to decide. And I have decided to stay here."

Dexios slowly turned his head. Grief had aged him terribly, cutting deep lines into his mud-spattered cheeks and adding serpentine blood vessels to the whites of his eyes. A shaking hand pushed weakly at Nambe's shoulder.

"Go. Away."

"No."

Dexios bared his teeth. "There is nothing more to do here, slave! Return to Thena. Warn the basileus. Leave me in peace."

"The final rites, Master. The dirges. The libations. We must bury all of them with honour, lest their shades be doomed to wander the shores of Tartarus for all eternity."

"I …" the strategos faltered, unable to continue. Fresh tears wet his face. "You are right. I am the harbinger. That is all I am now. I will ensure that the shades of the men who died here find solace in the arms of Charon, and I will return their shields to their families."

Nambe chose his words carefully. "That is an … arduous task, Mast— Dexios. The tauros slaughtered hundreds, and we are but two men. It will take weeks."

For an instant, Dexios's grief was replaced by anger. "It will take as long as it must. Such is my penance. I deserve this. I should have seen it. By the Gods, I should have seen it. And I will spend the rest of my days trying to make up for my stupidity."

Nambe sighed. "Then, we had better get started. There are picks and shovels back at the forward camp; the slaves use them to dig the latrines and defensive ditches. I will retrieve some."

Dexios mumbled his consent. One hand brushed absently against Keres's hair. Felt the half-healed bruise on his temple. *This is not the way it was supposed to happen,* he thought sadly. *It should be me lying there in the mud and you mourning me. You and your brother were the only truly good things that ever happened to me, and now you are both gone.*

A muted clang of metal brought him out of his

introspection. Frowning, he stood, his hand moving to his scabbard. Another clang. It was coming from the rear of the phalanx. Or at least, where the rear had been before the rout. Dexios drew his xiphos and began picking his way through the horrendous landscape of broken shields and fallen bodies. He passed several enormous tauran corpses, each brought down by a dozen spears. Each surrounded by a dozen slain Tyrreans.

How did we ever think we would beat them? Dexios wondered. *There is nothing in all of Tyrris that is strong enough to stand against such creatures.*

Another clang, much closer. It appeared to be coming from under the body of a tauros, his smoky-grey hair drenched in blood. The beast was definitely not the one making the noise: two arrows protruded from the back of his skull like an ant's antennae. Dexios prodded at a bony horn with the tip of his xiphos.

"Is … is anybody there?" came a hopeful voice. "I appear to be, um, stuck."

"Hold on!" Dexios replied, sheathing his weapon and grabbing one of the tauros's tree-trunk arms. He braced, then pulled, his sandals slipping in the mud. Despite his best efforts, the corpse refused to budge.

"Heavy bastard, isn't he?" the voice continued. It didn't seem particularly worried. "I've been trying to shift the bugger for what feels like hours."

"We need to work together," Dexios said, wiping at his forehead with the back of his hand. "You push. I pull. On the count of three! One … Two … THREE!"

He yanked as hard as he could. With a sickening squelch,

the body slithered sideways, revealing an impressive hooked nose and thin moustache.

"Strategos!" Krinne beamed, showing off two shiny gold teeth. "Thank Hera! I was beginning to suffocate under there. Must be one of the worst things I have ever smelt, and that's saying something. I once knew a misthios who had a yeast infection so bad …" he trailed off, his eyes scanning Dexios's face. "Gods, you look terrible. What happened?"

"Polydius's betrayal and my ignorance got my son killed," Dexios growled. He placed a foot on the chest of the tauran corpse. "And I am trying to decide whether or not you played any part in it."

Krinne suddenly became aware of the precarity of the situation. His moustache quivered. "Wait, what? Why in Tartarus would you think that? We're mercenaries, not traitors. Besides, we're still owed half our pay. How are we supposed to get that now, eh?"

"Perhaps Polydius paid you even more *not* to fight."

"If that's what you think, you're either blind or stupid. I saw you, up on that hill, sitting all proud-like on your stallion. I'm sure you had a great view of us misthios, down in the muck, facing off against two hundred tauros with sticks and string." Krinne struggled to move, but the lower half of his body was still pinned.

"We should have retreated after the first two volleys," he added. "But I ordered a third. I reasoned that if we could bring a couple more of 'em down, that would be two less for the phalanx to worry about. Didn't matter in the end, of course, but at the time it seemed like the right thing to do. Lost four men who were too slow to get out of the way. The rest of us circled round the back of the main force and loosed what we had left over the front line."

He gazed defiantly into Dexios's bloodshot eyes. "Not the most logical tactics for someone who had been paid to let you die. Anyway, I've said my piece. Either you believe me or you don't. So, kill me or help me out from under this stinking pile of hair before I choke on my own vomit."

Dexios stared back at the mercenary. He didn't especially like the man. Krinne was brash, vulgar, self-centred, greedy, and far too talkative. But a liar? A coward? Maybe not. Dexios removed his foot from the slain tauros and held out his hand to pull the misthios free.

"Thank you." Somewhat miraculously, Krinne still had his composite bow across his back. He unslung the weapon and ran his fingers over the polished horn, searching for cracks, then turned the core over and checked the layered sinew on the opposite side. His teeth clicked together in a satisfied smile.

"Not a single scratch," he said happily. "I thought that cross-eyed old southerner was trying to fleece me, but it appears I got what I paid for." He began loosening the string, then stopped as his brain finally caught up with the horrific scenes before his eyes.

"What … How badly did we lose?" he asked, taking in the scattered piles of dead hoplites and the shields that lay abandoned in the muck. The crows had arrived, drawn by the stink of blood and decay. They circled the battlefield, obsidian eyes scanning the corpses below.

"It was a massacre," Dexios replied, picking up a battered bronze helm. The thin layer of protective metal had been nowhere near strong enough to resist the double-handed blows of the tauros.

"I've seen worse," Krinne said, carefully wrapping his bowstring in a piece of leather that he kept in a pouch at his belt. "Your plan was a sound one, Strategos. It was Polydius who had these men killed, not you."

Dexios grunted. "That remains for Persephone to decide. I will know my fate when my shade steps into the Halls of Judgement."

"Master?"

Nambe was carrying a pair of shovels over one shoulder. Behind him trailed a score of men clutching pickaxes; slaves for the most part, along with a scattering of unarmed soldiers. "Found this lot at the forward camp," he said darkly. "Deserters. Three of them were on horseback. They must have stayed hidden while the main force passed through then returned to scavenge whatever remained. I persuaded them it would be in their best interests to help us bury the dead before the crows took them."

"What, you managed to convince them to come back here just like that?" Krinne asked incredulously.

Nambe turned his gaze on the misthios. "No. I was forced to kill two of them before the rest would listen to reason. An unfortunate necessity."

"Hah." A burble of laughter escaped Krinne's lips until he saw that the southerner was deadly serious. His smile faded as quickly as it had come.

Nambe glanced at Dexios and shrugged, making the scales of his strange armour ripple like a shoal of fish. The strategos was sure his former slave was not exaggerating. He had never seen Nambe lift his kopis in anger. And he knew why. The man's former master had been an unapologetic sadist, inflicting pain on his 'property' for no other reason than the pleasure of doing so. Dexios had seen the scars.

If Nambe had killed those men, then it had been the only way.

"Unfortunate," Dexios agreed. "But effective. Cut off the head, and the body will die."

"Unless it's a hydra," grumbled Krinne, sheathing his bow and accepting a shovel.

Dexios ignored him. "Tyche has blessed you!" he shouted to the group of reluctant labourers. "She has offered you another lease of life! Help me now and, Hera willing, the basileus will forgive your past transgressions. I need you to dig a trench. Eight feet wide. Shields in a pile on the side. I'll return them to their next of kin. Begin."

It was hard, back-breaking work and would have been even harder if the tauros had not churned the earth and the blood of the dead had not softened the soil. Dexios drove at the ground relentlessly hour after hour, heedless of the blisters forming on his palms or the aching pain in his shoulders and biceps. It was something to do. Something to stop him from thinking of Keres.

The trench was filled as fast as it was dug, the corpses piled two or three layers deep. Dexios recognised many of the cold, stiff faces. Men he had fought with for years, ephebes he had seen at the trials, the wine merchant who had bought a third of last season's harvest. Tychos, the stonemason's son. Helydices. On and on, a morbid parade of all those he had failed.

"The shores of Tartarus will be full," said Nambe, heaving another body into the trench. "And therein lies another problem, Master … I could only find three of the four money pouches I had secreted in your quarters before the assault. There are not enough obols to pay the ferryman's toll for everyone."

Dexios cursed softly. "Then, we must do what we can. The youngest first, then the weakest. Let us pray to Hera that the shades denied passage will not go mad from their forced detention. Once we reach Thena, I'll ask Letho to send a priestess of Hera with the obols for those we could not honour. And stop calling me Master."

It was dark by the time they had finished. Nambe sent the exhausted labourers off looking for kindling, and soon a large bonfire blazed on the edge of the mass grave.

"We are done," Dexios said tiredly, throwing down his shovel and stretching his arms wide to make the bones in his spine crack.

"Not quite," Nambe replied, pointing at one last corpse that lay apart from the rest. Keres. "You need to decide what you wish to do with your son. We could dig a separate grave, perhaps? I fear returning him to the family crypt in Thena is not a viable solution. A week on the road under a hot sun will wreak havoc on the soft tissue."

"He stood with the phalanx. He should rest with them. Place him in the trench with the others."

Nambe and Krinne lowered the strategos's son carefully into the trench. Dexios knelt and prised Keres's clenched jaw open long enough to slip a silver obol into his mouth.

He stood, gathering his thoughts. Dexios had pronounced many funeral orations in his long years as strategos, but now words failed him. Nothing he could say would convey the heart-wrenching loss he felt. The hole deep inside his soul that would never heal.

"Here lies a host of brave men," he began hesitantly. "The bravest I have ever known. They felt fear, but they did not waver. They felt tired, but they did not fall."

There was a sound like a beating drum. Nambe had made a fist with his hand and was thumping his chest rhythmically. Others took up the call.

"They were abandoned, but they did not give up," Dexios continued. "They were overwhelmed, but they did not flee. They brought pride to Thena. Pride to their wives. Pride to their children." His confidence returned, buoyed by the hammering of fists. "And, in doing so, they have become immortal! For we will not forget what they did here. We will not let the memory of their courage fade away!"

Tears clouded his vision. He blinked them away. "Let us not be sad! Let us rejoice! The shades of these valorous warriors will reach the shores of Tartarus, and when Charon brings them before Persephone to be judged, what will she see? Heroes! Legends of Tyrris! And so, she will smile; and the gates of Elysium will open, welcoming them to an eternity of wonder! Praise Persephone! Praise Hera! May her light guide these shades to their final resting place."

"Praise Hera," Nambe repeated half-heartedly, seizing a shovel and throwing the first clump of dirt into the trench. Dexios fell silent, watching as the mud slowly obscured his son's face until, at last, it disappeared from sight.

♋

"We only have three horses," Nambe said to Dexios. They

were sitting with Krinne by the bonfire, too exhausted to move. Twenty feet away, a pyramid of bronze gleamed in the light of the flames. Over a hundred aspides. Memories of the fallen.

"What else?"

"A week's worth of supplies. Your tent. One of the supply wagons and the ox to pull it. Just about enough to get us all back to Thena if we're parsimonious. To be honest, we're lucky to have anything at all. If the tauros had thought it worth taking a detour to our forward camp on their march south, they could have burnt everything there to ash with little effort."

"And the pigeons?"

"Gone. The coop was empty. Polydius's work, I'd wager. Or one of his lackeys. Depriving us of a way to warn Letho, if you think they are still heading straight for Thena."

"It seems like the next logical step. With the loss of our phalanx, the polis is vulnerable."

"Vulnerable perhaps, but not defenceless, Dexios. Those walls can be held by the men the basileus has left. Besides, doesn't Polydius only have two hundred heavy cavalry? He won't take Thena with so few."

"Two hundred cavalry and a horde of tauros. And who knows what else? He could have been lying to us about the strength of Ruxia's forces just like he has about all the rest. I wouldn't trust anything that spews forth from that traitor bastard's mouth."

"Agreed."

Dexios stared moodily into the fire. "Did you search his tent?"

"Aye," Nambe confirmed. "Empty ... Actually, that's

not quite true. He did leave one thing, but it is barely worth mentioning; a juvenile attempt at insulting you."

Dexios smiled bitterly. "I think we are beyond petty insults now, Nambe. He killed my son. What was it?"

Nambe sighed and produced a well-worn slip of parchment. "The words of the Oracle." He handed it over, and Dexios saw three words illuminated in the firelight.

You will win.

"She was right," he murmured. "The Oracle was right. She never lies." His gaze returned to the bonfire.

He had only consulted the Oracle once in his long, illustrious career; before embarking on the campaign south across the Straits. She had given him some cryptic reply about heeding the flight of the gulls. He hadn't understood at first. Then, on the very morning his six triremes were set to cross the channel, the sky above Krene was filled with birds. Dexios had decided to delay the departure, pulling his men off the ships and back to the comfort of the garrison. Hours later, a violent storm had hit the coast, destroying half his ships. Half his ships, but none of his men.

The Oracle never lies.

No matter what the question is. No matter how ludicrous, how impossible.

All legends begin with a truth.

He felt it. The tingling of an idea so far-fetched that yesterday he would have laughed at the insanity of it. But not today. Today, his son was dead, and he would do everything in his power to bring him back.

Everything.

"Send the men south with sufficient supplies, the aspides, and the wagon," he said. "Impress on them the importance of returning the shields of the deceased and what they risk if they fail Thena a second time. They must, of course, avoid the tauros at all costs. If the way to Thena is blocked, they should make for Boena. Let us hope the basileus there has not fallen for Ruxia's tricks."

"Master?" Nambe looked puzzled.

"Krinne. You are still a misthios, yes? I am in need of your services. I cannot pay you upfront, but you know me. You know I always honour my debts. What do you say?"

The archer stroked the thin tuft of hair on his upper lip. "I'm sure the rest of the lads will be heading for Thena. We mercenaries are drawn to the fires of war like moths to a flame. Makes sense for me to head there too."

"We're not going to Thena."

Krinne's fingers stopped mid-stroke. "What? Where then?"

"I must consult the Oracle."

"Why?"

And as Dexios uttered the word, the tingling in his spine grew and grew until it reached his heart, and for the first time since the death of his son, he felt a slight flickering of hope.

"Panacea."

19

CONFORMITY

"There is no greater demonstration of love than to sacrifice oneself for others. When the Ruined sought to enslave mankind, Hera was the first to have the temerity to resist. When the Ruined tried to tear down the great palace of Olympus, it was Hera's courage that pushed them back. And when, finally, the Ruined were vanquished, it was by Hera's mercy that their lives were spared."

THE TEACHINGS OF HERA, VERSE 5.4

LENA MARCHED PURPOSEFULLY through the bustling stalls of the agora in the direction of the temple of Hera. She had told no one of her conversation with the basileus, not even Makar. She glanced down at her left hand, where a silver signet ring adorned her index finger. A gift from Letho and not just a pretty bauble. It would allow her unrestricted access to the palace at all times. Derka had nearly fallen off his stool when he had seen her wearing it.

She passed a wine merchant and stopped for a moment to gaze at the rows of amphorae. How long had it been since her last cup? A day? Two days? Enough to start to make her feel nauseous and sweaty. It was as if a part of her was missing. A part of her *brain*.

And I haven't been sleeping well, she thought. *Although, that's probably not helped by the fact that every time I've gone to bed recently something terrible has happened.*

She reached the western edge of the agora and stared up at the austere facade of the temple of Hera, a massive monochromatic slab of marble that seemed to leach all sound and colour from its surroundings. Twin statues of the goddess wielding a sword and spear protected the columned entranceway, their stern gaze scrutinising Elena like she was some sort of insect. A priestess stood at the top of the steps, the left side of her head shaved down to her scalp, the right a cascading stream of auburn locks.

"Yes?" she asked, raising a disparaging eyebrow. "What brings you to Hera's sanctuary?"

Elena was acutely aware of her dishevelled appearance. "I need to speak to one of the priestesses here," she said.

"I see."

"Um, on the orders of the basileus." She flashed the ring.

"I see. And you are?"

"Sophistes Elena."

"Well, Sophistes. The disciples of Hera are always ready to help our illustrious leader. Who is it that you seek?"

"Graycea. A priestess of a certain age, who—"

"I know who she is. And what she is. A disgrace to the temple. You'll find her in the kitchens, cleaning the chamber pots or doing some other menial task we normally leave to the slaves. It's all we dare entrust her with now after her repeated affronts to our beloved goddess. Why she is still allowed refuge here, I cannot comprehend. I'd throw her out onto the streets myself if it wasn't forbidden by our creed." She pursed her lips. "Turn right just before the main entrance to the temple and follow the corridor to the kitchens."

"Thank you," Elena replied, making the sign of Hera. "You have been most helpful."

"Hera protects," the woman agreed and turned her attention elsewhere, effectively signalling that their conversation was over. Elena slipped past the priestess, out of the sun's hot glare, and into the cool of the temple. She had expected the interior to be smothered in silence, but a metallic clanging from one of the corridors rendered any attempt at tranquillity quite impossible. As she followed the sounds, they became further enriched with a smattering of curse words that punctuated the louder bangs.

"Hera's saggy tits!" an elderly female voice exclaimed as Elena entered the slave quarters. The woman in question was sitting on the floor in the midst of a pile of chamber pots, her chiton hiked up around her thighs and a dirty cloth in one hand.

"Graycea?" Elena asked tentatively. Her nausea reared its ugly head once more as she got a whiff of the questionable odours emanating from the pots.

The woman threw down the cloth and glared at her. "Who wants to know?"

"Sophistes Elena. Here on the orders of the basileus."

"Hmmph. What's that idiot gone and done this time?"

Elena was beginning to like the grumpy old priestess. "Nothing, actually. He just thought you could help me with something. You are still a follower of Hera? Your hair, it's … "

Graycea tugged at a clump of her stringy, silvery-grey strands. "Hah! Grown back. I stopped shaving it off before you were born, child. Stupid tradition. Hera never chose to mutilate herself; I don't see why we should just to prove our loyalty. As I said, stupid tradition. One of many. What do you want?"

Elena glanced around at her surroundings. "Perhaps we could go somewhere more … agreeable?"

Graycea sniffed and picked up the cloth again. "'Fraid not, child. Chamber pots need to be cleaned, then it'll be time to start preparing the cauldron for today's meal. We can talk while I work."

"I hope you don't use the same cloth for both."

The old woman let out a jubilant cackle. "Haven't done so yet, child, but it's not a bad idea. It would certainly add a bit of flavour to the stew!"

Elena smiled despite herself. "Why do they treat you like a slave?"

"They are punishing me for some of my more … extremist opinions. And as it is forbidden by law to harm or ostracise a priestess of Hera, this is the next best thing. Jokes on them, though. This is infinitely preferable to giving out sermons and listening to rich buggers whine about their problems all day long."

Elena felt her stomach churn. She wasn't so sure. She took a deep breath, which only made it worse.

"What sort of opinions?"

Graycea cocked her head and looked Elena in the eye. "About the passage of time. About remembering our past, mistakes and all." She gestured all around her with the damp cloth. "This place wasn't always a shrine to Hera. It was initially built to venerate her husband. Then the war happened, and the victors scrambled to scrub any mention of the Ruined from the annals of history. Smashed the altars. Ripped up the mosaics. There used to be four enormous bronze statues mounted on the temple roof. Guess where they are now?"

"I don't know," Elena said, trying to avoid thinking about the smell.

Graycea tapped a dirty fingernail against a chamber pot, making it clink. "Melted them all down and used them for these. Who says Hera doesn't have a sense of humour?"

Elena found she wasn't particularly surprised to learn this. Her own mother had been a priestess in the temple of Artemis and had groomed her daughter to follow in her footsteps, providing her with the education she would need to fulfil such a prestigious position.

It was, as with many things her mother did, a road paved with good intentions. The priesthood, or hiereiai, was one of the only areas of Tyrrean society where women could hold a position of esteem and strive for something more than the traditional tasks of maintaining the household and raising children.

Unfortunately, the more the young Elena became embroiled with the inner workings of the hiereiai, the more she realised that under that golden sheen of benevolence lurked a rotten core of arrogance, narcissism, and hypocrisy. The age-old tradition of appointing priestesses through inheritance or from the upper echelons of the Tyrrean elite had slowly but steadily alienated the hiereiai from the middle and lower classes, leading to pronounced favouritism towards the rich and the influential.

Elena's years of disillusion had culminated in an explosive shouting match between her and her mother that had been so loud it had rattled the offering bowls placed on the temple altar. Now, over a decade later, she could not remember everything that had been said, only that anger had twisted and distorted her words into hooked barbs, which had torn a terrible rift between them. A rift that would never heal.

The next day she had left the temple. And left her mother.

A rumbling clang yanked her back to the present. Graycea had finished with the chamber pots and was dragging a huge cauldron across the floor.

"Decided to get another cloth," she said when she saw Elena looking at her. "Most of the hiereiai are pompous cretins, but some of them are all right. Besides, I eat out of the same pot as they do. Now, are you going to stand there daydreaming for the rest of the morning, or tell me why you've come here?"

"There's been a murder," Elena said, pushing her memories back into the far recesses of her mind. "Several, actually."

"Sorry to hear it."

"Ah, um, yes. One of the corpses had a very unique wound: four evenly-spaced circular marks in the centre of its chest, slightly wider than an arrow's shaft."

Graycea didn't reply straight away, her wrist flicking back and forth as she vigorously attacked a particularly resistant patch of congealed food.

"Again," she said eventually. "This has happened before. The basileus sent his hound sniffing round here, barking and growling like the obedient little dog he is. I told him what I thought the marks meant, and he laughed in my face."

"That was not very nice," Elena tutted.

"No. Tell me, child. As the garrison's sophistes, what subjects do you teach your budding ephebes?"

"History and geography mostly. Military strategy. Culture. I help those who cannot yet read or write properly. A little music — when I have to — and the rudiments of mathematics."

"Culture. You mean religion?"

"Not really. There's no need. All the ephebes are sons of Tyrrean citizens; that sort of thing has been drummed into their brains since they were born."

"A pity." Graycea put aside the cloth and washed her hands in a small basin of water. "And what place do the other races have in your teachings?"

"Other races? Oh, you mean the tauros? Or the martichoras? We study them quite intensely. Social structure, anatomy, combat tactics."

"So, how to murder them."

Elena began to feel uncomfortable. The woman's tone was becoming considerably more condescending.

"Not only that. We … I try and paint a more complete picture. The kosmetes and I discuss the contents of my tutoring in great detail."

"This is the problem, you see," Graycea said, springing to her feet with a spryness that belied her age. "The kosmetes has orders from the temple of Hera, and the temple has the perfect stranglehold over what is to be remembered, and what is to be forgotten. To disobey them is to" — she spread her arms — "end up like me."

"And what exactly should I be teaching, then?" Elena asked irritably.

"Mythology. Lore. Ancient history. Anything from before the Ruined were banished. What do you know of harpuia?"

"Harpies? They are ancient legends, supposedly servants of Ze— of the Ruined." Elena screwed up her face, trying to remember. "They were used as instruments of punishment … to bring pain and torture to the guilty. They abducted evil-doers and brought them to the gates of Tartarus."

"Aye," Graycea said in a small voice. "And just as the tauros are half-man, half-bull, so the harpies are half-woman, half-bird. Tall, raw-boned, winged … and taloned. Four thin claws that extend from each finger. As wide as an arrow's shaft."

Elena stared at the old priestess, trying to decide if she was joking. There was no humour in her rheumy eyes.

"So, that's what you told Crenate? That the marks were made by a servant of the Underworld? I mean … the man's certainly not very open-minded, but you must admit that it sounds a bit far-fetched."

"Why? Tauros were once creatures of myth and now they are so numerous it takes an alliance of poleis to stop them. Martichoras have been sighted several times in the lands across the Straits. We have proof that these beasts exist. Why should it be any different for the harpuia?"

Elena sighed. She was beginning to see why Graycea was cleaning chamber pots instead of performing libations.

"I didn't say it was impossible," she said. "Just unlikely. I am a sophistes. My entire profession is based upon separating fact from fiction. Everything we teach must be substanti-ated. Harpuia … I'm sorry but as far as I know, no one has ever even *seen* one."

Graycea smiled sadly and slipped her chiton off her left shoulder. Four circular scars ran parallel from clavicula to breast.

As wide as an arrow's shaft.

"I have," she said.

Elena's eyes widened in surprise. She leant forwards, forgetting herself, and traced one of the puckered wounds with the tip of her finger. "In … incredible. Did you show Crenate this?"

"After how he laughed at me? Of course not. Sent him scampering back to his master with his tail between his legs."

"When did this happen? How did you survive?"

Graycea rearranged her chiton. "It was a long time ago. When I was a young woman, younger than you are now. There was a tauran incursion in Lendes, and Thena was called upon to honour age-old alliances. A small phalanx was drafted — veterans mostly — and sent north. I was chosen to accompany them as a representative of the temple of Hera. A prestigious position, but not unreasonable considering I was a highly-respected member of the hiereiai at the time." Her mouth twitched. "Probably because I knew when to hold my tongue. In any case, the march north was uneventful, and we soon reached the spot where the tauran herd had last been seen; the burnt-out remains of a small farmstead.

"The strategos — the father of that Dexios fellow — decided that the main building was easily defendable, so the hoplites barricaded the doors and windows, and we shored up there for a few days while scouts were sent into the surrounding forest to try and pick up the tauros's trail.

"Only the richest soldiers had slaves with them, so the rest of us were forced to contribute to the daily running of the camp, even a lofty priestess of Hera like me. I found myself on water duty, the farmstead well having been polluted with copious amounts of tauran dung."

She was interrupted by a couple of adolescent female slaves, their shaved heads and near-identical grubby chitons making them look like twins. They began clearing away the chamber pots, mumbling apologies for the clangour.

"I went into the forest alone, without an escort," Graycea continued, abandoning the cauldron. "The scouts had surveyed the land closest to the farm and had assured me it was quite safe."

"Except it wasn't," Elena said.

"No. Either they had done their job poorly, or the tauros were far more intelligent at hiding their tracks than the hoplites thought possible. I expect it was the latter. One of the beasts found me as I was filling an amphora with water from a stream. The first and only time I have ever seen one of those creatures in the flesh." She shuddered at the memory. "You can read about them. Hear others talk about them … nothing can properly prepare you for their sheer size and stench. Taller than the tallest man I knew, covered in coarse grey hair and crimson paint. Then there is the smell … salty sweat and rotten flesh … I remember trying to run, pleading with my legs to move, but I ended up just standing there staring at him stupidly.

"The tauros bore no weapons — not that he needed any. His massive hands could have torn me in half with little effort. I felt him grasp my shoulder and pull me towards him. My cheek brushed against that disgusting, unkempt hair. I think … I think I had my eyes closed … I was praying to the Gods, screaming and ranting for them to come and save me. It was then that I felt something wet and sticky spatter all over my face, followed by an excruciating stab of pain just above my heart.

"The tauros gave a surprised bellow and dropped me. The tips of four bony talons had erupted from his chest, boring through the beast's flesh before entering my own. I watched through a haze of pain as the talons retracted with a sickening squelch, doing even more damage to the dying tauros. He slid to the ground, revealing my saviour."

A chamber pot clanged, nearly making Elena jump out of her skin. The slave responsible gave a wan smile.

"I … I couldn't see the figure clearly," Graycea said. "Tauran blood was dripping into my eyes, and the pain was making it hard to focus." She shook her head in frustration. "All I remember are two crimson-soaked claws and that fiery, piercing gaze as if I were looking into the depths of Tartarus itself. And maybe I was."

Elena stuck a fingernail in her mouth and chewed on the tip. That was it? A thirty-year-old testimonial by a disgraced priestess known for her … irrational convictions? She struggled to keep her disappointment from showing on her face. There was nothing of use here. Another dead end. After a week's investigation, she was no closer to finding out the identity of the killer.

It was time for her to leave.

"Thank you for telling me this," she said, removing her finger. "I can see that it is important to you."

"More than that," Graycea replied softly. "It changed my life. It made me realise that Hera was incapable of protecting us, that perhaps she was not so infallible as the temple would have us believe. Once the phalanx had eliminated the rest of the herd and we returned to Thena, I started pushing back against the hiereiai."

Elena was only half-listening, but something the priestess had said didn't quite add up. "I don't understand. Why did you lose faith in Hera? You told me you prayed to the Gods and were saved."

Graycea locked eyes with the sophistes. "And that is why I spoke of the harpuia. I prayed to the Gods, yes. But in my hysteria, I didn't pray to Hera."

Something akin to religious zeal glistened in the depths of her old, yellow-tinged gaze.

"I prayed to the Ruined … I prayed to Zeus."

20

CONVERSATIONS

"Money can buy many things. Power. Influence. Luxury. But all of these are meaningless when the shade leaves flesh behind and comes to stand before Persephone in the Halls of Judgement. There, only one's actions in life matter. The weight of one's conscience. Understand that only a single coin is needed to claim eternal happiness, and that is the obol used to pay the ferryman's toll."

THE TEACHINGS OF HERA, VERSE 7.9

"So, WHAT DOES this Oracle woman look like, then?" asked Krinne, grasping the reins of his grey palfrey with the white-knuckled grip of a man who would rather be anywhere else than stuck on a horse.

"That is one of her many mysteries," Nambe replied. His twin kopis blades poked up from his back like iron horns, and the scales of his armour reflected the light in a myriad of different ways as he shifted in the saddle. "No one really knows."

"How is that possible? She must see hundreds of applicants every year."

"Indeed. Thousands, probably."

Krinne tugged his steed sideways, narrowly avoiding the low-hanging branch of an olive tree that was encroaching onto the main road. His palfrey whinnied irritably. "Then, how?" the misthios insisted. "Are they all blindfolded?"

"Wouldn't work. She needs to see their eyes. No, it's even stranger than that. She appears differently to each and every supplicant. Sometimes it's a familiar visage: a loved one, a mother, wife, or daughter. Others see a warrior, a priestess, a crone …" Nambe chuckled at the look of scepticism on Krinne's face. "You don't believe me, do you?"

Krinne wrinkled his nose. "Doesn't matter what I think. Dexios is paying me to fight, not to have an opinion." He jerked his head further up the road where the strategos was sitting astride a muscular stallion the colour of burnished copper. He was slumped unhappily, his head bowed. Keres's aspis was tied to the horse's right flank, the diving hawk hidden by a leather cover.

"That's what always bothers me about you, misthios," Nambe said. "You *choose* to surrender your free will. You knowingly give up something that a slave dreams all his life of having."

"A rather crude way of looking at things. We have the choice of who we serve and for how long. Most of us won't take on a contract that involves killing women or children. We avoid rape, murder, torture …"

"You kill men for money. Is that not murder?"

Krinne shrugged. "A man who takes up his spear and shield is no longer just a man. He is also a soldier. I kill *soldiers*."

"For money."

"Hera's saggy tits! When you have an idea buzzing around in that big round head of yours you just can't let it go, can you? Sure, for money. And do you know what? Some people actually *like* not having to shoulder a thousand different responsibilities every single day. The only thing I need to decide is how to spend all the silver I'm earning. I find that simplicity … liberating."

"Fair enough," Nambe said, his tone implying that he was putting an end to the conversation. The two men rode on for a time in silence, sweating in the heat of the early afternoon sun, the clopping of their horses' hooves mingling with the humming of the cicadas. They had been journeying southeast towards Eldenstar Lake for a couple of days and had yet to come across another living soul. It was as if they were the last three men alive in all of Tyrris.

"And what about you, then?" Krinne said after a time. "Dexios isn't paying you anything. Quite the opposite in fact. You could be back in the arms of your wife instead of out here in the middle of nowhere. Why go with him to the Oracle? You seem to be a reasonable man, or at least reasonable enough to see that we have left logic far behind and are careening headlong into ludicrous delusion."

Nambe glanced ahead. Dexios was out of earshot, staring blankly at nothing in particular.

"Two reasons. The first is personal. A short tale from the past, if you would indulge me?"

Krinne shifted in the saddle. "Anything to take my mind off how this nefarious creature is bouncing my balls around like two ripe plums."

"You … have quite a colourful language, misthios. You're from Atlis, right? Do all of you speak like that?"

"Dunno. I doubt it. I'm the son of a mercenary, Nambe. Never received a formal education. Never was an ephebe. I picked up all I know from battlefields, tavernas, and whore-houses. Not gonna apologise for it. Tell me your story."

"Right. So, you may already know this, but Dexios pur-chased me from a man in Carenos during Thena's campaign against the men of the south. The strategos pushed inland, winning several decisive victories against the enemy that culminated in the signing of a peace treaty … a treaty rein-forced by the gift of several wagons of tribute."

"Ah … now you have my attention. What sort of tribute?"

"Gold, mostly. Silks. Spices. Enough to pay for the whole campaign and make Letho even richer than he already was. Although Dexios still needed to transport it all back to Thena. Having lost several hoplites to the heat of the desert, he decided to return to Carenos by a slightly different route: he would march north as far as the coast, then follow the cliffs westwards. A longer path, but one that avoided the sand dunes almost entirely.

"What he hadn't taken into account was just how treacherous those roads were. One of the wagons hit a rut and tipped over …"

"Ouch. Bad news for the driver."

"Yes … I was the one driving it. I was thrown from the wreckage and rolled off the edge of the cliff. By some small miracle, one of my flailing hands managed to find purchase on a jutting outcrop of rock. The strategos was the first to reach me, just as I was losing my grip. He lay down flat on his belly and caught my hand before I fell."

"He pulled you up?"

"He didn't have the strength. So, I just hung there, suspended from his arms, waiting for the other hoplites to arrive, while the contents of an entire wagon of tribute rained down all around us. I saw uncountable riches tumble off that cliff. A golden headdress worth five times the price he paid for me. A necklace of lapis lazuli that would buy a complete bronze panoply. Rolls of silk. A barrel of wine. He could have stopped any of them from falling into the ocean. All he needed to do was let go of my hand. I was a slave. I was expendable. Yet, he held on."

"Basileus can't have been happy."

"He was *livid*. But I think the other two wagons helped smooth things over."

"I'm sure. So, that's why you're following him now? To repay a debt?"

"One of the reasons."

Krinne took one hand off the reins, reached carefully into a pouch on his belt, and withdrew a toothpick. He stuck it in his mouth and began prodding at one of the gold molars.

"What's the second one?"

"Catharsis."

"You think being spurned by the Oracle will help him deal with his son's death? Gods, Nambe! How?"

"I will try to explain. Ever since I've known him, the strategos has insisted on being the one to return the shields of the slain to their families. And when I could, I went with him."

"He ordered you to?"

"No, never. I offered. No one deserves to carry such a burden alone. Gods … the number of men and women we tormented. The sorrow we caused. After a time, Theneans began to dread the sight of his crimson cloak and plumed helm … and to hate the man who wore them."

"It is a stupid tradition."

"No, it is a necessary one. It reminds the strategos that he is commanding living, breathing men and not clay figurines."

Krinne laughed.

"What's so funny?"

"My predecessor taught me the exact opposite. 'Never learn their names' he used to say to me. 'Never get too close.' Charon's balls, if I had to visit the families of each and every misthios who died under my command …"

"Perhaps. But look at it another way. The Thenean hoplites went into battle knowing that if they fell, Dexios would pay the ferryman's toll. That their shields would not be lost in the mud and blood of faraway lands. It must have been a comforting thought."

"And that's cathartic?"

"No. What I was trying to say is that I have seen how people react to death and that the first emotion is always the same: denial. A grieving father would refuse to accept the aspis, claiming it was not quite identical to the one once carried by his son. A distraught brother would demand to be shown the corpse of the deceased as proof of his passing.

"Grief is not a thing to be rushed. Nor is it a thing we can control. We suffer it. The misery. The regret. We cannot scrape it away with a strigil, or force it from our minds with a cup of watered wine. It must be left to run its course, like the flow of pus from a wound. What the strategos needs now is support and understanding, not incredulity and confrontation."

"That's a particularly roundabout way of saying you are going to wait and watch him fail," Krinne remarked.

"It's the only way. He will not listen to us. But he *will* listen to the Oracle. And she will put an end to this ridiculous farce. She will shatter his last, lingering thread of hope … and, just like he was for me, I will be there to catch him when he falls."

♋

The temple of the Oracle was situated on a small island in the middle of Eldenstar Lake, a vast expanse of cerulean blue too wide to see across. Dexios stood on the pebbled shore of the northern bank, his vision filled with the softly undulating water that stretched as far as the horizon. A sudden gust of wind tugged playfully at his cropped hair. He took a deep breath, slipped off his sandals, and let the cool liquid lap around his aching feet.

He splashed some water on his face, his fingers lingering long enough to feel the gauntness of his cheeks and the prickly hair of his beard. His bronze panoply was carefully packed away in the saddlebags, and the sky-blue chiton he now wore hung loosely from his frame. When had he last eaten? Before the battle? That can't be right; that was days ago. He prodded at his nose and winced. Nambe's timely intervention had reset the bone nicely, but there was still a great deal of swelling. He was so banged up he doubted even Keres would recognise—

Gods!

It was not the first time it had happened — that his brain had simply forgotten that his son was dead. It only lasted for a moment, but each new mistake sent a fresh spike of agony coursing through his body as reality set in once more. Like awakening from a dream.

A single tear escaped the corner of one eye, running down his cheek to mingle with the droplets of lake water. He had known loss before. He had known grief. But never like this. Never had he felt such pain.

His hands were trembling again. He stared at them until they stopped.

"Strategos?"

He turned to see Nambe looking at him anxiously. For an instant, he felt an irrational pang of envy at this man, always so calm and composed. Then it faded away as if it had never been there at all.

"He was my guiding light. Whenever I dreamt of the men I had sent to die ... whenever I felt lost, it was his face that drew me out of the darkness."

"I know."

"When I was on campaign, it was not the vineyard I missed or even Melia. It was *him*. I ... never told him that. That he was the one who brought me home."

"You didn't need to. Keres could see it in your eyes, I am sure."

Dexios looked out over the tranquil water. "When he is returned to me, it is the first thing I will say to him."

"If that is your wish."

"If that is my wish ... Nigh on twenty years I've known you, Nambe. I've heard that tone of voice enough times. You think me a fool. But madness and grief are not the same thing. What if your own son was taken from you? Would you not do anything — no matter how tenuous — to get him back? It is not madness that has set me on this path, it is love."

"Some say that love is but another facet of insanity. An emotion we cannot control."

"You didn't answer my question."

"If it were my own son? I … I cannot say. I would like to believe I would know when to let go."

"You are implying I do not. You are wrong. If the Oracle's words do not bring me comfort, then we return to Thena, and I will hang my son's shield next to mine. My two failures."

"You are sure?"

"I swear it. In Hera's name. This is my first and last folly."

"I will hold you to it."

Dexios smiled. "I know you will. That is why I am glad to have you with me." He lifted his palm to ward off the glare of the sun and scanned the horizon until he spotted a dark mound-like smudge. "The only way to reach the temple is by boat," he said, pointing. "We'll find one in Dimmani, about a quarter-mile away if I remember correctly. If we follow the western shore of the lake, it will lead us there."

"Oi, you lot! If you've quite finished jabbering," Krinne called from the top of the slope that led down to the bank. "My balls look like two overripe tomatoes! Can we continue this discussion in Dimmani? Preferably with some goat's cheese and a glass of watered wine?"

Nambe rolled his eyes. "We had best proceed, Strategos, before the misthios's … lower appendages suffer any more damage."

"Aye," Dexios replied, grudgingly leaving the cool waters of the lake. "Although Krinne will be disappointed. There's no alcohol allowed in Dimmani, on the orders of the Oracle herself. Those who come before her must be pure in body and mind."

"No daughters of Aphrodite either, then," said Krinne, overhearing.

"No … No drinking and no whoring. But we can probably find you some goat's cheese."

"You know what, Strategos? At this point, I'll take what I can get."

21

ORACLE

"What people fail to comprehend is that being forced to always tell the truth does not exclude the Oracle from prevarication. Her power resides in the fact that she can choose just how much of her vision she reveals to others. And sometimes, a partial truth can have far more disastrous consequences than an outright lie."

GRAYCEA, PRIESTESS OF HERA

I T WOULD BE generous to call Dimmani a village. There were only four white-washed stone buildings lined up along the edge of the lake, with a minuscule jetty tacked onto the furthermost one. Close to fifty tents were pitched around them, the muddy-brown and dark green colours of their awnings making them look like a scattering of fallen leaves.

"Don't tell me all these people are here to see the Oracle?" Krinne asked, his moustache twitching. "We'll be here for days!"

"And you'll be paid for each and every one of them," Dexios retorted sharply. "What does it matter to you how long we must wait here?"

"All right, all right, no need to get all crotchety. I was just making an observation."

"Well, keep it to yourself next time. We might not have

to go to the end of the queue. Being a strategos has certain … privileges." He pointed at the jetty. "That is where the only boat that leaves for the island is to be found. Old Charon, the ferryman, decides who may cross."

"Old Charon? Why is he called that?"

"You'll see."

They passed through the shanty town of tents. Most of the supplicants bore some sort of affliction: poxes, pustules, putrid wounds, or swollen glands. A man rolled by on a wheeled plank of wood, both legs severed at the knee. Everywhere Dexios looked he saw the consequences of war; limbs lost in the crush of the shield wall, stomach wounds caused by xiphe or spears, eyes torn from sockets by the tip of a javelin. The air was filled with the unpleasant stench of impending death.

He had redonned his panoply, and those who recognised the plumed helm of a strategos pushed towards him, arms raised as if he would somehow be the one to heal them. Weak hands pawed at the hem of his cloak as he passed.

"Why do these people come here?" asked Krinne. He had been uncharacteristically silent since they had entered the village. "These … half-men and women." He led his horse around a catatonic young girl lying on her back in the dirt, staring uncaringly up at the sky. "The shores of Tartarus call to them. It would be better for them to spend what time they have left making their peace with the Gods."

"They are convinced that the Oracle will lead them to a cure," Dexios replied. "And if the stories are to be believed, sometimes she does. Supplicants on the brink of death return from the temple instilled with a new sense of vigour. Fevers are lifted. Wounds are healed—"

"Limbs regrown."

"No, nothing like that," Dexios admitted. "But a single miracle is often enough to ignite hope in a thousand minds." Keres's lifeless face flashed before his eyes.

Hope, he thought. *Such a strange emotion. So tenacious and yet so fragile. We cannot rid ourselves of it, however hard we try, such is the strength of its grip around our hearts. But it can be shattered in an instant by a single word. Shattered and lost forever.*

Gritting his teeth, he pushed the image of his dead son away.

A few minutes later, they reached the jetty. Five hoplites clad in silver thorakes and bearing the star-adorned aspides of Eldenstar Lake blocked the way, their spears crossed. A dozen or so supplicants in various states of decay were huddled just out of weapon range, pleading to be let through. As Dexios watched, one of them came too close and received a spear-butt to the gut along with a barked order to stay back.

"Who in Tartarus are these pompous malakas?" he muttered, dismounting with a frown. "Silver thorakes. Ridiculous." He turned and handed the reins of his stallion to a waiting slave.

"Need any help, Strategos?" Nambe asked.

"Five idiots in armour that must be twice as heavy as they are and incapable of stopping anything sharper than a fingernail? I think I can handle it."

Dexios pushed his way through the crowd as politely as he could. He heard the whistling sound of a spear shaft and caught the length of ash wood in both hands. With a sharp tug, he pulled the surprised guard out of formation. The man tripped over his own shield and hit the mud hard.

"That was probably the worst defensive stance I have ever seen," Dexios said, holding out his hand to help the man up. "You didn't even anchor your feet. Who trained you?"

The guard had lost a greave in his tumble and was trying to reattach it, hindered by the fact that his thorakes prevented him from bending over properly. "I ... um ... Lendes garrison."

Dexios tapped his helmet. "Do you know what this means, lad?"

"Um. Strategos."

"EXACTLY!" Dexios bellowed, causing the guard to jump backwards a few feet. His fellows looked at each other warily.

"You *will* address me by my rank when you speak to me, soldier. You are a disgrace! All of you! Gods, the man behind you is holding his aspis in his right hand and his spear in his left! Anyone with a modicum of tactical sense could cut all five of you down before you even managed to form a shield wall. I will be reporting this to your kosmetes. Now, I have business with the Oracle. Please stand aside."

The guard ran his tongue over his lips. "Um. You will need to register with one of the administrators. Um ... Strategos."

Dexios felt the comforting presence of Nambe and Krinne at his back. "Look," he said, trying to keep his tone as light and friendly as possible. "My companions and I are in a hurry. We are going to step onto that jetty behind you, now. I suggest you allow us to do so."

The guard took in Nambe's massive armoured form and Krinne's composite bow. Duty and self-preservation waged war in his mind for a fraction of an instant, then he made the sign of Hera and moved aside.

Dexios, with a nod of thanks, brushed past him onto the boardwalk. A large flat-bottomed boat bobbed at its moorings at the far end. Before it waited two bald slaves and a tall, skeletal figure wrapped in multiple layers of mud-coloured robes.

"Old Charon, I presume?" Krinne asked.

"Yes. As you can see, the resemblance to his representation in the old scrolls is uncanny. It is said he has been taking supplicants to meet the Oracle for the last fifty years. Whatever his name once was, it has long been forgotten."

Old Charon bent his neck as they approached, the wet planks of the jetty creaking under their feet. Sunken eyes peered out at them from a face lined with a thousand wrinkles.

"The ferryman awakes," he rasped in a dry voice. "Cross my palm with silver, that thy fortune may be known."

Dexios felt his heart sink. Gods! How could he have been so stupid? The toll! They would never be allowed to traverse the lake without an offering. And every last obol he possessed now lay in the mouths of the slain.

"Nambe?" he asked hopefully. The southerner shook his head. Dexios turned to Krinne.

"Sorry, Strategos," the misthios said. "Remember what I told you?" He opened his mouth and tapped at his two gold teeth with a grimy nail.

Hope. Shattered in an instant.

"Then, we can go no further," Dexios said, each word of regret piercing his soul like a spear. "Hera is punishing me for my selfishness. We should never have abandoned Thena."

"Prithee," croaked Old Charon. "Thy servant named thee 'Strategos'. Be that your true calling?"

"Aye. Strategos Dexios."

"Of Thena? I was given instructions that if the one carrying such a title was to grace these shores, I was to hasten his passage over wind and water without charge."

Dexios felt that elusive hope return. Slowly. Warily. Like a frightened animal.

"Given instructions by whom?" he asked.

"Her magnificence. The Oracle. The Lady of the Lake."

Something inside him fought to be heard. *Why?* it questioned. *Why me? Why now?* The voice was quickly smothered by another, a triumphant roar.

Soon, you will see your son again.

"And the others?" he heard himself say.

Old Charon turned his wizened features to Krinne and Nambe. "The Lady spoke only of you, Strategos. If your servants cannot pay their way across the lake, then they must remain here and await your return."

"Go," Nambe said immediately. "Krinne and I will see what news we can gather here. There are supplicants from all the major poleis. Perhaps we can glean some insight into why Ruxia and Lendes betrayed us."

Dexios grasped the former slave's wrist. "Thank you, Nambe. In a few hours, all will be decided, and we will leave this place."

"Let the supplicant advance," intoned Old Charon. He drew his leather hood over his head and took up position at the stern of the ferry where a barge pole was thrust into the silt bed of the lake.

Dexios lowered himself carefully, his every movement

causing the boat to rock precariously. He was barely seated before two slaves untied the mooring ropes, and Old Charon sent the ferry out over the water with a strong push.

The noise of Dimmani faded away, replaced by the tranquillity of the lake and the soft rippling sound of the boat's prow cutting through the surface. The ferryman was silent, his long, bony arms rising and falling rhythmically as he used the pole to propel them effortlessly to the island temple.

It was close to twenty years since Dexios had last visited the Oracle, yet the temple had not changed in the slightest. A winding path led through a shadowy grove of orange trees to a single stone structure on a raised platform. The entrance was composed of eight marble columns that held up a triangular entablature decorated with a strangely asymmetrical frieze. The right-hand side depicted the three warrior goddesses — Hera, Athena, and Artemis — riding their chariots into battle. The left side was completely blank as if the enemies whom the goddesses were charging towards had been scrubbed away.

Dexios removed his helmet and passed under the entablature into the gloom within. The interior was close to fifty feet long. More columns lined the walls, interspaced with iron braziers. The smoke from their fires gave off the strong, musky smell of cinnamon. There were no other furnishings, no ornamentation, only metal and stone. At the far end, the Oracle waited patiently, her hands clasped in front of her. She was clad in a tight black chiton while a gossamer veil covered her face and hair.

"My Lady?"

His voice echoed uncomfortably across the sparse chamber.

The Oracle raised a hand in greeting. Dexios approached and knelt at her feet, remembering the last time he had made obeisance here; young and brash, wearing his burnished bronze breastplate and plumed helm, exuding a recklessness that only harsh years of conflict would eventually erode away.

A pale hand went to remove the veil. Dexios steeled himself, already knowing the face he would see. The only woman who had brought him so much joy, and so much pain.

He raised his head and looked up into the hard, cold eyes of Melia.

"Strategos," the Oracle said. The resemblance was uncanny. The angular cheekbones. Skin like porcelain. Even her voice perfectly imitated that of Dexios's estranged wife.

"Oracle."

"Time has not been kind."

"Time is kind to no one, Lady. Except to you, perhaps."

She stroked her own cheek. "A beautiful woman. She came to me before you were wed. Did she ever tell you that? No, I suppose she wouldn't have. She asked me what the marriage would bring her."

Dexios felt a chill of fear. "And your reply?"

"I told her that it would be the source of her greatest joy and her greatest pain."

"Oneiros." A whisper.

"Yes." The Oracle looked at him quizzically. "You think she blames you for his death?"

"I know she does."

"No. She had the knowledge I gave her. The prescience. She could have spared herself the grief. Spared both of you."

Dexios shook his head, recalling his wife's harsh words. "She ... she hates me."

"The only person Melia hates, Strategos, is herself."

Dexios blinked. The cloying odour of the spices and incense was making it difficult for him to think. He tried to remember the last time he had seen Melia happy. The last time he had seen her smile. How long had she been decaying from the inside out, slowly devoured by her own guilt?

"It ... it doesn't matter," he said. "It is ... too late. Too late for us. Too late for Oneiros. But it is not too late for Keres."

"The second son."

"Yes."

The Oracle tilted her head. "You wish to know the location of Panacea."

Dexios swallowed as the last word echoed off the stone columns. "I do."

"Even if it costs you your life? If Thena is burnt to the ground? If those you love and respect are butchered and left in the gutter to rot?"

A young Keres chasing butterflies through the blossoming vines. Shrieking with delight.

Saddling a horse for the first time, happiness and pride etched on his boyish features.

Keeping pace with Dexios as they ran across the estate together, pursuing the rising sun.

His bruised face smiling in triumph as he crossed the finish line at the ephebic trials.

"Yes," Dexios said.

"For all these things will happen if you decide to tread

this dark path, Strategos. It is a path that leads to suffering, misery, and pain."

He stared at her defiantly. "I … I have to try. It is the only thing keeping me from madness."

The Oracle sighed. "So be it. I cannot refuse your request despite every fibre of my being screaming at me to remain silent. The Gods did not gift me with the location of that which you seek, only the one who can help you return your son to you. Listen well. *To the east, between ivory bone, the last of the blasphemers hides in ruinous exile.*"

Dexios repeated the sentence several times. "To the east, between ivory bone …"

His heartbeat quickened. *I know where that is!*

"I have nothing more to give," the Oracle said. "Father. Strategos. Harbinger. When you are on your knees, awash in the blood of a dead God, and your heart is torn apart by grief, remember that I tried to dissuade you from this path. Go now, and know that your selfishness may well have doomed us all."

Dexios rose to his feet. "No pain can be greater than what I already feel," he replied simply, and bowing respectfully, he left her alone.

The Oracle waited a moment, then clapped her hands twice. A figure detached itself from the shadows. "My Lady?"

"Send a pigeon to Polydius," she said. "Tell him he was right; his story of Panacea was enough to lure Dexios here. I have fulfilled my side of the bargain. I have sent the strategos straight into the jaws of the trap."

She dropped the veil down over her face, and Melia's features disappeared into darkness.

"I have sent him to his death."

22

HOMECOMING

"Choosing a decoration for one's aspis is possibly just as important as the ephebic trials themselves. It is the symbol a soldier will carry for all his life, a part of who he is. The kosmetes encourages us to find something unique, something to distinguish us from the others in the phalanx. It is only much later that we understand why. When among the slain, we discover corpses that are so badly mutilated ... so horribly disfigured, they can only be identified by the markings on their shields."

CERBRIONES, 'ALALAGMOE'

RIDICULOUS! THOUGHT ELENA, hurrying away from the temple of Hera as fast as her feet could carry her. The priestess was obviously delusional, bordering on heretical. Being admitted into the basileus's inner circle was one thing, impiety was something else altogether. She cursed her curiosity for leading her here.

And uttering the name of one of the Ruined out loud! In the confines of the temple of Hera! It was practically suicide. There was no way that Graycea could escape divine retribution. The only question was how long she still had left to live. A pity really.

After a while, Elena began to wander aimlessly, allowing her feet to drag her where they wanted to go. Comforting muscle memory took over, leading her steadily away from the bright, open expanse of the agora and into the seedy back alleys. Her double-knotted belt and untidy blonde hair drew less attention here. Besides, she was a familiar face.

She stumbled to a halt before a large door. Faded crimson paint was peeling from the dry wood like bloody tears; a lingering memory of long-lost opulence. A sign hung over the entrance, attached to the wall with a length of rusting chain. A bunch of grapes under a foaming waterfall. *The Sodden Vine*. A taverna. Her second home.

She pushed open the door with a sigh. The barkeep looked up from the kylix he was polishing with a hopeful look that quickly transformed into a scowl.

"Oh, it's you."

"It's me."

"Been a while. Was starting to wonder if something had happened to you." There was no empathy. No compassion. Just the eventuality of losing a paying customer.

"Oh. No, just been busy, that's all."

The barkeep set the kylix down and picked up another. "A glass of watered red?" he asked, changing the subject. "Sun's still up, but the sky's darkening. I'm sure your usual crowd will be along shortly."

"That would be perfect, thank you. If you could add it to my tab?"

The frown returned, sending angry wrinkles worming up the man's ample forehead. "Elena, your tab is getting longer than that of all my other patrons put together. When are you going to settle your debts so I can retire?"

"It can't be that much."

"Buy myself a nice place out in the country. Never have to serve a kylix of wine again."

"Next week. I promise."

"Melt down the wax tablets. Become a candlemaker."

Elena rolled her eyes "Fine. *Fine.* Tomorrow."

The barkeep grunted and waved her away. Elena found a quiet spot in the corner, far from the door. There were only two other customers, and both were fixed on whatever drink they had ordered with needle-like focus.

The tavernas were one of Thena's greatest social divides. The richer Tyrreans had no need of them: their wine cellars were always fully stocked. They entertained each other with symposia: glorified drinking parties where men and women reclined on pillowed couches in the host's andron and discussed a wide range of frivolous subjects.

For the less fortunate, those who had neither the space nor the means to organise such lavish affairs, the tavernas were the only real alternative. A handful of obols to forget the worries of the world. An enticing proposition, especially at the bottom of the social ladder where worries were not in short supply.

The barkeep slammed a cup down onto the table with enough force to make the wine inside slosh around dangerously. "Savour it. There'll not be another until you pay me what I'm owed."

"Of course," Elena replied, smiling sweetly. She took the kylix in both hands and stared at the purple liquid within. When had her drinking turned into a daily occurrence? It had started as a means to escape the long weekends alone at the garrison. Then once or twice a week, to blow off steam after a particularly bad day. And later … slowly … what was once exceptional had become routine.

Elena remembered the nausea she had felt earlier. The trembling fingers. It was getting harder to control. She needed to stop. She took a deep breath, involuntarily letting the wine's fruity aroma flood her senses. Her mouth watered.

Just a few more days, she thought to herself. *When the ephebes return. When Galleas returns. Then I will put an end to it.*

She lifted the kylix to her lips.

"Sophistes?" The voice conjured up visions of reed pens and musty parchment.

Elena put the cup down carefully and turned, already dreading who she would see.

"Derka. Always a pleasure."

Letho's slave looked completely out of place in *The Sodden Vine*. His pallid skin had taken on a waxy sheen, and his long fingers jittered as if searching for their beloved abacus.

"If only I could say the same. The basileus demands your presence."

"Oh." Elena glanced at the signet ring. It suddenly seemed to weigh much heavier. "Um. Very well. How did you find me?"

Derka smiled thinly. "We are aware of all of your … regular haunts. It was simply a matter of checking each one."

"He said right away?"

The wine sat on the table, undrunk.

"Yes. Down by the main gate." Derka's smile vanished. "The phalanx has returned."

♋

The hoplites appeared on the horizon in scattered groups of twos and threes, faces caked in dust and dried blood. Elena joined Letho who was waiting for them in the shadow of the city's walls, surrounded by his honour guard and an anxious crowd of Theneans. The basileus was stoic and still. Only his fingers moved, twisting the jewelled rings on his hands as if the motion would somehow change what he was seeing.

Behind the vanguard came the wounded. The fortunate ones could still walk, bandages wrapped around their heads or chests. As they drew closer, Elena could discern some of the gruesome consequences of the tauros' terrible strength. An eye ripped from its socket. A shattered cheekbone. A broken nose. An ear torn clean off, leaving a ragged hole of cartilage and skin. Armour dented and scarred. Shields punctured by bovine horns, their painted heraldry defaced. Among the soldiers, she saw one or two of the ephebes she had spent the last year teaching, the remnants of their boyish innocence snatched away.

And to the rear, the supply wagons, their amphorae of wine and crates of food replaced by rows and rows of grievously injured hoplites. Mercifully, the carts were covered by an awning and curtains, but nothing could be done about the stench; that overpowering, slightly sweet smell of slowly-decaying flesh.

A man whom Elena didn't recognise was the first to reach the gates. He wore a full panoply of bronze, his helm topped with the tattered remains of a horsehair plume. A lochagos, then, one of the front-liners. The soldier sought out Letho in the crowd and made the sign of Hera. "Lord," he said tiredly. "We have failed." His aspis slipped from his tired grip and fell to the ground with a crash.

The metallic ringing acted as some sort of signal to the mass of bystanders. They surged forwards, streaming past the lochagos towards the returning phalanx. Women called out for their husbands and sons, harassing the tired survivors for any news of their whereabouts. Children ran up and down the line, screaming for their fathers. Soon, cries of elation and wails of grief intertwined as people discovered the fates of their loved ones.

The unsettling disharmony of sound was enough to bring tears to Elena's eyes. She had spent years teaching military strategy. Describing some of the great battles in Tyrrean history. Studying … from a distance. But *this* was the reality of war.

She thought back to the last time she had seen Galleas.

War does not only destroy. It can create. Poverty and famine. Sickness and disease.

Orphans and widows.

"What happened?" murmured Letho. He spoke softly as if he was talking to himself. The basileus seemed perplexed rather than upset. "We had the numbers. We had the choice of terrain. We knew when and where the tauros were going to arrive. How could we lose when the scales were tipped so heavily in our favour?"

Emotion crackled like wildfire before the gates of Thena. For every wife held tightly in her husband's embrace, another was left alone by the roadside. Children laughed. Children cried. The lochagos had not moved from his spot, staring at his fallen shield with dull, vacant eyes.

"Report," Letho said to him. "Report, soldier!" he

repeated when he received no reply. "Why was a pigeon not sent? Where is the strategos? Where is Galleas?"

"I … I don't know. We were betrayed, Lord. Ruxia … Polydius …. They are in league with those *animals*. We tried to stop them. By Hera, we tried." He lifted his left arm. It was covered in bruises. "They *pummelled* us. Again and again. I could hear the wood of my aspis cracking. The metal coating twisting." He gave a mirthless chuckle. "How could we have ever thought we were capable of stopping something so massive? So powerful?"

"GODS!" Letho shouted. "May Cerberus devour their rotten corpses for all eternity!"

The basileus was so angry that he was forgetting to maintain his benign charade, allowing parts of his real character to filter through.

"May their treacherous shades be tortured in the fires of Tartarus! May Persephone castrate them and feed their shrunken balls to the vultures! What Ruxia has done today is unimaginable. And unforgivable."

"Lord …" the lochagos began, but Letho didn't hear him.

"Never in our long history has a Tyrrean stooped to allying himself with the tauros. It was an unspoken agreement. A line not to be crossed. This heinous act will not go unpunished. When the other city-states hear of this, they will be chomping at the bit to eradicate every last Ruxian."

"Lord, they are coming here."

"I will … What?"

"The tauros. They are marching south. My scouts confirmed it. The beasts are moving slowly as they have calves with them. Nevertheless, they are nearly upon us. Tonight, or tomorrow at the latest."

"Malaka! You're only telling me this now?"

"We had no means of contacting you sooner. The coop was destroyed, and the Ruxians had set the horses loose."

"Then, you should have abandoned the wounded and marched day and night until you got here," Letho snarled.

A flicker of defiance returned to the lochagos's eyes. "Forgive me, Lord, but there was no way I was leaving those men to fend for themselves."

"Are you sure they will attack Thena?" Elena asked, hoping to steer the conversation in a different direction. "Tauros are nomadic so the city would be of no use to them."

"Not to them, no," Letho answered. "But Ruxia? That rat-faced Xenokrates has been looking to expand his territory for a while. I just never thought he'd have the balls to do it. Turns out, he doesn't. Which is why he's stooped to getting into bed with bulls and cows."

"What could he have possibly offered the tauros—"

"That's not important." The basileus tapped one of his honour guard on the shoulder. "Get everyone back inside. The wounded are to be sent straight to the infirmary, the able-bodied men to the garrison. Have the palace slaves serve them food and watered wine." He thought for a moment.

"DERKA!"

"Here, Lord." The pasty northerner appeared completely unfazed by the surrounding pandemonium.

"Bring Crenate here. And find a squad of men willing to ride to the vineyard to fetch my daughter. I'll pay them twenty drachmae each if they can return her to me before sunset."

"Yes, Lord."

"Just my daughter, Derka, do you understand? The slaves will have to fend for themselves."

Elena baulked at hearing this but kept her mouth firmly shut. Now was not the time to anger the basileus further. She thought of the half-dead assassin kept prisoner under the palace. The way his sightless eyes sought the light.

"Elena?" The basileus was looking at her impatiently.

"Lord?"

"Snap out of it. I need you focused. Your knowledge of military history will be useful. Come, we'll meet Crenate on the gatehouse roof; it's as good a place as any to survey our defences."

He stormed off, the crowd of onlookers parting to let him through. Elena was left alone with the lochagos.

"You didn't answer his question about Dexios?" she prompted. "About Galleas?"

He shook his head. "I … I don't know, Lady. The strategos was alive when the pipes sounded the retreat. Galleas … I cannot say. We wanted to return to the field of battle but the tauros were snapping at our heels. We couldn't go back. We … couldn't go back."

The broken man sank to his knees before the gates of Thena and began to weep.

Most of the buildings in Thena were covered in sloping tiles, but the defensive wall was much, much older, dating back to the very first days of the city. As such, the gatehouse roof was square and flat. A large sheet of red fabric attached to wooden poles driven into each corner offered some protection from the sun.

The basileus stood close to the edge that overlooked the plains. He was silent once more, fingers moving up and down his hands, turning the rings. The canopy above added a reddish hue to his features, making it appear as if he was covered in blood.

Elena watched him fidget and thought of Galleas. She missed the curmudgeonly old kosmetes more than she'd like to admit. Perhaps it was because, despite his constant grumbling, he was the only person in Thena she could truly call a friend. And because, behind all that niggling and nagging, she knew he cared about her.

She supposed that their strange relationship worked because each could offer the other something they were missing. Elena, who had never known her father and wanted nothing to do with her controlling mother, found in Galleas a surrogate parental figure to latch onto. The kosmetes, on the other hand, gained the talkative, headstrong daughter he never knew he wanted.

He's still alive, she thought. *He has to be.*

Crenate arrived, panting. His palms banged against his decorated linothorax as he made the sign of Hera.

He even sounds like a dog.

"What's this nonsense about a tauran attack?" he barked. "And where in Tartarus is my son?"

Letho gave a tut of displeasure. "Compose yourself, Captain. You will speak to me with respect, or I will have another take your place."

Crenate's eyelid twitched as he tried to master his emotions.

"Apologies … Lord. Has my son been found?"

"Not as yet, no. Derka is overseeing a full head count. We will soon have a much clearer picture as to who survived—"

"—and who died."

"Precisely."

Crenate took a pale green leaf from a pouch on his belt and popped it into his mouth. He began to chew noisily.

"Always knew that Polydius was a bastard," he growled. "We should have slit his throat and sent him back to Ruxia in a box. It'll take more than a few cows to stop my son. He's out there. Somewhere."

"I didn't summon you to hear your complaints, Captain. With Dexios and Galleas both missing, command of the walls falls to you. I would hear how you propose to defend Thena."

Crenate masticated thoughtfully.

"The walls are strong. Limestone from the eastern quarries. Fifteen feet high and two feet thick. The cows are too big and stupid to attempt to climb them."

"Sophistes, what can military history teach us about tauran siege tactics?"

It took Elena a moment to realise that the basileus was talking to her. "Oh, um, nothing, Lord. There are no records of tauros attacking a walled city. Then again, as I said when Polydius first arrived, this is the first time a horde this size has ventured south of the Dorias Mountains. We cannot reliably predict how they will react."

Crenate hawked and spat a wad of something green and sticky. "Look, Sophistes. With all due respect, they're animals. Beasts. They're about as smart as the horse you ride or the ox that ploughs your field. They can barely hold a club, let alone build a ladder. As long as the walls hold, we'll be safe."

"We still need men," Letho reminded him. "And, more importantly, weapons. Most of which were lost in the north with the phalanx."

"Spears and shields. Neither will be useful here. Javelins are what will work best. Javelins and slings."

The basileus smiled grimly. "You shall have both. Along with every hoplite able to hold a blade. And when the tauros come to take our city, they will be met with a storm of iron and stone. They will be met with vengeance. They will be met with death."

♋

Elena lingered on the gatehouse roof long after the two men had left. She felt slightly at a loss as to what to do next. It seemed that the basileus had given orders to everyone except her. The signet ring on her finger glinted mischievously. Did Letho truly want her to be part of his inner council, or was it just some flight of fancy … a bribe to make her forget about the strange murders and the basileus's indiscretions?

Her hairnet was beginning to itch. She loosened one of the cords and allowed her blonde curls to spring free, fully aware that she now looked like she had been hung upside-down in a hurricane for a few hours. The second knot in her belt had come undone and she retied it irritably, yanking the two pieces of fabric together in frustration.

She peered at the sundial down in the courtyard below. The gnomon's shadow was approaching the final line, indicating that the day was drawing to a close and Thena's gates would soon be shut.

And so, another lonely evening begins, thought Elena. Unless she returned to *The Sodden Vine*, of course. The barkeep had probably kept that kylix of wine for her. It would be a pity to let it go to waste. Her mind made up, she gazed out one last time over the plains. A fast-approaching cloud of dust caught her eye.

Riders.

Elena descended the rickety wooden ladder as fast as she dared. She arrived at the bottom in time to see six exhausted horses pound through the gates with a clattering of hooves. The men whom Letho had sent to fetch his daughter had been successful. Melia dismounted gracefully and strode over to where Elena was standing. Dexios's wife was wearing a dark blue himation, her black hair pulled back tightly into a rigid bun that further accentuated her angular features.

Not even a speck of dirt on her cloak or a single hair out of place, Elena thought enviously, wishing she had not removed her hairnet.

"Sophistes," Melia said with a smile that came and went faster than a flash of lightning. "I take it my father sent you here to greet me?"

"Um … yes?"

"Typical. Always too busy to come himself. My husband has still not returned either?"

"No, Lady."

"Hmmm. That's unlike him. I hope he hasn't gone and got himself captured or anything stupid like that. Father didn't speak to him for a month last time that happened.

Said if it ever happened again, he'd seize the vineyard to pay the ransom money."

Elena tried to think of a suitable response. Melia obviously had no idea just how dire the situation was. For exactly how long had Dexios been honey-coating the darker side of his profession?

"I did not see Keres among the wounded either, Lady. The survivors have taken up temporary residence at the garrison. Someone there may know where he is."

Melia brushed the words aside with a wave of her hand. "He must be with his father. Dexios promised to keep him safe. They'd better get back here fast. This exasperating distraction is delaying the grape harvest far beyond what I deem to be acceptable. The slaves will have to—"

"Did ... did you just call the tauran incursion an ... *exasperating distraction*?"

"Yes. My father's perpetual squabbles with our neighbours seem to be getting longer and longer every season. The—"

"There was a *battle*. People *died*."

"I do wish you would stop interrupting me. People die every day, Sophistes."

"You ... you really have no idea, have you? That while you are flitting from symposium to symposium playing queen bee, your husband and a host of good men are fighting to protect Thena?"

"I don't see how that's relevant to—"

"That while you sip your watered wine and giggle over the latest gossip, Dexios is pouring out a libation for the dead and preparing their shades for Charon's embrace?"

"Enough, Sophistes!" Melia snapped. "My private life and personal opinions are no concern of yours."

Elena stared at the other woman defiantly. At that exact moment, something slipped, and for a fraction of a second, she glimpsed the real Melia, the one hiding behind that cold exterior: a tired, scared, guilt-ridden wife and mother.

She knows, Elena thought. *Of course, she knows.*

Then the setting sun dropped behind the roof of the gatehouse, and the vision disappeared with the last rays of light.

"I will not be residing in the palace," Melia said as if nothing had happened. "I can't abide Father when he's in one of his moods. One of my cousins will be happy to receive me, I'm sure."

She turned on her heel with a swish of her himation and walked back to her horse. There, she paused for a moment, fiddling with a large object attached to the beast's saddle-bags. It was an aspis, sheathed in old, cracked leather. Melia held the shield awkwardly with both hands.

"I have one more request. Would you please make sure this gets to the palace? It is … important to me. I would like to see it kept safe."

Elena nodded. "It's your husband's, isn't it?"

"It is. My greatest hope is that one day he'll have the courage to display our heraldry once more and that things will go back to how they were before …" Melia trailed off, embarrassed. "I'm … I'm sorry, I don't know why I told you that. Give my regards to my father."

May Hera give you strength, Elena thought, watching as Melia rode away.

Behind her, the gates of Thena slammed shut with a metallic shriek.

23

ADULATION

"Madness and irrationality are not the same thing. On the contrary, a person suffering from depression or dementia may be more epistemically rational, as they will adopt a completely delusional hypothesis in an attempt to explain the unexplainable."

BASILEUS LETHO, 'RUMINATIONS'

EXIOS FOUND NAMBE and Krinne playing a game of tavli, surrounded by a circle of eager-eyed onlookers.

"Ma—Strategos," Nambe said in surprise, dropping his dice, which rebounded off the edge of the board and rolled away under the foot of one of the bystanders. "We did not think to see you back here so soon."

"So, this is what you meant by 'search for supplies'," Dexios said cheerfully. He felt more alive than he had in the last ten years as if the Oracle's words had physically restored his youth. "I can see why you were in such a hurry to see me off."

"It's not that at all," replied Nambe hurriedly. Dexios was amused to see the usually calm slave becoming rather flustered. "We toured the camp as I suggested. Spoke to a few supplicants. Unfortunately, we learnt nothing of note:

only that the tauros are heading south towards Thena much as we had already surmised."

There was an appreciative roar as Krinne threw two sixes. The misthios grinned.

"And then you decided to settle down here and partake in some gambling, one of the things specifically forbidden by the Oracle."

"Not gambling if we don't bet any money," Krinne corrected, one hand moving his checker up the board. "We're playing for the pure joy of the game."

"Your joy, you mean," grumbled Nambe in disgust. "That's the third time you've beaten me in a row!"

"A soldier's experience," said Krinne loftily, bowing to his audience.

"Or loaded dice," retorted the southerner under his breath.

"Well, there won't be a fourth," Dexios said. "I have promising news." He told them both of his meeting with the Oracle, forcing himself to keep calm as he related her prophecy.

"Panacea … exists?" Nambe asked with a doubtful frown.

"Not only does it exist, but she told me where to find the one who can lead us to it," Dexios replied, barely able to contain his excitement. "To the east, between ivory bone. So simple even a child could figure it out."

"The Horns of Celiston lie to the east," Nambe concurred. "I would imagine we will find our answers there. But, Strategos …"

"You are going to ask me if I am sure I wish to continue, aren't you?" Dexios asked. "How can I not? You know as well as I do that the Oracle never lies. She is compelled to tell the truth. There is no question that I will find what I seek."

"And what of the rest? You have omitted the other half of the prophecy. The part involving suffering, misery, and death?"

"An overreliance on melodrama, as is her way. Nambe, I am fully committed. There is nothing you can do or say to sway me from this course."

Nambe gave a resigned sigh. "Then, I will stay by your side and see it through."

Dexios clapped him on the shoulder. "I knew you would. Keres will be pleased to see you standing next to me when he is returned to us. Krinne! Up for a little more adventuring? I'll make it worth your while!"

The misthios stroked his moustache pensively. "How much riding does it involve?"

"A day or two."

"Gods … same pay?"

"Once my son is returned to me, I'll double it."

Krinne's eyes lit up. "You don't say? That'll be enough for another gold tooth. I'm in."

"Excellent. Nambe! Fetch the horses. The sooner we find our guide, the sooner I will see my son's smile again."

Hold on just a little longer, Keres, he thought. *I'm coming.*

The aptly-named Horns of Celiston were two rugged off-shoots of the Dorias Mountains that curved away then back towards each other like a scorpion's pincers. They encircled a bowl-shaped valley, protecting it from the worst of the sun and nourishing its soil from glacial streams that trickled down from distant snow-capped peaks.

As a result, the valley was lush and verdant, even during the hot Tyrrean summer. It did not take long for the city-state of Lendes to exploit this microclimate by filling every available space with one of the most sought-after raw materials: ash wood.

Ash wood, or hardwood as it was also known, was tough and resilient, but also paradoxically light and supple. It could be used decoratively, but its real value was in weapons and, more specifically, the most important item a Tyrrean would own. The symbol of his passage from ephebe into adulthood and citizenship. The spear.

It took the companions another day of hard riding to reach the entrance to the valley. Dexios breathed an audible sigh of relief as he and his escort passed into the welcome shade of the ash trees. Looking up, he saw that the dense foliage hid the sun completely. It was strangely fitting that the feather-like leaves bore such a close resemblance to the tip of a hoplite spear as if the Gods were in some way sending a message.

The lumber camp was only a mile or so further into the forest. It was run by a jovial old Tyrrean with a peg leg and a long scar that, in his own words, ran from 'arse to armpit'.

"Tree fell on me when I was a young'un," he told the travellers with a grin that was missing more than a few teeth. "Before I were smart enough to respect 'em."

"I am sorry to hear that," said Dexios, gazing round at the stacked piles of timber, some over eight feet high.

"Ah, don't be. I cut that little bugger into a thousand pieces. Sold 'im off as firewood. Apart from one little chunk

I kept for meself." He rapped on his leg. "What brings ya to the Horns of Celiston? The only fellas we see round 'ere are merchants or bandits, and we don't much care for either."

Shadowy forms skittered between the rows of timber. Dexios saw that Krinne had unslung his bow and was casually stroking the fletching of one of the many arrows poking out of the quiver attached to his saddle. His own stallion whinnied. He could feel the nervous rippling of its muscles beneath his thighs.

"Then, you are in luck, friend," he said as amiably as he could muster. "For we are soldiers, sent by the Oracle on a mission of utmost importance. Strategos Dexios of Thena, at your service."

"Strategos, eh?" the other man said. "Where's yer panoply?"

"Safe in my saddlebags. The sun takes great pleasure in torturing fully-armoured men during the summer."

"Wouldn't know anything about that," the woodsman sniffed. "'Aven't stood in a phalanx since I was an ephebe. Losing a leg makes the whole *standing* part far too complicated. Let's say I believe ya, for now. What did Hera's mouthpiece say to ya?"

"That someone here could lead us to what we seek. An ancient artefact called Panacea."

"Never 'eard of it. And I doubt any of my men 'ave either. We're simple folk, Strategos. Most of us come from the surrounding villages, and I know for sure none of us 'ave ever been any further than Lendes. Maybe the Oracle was mistaken."

"Impossible," said Dexios firmly. "She has never been wrong. Is there anyone else here besides you?"

The woodsman thought for a moment. "Only Piraeus, the old 'ermit. Weird fellow, that one. Not quite right in the 'ead, if ya get me." He tapped his finger to his temple emphatically. "Not sure 'e'll be any 'elp, I'm afraid. Poor bastard was already 'ere when I arrived forty-odd years ago, and I've never seen 'im leave that filthy old cave of 'is."

Dexios spared a glance over his shoulder at Nambe, who was waiting silently. The southerner nodded.

"We'll speak to him."

"Fine by me. It's not far; the dirt trail to the north will take ya there. Just don't expect too much."

"I never used to," Dexios replied with the ghost of a smile. "But I am starting to believe that optimism is just another word for hope."

And kicking his horse's flanks, he rode away without waiting for a reply, the stacked piles of ash trunks towering over him like unscalable cliffs.

"Apologies," murmured Nambe to the startled woodsman. "His impatience grows with every step we take closer to our goal."

The old man stared at the rapidly receding cloud of dust. "Seen a few like 'im in my time. Driven. Eyes always fixed on the 'orizon. People like that forget ya need to look down at your feet once in a while to check where yer going. 'Specially if yer walking along the edge of the abyss."

"Aye," agreed Nambe. "That's why I'm here … to catch him when he falls. Thank you for your time."

"Don't mention it. 'Been nice to see some folks that didn't want to rob us or swindle us. May Hera protect ya."

"And you."

"Trust me, lad. If that crotchety old bugger's 'aving one

of 'is bad days, you'll need 'er protection far more than I will."

♋

The area around the hermit's cave had been completely cleared of trees by the loggers, leaving behind a desolate wasteland of hard soil and hacked stumps. The omnipresent charcoal-grey clouds that hung over the twin prongs began to roll down into the valley as the day drew on, leaching the colour from the landscape and further adding to its unnatural atmosphere.

Dexios slowed his horse to a trot, carefully navigating around the broken trees and gnarled roots that pushed up through the scarred earth like the hands of the dead. The rampant deforestation had driven away any wildlife, and the place was eerily silent.

This is what the shores of Tartarus must be like, he thought. *A lifeless wilderness of mud and rot. This is where Keres must be now, surrounded by the moaning shades of his fellow soldiers. Waiting to cross the river. Waiting to be judged. My son. Alone and afraid. He will not have to wait for much longer.*

The cave was easy to spot, a gaping maw cut into the base of a trio of steep hills that lorded over the desecrated woodland. The advancing clouds were creeping over the three summits, shrouding them in a veil of mist.

Dexios reined in his horse a hundred feet or so from the cave entrance and slid from the saddle, tying the beast to a ragged tree stump and retrieving his panoply from the saddlebags. The pounding of hoofbeats, strangely loud and echoing, heralded the arrival of his two companions.

"We leave the horses here," he said to them, snapping his breastplate closed and fastening the pins. "No need to scare the poor man."

"Which is why you're putting on your armour," said Nambe wryly as he dismounted with a harmonious jingle of metal scales.

"I'm impatient, not stupid, Nambe. We have no idea what we'll find in there. Gods, the foreman could be sending us into a trap for all we know."

"He certainly seemed a bit off," Krinne agreed, stretching his legs with a satisfied sigh. "Did you see how his eyes kept darting left and right like he was searching for something? I've seen that look plenty of times before. Mostly just before someone tries to fleece me. Besides, doesn't smell right."

Nambe glanced at the misthios's large hooked nose. "It doesn't *smell* right?"

"Laugh if you want. But this nose has got me out of plenty of sticky situations. My mother always used to say that I may not have been gifted in looks, but the Gods had more than made up for it with my sense of smell."

The southerner took a dubitative sniff. "And what are you smelling right—"

"Enough!" Dexios cut in, adjusting his helmet. "It doesn't matter. I am not turning back. *We* are not turning back. Now, stop prattling and cover my flanks."

He moved closer to the cave mouth, hands held out, palms turned skywards.

"Piraeus?" he called. "My name is Strategos Dexios and I—"

A rock the size of an apple whistled past his ear, close enough to ruffle the horsehair of his helm.

"GO AWAY!"

"We have been sent—"

Dexios was ready for the rock this time. He ducked, letting the missile sail harmlessly over his head.

"Sent by the Oracle," he tried again.

Silence.

He braced for another stone barrage, but none came. A shadow moved. Darkness within darkness. "Which one?"

The voice was cautious yet curious.

"What do you mean 'which one'?" Dexios replied.

"The Key, the Serpent, or the Torch?"

"I don't …" Dexios trailed off, at a loss for words.

"Idiot boy. And you call yourself a strategos? I'd go back to the sophistes who trained you and ask for some sort of compensation if I were you. They've obviously botched your education."

Dexios heard Nambe unsuccessfully trying to disguise his chuckle with a cough.

"Now, hold on a minute—" he began hotly.

"No, I don't think I will." Piraeus emerged from the cave, blinking as his eyes adjusted to the light. He must have been tall once, taller even than Nambe, but age had not been kind to his old bones. His back was as curved as the crescent moon, his twisted spine making his head and neck jut forwards from his body like a disgruntled turtle. A long, scraggly beard dangled from his pointed chin almost as far as his knees. He shuffled towards them, using a cane of ash wood to keep his balance.

"What did the Oracle say?" the hermit asked. He was

close enough now for Dexios to see his eyes. They were the colour of blue ice, shrewd and penetrating, at complete odds with his aged, worn body.

"That you could lead us to Panacea."

"HAH!" Piraeus grinned, revealing dirty-yellow teeth. "You must have met the Serpent. She's the only one stupid enough to spout such idiocies."

Krinne muttered something, his hand running up and down his bowstring in an effort to calm himself.

"I hear you misthios," Piraeus said, pinning the archer with his keen gaze. "You think I'm mad. Well, I won't keep you. Give my regards to the Oracle."

He turned and began to hobble back the way he had come, leaning heavily on his cane. Dexios saw that the hermit was barefoot, his skin cut and bruised from the dirt and loose stones.

"Wait!"

He shot a dark look at Krinne and raced after Piraeus, catching up with him just as he reached the mouth of the cave. "Forgive my friend," he said, laying a restraining hand on the hermit's arm. "He spoke rashly. I need your help. Please."

Piraeus studied him thoughtfully. "Something has happened to you, Strategos. You have lost someone important, am I right?"

"I … yes. My son."

"Hmm. And what would you do to get him back?"

"Anything," Dexios answered without hesitation.

"Then, step into the cave."

Dexios tried to discern some hint of what the old man was thinking in the depths of those crystalline eyes, but all he could see was his own tired reflection like he was staring into his polished aspis. *Another trial,* he thought. *Another test.*

"Wait here," he said to his two companions before advancing into the cave.

The interior was … disappointingly empty. Pearly drops of rainwater glistened on slick, damp walls. Clumps of lichen clung to the wet surface like hairy spiders. At the far end was the cave's only perceptible feature: a single block of roughly-hewn stone, illuminated by a natural shaft of light.

Dexios moved towards it, his sandals squelching on patches of moss. The stone was marble, not granite as he had originally surmised. There were no marble quarries in Lendes. It must have been dragged here from somewhere else. His hand brushed the smooth surface. No, not quite smooth. There was something carved there. His fingers felt several worn indentations. He traced them slowly, letting his touch reveal the shape. A triangle. A zeta. Turned on its side.

A thunderbolt.

He heard the tell-tale tapping of Piraeus's cane behind him.

"You are no hermit," he said softly without turning round. "You are a priest."

"I am. Not *a* priest. *The* priest. The last remaining worshipper of Zeus. And this is his final temple."

Dexios whirled, whipping his xiphos from its scabbard. "Blasphemer," he said scathingly. "You cannot be the one of whom the Oracle spoke. She speaks for Hera. If she knew you were here …" He lunged at the old man, who made no move to avoid him. The tip of the iron sword slid through

Piraeus's long beard and pricked his throat, deep enough to draw blood.

"You dare utter the name of one of the Ruined. Worse, you … show him reverence? Give me one good reason why I should not kill you where you stand."

"Because he has spoken to me," Piraeus said calmly, ignoring the trickle of crimson staining his chiton. "The Oracle's prophecy was correct. Zeus has revealed to me the location of Panacea."

24

TRUCE

"Unfettered ambition is a dangerous thing. It becomes a thirst that can never be quenched. A hunger that can never be sated. It takes and feeds and devours and destroys until, in the end, there is nothing left."

CERBRIONES, 'ALALAGMOE'

THE TAUROS ARRIVED at dawn.

They set up camp about four hundred feet from the walls of Thena, well beyond javelin range. Elena watched from the relative safety of the gatehouse with a mixture of fear and wonder. She had spent years studying tauran history, biology, and sociology, but now, seeing the hulking beasts for the first time in the flesh, she realised how incomplete her knowledge was.

The yellowed, dog-eared, dusty scrolls that she had dug up from the garrison archives had been written *by* military men *for* military men. Battle reports. Herd sightings. A single autopsy from the physician focusing more on tauran weak spots than providing a comprehensive guide to their anatomy. They were statistics and numbers, with no mention of social structure or hierarchy.

The early morning light painted a different picture. Even at this distance, Elena could easily distinguish the heifers and calves. The female tauros, while still muscular, were smaller and slimmer than the males. They wore shirts or tunics of animal skin, and several even had jewellery of some sort that glimmered as it caught the sun. Calves of both sexes ran playfully through the camp, their guttural laughter carried to Elena's ears by the wind.

The abundance of markings and body paint among the male tauros were obviously tribal decorations. Each herd had its own unique colour, and from her position atop the walls, Elena could make out ten different hues grouped together in discrete areas of the camp. By far the most numerous were those bearing deep purple motifs, outnumbering some of the other tribes by two-to-one.

To the rear, conical tents rose from the earth like lumpy anthills. Many already had strands of grey smoke spiralling from flaps at the top, presumably from cooking fires. There were no defensive structures, not even a perimeter of stakes or a ditch. No sentries. They looked more like a group of settlers than a ferocious warband.

But Elena had been there when the hoplites had returned and had seen the despair in the eyes of a hundred soldiers. Heard the cries of the widows and children. No. Before her lay the enemy. There would be no mercy shown. And no mercy given.

She heard a soft squelching sound and didn't need to turn around to know that Crenate was standing behind her.

"No civilians on the wall," he growled. He had squeezed a leather helmet on over his prominent forehead, and the cheek flaps hanging down on either side of his face only enhanced his canine expression.

Elena flashed the silver signet ring in reply.

"Hera's tits, I don't know what the basileus was thinking,

giving you that," he said with a scowl. "He doesn't need any more advisors. Especially not a—"

"Woman?"

"I was going to say troublemaker."

"Yeah, sure you were. It's a big wall, Crenate. I'm confident that if we are careful, we can avoid running into one another."

A sudden wave of nausea hit her, and she gripped the stone parapet tightly to stop herself from falling. A not-so-subtle reminder from her body that she hadn't had a drink in days. She had come close last night, but after bringing Dexios's shield to the palace, she had hurried to *The Sodden Vine* only to find it closed.

I will not embarrass myself in front of this misogynist spawn of Tartarus again, she promised herself. She focused on her breathing. In and out. In and out.

"Are you all right, Sophistes?" Crenate asked, his tone of voice implying that he didn't care one way or the other. "Maybe you should go and have a lie-down. You look paler than my son's spotty backside."

A warm flush of anger sent the sickness scurrying back down into the depths of her belly. "I am fine, thank you, Captain. Just a bit tired. Now, if you'll excuse me, I feel I need to stretch my legs."

She forced herself to walk away slowly, feeling his eyes bore into her back. The ramparts stretched out before her, curving eastwards then southwards as they followed the city limits. Soldiers were stationed every three or four feet; a mix of polis guards, reservists, and the several hundred hoplites from the phalanx still in fighting condition.

The defenders had exchanged their spears and shields

for javelins: shorter, lighter weapons weighted at the front to give a heavier impact. The number of javelins each man had stacked in front of him depended on his proficiency: the skilled throwers had five or six in reserve whereas the more inexperienced had only a couple to be used at close range.

Elena moved down the line. A few of the soldiers made the sign of Hera or mumbled a brief greeting, but most ignored her, their tired, red-rimmed eyes staring at the tauran camp in the distance. Crenate had begun to man the wall the previous evening, brushing aside complaints from the phalanx's weary lochagos. The lack of sleep and trau-matic events of the last week were having a disastrous effect on troop morale.

But Crenate doesn't see that, Elena thought, smiling at an exhausted ephebe, one of Helydices's former lackeys. *He is used to commanding professional soldiers, not merchants and craftsmen. Not men who put on their armour for a couple of days every few months for obligatory training, then put it away and forget about it again.*

There was another problem. One that had run rampant around Elena's head last night as she lay on her back staring at the ceiling: whatever the outcome here before the city wall, Thena had already lost.

If Derka's calculations were correct — and having come to know the man, Elena had no doubt they were — then over two hundred hoplites had lost their lives due to Ruxia's deception, either killed on the field of battle or succumbing to their wounds on the return trip south. It was not only a grievous military defeat, but also a terrible blow to Thena's economy.

Fields would not be harvested. Quarries would not be

mined. Cattle would not be fed. Fresh meat and fish would rot and decay. The two hundred shades now wandering the shores of Tartarus were only the beginning. Soon, winter would come, and without enough wood to fuel the fires or enough grain to feed the Theneans, hundreds more would be lost from cold and hunger.

Elena sighed as the realisation hit her. *This* was why Letho had made her part of his inner council. He had a slew of military men that bombarded him with advice on strategy and tactics, but none of them would have anything useful to say once the assault was over. When they would have to deal with the consequences. The basileus didn't need her to crack the egg. He needed her to pick up the shattered pieces.

She reached the nearest tower. A priestess of Hera was preaching to the surrounding hoplites in a bored voice. It was Graycea, barely recognisable in a clean white chiton, her long silver hair bound and braided.

"Sophistes," she exclaimed, her apathetic eyes regaining their customary twinkle. "I didn't expect to see you here. Come to see the end of the world?"

"Don't be so dramatic. Thena will hold."

"That is for the Gods to decide."

"Really? Which Gods would that be?"

Graycea put a finger to her lips. "I told you that in confidence, child. Don't go and get me into even more trouble."

"Sorry … I'm tired, and I need a drink."

"Just like every other poor bastard stuck on this wall."

Elena smiled. "You included?"

Graycea gave a mock frown. "What makes you think I didn't volunteer?"

"Did you?"

"… No. A squad of town guard came to the temple in the middle of the night on the orders of the basileus. Apparently, his lordship had decided that having a priestess of Hera on the ramparts would be good for troop morale. Somewhat unsurprisingly, the hiereiai chose *me* for that honour. Unanimously, as it turns out."

Something in Graycea's contrite expression made Elena burst out laughing, causing the surrounding hoplites to turn and stare.

"Mistress?" one of them asked.

It was Makar. The lanky ephebe was kitted out in a battered bronze cuirass and an ancient-looking helm that was missing a cheek plate. He was gripping his javelin as if his life depended on it.

"Gods!" Elena exclaimed. "Makar? Does your father know you're here?"

"It was him who told me to come," he replied reproachfully. "I have my spear and shield now, Mistress, remember? I am part of the reservists. The one in ten who were chosen to stay behind to defend Thena."

"Even so …"

"I will finally have the chance to prove my worth. To prove myself to my father. I know what he thinks of me. His disappointment drips from him like foul sweat. He doesn't think me capable of hurting another living thing, let alone killing one. He believes me to be weak."

His hand twisted on the shaft of the javelin. "And the weak deserve to be left by the wayside. Left to die."

Elena recoiled from the bitterness in his voice. "Refraining from violence is not weakness," she countered. "Nor is being repulsed by the act. Aggression is the easy path.

The simple path. True bravery lies within those who take the harder road to victory. One that is paved with reason, discussion, and compromise."

Graycea nodded approvingly.

"I ... I wish my father shared that sentiment," Makar admitted. "But he does not. Do you see what I am wearing?" He banged his free hand against his cuirass. "This is his panoply. Bearing the marks of numerous battles. See the deep scratch below the ribs? He told me it was from the tauros that took his arm. This is what he was, Mistress. And so, this is what I too shall strive to be."

Another child yoked to the ambition of an adult, Elena thought. How many sons and daughters were forced along a path they did not want to walk by overbearing parents? Passion and opinion are not hereditary. Differences should be celebrated, not repressed. If Elena had submitted to her mother's control, she would be a priestess of Artemis by now. Makar had neither the physical qualities nor the mindset of a soldier. Desha should let it go.

She opened her mouth to say something when a movement over Makar's shoulder made her pause. Another great cloud of dust was on the horizon, drawing steadily closer. Bigger even than Melia and her escort. More riders.

"Friend or foe?" Graycea asked, following her gaze. "These old eyes aren't what they used to be."

"I'm not sure. Makar?"

His brow wrinkled as he concentrated. "Definitely cavalry."

"Any heraldry? Banners?"

"I don't ... it may be a trick of the light, but it looks like purple."

"Ruxia," said Elena ominously.

♋

In the time it took the Ruxians to reach the city walls, Letho had been summoned. He stood next to Crenate, surrounded by his honour guard, their gleaming panoplies shining like beacons atop the gatehouse.

"Ah, my newest advisor," he said laconically as Elena arrived, out of breath.

"L … Lord," she puffed.

"Not the best time for a morning stroll, Sophistes."

How can he be so calm? Elena wondered, searching his face for any sign of stress and finding none. Then she remembered how he had changed that day in the palace gardens. *His emotions are a weapon,* she thought. *To be drawn when needed then sheathed and forgotten. Gods! How I have underestimated him.*

"Apologies, Lord."

The riders drew up in perfect formation before the city gates. One nudged his horse forwards and removed his helm. It was Polydius.

"Truce!" the strategos called. "In Hera's name!"

"He is within javelin range, Lord," Crenate growled.

"He … has invoked the sacred truce," Elena said. "Killing him now would be a direct affront to Hera."

"Enough nattering," Letho ordered. He slid one of his rings up and down a plump finger. "I think I will talk to this traitor," he said finally. "He has awakened my … curiosity."

He edged closer to the parapet.

"You speak of Hera, yet you align yourself with these

godless creatures." He pitched his voice well, and it echoed off the high walls, heard by all.

Polydius smiled. "It is good to see you, Basileus. And Thena, too. There is nothing quite like coming home." His horse stamped its hooves, and he laid a calming hand on its neck. "You are wrong, you know. The tauros have their Gods. And their priests. They are just not the same Gods as ours. They are more like us than you think."

"Like *you*, perhaps. Like Ruxia. What could have possibly driven you to such an act of stupidity? You have not just betrayed *us*, you have betrayed all of Tyrris. And for what? More land? More wealth? It doesn't matter what happens here. Even if you win, you will have to contend with the other poleis. They will never let this go."

"Perhaps. Although silver can be a convincing argument. The mines of the Dorias Mountains run deep."

"Deep enough to buy a horde of tauros."

Polydius's mouth twitched. "That is not what we promised them. The Lendians, on the other hand, were in great need of funds to rebuild their outposts. It seems there are more and more tauran incursions into Tyrrean territory."

Letho was silent.

"I … the bleeding of the phalanx was regrettable," Polydius continued. "That was not part of the plan. I thought that they would break as soon as we abandoned them. They … resisted. Like a tenacious barnacle that refuses to let go of its rock. So many killed, and still they held. K'vath was impressed."

"K'vath?"

"I suppose he is their leader. He speaks for them, in any

case. The alpha of the largest herd. He did not expect to lose so many of his kin."

Letho sighed. "How did it come to this, Polydius? Your mother gave birth to you not five hundred yards behind where I am standing now. I was the one to give you your spear and shield. You … you fought for Thena. Bled for Thena. You sat in my andron. Drank my wine … We may not have been the closest of friends, but there was mutual respect at least. How could you betray all that? How could you betray the place where you were born?"

Polydius shook his head sadly. "I could try to explain, but you wouldn't understand."

"Then, I pity you, Strategos," Letho said. "I can only begin to imagine the torture Persephone will inflict upon your shade when it is dragged screaming into the depths of Tartarus."

"If that is my fate, then so be it. That being said, I am hoping to delay my journey there as long as possible. And I will not be alone. We have all sinned, Letho. Even your beloved strategos."

"Where is he?"

"K'vath spared his life. I thought he might. The tauros have a terrible tendency to show leniency towards an enemy they respect. I had several contingencies in place. A number of juicy pieces of bait. His choice was … surprising, but the end result is the same. Dexios is dead."

The basileus's eyelid flickered. His finger tightened around the ring he was playing with. Squeezing. Crushing.

"I am not getting any younger," he said to Polydius. "Let us dispense with the pleasantries. Say your piece, and go play farmer with your cows."

"Gladly. I have been charged to tell you that Ruxia desires your land, not your lives. Any who wishes to leave Thena may do so now and will not be harmed. I swear it, in the name of Hera."

"You would have us leave? There are families here whose ancestors helped build this city. Gods, *my* ancestor helped build this city. And where would we go? None of the other poleis is big enough to take us all in. You would condemn us to a life on the road, begging and scraping our way through Tyrris? Forever without a home? That, to me, is a fate worse than death."

Polydius shrugged. "I expected as much. I had to try. For old times' sake. I will tell K'vath to prepare. The next time we meet, Lord, I intend to kill you."

"Oh, one last thing." He untied a plain canvas sack from his saddle and held it up for all on the wall to see. "Remember when I told you I had several contingencies? This one didn't work out."

He let the bag fall to the ground. It hit the parched, dry soil hard enough to dislodge its contents.

Elena let out a shriek of horror as the soft dawn light illuminated the severed head of Kosmetes Galleas.

25

CONFRONTATION

"To write the names of the Ruined is blasphemy. To speak the names of the Ruined is blasphemy. To encourage heretical acts in any way, or to refuse to denounce those who commit them ... is blasphemy. In all cases, the punishment is the same: lapidation by those who remained faithful. And may your shades find redemption in Charon's embrace."

THE TEACHINGS OF HERA, VERSE 10.4

"LIES," DEXIOS SPAT, his voice rippling with anger. "The God you worship is a deceiver. Tyrris was almost torn apart by his arrogance and hubris. If not for Hera, we would all have perished."

"Is that so?" Piraeus asked, wincing as the xiphos scraped against his neck. "Is this what the hiereiai teach?"

"It is common knowledge," Dexios said contemptuously. "Everyone knows the story of the Ruined."

"Then, enlighten me." Piraeus raised his left hand slowly and pushed the blade away. "If you believe in the Oracle, then you must believe she sent you here for a reason."

"Pah! More games!"

"Perhaps. But a game worth playing. Now, either kill me or talk to me. I'm getting tired." He grimaced and arched his back. Dexios heard something crack. The hermit limped over to one of the larger rocks scattered over the cave floor and used his cane to help him sit.

Dexios took a deep breath. What was he doing? He had never drawn his sword on an innocent before. His grief was making him irrational. Gods! He used to pride himself on his self-control. Everything was unravelling. A drop of the hermit's blood still glistened at the tip of his sword. He stared at it guiltily. For an instant, he imagined Keres standing beside him, a disapproving look on his handsome face. Another deep breath. He wiped his weapon clean on a piece of moss and sheathed it.

"Very well," he said. "I will indulge you." He closed his eyes and dredged up the memory of his wife, Melia, telling the tale of the Ruined to their two sons. Back when there was still a spark of joy in her gaze. Before it was snuffed out by the glacial cold that now encased her heart.

"Zeu … the one known as the greatest of the Ruined was a lustful, arrogant, deceitful God. When the great Goddess Hera refused his advances, he disguised himself as a cuckoo and took her virginity, forcing her to marry him out of shame. Yet, marriage did not satiate his voracious appetite. He spread his seed far and wide with no thought of the consequences. Wars were fought over false accusations and broken promises. For centuries, Hera suffered her husband's many infidelities until, at last, moved by the pleas and prayers of Tyrris, she decided to act. She asked him to stop."

Dexios opened his eyes and glanced at Piraeus. The old hermit was listening intently, both hands resting on the top of his cane.

"The Ruined God flew into a great rage. He tried to strangle Hera on the spot, but she escaped, fleeing in panic into the depths of Olympus. Her husband followed, calling on his brothers and sons to lend him their strength. And so, a colossal battle was fought on the very slopes of Olympus itself. Brother fought against sister. Mother against son. Husband against wife. Their conflict wrought havoc on the lands below. Earthquakes. Tidal waves. Tornados. Fire and lightning. Thousands died.

"In the end, Hera triumphed. The Gods are incapable of killing their own kind. Instead, the Ruined were banished, exiled from Olympus, and cursed to roam the lands of Tyrris until they faded into obscurity. Belief is what gives the Gods power. Without it, they are nothing. Hera had the names of those she had defeated struck from the annals of history. Their temples were torn down and the stone used to build even greater places of worship. Statues, carvings, paintings, mosaics … all destroyed. They were to be forgotten. Ruined. And so, by Hera's grace, peace was restored to Tyrris."

There was the sound of clapping. "A good tale," Piraeus said. "And well told. All the best lies spring from a grain of truth." He rubbed at the mark on his neck. "My father spun me a different yarn. A story passed on to him from his own father. An oral tradition, dating back centuries."

He reached over to the wall of the cave, pulled off a strip of moss, held it over his mouth, and squeezed. Droplets of water dripped into his mouth.

"As I said, the greatest lies have a modicum of truth. Zeus was, in the words of my father, imperfect. He had his faults, as do we all. Some would argue that our flaws are an integral part of who we are. His satyriasis gnawed at him constantly, filling his mind with forbidden cravings. His adultery was the unfortunate consequence."

"A serious crime," said Dexios. "A direct violation of the sacred laws that bind a family together. In Thena, the punishment is public humiliation or death. Banishment would be seen as leniency."

"That is for the Gods to decide. Zeus is reviled not for his infidelity, but for the suffering he caused. And this is where the lies begin. For it was Hera, in her jealousy, who sowed the seeds of discontent. Hera who whispered fallacies in the ears of the fathers and husbands whom Zeus had wronged. Hera who pitched the men of Tyrris against one another in bloody conflict and mindless violence."

Piraeus locked his cerulean eyes with Dexios's and held them fast. "It was Hera who gathered Athena, Artemis, and Persephone to her side and cornered Zeus in his chambers. Who instigated the devastating civil war that tore the land apart. Who is responsible for the years of pain and suffering inflicted on the Tyrreans. Hera. Not Zeus."

"You … you should not speak his name. It is forbidden."

"Forbidden by her, and she cannot reach us here. This is *his* temple. One of the last. Hidden from her scrutiny."

Dexios was shaking his head in disbelief. "You are as gullible as your father. Placing your faith in a simple story."

"This coming from a man brought here by a nonsensical prophecy spoken by a charlatan."

"That's different. The Oracle speaks only the truth."

"Does she? How can you be so sure?"

Dexios felt his frustration bubbling to the surface. "It is common knowledge. Besides, I consulted her once before and thanks to her auspicious warning, I saved the lives of over half my command."

"A man consults the Oracle, and she tells him he is

going to die. The man is distraught by the news. It occupies his thoughts to the extent that he cannot concentrate. He trips over a stone in the road and falls into the path of a galloping horse, his skull crushed beneath its hooves."

"The prophecy came true."

Piraeus wagged a bony finger. "It did. But would the man have died if he had not consulted the Oracle? Veracity and common knowledge are not synonyms, Strategos. If everyone told you that the sun was blue, you would not believe it, for you can see with your own eyes that it is yellow."

"The story of the Ruined is carved into the walls of the temple of Hera," Dexios countered. "It is written on the scrolls and tablets of Tyrris's sophistes."

"It was carved, yes. Carved into the stone of the temple of Zeus. A final desecration before Hera took it for herself."

He is a competent orator, Dexios thought. *Neither pleading nor forceful. His voice calm and patient. He is extremely convincing. Just not convincing enough.*

"I … thank you, old man."

"You thank me?"

"Yes. One of my companions, Nambe, believed I was losing my mind, and for a time I was afraid he might be right. But it seems I still have some common sense, for even I can see that you have been left alone for too long. You have become wrapped up in your own self-delusion."

"You don't believe me?"

"I do not. You say you are a priest. That your God speaks to you. But you have no proof. I admit, you too tell a fine tale. But that is all it is. A whimsical falsehood, kept alive by a man who has nothing better to do than shout at the wind. You blaspheme and you plot … yet, I do not believe you pose a serious threat. And I do not kill innocent men. For that, and for my son, I will leave you alive. I will not even reveal your presence here. You may live out your days in peace, the last decrepit member of a dying cult. And when you are gone, the names of the Ruined will fade even further from memory."

Piraeus smiled as if expecting this. "And what of Keres?"

"I will find another way. Perhaps I misinterpreted the Oracle's words."

There was a rumble of distant thunder from outside the cave. A storm was approaching. It was time to leave.

"Then, may the Gods protect you on your journey, Strategos."

Something in the priest's voice filled Dexios with a sense of unease. He nodded curtly and strode hurriedly from the cave, nearly bumping into Nambe and Krinne who were hovering near the entrance, trying unsuccessfully not to look like they were eavesdropping.

"Well?" asked Krinne innocently.

"A dead end, as I'm sure you heard," said Dexios. There was another grumble from the clouds above. The descending mist was thick and heavy, completely engulfing the hilltops. "Back to the horses. We ride for the Lendian lumber camp. The foreman seemed hospitable enough; let us see if he will let us stay the night."

A flash of lightning lit up the broken tree trunks, casting strange shadows. They needed to get away before the rain hit and transformed the muddy terrain into a treacherous quagmire.

Dexios started back down the slope, his unease growing.

A nagging thought tugged at his mind. A glaring mistake. He stopped suddenly as it struck him.

"I never told him my son's name."

"Strategos?" Nambe queried.

"He asked me about Keres. I never said his name."

He wheeled round. Piraeus was silhouetted against the cave's entrance, his long beard buffeted by the rising wind. He was smiling.

"Bastard," Dexios snarled. "More lies. I was too kind to the old malaka."

"Strategos," Krinne warned.

"No, enough is enough—"

"Not the hermit." The misthios pointed towards the treeline. A man was standing on the very edge of the clearing, dressed in bronze plate and helm. A decorated aspis rested against one shoulder. Another flash of lightning revealed a stylised 'rho'. Ruxia.

Some sixth sense made Dexios dive to the ground. A hollow stone whined past his head as he hit the earth. "COVER!" he yelled.

More hoplites appeared from the shadows of the towering ash trees. Ten. Twelve. All were wearing a full panoply apart from two slingers clad in light, manoeuvrable linothoraxes. With a flick of his fingers, their leader gave the order to spread out, cutting off all avenues of escape.

Dexios crawled forwards, his greaves pinching his calves, his thorakes scraping against the mud and loose scree. He reached one of the wider stumps and put his back against it. Krinne was crouched behind a rock to his left, compound bow held tightly in one hand and an arrow in the other.

Nambe was still in the open, his massive body pressed flat against the dirt.

"Krinne," Dexios hissed. "Can you hear me?"

A missile slammed into the side of the trunk he was hiding behind, burying itself in the wood. A second shot kicked up clods of mud inches from Nambe's face.

"Krinne!"

The misthios nodded.

"Nambe won't last long out in the open. I'll draw their attention. Wait until the time is right." He paused. "And don't miss. There'll be no one left to pay you if I'm dead."

He removed his helmet. There was an enormous scratch along the left cheek plate and two gaping holes in the horse-hair. Nambe would not be pleased. He picked up one of the large branches that littered the ground. Balancing his helm precariously on one end, he poked it around the side of the stump.

There was a familiar whistling sound, and a stone punched through the right eye socket. Seconds later, the plume lost another great tuft of hair.

Now, Krinne! Dexios willed silently. He turned to see that the misthios was already rising from his hiding place, an arrow nocked and drawn, one eye closed as he took aim. The bowstring thrummed, and fifty feet away a slinger gave a startled cry as feathers seemed to sprout from his forehead. He keeled over backwards, his sling slipping from his grasp.

The surviving slinger recognised the danger and fled for the safety of the trees. Krinne's arrow caught him in the shoulder with enough force to spin him around. He opened his mouth to cry out but another shaft drilled into his neck, silencing him forever.

Nambe was on his feet, mud dripping from his shaved head. He had drawn his twin kopides. "Your orders, Strategos?"

"Close formation," Dexios said, yanking his xiphos from its scabbard. "They'll try to separate us. We can't let that happen or we'll be cut down. Krinne, do what you can."

"That's what you pay me for, Dexios. Bastards have helms and shields, though. Not many openings."

"Then, make some."

Something wet hit his shoulder guard with a plinking sound, then a dozen, then a score more. Big fat droplets of rain tumbled down from the heavens as the clouds finally decided to discharge their bounty.

The Ruxians moved in, tightening the net. Dexios smiled at his two companions and raised his sword high. "Hera, grant us your strength!"

The Ruxians charged.

Krinne had time to loose one last arrow. It slammed into an aspis and stuck there quivering. Then the enemy were upon them in a flurry of swords and spears.

Dexios batted away a probing spear tip, his counter-thrust screeching across his opponent's breastplate. A xiphos came hurtling towards him from the left. He twisted, taking the blow on the shoulder, and kicked out, feeling a satisfying crunch as his sandal connected with the other man's fragile wrist bone.

The spearman advanced, aspis held high. That was a mistake. The spear and shield were a devastating combination in the ranks of the phalanx, where each hoplite's weaker right-hand side was protected by his neighbour. Even three or four soldiers fighting together as a cohesive unit could hold off an opposing force several times their size. But the Ruxian officer had prioritised encircling his prey instead of consolidating his formation. It was the wrong decision.

Dexios suddenly darted to his left. His opponent, his peripheral vision restricted by his helm, reacted far too slowly. The strategos moved behind him and slashed low, aiming for the calf muscle. Another weak spot. The clip-on greaves offered excellent protection from the front but left the rest of the leg exposed. The xiphos bit deep into the soft flesh. Dexios's exultant cry mingled with the wounded man's scream. He drew his blade free in a spray of blood and used the moment of brief respite to see how the others were faring.

Nambe was facing off against a duo of Ruxian hoplites, his twin kopides flickering like flames as he parried and countered. He wore an expression of intense concentration, the rain cutting lines through the mud on his face.

Krinne, his thin moustache plastered to his upper lip, had dropped his bow and drawn a dagger. The five-inch length of iron looked laughably inadequate compared to the ash wood spear held by the Ruxian opposite him. There was no way Krinne could get close enough to be any sort of threat, and the spearman was slowly pushing him back.

He needs help, Dexios thought, readying his xiphos. Then someone barrelled into him from behind. He hit the ground hard, biting his tongue. Hot blood exploded into his mouth. He gagged and tried to turn, but a hand pressed down on the back of his head. Muddy slime found its way into his nostrils, suffocating him.

His mouth opened reflexively, and more of the foul stuff was pushed inside. He struggled and squirmed, but his opponent held him fast. His lungs began to burn. Panic overtook him, his heartbeat rattling around his brain, louder and louder, drowning out all else.

Hera give me strength.

With a roar of anger, Dexios flailed blindly with his arms and felt the pressure on his head relax slightly. He rolled in the mud, slithering onto his back, and found himself looking up into the hateful gaze of the Ruxian officer. A fist crashed into the side of his skull. His vision blurred.

"You're lucky Polydius wants you alive," the officer spat, rain dripping from his hair and beard. "Otherwise, we would have stabbed you all in the back as soon as you entered this awful place." He leant close. "He only said *alive*, mind you. I don't think he'll be *too* upset if you're missing a limb or two."

Dexios smiled amiably and head-butted the Ruxian on the nose as hard as he could. There was a sickening crack as the bone shattered, drenching the strategos with warm blood. The man's yell of pain and surprise was lost in another booming roll of thunder.

Dexios's questing hand closed on his fallen xiphos. His fingers curled around the hilt. With the last of his strength, he rammed his blade upwards through his opponent's jaw and on into his brain. The Ruxian's eyes went white, and he collapsed, his body twitching and jerking like a fish out of water.

"Thank you, Hera," Dexios murmured, tilting his head skywards and letting the rain wash the blood from his face. He opened his mouth and used more water to rinse out the worst of the mud and gore. That had been close. Too close. He was becoming far too old to roll around in the muck.

"Strategos." The voice was calm and menacing. He

turned and saw Krinne had been forced back against the rock, the tip of a spear tickling his throat. Nambe was on his knees in the centre of a ring of swords.

"Strategos," the voice called again over the thunder. A muscular Ruxian stepped forth from the circle of iron blades. He was old for a hoplite, older than Galleas even, his right eye socket a mass of wrinkled scar tissue.

Dexios started to rise.

"No, no. Stay down in the mud. On your knees. Where you belong. As you can see, it is over. Drop your weapon or we kill your friends."

"What's to stop you from murdering them anyway?"

A look of annoyance crossed the veteran's face. "We are not monsters. Polydius only needs you. I swear by Hera that if you come with us, we will release your companions unharmed."

"Run, Strategos," Nambe growled. His advice earned him a backhanded slap.

Gods. I've been selfish, Dexios thought. *I should never have dragged these two brave men into this. I have led them to their deaths.*

"I cannot submit," he said with an apologetic shrug. "Polydius will either torture me to obtain information on Thena's weaknesses or use me as leverage against the basileus. I am sorry." He looked at Nambe. "Truly."

"So be it," said the Ruxian. "Honourable but stupid. Start with the slave. Slit his throat, then—"

"May Zeus, the benevolent father, protect you."

Piraeus stood with his arms outstretched as if he were trying to pluck the swirling storm clouds from the sky. His chiton was soaked with rainwater, his long beard a sodden mass of dirty white hair.

"May Zeus, the eternal warrior, grant you victory."

"Who in Tartarus is this idiot?" asked the scarred veteran.

Something was changing in the air. An acrid, metallic smell. Dexios could taste it on his swollen tongue. Almost touch it. A vibrant thrumming of anticipation.

"May Zeus, the learned scholar, share his wisdom."

"Kill him!" the Ruxian shouted. "He dares to utter the name of one of the Ruined! Execute the blasphemer!"

Two hoplites started up the slope, their sandals sticking in the rain-slick mud. Piraeus gave them no heed. His eyes bored into Dexios, and his next words were for him, and him alone.

"May Zeus, the paradigm of justice, punish your enemies."

Dexios understood.

"DOWN!" he yelled. "GET DOWN!"

An iridescent bolt of lightning exploded from the raging storm clouds, hurtling earthwards and grounding itself on the metal tip of an unfortunate Ruxian spearman. He let out an agonising scream as white-hot tendrils crackled over his armoured body. His bronze helm melted, liquid metal eating into his skull and stripping the flesh from his face. The scream became a moaning gurgle, a final, desperate plea, before stopping altogether.

The deadly radiance was far from satiated, however. Sizzling offshoots arced out hungrily from the burning corpse in search of easy prey. The Ruxians surrounding Nambe were the perfect targets. A writhing bolt hit a soldier in the face, causing his eyes to burst from their sockets. Another felt a forked tongue brush against his scalp, followed by a terrible pain as his hair was set on fire.

The survivors scattered.

Dexios watched with morbid fascination, unable to tear his gaze away from the massacre. His ears were ringing from the deafening boom of thunder that had accompanied the lightning. Piraeus had not moved, his arms still raised, his lips trembling as he prayed to his God.

With a blinding flash, a second bolt lit up the sky. It missed the spearman threatening Krinne by a couple of feet, pounding the ground next to him with earth-shattering force. The resulting shockwave threw both men into the air. Krinne, his back still against the large rock, was lucky. The Ruxian was less fortunate. He spiralled madly across the clearing before crashing into a tree trunk, impaling himself on one of the serrated edges. His hands grasped feebly at the fist-sized chunk of wood protruding from his torso, then fell limply to his sides.

Dexios shook his head in amazement. This was a … slaughter.

"Stop," he croaked. The throbbing in his ears was so loud he couldn't even hear his own voice. He struggled to stand, but his sandal slipped on a slimy patch of sludge, and he hit the mud hard enough to push the air from his lungs.

He lay there on his back, trying to catch his breath as the rain pelted his face and body. He was tired. So tired. A spear of light blazed across his vision, burning its brilliance onto his retina. It exploded somewhere behind him.

If this is the end, so be it, he thought. *If Keres cannot join me in life, then my shade shall join his in death.*

A shadowy figure obscured the flashing storm clouds, sheltering him from the rain. Piraeus smiled triumphantly.

"You asked for proof, Strategos. Is this proof enough? My God is real. And he is kind. He wishes you to see your son again. Will you let him help you?"

Dexios looked up as more lightning tore the sky in two. The wrath of Zeus. An undeniable demonstration of unbridled power. What terrible havoc such power could wreak.

Suffering, misery, and pain.

'The Oracle always tells the truth.' His own words, returning to haunt him. For she had warned him that this time would come. When he would find himself at the crossroads between absolution and heresy. To save his son, he would have to abandon everything he believed in. To step away from Hera's light. To embrace the darkness.

Misery and pain.

He sighed. In his hubris, he had somehow managed to convince himself that he could avoid submitting to his fate. A foolish notion. He had never been in control.

"Dexios?" Piraeus asked again.

There was no choice. No decision. A single path stretched out in front of him, cold and uninviting.

"I accept your help," he said, the words stale and bitter in his mouth.

"Excellent. Then, I will guide you to Panacea."

"Where? Where can I find my son's salvation?"

"In the same place it has always been."

"*Where?*"

"In the city of Thena."

26

ASSAULT

"Every defensive force should theoretically have a number of significant advantages over their aggressors. In reality, these advantages are fleeting and rely on an experienced, competent commander to exploit them correctly."

CERBRIONES, 'ALALAGMOE'

ELENA FOUND HERSELF unable to tear her gaze away from Galleas's severed head. The pale bluish tinge around the lips. The flecks of dried blood encrusted in its beard. The lolling tongue, thick and bloated. Like a purple slug.

It's not him. It can't be him. This isn't real.

Crenate was the first to break the silence. "You must return to the palace, Lord," he urged. "It's not safe here." The basileus removed his silver circlet and ran a hand through his hair. He nodded.

"You too," the guard captain added, glowering at Elena.

No way, she thought. *I want to see the bastards who did this suffer. I want to see them bleed.*

She planted her feet stubbornly. "I'm staying."

"Sophistes ..."

"Oh, let her do what she wants, Crenate," Letho said,

his voice betraying his tiredness. "Just make sure you apprise me of any changes."

Elena, her face flushed with adrenaline, focused on the tauros once more. The calves and heifers had vanished behind the tents, while the males were arming themselves and joining the front line where an enormous dark-skinned tauros with a missing horn and purple markings was organising the new arrivals into ranks. Colours flowed together and then separated again as the different herds were split from one another once more.

A wily strategos would often build his phalanx in the exact same way, placing friends and family members near each other. The reasoning was obvious, and a little macabre: a hoplite would fight harder to protect someone he knew than someone he didn't … and if he was ever unfortunate enough to witness a comrade or a loved one fall to the enemy … his hate and rage would make him fight harder still.

And now the tauros were doing the same.

"Stop gawking at the cows and listen to me," Crenate roared from his perch on the gatehouse. "I know most of you. Seen you at the training grounds. Half of you throw like you piss: too fast and without aiming properly."

Such a way with words, thought Elena, putting some distance between herself and the guard captain in an attempt to avoid being spattered with green expectorate.

"Take your time, and make sure you're standing straight. Weight on the rear leg, hips facing forwards. Nice tight grip on the shaft."

A drum began to boom out over the plains, soon joined by another, and another. The tauros front line rippled.

Then began to move.

"When I give the order to throw, bring your arm in hard and fast." Crenate was yelling now, fighting to be heard over the pulsing beat. "Elbow raised high. Pick your targets. Make them count."

Hundreds of hooves pounded the dry earth, sending vibrations rippling outwards towards Thena. Elena pushed a wisp of blonde hair from her eyes and laid a hand on the parapet. The ancient stone was *thrumming.*

"Hera give me strength," she said softly just as further down the line Graycea began to preach once more. Although there was something different in her tone of voice. The bored dullness replaced by a more vibrant sound.

"Oh, Great One, hear us! Let us stand in the protection of your shadow once again. Let your arms envelop us. Let them shield us. For we will feel no fear when we are nestled in your warm embrace."

Great One? What is she playing at?

Elena spared a glance at the old priestess of Hera. Graycea had tilted her head back as far as her wrinkled neck would go, turning her face to the morning sky. Whatever she was doing, it was having some effect. The hoplites around her stood straighter, their exhaustion momentarily forgotten.

The drum beat quickened, the tauros accelerated, and the advance became a charge.

"STEADY!" Crenate ordered, lifting his hand high above his head. All along the wall, men waited for the signal.

Less than two hundred feet of open ground separated the enemy from Thena. Close enough for Elena to make out all the small details she had missed before.

How the tribal markings enhanced the numerous scars each warrior bore.

How the larger, stronger beasts formed the vanguard while the grey-skinned tauros brought up the rear.

How the unarmed veterans protected their weaker bodies with voluminous cloaks made of animal hides.

"RAISE!"

How the colossal thigh muscles moved in time with the hammering of hooves.

How the bulbous nostrils flared and snorted with exertion.

How the cacophony of battle cries seemed to shake the very foundations of the earth.

"THROW YOU BASTARDS! THROW!" Crenate yelled, whipping his arm down like a scythe.

The javelins took flight, arcing over the parapet with a wrathful humming sound. A hail of iron fell among the charging tauros, and for the first time in her life, Elena heard the creatures bellow in pain as a slew of missiles penetrated bovine flesh.

Yet still, they came.

Elena watched in horror as one of the tauros lumbered on, six wooden shafts hanging from his back like the quills of a porcupine. Another, his right arm pierced by a duo of javelins, simply transferred his maul to the other hand, leaving his wounded appendage to flop uselessly against his torso as he advanced.

Only a dozen had fallen, nearly all from the front line, their corpses unceremoniously trampled into the chewed-up earth by the other herds.

Crenate called for another volley. More of the beasts were sent to the shores of Tartarus — or wherever their shades went when pulled from their dead bodies. Then they reached the gates.

"We have them!" the guard captain exclaimed, stepping aside to allow a trio of sweating slaves to run past with the last of the javelins. "Those doors are oak. Reinforced and nearly a foot thick."

Elena peered over the parapet. The tauros were frighteningly close. Their leader, the one Polydius had called K'vath, was the first to reach the gates. He kicked aside the decaying head of Galleas, then reached out and ran his hand across the weathered planks. Elena saw that he was missing his middle finger and recently, judging from the red scab covering the wound. K'vath stepped back, hefted his colossal battle-axe pensively, then swung hard at the door.

The crack the blade made as it entered the wood resonated like a death toll.

"Crenate ..." Elena began.

K'vath gave a guttural growl, and the horde surged forwards once more to beat against the doors with axes, cleavers, and mauls. The grey-pelted veterans encircled the younger tauros protectively.

"Crenate ..."

"It'll hold. Long enough for us to kill them all at least. JAVELINS! TAKE AIM! I WANT TO HEAR THESE COWS SQUEAL!"

He stalked over to the other side of the ramparts and glared down into the courtyard where slaves were dragging large rocks and pieces of wood towards the gatehouse in a last-ditch effort to reinforce the doors. Elena watched him absently, his impatient instructions sounding distant and muffled. He was ordering the slaves to bring boulders to the gatehouse roof. Gods! Why hadn't all this been done last night?

Because he was convinced that they wouldn't reach the walls, she thought in disgust. *Because despite my repeated warnings, despite the tales of horror brought to us by the broken, hollow-eyed survivors of the phalanx … he still calls them cows. Cattle. And we are paying for his delusional ignorance with our lives.*

"Crenate, maybe we should send word to the basileus—"

"NO! I can handle this. I WILL handle this." He returned to the parapet, bumping against her shoulder as he passed. He raised his arm once more, studying the mass of beasts attacking the gate. The veteran tauros were removing their cloaks, revealing something strapped to their backs.

"What …" Crenate faltered, his hand wavering. A flash of polished metal. Another.

Anguished cries spread along the wall as the defenders saw what the tauros had been hiding. Bronze shields. The shields of the fallen. The shields of the Thenean slain. Covered in muck and blood. Tarnished. Despoiled.

The hoplite's aspis was the most important part of his panoply. There was no greater shame than to lose one's shield. And for it to be taken by the enemy, to be *sullied* in this way, was inconceivable.

Elena felt a terrible sadness as the veteran tauros raised the shields high to protect their younger brethren. She could see dozens of stylised 'thetas' through the layers of grime. Paintings and etchings of animals mingled with more fantastical drawings of gods, heroes, and mythological creatures. The personal heraldry of the dead, displayed for all.

"No …" came a whisper. It was Crenate. He had seen the shield belonging to his son. The aspis had been badly dented, a hoofprint obscuring much of the lion's lower body and tail, but there was no mistaking what it was.

"He is not dead. He can't be dead."

A horrendous splintering sound came from below. The gate would not hold.

"Crenate!" Elena cried. "The men await your orders. Loose the javelins."

"No … no that would not be right," the guard captain answered in a strange voice. "We would risk further damage to the shields. They must be passed on intact to the next of kin. It is our way."

"There will be no one to pass them on to if the tauros break through that door, Crenate! Give the order."

"Wouldn't be right," he mumbled apologetically. His puffed-up chest deflated, and he lowered his arm slowly. "What would Helydices think if I disfigured his shield? He's only had it for a couple of weeks."

"YOUR SON IS DEAD!" Elena screamed into his face. Crenate stared back at her with vacant eyes.

"GODS!" she yelled at no one in particular. Taking a deep breath, she shouted as loudly as she could. "JAVELINS! LOOSE JAVELINS!"

The nearest hoplite looked at her in confusion. "But the captain said—"

Elena raised her hands in exasperation and grabbed the man's javelin, hurling it from the wall. It was a poor throw, but it clanged off one of the shields with enough force to rouse the nearby defenders from their stupor.

"THROW!" she cried again. "THROW, OR ALL IS LOST!"

Three more javelins soared skywards from her right

before slamming into the raised shields. Elena turned her head to see Graycea screeching obscenities at anyone who could hear her. Makar was among those who were listening, grabbing fresh missiles from his reluctant neighbours, and hurling them at the tauros near the gate.

The sporadic throws grew in intensity as more and more of the hoplites realised the danger. A few well-aimed javelins began to slip through the gaps in the raised row of shields, and the defenders were rewarded by muffled grunts of surprise and pain.

Elena let out a sigh of relief and marched over to Crenate who was still staring at his son's shield. "I need you," she snapped. "I'm a teacher, not a fighter. Tell me what to do!"

"It doesn't matter," he replied serenely. "My son is gone. Nothing else matters."

She slapped him hard across the face. Her palm burned with the force of the blow. "Pull yourself together! Thena needs you, Captain! We need to stop them! How do we stop them?"

He looked at her, his stony face cracked and brittle. A tear rolled down one cheek. "I ... I don't know."

"Tartarus take you!" she cursed, forcing her tired, alcohol-deprived mind to think. There was nothing in recent Tyrrean history that would help her. A phalanx never attacked a city directly. It would be suicide. The shield wall offered incredible protection from the front but was completely useless in a siege, its lack of manoeuvrability and its vulnerability to missile fire making it a tempting target for those who held the higher ground. Consequently, skirmishes between Tyrreans mostly took place on flat, unobstructed land where the phalanx was at its most dangerous.

The ominous sound of a plank splitting in two pulled her from her thoughts.

Right.

"TO THE GATES!" she yelled. "HERA COMMANDS IT!"

She grabbed the nearest soldier. "You! Go to the palace. Fast as you can. Tell the basileus the wall is breached. Don't come back until you have his reply!" He looked at her in befuddlement.

"NOW, SOLDIER!" She pushed him towards the ladder leading off the wall. Hiking her chiton up around her knees, she made for Graycea as fast as her legs would carry her.

"They're breaking through! We need to form some sort of defensive line to stop them from running rampant through the residential areas. You are a priestess of Hera, whether you like it or not. They'll listen to you. Tell them their goddess summons them to defend Thena."

Graycea gaped at Elena as if she were mad. "Defend Thena? With what? A handful of javelins? Crenate told the men to leave their spears and shields back at the garrison with the wounded. How will they form a shield wall without any shields?"

"They can't," interrupted Makar in his quiet voice. He bore a look of grim determination. "However, a small group of us could slow the tauros down long enough for the rest of the defenders to regroup and retrieve their weapons. Maybe even mount some sort of counter-attack."

"Not you, Makar, I wasn't talking about you."

"That's not for you to decide, Mistress. My fellow ephebes fought and died while I relaxed with a kylix of watered wine before sleeping in my nice, warm bed. I should have been there with them. My place was in the phalanx."

A group of men were slowly congregating in the court-yard below. Reservists. They looked tired and desperate. The phalanx had outnumbered the tauros three-to-one and still lost. What chance did this pitiful band of hoplites have?

"The basileus gave the order—" Elena tried to say.

"The ennea? He sought to protect the weak by offering us a way out. The other reservists are all like me. Misfits. Unwanted. Denied a chance at glory. This is my chance, Mistress. The Gods have offered me a way to redeem myself."

He straightened his antique helmet and made for the ladder. Elena stared at his retreating back, thinking furiously for a way to change his mind.

"Redeem yourself from what?" she shouted after him. "You've done nothing wrong!"

"Tell that to my father," he replied, one sandalled foot already on the top rung.

"Stop!" Elena cried, but her desperate plea was drowned out by a deafening roar of triumph. The tauros had rent a great hole in one of the wooden planks and were working to lever the crossbar from its supports. A half-hearted volley of javelins ricocheted off the dead men's shields with a metallic clatter.

The hoplites who had answered the call-to-arms were attempting to organise themselves into a square. Makar was in the first rank, next to the lochagos who had led the shattered phalanx back to Thena. From her elevated position on the gatehouse roof, the little group of men looked laughably small. They would be swept away in an instant, grains of sand against the tide.

"Time to leave, girl," Graycea said as she hurried past. Elena realised she was one of the last defenders still on the wall. The other survivors had either fled or joined the last-ditch stand of the men in the courtyard below.

There must be something I can do! she thought, her eyes roaming the near-deserted ramparts before alighting on the statue-like form of Crenate. The town captain was completely immobile, his jaw locked tight.

"Captain, your men need you!"

He cocked his head to one side. "It is too late." He smiled, something Elena had never seen him do before, and his joyous expression was so alien, it made her want to scream.

"Can you hear the sound of a boat's prow breaking the waves, Sophistes? It is Charon, come to take our shades to Tartarus. Come to take me to my son. I will be with him, at last."

I've lost him, Elena thought. The paved stone beneath her feet trembled. Old oak creaked and buckled.

"WATCH OUT!" she yelled as the city gates exploded inwards, and the tauros flowed into the courtyard in a maelstrom of hoof and horn. They stampeded into the waiting hoplites without slowing. The lochagos was one of the first to die, his skull crushed by a spiked maul.

The return swipe caught Makar in the chest, and Elena looked on helplessly as the young ephebe was thrown through the air by the force of the blow, landing heavily near an abandoned cart.

He did not get up.

27

CONSTELLATIONS

"Do not spend too much time worrying about your legacy, or how people will talk about you when you are gone. Unkind words hurt much less when you are no longer around to hear them."

GRAYCEA, PRIESTESS OF HERA

I
T WAS THE first time that Dexios had looted a corpse. He had seen his fellow soldiers do so many a time, grubby hands pawing at the clothes of the dead, rifling through pockets, and tugging jewellery from swollen fingers. A final humiliation, as if defeat was not already enough.

Most hoplites would argue that it wasn't really *stealing*. The shades had already departed, fleeing the cooling corpses for the warmth of Charon's embrace. All that remained were uncaring sacks of meat and bone, which had no further use for the world's mundanities.

Dexios tried to keep that thought firmly at the front of his mind as he searched the dead Ruxian officer. He found a silver medallion around the man's neck and snapped the chain so that he could pull it free. A well-crafted piece engraved with some sort of bird of prey and the letter 'phi'. The initial of the deceased's wife perhaps? Or his child?

"Everything all right, Strategos?" asked Krinne. The wiry little misthios was sitting on a broken tree trunk, meticulously running a length of serving thread up and down his bowstring to remove the drying mud and debris. A ball of wax was next to him, ready to be rubbed into the string once it was clean and dry.

"These men were only following orders," Dexios said, moving on to another corpse. "Fulfilling their duty. It does not seem … honourable to pilfer their most precious possessions."

Krinne shrugged. "If Piraeus hadn't intervened, we would all be dead, and one of these bastards would be prying my gold teeth from my stiff jaw. There is no honour to be found here, Dexios, for any of us. Besides" — he stole a furtive glance at the temple of Zeus — "theft is a lesser sin than blasphemy."

"If you have something to say, Krinne, just say it."

"I don't trust him."

"Neither do I. But my trust was already a hard thing to earn before Polydius betrayed us all. Now … Gods, I'm not sure I'll be able to truly rely on anyone ever again. You, for example. What's to stop you from switching sides when Ruxia comes calling? They must have enough silver to bury you from head to toe in the stuff. How much is my death worth?"

Krinne smeared a generous gob of wax onto his fingers and began wiping it along the bowstring. "A fair point. Although you haven't even paid me yet. It wouldn't be good business to kill you before then."

Dexios shook his head ruefully. "Everything's a joke to you, isn't it?"

"Not everything. There is one thing I take very seriously."

"And that is?"

"Honouring a contract. That son of a whore, Polydius, only paid my men and me half the agreed-upon sum before throwing us to the wolves. He welched on our deal. Bastard. I'd rather shave off my moustache than work with him again."

"He also betrayed you and tried to have you killed."

"Yeah, so he wouldn't have to pay us. The skinflint."

"That is a rather … unique way of looking at things, but as long as it works in my favour, I'll not question it further. Does that mean you are coming with us to Thena?"

"I'm staying with you until you pay me, Strategos, or until I'm forced to collect payment myself. And as I said, you're no use to me dead, which will probably happen soon unless I'm around to keep an eye on the priest."

"We will both be doing that." Nambe had joined them, holding a Ruxian cloak bulging with valuables. "He serves a duplicitous God."

"You believe him, then?" asked Dexios.

Nambe jerked his head towards the two charred craters that scarred the earth. The rain had faded as quickly as it had come, but there was still moisture in the air that hissed and steamed from the intense heat. The mud around the craters had fused and vitrified into a solid, glassy crust.

"I cannot ignore what happened. The way the lightning was drawn to our enemies and avoided us completely. But he is hiding something."

"I can smell the stink of secrecy on him," Krinne agreed. "Besides, no one does anything for free. If he's leading us to Panacea, then it's in his best interest. I'm just not sure why yet."

"Then, we don't let him out of our sight," Dexios said.

"Even at night. We'll take turns standing watch. Once I have Panacea, we'll cut him loose, and he can hobble off back to his cave. Agreed?"

"Aye."

"Aye, Strategos."

"Good. What have you found, Nambe?"

The southerner spread the cloak out on a tree stump, revealing its contents. A half-dozen rings, a belt buckle, an ornate scabbard, three necklaces, and a handful of drachmae.

"A pittance," Krinne said with a twitch of his hooked nose. "Barely worth the effort. Lucky we still have the horses or our trip south would have ended before it had even begun."

Dexios nodded. The first thing they had done after the unnatural storm had abated was check on the animals. Miraculously, they were still where Nambe had left them, anxious and skittish but otherwise unharmed.

Steeds bred for war, thought Dexios. Trained since they were foals to tolerate the loud, stinking chaos of battle. There was a rumour that the Thenean stablemaster liked to lead his colts to the artisan's quarter, where the ringing sound of the blacksmith's hammer mingled with the smell of butchered animals that emanated from the slaughterhouses. Supposedly, it helped the beasts grow accustomed to the stench of blood and death.

His gaze fell on the small pile of trinkets. He added a trio of rings and the silver medallion. "We need another horse for the priest; our own animals are loaded down enough as it is. And supplies. The men at the lumber camp may be willing to trade …"

From strategos to common thief, he thought. *Curse you,*

Polydius, for turning me into this. And curse you for sending these men here.

"I want sufficient coins set aside for proper funeral rites," he added.

"Bastards don't deserve it," Krinne muttered.

Nambe raised an eyebrow. "You would condemn their shades to wander the shores of Tartarus simply for following orders?"

"The orders they had to kill us, you mean?"

Dexios took a step towards him. "I understand that you are angry, but you are directing your hate towards the wrong people. Punishing these men will neither hurt Polydius nor curb your vengeful thoughts. We should see to it that they have the means to pay Charon's toll."

Krinne didn't flinch. "You both have a strange sense of priorities," he said. "I won't stop you. But I won't help you either. You'll find me waiting by the horses when you are done. With Piraeus. Don't take too long."

Dexios took a handful of coins and gestured for Nambe to do the same. They went from corpse to corpse, administering the final rites. An obol or drachma in the mouth followed by a short prayer to Hera. One man's jaw had been turned into a mass of fleshy slag making it impossible to pry open. Another's helmet had been melded to his face, the molten metal completely covering the skin beneath. Dexios forced Charon's toll in between his stiff fingers, hoping that it would suffice.

"What now?" Nambe asked. "We have no shovels to bury them, and the bodies are still far too wet for a pyre."

"We'll pay the loggers to come up here tomorrow and dig a trench."

"As you wish."

Dexios stretched, cracking the aching vertebrae in his back. His injured nose throbbed. Damn thing had barely started healing before that malaka had shoved him face-first into the muck. He hoped it wasn't broken again.

He looked down at the row of Ruxians. Was this to be his legacy? The strategos who buried both the men he lost and the men he killed? He knew full well what the soldiers under his command called him, and what it meant. Harbinger.

The herald of grief and death.

Dexios exhaled a long, weary breath and traipsed back to Krinne and the horses. His battered helm was waiting for him on a nearby rock where he had left it. He slammed it onto his head, patted his stallion's neck affectionately, and used the rock as a stepping stone to help him into the saddle. One sandalled foot brushed against his son's aspis.

A legacy can be changed, he thought. *Once I find Panacea. Once Keres is returned to me …*

I will no longer be known as the Harbinger. I will be known as the man who brought his son back to life.

If the lumber camp foreman was surprised to see the travellers still alive, he didn't show it. The old woodsman must have known about the ambush and was possibly even the one who had warned the Ruxians that their prey had arrived at the temple of Zeus. Dexios found that he didn't care. All he wanted was to head south as soon as possible, back to

Thena. And that meant a horse for Piraeus and supplies for the journey.

He let Krinne do the haggling, wandering the rows of cut tree trunks while he waited and using the time to try and calm his frazzled mind. When he returned, both the misthios and the foreman were out of breath, their flushed faces making it look like they had just competed in the ephebic trials.

"We've been robbed, Strategos" panted Krinne, his moustache quivering. "Old greybeard here has swindled us out of enough jewellery to purchase a small polis."

"And who in Tartarus am I going to sell it all to, out 'ere in the middle of nowhere, eh? Trader won't be up 'ere for another two weeks and 'e'll probably only buy a few pieces. It'll be years before I get rid of it all. In fact, now I think about it, I should ask for—"

"Pay the man what he wants, Krinne," Dexios cut in wearily. "Let's not waste what little daylight we have left."

Krinne muttered something obscene and undid the knotted cloak. The foreman sent one of his men to fetch a mount for Piraeus, a huge piebald stallion almost as muscular as their own war horses. The priest of Zeus eyed the beast with a mixture of fear and contempt. It took him three tries to hoist himself into the saddle. He sat there stoically, his long beard brushing against the horse's mane.

They rode well into the night, stopping only when fatigue threatened to overwhelm them. Dexios led them to a grove of olive trees near the side of the road. He set about removing his panoply while Nambe started a small fire. Piraeus kept apart from the others, rubbing his bruised thighs.

They ate in silence, too tired to speak. Nambe volunteered for first watch, and Dexios accepted gladly, drifting off to sleep as soon as his head hit the rolled-up cloak he was using as a pillow. He dreamt of Keres. The same dream he had been having ever since his death. Of them running side-by-side through the vines, the sun warm and inviting on their skin. The smell of ripening grapes.

Krinne shook him awake what seemed like moments later. Dexios squinted bleary-eyed at the sky and saw that the moon had shifted position, bringing Tyrris closer to dawn. He yawned. "My turn?"

"Aye. I warn you though, Strategos, that priest is a weird one." Krinne pointed to a spot by the fire where Piraeus sat cross-legged, staring into the flames. "He's been like that for hours. Doesn't move. Doesn't sleep. Nambe told me it was the same when he was on watch. I don't like it."

"Try to get some rest," Dexios replied, wiping a speck of particularly tenacious grit from his eye. "I'll make sure he doesn't murder you in your sleep."

Krinne gave a sigh of exasperation and headed for his bedroll. Dexios pulled himself up into a sitting position and turned his gaze to the stars once more. Distant constellations twinkled high above his head. The katasterismoi. The stars placed by the Gods. It was one of the many ways that the Pantheon reminded humanity of what would happen if they defied their rulers.

Orion, killed accidentally by Artemis due to Apollo's trickery. Callisto, seduced by Zeus and murdered by Artemis. Cassiopeia, the victim of her own hubris … a hundred different tragedies playing out across the sky, night after night.

A hundred different examples of the Gods' callousness, impatience, greed, and wrath.

And, if the stories were true, the worst of them all was Zeus.

Dexios added some kindling to the smouldering wood. He glanced over at Piraeus. The old priest sat as still as a statue, the glowing embers of the dying fire reflected in his eyes.

"You knew my son was called Keres."

Piraeus didn't answer for so long that Dexios began to think he hadn't heard him, then the old man blinked once and turned his head.

"Zeus revealed the names of both your dead children to me, Strategos. Keres and Oneiros. He told me it would help convince you."

"I don't understand. How can he even know such things? He was banished along with his brothers. Olympus is closed to him."

"It is not a *place* that gives a God his power. It is people. Faith. *Belief.* A God's strength waxes and wanes constantly, even for Hera. For years after his exile, Zeus was weak, only surviving thanks to a meagre group of ageing priests like my father who continued to worship him daily. Now … there is a change coming. Hera has overstretched. Her once benevolent reign is slipping into something more authoritarian. More tyrannical. Adulation fades, replaced by fear."

"And fear of Hera leads men to pray to other Gods."

"Yes. Every desperate plea, every cry for help, fills him with energy."

"The lightning."

"It is one of his gifts. Lost to him for a long time. But, like many things, it is returning."

Piraeus did nothing to hide the gleeful tone in his voice. Dexios tended the fire with the charred tip of an olive branch, thinking about what he had heard. *What would Zeus's return mean for Tyrris?*

"He is still angry," he said.

"Anger is not even close to describing the extent of the rage he feels. It is beyond anger. It consumes his every breath."

"He wants to return to Olympus, doesn't he? That is the final goal. To take back his rightful place from Hera?"

Piraeus nodded. "Would not you wish to do the same, if you were unjustly forced from the home you had built with your own hands? Your power stripped from you? Your name erased from history? A day will come when he will gather an army and ascend the slopes of Olympus. But for now, the way is blocked. The Citrine Wastes remain impenetrable."

"The Citrine Wastes? I have not heard of this place."

"Few have. It lies far to the north, beyond tauran territory. It is said that it was once a green and fertile land filled with birds and beasts, unsullied by man or tauros. A natural paradise in the shadow of Olympus's great peak. Then the Gods went to war, and it became a battlefield. Fire blackened the soil. Lightning split the sky. Years of destructive energies shattered the earth and twisted the few pitiful creatures that survived into ghoulish abominations. Even the very air was tarnished. It became the sickly shade of toxic yellow that gave the Wastes their name. It became death."

"Death to the Gods?"

"You mean Zeus? I don't know. Before, in his weakened

state, maybe. But now, with his strength returning? He could traverse the Wastes, I think. Yet, it would cost him."

Dexios scratched at his unkempt beard. He could detect no lies in the priest's words. Piraeus obviously fully believed everything he was saying, no matter how fantastical it seemed. Although … there was still one important question he had not answered.

"Why Panacea?"

Piraeus's eyes flickered. "What do you mean?"

"Why help me find Panacea? What advantage does he gain?"

The priest licked his lips. "Zeus is a benevolent—"

"No more games. Tell me."

"It … I do not know the details. I only know that by killing Panacea you will aid my patron."

Dexios felt a shiver run down his spine. "What did you say? *Killing?*"

Piraeus looked at him incredulously. "Of course. I thought you knew. Panacea is not an object. It's a person. And only their death will bring your son back."

28

FLIGHT

"To accept defeat in battle is not the same as giving up. As a commander, it simply means that saving the lives of your own men has become more important than taking the lives of others."

CERBRIONES, 'ALALAGMOE'

MAKAR'S HAND TWITCHED.

I have to go, Elena thought. *I have to help him.*

She tore her hairnet from her head and searched around desperately for a weapon. Her eyes alighted on Crenate's xiphos, still in its scabbard, untouched.

"Crenate?"

The guard captain didn't reply.

"I'm taking your weapon." Her fingers closed around the grip. She drew it forth carefully and stuck it in her belt. The movement appeared to finally rouse Crenate from his dazed indifference. He blinked slowly.

"It's too late, Sophistes. Far too late."

"For your son, perhaps," she said, her voice cold. "Not for Makar. Or all the others who are buying time with their lives. Oh, and you will not see your son in Tartarus, Captain. He died a hero. Elysium will welcome him with open arms. You, on the other hand, will die a coward."

Elena turned her back on him and ran for the ladder,

the screams of the hoplites and the bellows of the tauros ringing in her ears. Reaching the courtyard was like entering Tartarus itself. Everywhere she looked, she saw Theneans suffering. Tauran axes tore through leather armour and the skin beneath in gory displays of unstoppable violence. Huge hammers pummelled flesh and cracked bone. The smooth stone beneath her feet was already slick with blood and fouled by the bodily waste of a dozen corpses.

Elena recognised K'vath, the colossal alpha, in the thick of the melee, lashing out left and right with his powerful fists. He grabbed hold of a terrified reservist and ripped the man's head from his neck with a guttural roar. A crimson geyser fountained up from the ragged hole, drenching the tauros as he raised his gruesome trophy high for all to see.

Makar. I have to find Makar.

She had not yet been spotted, but that would change as soon as she ventured into that … nightmare. Squinting through the rolling mass of men and monsters, she spied the top of the overturned cart less than fifty feet away.

May Hera guide me.

Holding Crenate's xiphos out in front of her like a divining rod, she took a step forwards, then another, her eyes constantly searching. Her heart was beating so fast it felt like it would burst from her chest at any moment.

She edged carefully around a dead body that had been hacked in half, only held together by a thin coil of intestines that stretched from the mutilated torso to a pair of pale, blood-spattered legs.

If I ever get out of this alive, I will never touch a cup of wine again, Elena vowed, wincing as her sandal trod in something soft that squelched under her foot.

A hoplite appeared out of nowhere, and she bumped into his back, narrowly avoiding running him through with her sword.

"I'm sorry," she stammered. "I'm trying to find someone. He may be hurt. Can you help me? Please?"

The man turned. Elena looked upon his face with horror. The skin had been beaten into a pulpy mass of glistening red, his eye sockets two cavernous, empty holes.

"Mother?" he asked. "Is that you? Are we going home?" He stretched out an arm, and Elena ducked guiltily under his searching fingers. He stumbled back towards the fighting, still calling softly.

I can't do this.

Her stomach cramped painfully. She was going to be sick. Her throat spasmed, and she spat out a mouthful of bile.

Makar!

She could see his recumbent form now. His helmet had been knocked from his head, freeing his sweaty black hair that fell like a mask over his face. The old bronze breastplate inherited from his father bore a fresh furrow running diagonally from abdomen to shoulder. It shifted almost imperceptibly. He was still breathing.

This knowledge gave Elena the strength to cover the last few feet. She shoved Crenate's xiphos unceremoniously back into her belt, then knelt beside the ephebe, and brushed the hair from his eyes.

"Makar?" she called softly and was rewarded with a tired moan.

"Go away."

"We are out of time. The courtyard is lost. The tauros

will soon have free rein to pillage the city. Where is your father?"

He looked at her, groggy and confused. "I ... At his workshop, probably. Where else would he be?"

"He won't be safe there. The palace or the garrison is our best hope of survival. Come on!" She stood and held out her hand.

Makar coughed. A thin trickle of blood escaped his lips. "I won't run from battle, Mistress. I'm not a coward."

Elena gave a laugh that bordered on hysteria. "Look around you! This is not a battle, Makar, it's a massacre! You've done all you can. We can't save them. But we can still save your father."

For a moment, a silent war waged behind his eyes, then he reached out with a skinny arm and took Elena's hand. She pulled hard, surprised at his weight. Makar swayed unsteadily, took one wobbling step, and half-fell against the side of the overturned cart.

"Just give me a minute to catch my breath," he said, his voice slurred.

"We don't have a minute! Loop your arm around my neck, and lean into me. I can drag us as far as your father's workshop."

"Can't do that, Mistress. What if someone saw us? Wouldn't be proper ..."

He's becoming disorientated, Elena thought anxiously. *We can't stay here any longer.* She leant closer. The movement saved her life. Something heavy whistled through the space where her head had been seconds before, the displaced air from its passage tickling the nape of her neck.

Elena smelt earth and sweat and blood and death.

She turned slowly, already knowing what she would see. The tauros loomed over her, his lips peeled back in an ugly snarl, the stringy hair of his pelvis and thighs matted with human blood. He wielded a crude, cleaver-like slab of metal flecked with rust and small white chips that could only be shards of bone. Deep-sunken eyes glinted dangerously.

Elena recoiled until her back hit the side of the overturned cart with a thunk. They were trapped.

The tauros advanced unhurriedly, swinging the cleaver back and forth like a pendulum. *He's toying with us*, Elena thought. *Like a cat playing with its prey.*

"Get behind me, Mistress," Makar said, struggling to stand.

"Hera hear my prayer," Elena pleaded aloud, turning her eyes to the heavens. "Do not forsake us in our final hour. Do not turn away from your faithful servants." She drew the xiphos and raised it protectively. It looked tiny compared to the massive tauran cleaver.

"Throw me my sword!"

The voice came from above her head.

The Gods! The Gods had answered her prayers!

"ELENA!"

It was not the Gods but Crenate, balanced on top of the overturned cart, his gaze clear and focused once more. "My sword."

She tossed it to him with a crude underarm throw. He caught it by the hilt and leapt at the approaching tauros, raising the xiphos high over his head with both hands and screaming his son's name. The warrior-beast saw the danger coming far too late. Crenate, still in mid-air, brought his sword scything down, clipping the right horn before sinking deep into the creature's neck.

With an angry bellow, the tauros pushed the guard captain away, ripping the blade free in the process. Tauran blood, so dark a red it was almost black, gushed from the gaping hole. The warrior dropped his cleaver and pressed his stubby fingers to the wound in an attempt to staunch the arterial flow but the liquid founds its way through the gaps, coursing over his knuckles and down his wrists.

Crenate watched with contempt as the beast's lifeblood further darkened the once pristine-white paving of the courtyard. "May Hera accept my sacrifice," he said, kicking the dying tauros in the chest and knocking him onto his back. He sheathed his xiphos without bothering to clean it.

"I thought about what you said, Sophistes. You were right. I will not go to the shores of Tartarus a coward. Hera in her magnificence has allowed me to choose the manner of my death, and it will be by a tauran blade, just like my son. Leave here now. Get to the palace." He took a deep breath and roared "RETREAT! FALL BACK!"

The pitiful remains of the reservists attempted to dis-engage. Crenate nodded once in thanks and drew his sword once more. He charged into the fray.

Elena stretched her arm around Makar and hobbled towards the relative safety of the back alleys. The ephebe was having trouble putting one foot in front of the other.

A familiar figure emerged from the chaos. Graycea had a long scratch down one cheek, and her chiton was so covered in blood and mud it looked like she had bathed in the stuff.

"Let me help."

She hooked a scrawny arm under Makar's breastplate, and the three of them set off at a slightly faster pace.

"I crawled," the priestess said, her long hair hiding the expression on her face.

"What?"

"You were wondering how I am still alive. I lay down on my belly like a snake, and I crawled."

They finally reached the shadows of the alley, the screams of the beleaguered reservists fading as they moved further and further along the twisting, deserted pathways. Makar tripped on a loose stone and nearly sent them all tumbling. He apologised vaguely, gazing up at the red-tiled roofs as if discovering them for the first time.

It took a couple of wrong turns before Elena was certain they were on the right track. They passed a cracked statue of Artemis, her bow and quiver long gone, turned left at the following crossroads, and arrived at the small square bordered by Desha's workshop. The old man opened the door himself, his keen eyes taking in Graycea's bloody chiton and Makar's dented armour.

"We lost," he stated.

"We didn't even slow them down," Elena replied wearily. "It won't be long before they catch us."

Desha nodded and stepped aside to let them in. "Put him in the andron."

The two women staggered past the jewelled statue of Hera and lowered Makar onto one of the couches. Desha reappeared with a pewter cup filled to the brim with a foul-smelling liquid.

"Crushed arkeion and althaea," he explained. "When I was part of the phalanx, some of the other soldiers used to drink gallons of the stuff. Kept them going." He perched on the edge of the couch beside his son.

"Didn't take very good care of my armour, did you, lad?" he said, not unkindly.

"Sorry, Father."

"I've brought a little something to help you feel better." He put the cup in Makar's hand. The boy looked at it for a moment before lifting it to his lips.

"That's my boy." Desha took a rag from one of the pockets of his apron and wiped some of the filth from Makar's face. It was a tender and intimate gesture that took Elena by surprise. *He cares about his son*, she thought. *Despite his constant admonishments. He cares.*

Makar coughed again. "It was terrible, Father." His eyes had regained a hint of lucidity. "We were victims of our own stupidity. Always treating the tauros like animals. They are not. They *planned* this ... All of this ... Father, they used our own shields against us. The shields of the fallen."

Desha frowned. "If they are inside the city, we cannot fight them. I tried that before." He scratched at the stump of his arm with his remaining hand, as if the mere thought of the tauros was causing his wound to itch. "The garrison is a death trap. Our only option is to flee. There's a merchant in Boena who owes me a favour or two. He'll take us in until we can get back on our feet."

"And how exactly do we leave Thena?" Graycea said testily. "The only way out is swarming with tauros."

Desha's frown deepened. "I do not believe we have met ... Lady."

She cackled. "I'm no Lady! Graycea, priestess of Hera."

"Graycea. I know that name. Where have I heard it before?"

"It's common enough. Maybe you heard one of the other priestesses yelling at me. They seem to like screaming at me on a daily basis."

"Perhaps …" Desha didn't seem so sure. "I … Never mind. You asked how we can escape the city. You're right. I don't have the answer."

"I do," said Elena suddenly, remembering her conversation with the basileus. "Letho told me there are tunnels under the palace, tunnels that lead to all sorts of places. I bet one of them will take us beyond the city walls."

"And how do you propose we get inside?"

She smiled and showed him the silver ring on her finger.

"He gave you his seal? You're an advisor to the basileus himself? That's … impressive. He really must be desperate."

"Father!" Makar exclaimed.

"Apologies. My words were not meant to offend. It is merely an unusual strategy. Why you, I wonder?"

"Who cares?" Graycea said, rearranging her mud-spattered chiton. "If that ring gets us into the palace, then it's a good enough plan for me."

Desha gave a curt nod. "I have a small wooden box hidden in the back of the workshop, filled with some of my finer pieces. Things that for one reason or another never found their way into a customer's hands. They will buy us passage to Boena. Wait for me out front. Makar, fetch my xiphos."

"Yes, Father. Would you like me to remove your armour too?"

Desha paused in the doorway. "No, Son," he said

without turning round. "You have … shown courage in the face of the enemy. I believe you deserve to keep it. My pano-ply is yours."

"Th … thank you, Father," Makar stammered, his face flushed. "I will wear it with pride."

What's left of it, thought Elena, eying the deep cut across the breastplate.

Her gaze wandered to the spot on the floor where less than a month ago a man had been murdered. Those four cir-cular holes. She never did get to the bottom of that mystery. It seemed so inconsequential now, submerged by the tauran tide that threatened to overwhelm the city.

Graycea clapped her hands. "Right. Time to get moving. I don't know about the rest of you, but I need to wet my lips before we venture outside into certain death. Sophistes, care to join me for a cup of watered wine?"

Elena thought about it for a moment.

"No," she said finally. The craving was still there. Lurking. Whispering. But it no longer had the strength to compel her. It had lost control.

Here, at last, was a battle she could win.

She smiled.

"No, I don't think I will."

☙

It must have taken only ten minutes for Desha to finish preparing, yet to Elena, waiting anxiously with Graycea in the silent square outside, it felt like hours. Puffy white clouds had invaded the blue sky overhead, finally offering the inhabitants of Thena a brief respite from the scorching heat of the last few weeks.

A pair of crows alighted on one of the tiled roofs bordering the square with a scratching of talons that made Elena almost jump out of her skin.

"Always hated them damn birds," grumbled Desha, appearing in the doorway with his son. He produced a key from his belt and inserted it into a small opening that gave him access to the bolt inside. There was a click as it slid across.

"That won't stop a tauros, Father," Makar said.

"I know. I know. Just doesn't seem right to leave this place unlocked. I was …" he laid his palm flat against the workshop wall. "I was … happy here."

"We can come back. When this is over. We can rebuild."

"Ah, the optimism of youth. Come on, let's get on with it. Sophistes, lead the way."

"Right," Elena said.

I promised to keep the basileus's secret, she thought. *How will he react when I arrive on his doorstep with three other people?*

Another clatter from the far side of the square. It wasn't the crows this time.

Two men, dirty and dishevelled, one old and scrawny, one younger and more muscular.

Despite the grime and blood, there was no mistaking that face.

Dexios.

29

REVELATION

"Distraction isn't just about making a person look away from what you don't want them to see, it's about directing their mind towards something else. Something that captivates their attention so completely that it becomes an obsession."

BASILEUS LETHO, 'RUMINATIONS'

D EXIOS SAW THE column of smoke on the distant horizon and knew at once that they had arrived too late.

"Thena burns," he said to Nambe. "Polydius has managed to breach the gates." The southerner gave a non-committal grunt. He had been uncharacteristically reserved for most of their exhausting ride south, and Dexios knew why. Nambe suspected his former master was hiding something from him.

And he was right.

Piraeus's revelation as to the true nature of Panacea had hit Dexios like a punch to the gut. He had sat there, stunned, as the fire of hope that burned within him — the same fire that had given him the strength and willpower to continue after the loss of his son — had sputtered and died. He had been prepared to do anything to bring Keres back. Abandon his command. His wife. His basileus. Ally himself with the priest of a banished God. But ... murder? End one life to save another? Tartarus was filled with the shades of such criminals, damned to torture and suffering for all eternity. No. It was too much.

He had tried to press the old priest further, but Piraeus was adamant. He had told Dexios all he knew. Zeus would guide him to the one known as Panacea, and their death would free Keres's shade. It had been enough to send Dexios into a spiral of depression. Food lost its taste. The constant chattering of his companions irked him, and he purposely let his horse lag behind the others so that he could be alone with his thoughts.

It was on the second day, after a long, sleepless night, that something had stirred in the smouldering ashes of that once-bright fire. An inkling of an idea. No louder than a whisper on the wind.

What if Panacea deserved to die?

He had brushed the question aside, unanswered, overcome with guilt. But the following night, it had come to him again, slipping into his mind while the others slumbered. Panacea could be evil incarnate. A thief. A rapist. A child molester. A ... murderer. To trade an innocent life for that of his son was unthinkable, but an immoral, wicked, corrupt life? Someone who took joy in inflicting pain? Dexios would not only be helping Keres, he would be saving countless others from misery.

The thought refused to leave him, bouncing off the insides of his skull like an echo, growing stronger and stronger. It was a branch held out to a drowning man. A spark of warmth against the cold. Dexios tried to resist, to push the thought away, but whenever it left him, a vision of Keres

took its place. His son's eyes were always open and searching. Pleading.

He capitulated. He would face Panacea. Judge their
worth. If they were innocent, Dexios would return to
his vineyard and hang his son's shield next to his own. If
they were guilty … he would swing the blade of execution
himself.

Nambe could not be told. He wouldn't understand. The
southerner rarely spoke of his previous master, but Dexios
had gleaned enough over the years to know that he had been
a brutal, sadistic man, prone to unprovoked acts of violence.
He had treated his slaves like any other tool he owned: used
them until they broke then thrown them aside. Nambe still
had the scars to prove it.

I will explain it to him, Dexios thought. *I will make him
see that there was no other choice. He loved Keres too.*

He raised his hand to signal to the others. "Hold! This is
close enough. We need to see what we're up against. Krinne,
you are our best scout. Get as near to the gates as you can."

The misthios practically leapt from the saddle. "Of
course, Strategos. Anything is better than spending another
minute on that flea-ridden animal."

He flashed a sign of Hera and jogged away towards the
distant plumes of smoke, his bow jingling up and down on
his back. There was little cover to be found on the plains
before the city: the verdant grasslands had suffered terribly,
the merciless summer sun and weeks of drought transforming them into a desert of brown earth dotted with rust-red
boulders and twisted olive trees.

Dexios looked around for somewhere to hitch the
mounts and found a tall rock formation shaped like a spear

tip. He looped the reins of his stallion over the top and gave the beast a rub between the ears.

"You've only had that horse for a few weeks, and by Hera, I swear you already like him more than us." Nambe had an open canteen in one hand. He offered it to Dexios who raised his helm and took a grateful sip.

"I like him. He doesn't talk much. Never complains."

"The opposite of Krinne, then."

Dexios chuckled. "He has his flaws, as do we all."

"You have been uncharacteristically silent yourself. Is something other than Keres troubling you?"

"I … no. It is hard to see Thena like this."

"I hope the vineyard was spared. If this year's grapes are lost … we will face a difficult winter."

Dexios felt a surge of guilt. He had been so focused on finding Panacea that he had not spared a single thought for his home. His wife. Nambe's family.

"We can afford to lose the harvest. And I'm sure your wife and child are fine. Melia is the basileus's daughter; he will have taken steps to keep her safe."

Melia. He had abandoned her yet again. Just like he had abandoned her after the tragedy that had caused the unmendable tear in both their hearts, the ever-widening divide that neither of them could cross.

The loss of Oneiros.

He would not fail her this time. He would not fail Keres.

Dexios took another drink of water and passed the canteen to Piraeus who was sitting with his back against a rock, his eyes half-closed.

"Can you sense Panacea?"

"Not yet. I need to be closer."

"But why—"

"Always with the questions, Strategos. I have already told you all I know. Zeus will send me a sign. And if he does not, you may exact whatever punishment upon me you see fit. Now, leave me alone."

The priest had become more and more irritable as they approached Thena. Something was bothering him. There was an uncertainty in his gaze that hadn't been there before … an uncertainty bordering on fear. Dexios had seen Piraeus pray every day since leaving the temple, often for hours on end. Had any of those prayers been answered?

He let slip a tired smile. It didn't matter. He had come too far to turn back now. If Piraeus couldn't locate Panacea, then Dexios would find them himself, even if it meant interrogating every single Thenean citizen. He took a grey-blue sharpening stone from his saddlebags and settled down on a rock to wait, stroking the length of his xiphos calmly.

By the time Krinne returned, the morning sky was no longer a pure, unblemished blue. Dark clouds had appeared on the northern horizon, creeping steadily closer. Soon the long-suffering grasslands of Thena would have the rain they so desperately craved.

"The tauros have entered Thena," the misthios said. "All except the calves and heifers who are camped to the east. I found horse tracks, too. Polydius, I reckon, unless the cows have learnt how to ride."

"Thena was always his target," Dexios agreed. "It seems logical he would want to be there to see it fall. Is the wall defended?"

Krinne shook his head. "The ramparts are empty. There are two tauros standing watch before the gates, but they are facing inwards, towards the city. I think they have been posted there to stop people from getting out rather than getting in."

"Polydius should have manned the walls. After taking a city, the first thing every good strategos should do is prepare for a counter-attack."

"Maybe he hasn't taken it yet? Maybe he's overconfident? Or, more likely, maybe he's just a half-formed pile of congealing vomit with the brains of a slug?"

"I like the third option," Nambe said, tightening the straps of his dual leather scabbards.

"Whatever the reason, he's left us with an opportunity," Dexios continued. "We'll take the horses as far as the gates. Their speed will help us conserve the element of surprise."

"What about the tauros camp?"

"We'll give it a wide berth. Hit the two tauros on guard as fast as we can, then ride on into Thena."

"Let's just hope the rest of the horde isn't waiting for us on the other side."

"I'm confident they won't be. To control Thena, Polydius will need to take the garrison and the palace. His forces should be concentrated in those two areas."

"And if Panacea is in the palace?"

"We'll cross that bridge when we come to it. There are other ways to enter the palace besides the main gates. Only a fool would not leave himself an escape route or two. Get Piraeus back onto his horse. We ride."

Dexios unhitched his stallion and laid his hand briefly on his son's shield. Soon, it would be returned to its rightful owner. A muffled curse from nearby told him that Piraeus was attempting to mount his own horse, his beard becoming entangled with the reins.

"Nambe, to my right. Krinne, stay near the priest. Make sure he keeps up. May Persephone keep us from Charon's embrace."

"May Zeus grant us victory," Piraeus added sombrely.

Dexios lowered his helm back into place. Nambe had worked wonders on the trip south, repairing the broken cheek plate and replacing most of the horsehair crest. He tapped his heels lightly on his horse's flanks and felt the beast's powerful leg muscles bunch then release as it lurched into a canter. Another tap and the canter became a gallop, hooves pounding the sun-scarred grass of the plains.

The city walls grew closer at an alarming rate. Dexios could make out numerous fires in the lower levels, but the basileus's palace still appeared untouched, shining proudly from its perch at the top of Sisyphus Hill. To his left, roughly fifty cone-like tents marked the entrance to the tauran encampment. He angled as far right as he could, passing into the shadow of the ramparts, Nambe at his side.

The huge corpse of a tauros, a javelin stuck deep in one eye, was the first evidence of Thenean resistance. Dexios's steed bounded over the obstacle with an angry snort. More dead tauros lay beyond, some bearing hoofmarks on their bodies as if they had been trampled by their own kind.

Dexios drew his xiphos, his other hand still gripping the reins. The gates were in sight, the right-hand door so badly damaged that it had been torn from its hinges. Familiar feelings of anger and battle lust rose to greet him like old friends, and he embraced them, relishing the burning sensation that spread from his chest to his limbs.

The tauros will pay for what they have done. By Hera's light, they will pay.

Two of the colossal beasts stood in the ruins of the shattered gates, just as Krinne had said, their backs to the approaching horsemen. The thunderous beating of hooves made them turn, beady eyes widening in surprise. The larger of the two, his curling horns covered in dried blood, let out a panicked bellow and began to raise his cleaver. Then Dexios was upon him, xiphos arcing down. It hit the tauros on the side of his shaggy head and rebounded with a clang, unable to penetrate the hard bone. Dexios cursed and reversed his strike, slicing through the soft flesh of the beast's cheek and biting deep into his tongue.

The tauros roared in agony and dropped his weapon, fingers probing at the gaping hole in his face. Dexios leant forwards and pressed hard into the saddle, causing his horse to rear up. Two massive hooves slammed into the tauros's chest, cracking ribs and puncturing the lungs beneath. The creature's angry cries faded to a gurgle as he fought to draw breath. With a final gasping wheeze, he collapsed.

Nambe had already dispatched the second tauros with a precise cut to the throat. Dexios peered into the courtyard beyond, half-obscured by smoke. No more enemies lay in wait, only dozens upon dozens of dead Theneans; mauled, bludgeoned, and broken. Many he recognised: reservists spared the horrors of the phalanx only to die here, protecting their city.

His eyes alighted on the crumpled form of Crenate, one arm torn from its socket, the other still grasping a bloody xiphos. The 'theta' emblem on his linothorax was miraculously unsullied, perhaps a sign from the Gods that Thena was not yet defeated.

Dexios walked his horse slowly into the courtyard and dismounted, reverently closing Crenate's staring eyes. The corpse's skin was still warm under his touch. "May you find peace in Tartarus, Captain," he said softly. "I hope your shade will be guided to that of your son."

"These men died recently," Nambe said. "We are not too late! We can still help save Thena! Let us make for the palace and lend our strength to those who defend it!"

The palace. Letho. Melia. His wife might be in danger. He promised …

Dexios looked up to see Krinne and Piraeus passing through the gates. The priest was smiling. He caught sight of Dexios and nodded, pointing to the north. Away from the palace.

Who do I save? My wife, or my son?

He remembered his promise to her. As they lowered the body of Oneiros into the ground. As he held her in his arms, stroking her hair, swearing through his tears.

That it would never happen again.

That they would never lose another child.

Keres. It had to be Keres.

"I cannot go, Nambe," he said. "Not when I am so close to reviving my son. But *you* can. Take Krinne with you. Piraeus and I will search for Panacea."

The misthios frowned. "That's not the best of ideas, Strategos. I have yet to see even a single drachma of the money you owe. What if you get yourself killed before you are able to pay me?"

Dexios shook his head at the absurdity of the situation.

"If I die, my wife inherits all I own," he said. "My wife, who is trapped in the palace and who, incidentally, is the daughter of the basileus. I can assure you that saving her life will be extremely profitable."

"I will vouch for you," Nambe said. "If that is what the strategos wants." The last words were tinged with regret. The big southerner nudged his horse closer to Dexios and looked down at him sorrowfully.

"I ... I know why you are sending me away."

"Nambe ..."

"You have changed since Keres died. You have lost that part of you that helped you distinguish right from wrong. You have been keeping secrets from me, Strategos. And now you want me gone so I will not be there to witness whatever you are going to do."

Dexios removed his helm and held the other man's gaze. He was surprised to see that Nambe's eyes were filled with tears.

"I have made my choice, my friend. And I will suffer the consequences. This is how the world works. It is what the Oracle foretold. I am at peace with it."

"Then, let us confront this challenge together, as we always have."

"Not this time. This is something I must do alone."

Nambe started to reply, then stopped and shook his head sadly. "Then, may Hera guide your way, Dexios. I hope you find what you seek. Goodbye." He wheeled his horse and called to Krinne, gesturing towards the main street leading to the agora.

Dexios watched them leave.

"Goodbye, my friend."

A crackle of thunder overhead made him glance upwards. The blue sky was fighting a losing battle against the swirling grey storm clouds, the few remaining patches being slowly consumed.

"Zeus is with us," Piraeus said. His eyes were alight with the same cerulean fire as when they first met. "It is *him*, not Hera, who will light your way now, Strategos."

"Where?" Dexios asked wearily.

"Panacea is close. So close. Now is the time to unveil your son's shield. He will need it when he returns."

Dexios ignored the excited fluttering of butterflies in his belly and loosened the ties of the leather cover, freeing the hawk from its cage. The aspis gleamed as the bronze caught the last of the sunlight. Piraeus gave a self-satisfied nod. He seemed more confident somehow as if passing through the gates of Thena had restored his faith. He stepped over Crenate's body and headed for the rear of the courtyard. Dexios realised that the old man was no longer carrying his cane.

He slipped his son's shield onto his left arm and followed Piraeus into the back alleys. The priest never faltered, leading them unerringly through the warren of narrow streets until they reached a small square.

A crumbling stone fountain greeted them, dry and cracked marble topped with a worn statue of Persephone. On the far side of the square, four figures stood before the door to a large workshop. Two men and two women. One of the women turned, revealing a shock of blonde hair that Dexios recognised instantly.

"Elena," he called out. Her brow crinkled in confusion. "Dexios?"

A man pushed past her angrily. He was old and bearded, his right arm ending just below the elbow.

"Leave," he ordered. "Now."

The voice was deep and powerful, fuelled by the man's rage. It hit Dexios hard, and he took an involuntary step backwards, bumping into Piraeus.

Except it was not really Piraeus anymore. The face and eyes were the same, but the body was changing. Transforming. The crooked spine straightened with a crack of bone. Arms and legs swelled with newly-formed muscles that wriggled under the skin like worms, latching onto cartilage and tendons as they grew. Dry, wrinkled skin stretched until it was taut and smooth.

Thunder boomed across the confined space of the square, making Dexios's teeth rattle.

Piraeus now stood over seven feet tall, his chiton pressed tightly against his mesomorphic form. He raised one powerful arm skywards, and cerulescent sparks sputtered to life in the spaces between his fingers, snaking around his wrist like ivy.

Dexios looked into the priest's eyes. The irises were filled with bright blue lightning that hissed and buzzed chaotically as if looking for a way to escape its prison.

"No …"

… The Ruined were banished, exiled from Olympus, and cursed to roam the lands of Tyrris until they faded into obscurity …

… Fear of Hera leads men to pray to other Gods …

… Every desperate plea, every cry for help, fills him with energy …

… It is not a place that gives a God his power. It is people. Faith. Belief …

… And Dexios, lost in the depths of those twin glowing orbs of writhing fire, believed.

Zeus, first and greatest of the Ruined, flexed his fingers and laughed. "At last, I can show you my true face, Strategos. I did so much enjoy watching you fumble around in the dark like a blind beggar. Thinking you were in control. Now, pull yourself together. It's time to finish what we started."

He turned to Desha and grinned amiably. "Isn't that right … Brother?"

30

RESOLUTION

"The Ruined are lying, scheming, duplicitous snakes. Never to be trusted. Never to be forgiven. Olympus will not know peace until I have found a way to destroy them all. A way to tear the flesh from their treacherous bodies and grind their bones into dust. A way to make sure they can never return."

THE TEACHINGS OF HERA, VERSE 19.2

"**W**HY … WHY DID he call you brother?" Makar stammered.

"Because that's what he is," Zeus answered cheerfully. "Brother, won't you introduce me to your friends?"

Makar licked his lips. "I am his—"

"These are no friends of mine," Desha interrupted with a stern glare. "Two of Letho's lackeys. A soldier and a priestess of Hera sent to escort the sophistes and me to the palace."

"Hmmm. That's unfortunate. I am not quite ready for all of Tyrris to know of my newfound strength. The longer my dear wife is unaware of my existence, the better. That means no witnesses."

Zeus flicked his fingers. A blinding spear of pent-up energy streaked across the square, striking the head of the statue of Persephone and shattering the stone into a thousand tiny pieces.

"They are ants, Brother," Desha said. "Unworthy of your attention. Let them go. Who will they tell? To speak your name is heresy. They will not risk exile or worse by breaking the sacred law of Hera."

"Perhaps ..." Zeus frowned and took a step forwards. "Priestess ... I know you. Look at me."

Graycea raised her head and fought to hold the Ruined God's gaze, tears trickling down her face from the effort.

"You ... are one of my faithful. You have prayed to me many times."

"I have prayed to all the Gods," Graycea answered defiantly. "That doesn't mean I respect them."

"Oh, you don't have to respect us," Zeus said with an easy smile. "It is your *belief* that sustains us. Fear, love, hate, guilt, whatever emotions lead to that belief are inconsequential." He tapped a finger against his cheek in mock reflection. "However, this changes things. I am not in the habit of killing my followers. It always feels like throwing away a perfectly good amphora of wine. A waste. I gift you your lives. Stay or leave, it matters not." His voice became hard. "But do not intervene. Or I will melt the flesh from your bones."

"Liar." It was Dexios who had spoken, his eyes boiling with barely-contained fury. "What is this trickery? You *swore* you would lead me to Panacea!"

Zeus clicked his tongue in disapproval. "Careful with your choice of words, Strategos. It is not wise to insult a God. Panacea does not exist. It never did. An artefact that could cure any disease? Heal any wound? If we had the power to create such a thing, we would certainly not hide it away or leave it in the hands of mere mortals. And I would never have been forced from Olympus." He paused. "But the Oracle did not lie. She told you that I would help bring your son back from the shores of Tartarus. And I will."

"No ..." muttered Desha. "Don't do this, Brother."

"Tartarus, much like Olympus, is surrounded by a protective barrier. The barrier serves a dual purpose: to keep the living from entering the Underworld and, more importantly, to keep the shades of the deceased from leaving. It was exceptionally complex to build and maintain, even with our superior intellect. In fact, the first two attempts failed. We realised then that the only way it would work was if the barrier was intrinsically linked to one of us. My brother volunteered."

"Desha ..." Elena began.

Zeus let out a raucous boom of laughter. "Desha? Is that what you are calling yourself, Brother? Oh, the arrogance! You couldn't even give up the letters of your own name!"

"My son," Dexios growled.

"Oh, come on, Strategos, have you still not worked it out? My brother is the only one keeping Keres from you. If he is killed, the gates of Tartarus will open, and Keres will be free to return to the surface. To return to his family!"

"Desha ..." Elena repeated.

"Ssssssstay bbbbback," the old jeweller hissed through gritted teeth. Something was happening to his right arm. The knotted ball of scar tissue that formed the stump was throbbing; inflating and deflating like a beating heart. The scar was widening. Unravelling. The skin peeled back, revealing a glistening mass of crimson muscle surrounding a pulsating opening. It looked like the gory lips of a fleshy maw, slick with blood and fluid.

Desha screamed as a length of white bone exploded from the stump with a sickening squelch. The appendage bore a slight resemblance to a human forearm, with four long fingers ending in pointed claws.

Or talons.

Graycea's hand flew to her shoulder. "You!"

"Y ... yesssss," Desha said, panting hard. "You prayed to all the Gods that day ... even meeeee." His eyes flickered to Makar. "I have ... always tried to protecccct ... those I care about."

"A touching sentiment," Zeus said. "But a false one." He turned to Dexios. "You refuse to kill innocents. My brother fought to keep his place in Olympus, just as I did. Thousands upon thousands perished due to the energies we unleashed. He is a murderer. And he deserves to die."

There was another repulsive sound of tearing flesh, and four more claws pierced the soft fingertips of Desha's left arm. He sprang into the air with a snarl, sailing over the broken fountain towards his brother with his talons out-stretched. Zeus leapt aside at the very last moment, and a bony arm smashed into the paving slab where he had been standing, cracking it in half.

A ball of sputtering lightning appeared in the Ruined God's palm. He hurled it at Desha, who batted it away with a slice of his clawed hand. The missile careened wildly across the courtyard and slammed into the roof of the workshop where it exploded, showering Elena with broken tiles and dust.

"Help me!" Zeus yelled at Dexios. The strategos shook his head in confusion.

Desha charged, his left arm a blur. A horizontal cut removed most of Zeus's beard and ripped a hole in his chiton. He replied with a right hook that hammered into his brother's shoulder. Desha grunted in pain, drew his head back, and slammed his forehead into Zeus's jaw, sending him reeling.

"STRATEGOS!" Blood was streaming from the Ruined God's mouth. He winced and spat onto the stone paving. A broken molar gleamed pearly-white among the red-tinged spittle. Zeus cursed and raised his hand skywards in an attempt to gather more lightning, but Desha was already on the move, tackling his brother to the ground. A flailing talon scored a line across one cheek. A second severed the right earlobe in a spray of blood. Zeus gave an angry roar and flung Desha from him with a strength born of desperation.

The Lord of Tartarus's flight was halted by the stone fountain. His leg collided with the headless statue of Persephone and toppled it from its perch. Desha fell with it, landing on his back amid the broken remains of his former wife.

"I underestimated your strength," Zeus admitted, spitting another mouthful of blood. "There are a few who still believe in Hades, it seems." Sparks jittered down his forearm, coalescing along his fingertips. Tendrils of blue-white light whirled around in concentric circles above his palm, fusing into a burning globe of fire.

Thunder groaned. Something flashed in the angry clouds above the palace. Desha tried to rise but his leg gave way beneath him, and he collapsed again.

"There is a storm coming, Brother," Zeus said with a

gory grin. "It is nearly here. Can you hear it? The heralds of the sky rejoice at my ascension. Or, perhaps, it is a eulogy for the fallen." He raised his arm.

"NO!" Makar screamed. He tore himself away from Elena and charged at the Ruined God, his father's xiphos clutched tightly in one fist.

"MAKAR, STOP!" Elena yelled. She started after him, already knowing she would not reach him in time. Zeus turned slowly, almost lazily, to meet this new threat. He cocked his head to one side in bemusement. "What are you doing, soldier? I warned you not to interfere."

The ball of lightning took Makar full in the chest, knocking him off his feet. He rebounded twice off the stone paving and rolled to a halt ten feet from Elena, his legs twitching. The bronze breastplate had taken the full brunt of the blast and had partially melted, revealing a circle of charred flesh underneath.

Desha let out a strangled cry.

"Enough," Zeus said irritably. He stalked over to the recumbent form of his brother and dragged him by his wounded leg to where Dexios stood silently, his son's shield on one arm, his xiphos held in the other.

"Finish it. If you want to see your son again, finish it."

"I ... I cannot."

"Then, you are a coward. And a liar. You swore you would do anything. *Anything.* And now, by the will of Zeus, you have that chance."

"I ..."

"Decide. As a final courtesy, I will give you two minutes. Kill him, or it is I who will kill you and find another to do what you could not. There are plenty of grieving widows in this city who wish for nothing more than to see their children again."

Dexios cried out in pain and raised his sword, but he could not bring himself to strike. This was the line he couldn't cross. This last shred of humanity that his conscience refused to give up.

"This ... this isn't who I am."

He felt a hand paw feebly at his leg. Desha was staring up at him. He whispered something. Dexios removed his son's shield and bent down on one knee, placing the aspis face-up beside him. The Lord of Tartarus whispered again, too softly to be heard. Dexios leant as close as he dared, his ear brushing against the fallen God's mouth.

"Do it," Desha was saying. "It is the only way ... to save both your son and mine." His eyes went to Makar. "He ... is ... *fading*. A God cannot kill another God. If I die, he will inherit this gift. He will *live*. You must bring him to Tartarus. You must restore the barrier. The Oracle ... knows." He grasped the point of Dexios's xiphos and placed it on his chest. "Come, Strategos. *Harbinger*. You have done this many times before. A mercy killing. Do your duty."

"What are you mumbling about?" barked Zeus impatiently. "Enough. Decide."

"Please," Desha whispered. "Save him. *Please*."

"May Keres forgive me," Dexios said. He located the soft patch of skin under the bottom left rib and pushed. The sharp tip pierced the flesh easily, slipping under the bone. He angled diagonally upwards, slicing through the lung, severing the arteries, and puncturing the heart. Bright red blood welled from the wound, running down the iron blade and onto his wrist.

Gods can bleed, he thought absently. *And Gods can die.*

He returned his gaze to Desha, who was smiling. "Thank you," he managed to croak with some difficulty. "And tell her I was wrong ... I should have stayed."

Dexios withdrew his blade. "Tell who?"

"Per ... Persephone." His body convulsed. A myriad of conflicting emotions raced across the dying God's face. Confusion. Fear. Sadness. Hope. Then, with another jerking spasm, his jaw cracked open, and a boiling mass of dark grey steam exploded skywards like an erupting volcano. Dexios gave a startled shout and scrambled backwards, droplets of liquid burning his skin. With a snap, the jawbone dislocated itself from the rest of the skull, tearing the skin off the face as it was stretched impossibly wide.

There was a whoosh of converging energy, and the body burst into flames far brighter than any bonfire. The heat was so intense that the stone underneath began to blacken and fissure. Dexios watched, unable to look away, as hair turned to ash.

The Oracle's warning echoed in his mind, mocking and hollow.

When you are on your knees, awash in the blood of a dead God, and your heart is torn apart by grief, remember that I tried to dissuade you from this path.

Fat popped and sizzled. Flesh was sloughed from bone.

The unnatural fire was reflected in Keres's shield, making it look like the hawk was burning too.

I did this.

He felt a heavy hand on his shoulder. Zeus towered over him, his piercing blue eyes unreadable. "Needs must."

"He was your brother," Dexios replied in a bitter voice. "What kind of God butchers his own family?"

"What kind of man trades one life for another?"

Dexios looked down at the blood that stained his blade. "A … ruined one."

Zeus nodded. "You are beginning to understand. I have nothing left to lose, Harbinger. This was my last, desperate ploy. And it has succeeded. I feel it. Your son's shade is no longer trapped on the shores of Tartarus."

Keres!

"Take me to him."

Zeus's grip tightened. "That was *not* what we agreed."

Dexios felt a kernel of dread awaken deep in his gut. "I did this … all of this to be reunited with Keres. I need to see him. To be with him."

"No. That will not be possible. I have other plans."

Dexios wailed in anguish and lashed out angrily with his xiphos. Zeus tightened his grip on the strategos's shoulder. Pain coursed down his right arm, forcing him to drop his weapon.

"You dare attack me? Me! This is the gratitude you show after I have upheld my side of the bargain? After I have given your son his life back? I thought you were different, Harbinger, but you are like all men. Incapable of treating your masters with respect."

Zeus squeezed harder, making Dexios scream out loud as an intense, stinging pain raced down the length of his arm.

"I will do you one last favour. I will return your son's shield to him." Zeus strolled over to where the hawk-emblazoned aspis lay against the paving and pushed his large hand through the straps.

"NO!" Dexios cried through a haze of agony. "It is all I have to remember him by. Please."

"What would you do with it? Cover it up and forget about it as you did with your own shield? Did that work? Did it help with the death of Oneiros? Mistakes must be owned, Strategos, not hidden away. Keres will have better use of it than you."

"BASTARD!" Dexios tried to focus on the sword at his feet. If he could just get his fingers around the grip. He attempted to move his arm. Another wave of pain almost made him black out. His trembling legs could no longer hold his weight, and he stumbled, falling to the ground beside the charred corpse of the God he had killed.

Zeus smiled. "I have destroyed many for less than that, Strategos. But I am feeling magnanimous. You shall live to see me take back Olympus and return to my rightful place. Then, perhaps, when the temples of Hera have been torn down and her priestesses violated. When the followers of Artemis have been nailed to the city walls. When Aphrodite's children have been mutilated and exiled. Then I will seek you out. In the ruins of your sad, lonely life. And we will continue this conversation."

He gave a mocking half-bow and turned his back on his dead brother, raising both hands high over his head in a grim parody of the supplicating stance he had used when posing as Piraeus, the priest. A blinding bolt of lightning burst forth from above, streaking angrily earthwards and striking Zeus with a brilliant flash of energy so glaringly bright that Dexios was forced to close his eyes.

When he opened them again, Zeus was gone.

The storm clouds finally broke, releasing their gift of water over the embattled city of Thena. Dexios turned his face towards the sky and screamed. Raindrops mingled with the tears that streamed down his face.

He had failed.

31

AWAKENING

"May Persephone keep you from Charon's embrace."

THE TEACHINGS OF HERA, VERSE 1.1

THE SAND LOOKED like ash. Grey and flaky. Keres pressed down with his bare foot and watched thousands of tiny grains run through the cracks between his toes. He felt nothing. No prickly sensation on the soles of his feet. No itchiness where the sand stuck to his skin. Strange.

He pushed his hair back from his face and took stock of his surroundings. There was not much to see. A thick mist swirled lazily around his naked body, limiting his visibility to a half-dozen paces. Shadows moved within. Some appeared human, others took on strange animalistic forms. The head of a lion. The twin fangs of a snake. Coalescing and dissipating as he tried to focus on them.

Keres scratched at his neck and looked up into the pitch-black sky that hung ominously overhead. There were no stars. No moon. He blinked, forcing his eyes to adapt to the gloom. There were wrinkles in the darkness. Triangular shapes jutting outwards, like enormous teeth. Stalactites. It wasn't the sky he was looking at, but the roof of a colossal cavern.

He shifted uncomfortably. The irritating tingle in his neck was getting worse.

Gods!

Keres didn't even remember how he had arrived here. Wherever *here* was. He tried to ignore the stinging sensation and prodded at his tired brain. The phalanx. He had been standing in the phalanx. With Tychos and the others. Then …

Why was this so hard? It was like trying to remove a particularly recalcitrant splinter.

He tugged at the fleeting memory. The tauros. The shield wall. Blood and death. Trampled bodies. Broken limbs. He had … resisted. He had …

The feeling in his throat was suffocating. He coughed. Something moved. Panicking now, he coughed harder; great, wracking heaves of his chest and lungs. He thumped his torso with his fist as his breathing was reduced to short, pain-filled gasps.

Hera protect me. Don't let me die here in this forsaken place.

One last violent fit of coughing and whatever was lodged in his throat burst from his open mouth and spattered wetly onto the monochrome sands. A flash of silver.

Keres bent to pick it up with a trembling hand. An obol, stamped with the head of the basileus of Thena on one side and the letter 'theta' on the other.

A hysterical peal of laughter escaped his lips as he realised where he was.

Don't let me die here …

He was already dead. He was standing on the shores of Tartarus, and in his palm, he held the ferryman's toll.

The revelation had a surprisingly calming effect on his

addled mind. It is lack of purpose, his father had once told him, that leads to madness. Keres fingered the obol. He could feel the weight of it, but nothing else. Not the slight coolness of the metal, the embossed profile of Letho, the faint scuffs along its uneven edges. Was this death? To lose all feeling? All sense of touch?

I must find Charon, he thought, staring out into the mist. The ferryman would take him to the Halls of Judgement, and there he would have his answers.

His hand throbbed. The obol was glowing, emitting a soft, pale light. He held it out before him, and the mist fled before its brilliance. A way forward.

Keres took a deep breath and set off down the path created for him. His feet left no footprints, only fleeting indentations quickly swallowed by the sand. There was no way to retrace his steps. No going back.

He wandered for what seemed like hours, trying to ignore the multitude of shadows that flitted in and out of sight. Whenever he reached a dead end, the glowing obol pulsed brightly for an instant, and a new path opened. He began to lose all sense of direction. Without the sun or the stars to guide him, there was no way of knowing if he was getting closer to the shores of the great river and Charon's ferry. In fact, he might even be walking in circles. Round and round the same patch of sand until he collapsed from exhaustion.

He pressed on. He felt no hunger or thirst, only a slowly mounting sensation of dread as the talisman opened up yet another pathway that seemed identical to the last. Spectral forms swam in the mist. One drew his eye, larger and somehow more *tangible* than the others. It was moving towards him.

His hand reached mechanically for the xiphos slung under his left armpit before he remembered that he was weaponless … and clothesless.

"Charon's balls," he swore aloud, fully aware of the irony behind using that particular curse in his present location. He spared a glance over his shoulder. The pathway behind him had already been reclaimed by the rolling mists.

Are you afraid? The voice popped unbidden into his head. It was very similar to his own but sounded more confident. And smug.

"I'm naked and alone on the shores of Tartarus," retorted Keres. "Of course, I'm afraid!"

Of what exactly? You are already dead.

"I … shut up." He held out his glowing obol like a shield and cried out a challenge. "Shadow! Fiend! I see you! Lurking in the ether like a coward. Come out and face me!"

"Keres? Is that you?"

"Ty … Tychos?"

"Aye."

The stonemason's son stepped naked and blinking into the light. Keres's face split into a grin so wide it made his cheeks hurt. "My friend. It both pains me and brings me great joy to see you here. I was beginning to go mad." He put his arms around Tychos and pulled him close. They stayed entwined for a moment, then Keres released him with a sigh of frustration and looked down at his hands.

"I can see you and touch you, but I cannot *feel you*," he said, waggling his fingers. "Or smell your scent. It is as if you are both there and not there. Is this to be our fate?"

"I can imagine worse," Tychos replied with a smile that became a spluttering cough. He bent over, wheezing, and Keres saw a large circular welt on his friend's back. A badly-healed exit wound from a spear.

K'vath.

"You … saved me," he said, remembering. "You stood alone against that … monster."

Tychos shuffled his feet awkwardly. "You would have done the same. And I didn't really save you, did I? Only delay the inevitable by a few minutes."

"You're not wriggling your way out of this. It was one of the kindest things anyone has ever done for me. Accept the compliment."

"I—" Another heaving cough. "Gods. My throat is on fire. What in Tartarus happened to me?"

"The tauros pierced your lung, Tychos. You drowned in your own blood."

"There's something stuck in there. I can't get it out."

Keres held up his obol. "It must be Charon's toll. Hold on." He gave Tychos a few strong blows on the back with the heel of his hand. "It's stuck. Lean forwards." Locking his arms around his friend's waist, he jerked upwards and inwards five times. The final abdominal thrust was enough to expel the tiny disc, which span like a miniature comet through the mist to land on the grey sand.

"May Hera bless you," Tychos said fervently, bending to pick up his obol, which was already beginning to glow.

"Its light is leading us somewhere," Keres explained. "Although I'm not quite sure where."

"Anywhere is better than here."

"The legends beg to differ. There are places in Tartarus

where the shades of the damned are strapped to an ever-revolving ring of fire. Or crushed by falling rocks. Or torn apart by carrion."

"Only those who have been judged unworthy to enter Elysium."

"Exactly. They won't even need to use the scales for you. One look at the long list of your misdeeds and they'll be calling for the vultures."

Tychos made an obscene gesture and waved his obol around until a section of the mist retreated. "Most of those *misdeeds* were with you," he retorted, walking away so fast that Keres had to do a half-skip to catch up.

"Ah, but I was not the instigator. I will argue that I fell prey to your inescapable wiles and charm."

"Right. Like when you filled Galleas's helm with raw eggs."

"They were *your* eggs. You shouldn't have left them lying around."

"Or that other time ..."

Keres relaxed as the familiar drone of his friend's voice washed over him, numbing the pain in his throat. His hand snaked out and found Tychos's. They plodded ever onwards, bare feet sinking into the sand, making twin footprints that disappeared moments later. The shores of Tartarus were no longer intimidating. They were inconsequential, merely part of the journey that was leading to somewhere far greater.

He was in the middle of explaining a particularly elaborate prank that he had played on Nambe the previous summer when his right foot suddenly sank into the ground as far as his knee. He gave a cry of surprise and would have toppled over if Tychos hadn't been holding his hand.

"What in Tartarus?"

"Water," his friend said.

Keres frowned and looked down. His leg was immersed in a sluggish black liquid, so dark and thick that he couldn't see his toes. They had reached the banks of a river or large pool of some kind, stretching away as far as the eye could see until it became indistinguishable from the cavern roof.

"I ... can't feel it. No sensation of wetness. No cold. It's just like the sand."

"Huh." Tychos released his friend and cupped some of the strange water in his hand, watching with undisguised fascination as it dribbled between his fingers. "You're right. Nothing. My eyes are showing me something that my mind refuses to believe."

"You always were an idiot." The deep voice made them both whirl around. Helydices emerged from the fog, an obol clenched in one massive fist. His naked body was covered in purple bruises and what appeared to be hoof marks, as if he had been trampled by a horde of tauros. And maybe he had.

"Praise Hera," Tychos said, his voice cold. "For if you are here, then there is some justice after all."

The big man's forehead scrunched tightly. The muscles in his jaw clenched and unclenched.

We can take him, Keres thought. *Both of us together. Knock him into the water.*

"I meant what I said in the phalanx," Helydices said slowly as if uttering the words caused him pain. "I was wrong. It's just ... you were both always the centre of attention. Sophistes Elena adored you. Galleas praised you. I had nothing."

"You broke my arm!" Tychos exclaimed.

"I know … it was so hot that day. The heat, it gets to me … does something to my temper. Everything turns a shade of red, and I forget who I am. Keres … I never meant for that man to hurt you. I just wanted you to lose the race. To be forced to watch from the sidelines for once while I had all the glory."

Keres shook his head. "You're not making a very good case for yourself, Helydices."

"It was difficult. My father was … difficult. It has taken me a while to realise that wanting to grow up to be like him is not the same as wanting to grow up to be an honourable man."

"You cannot blame your father for your own mistakes."

"That's not what I meant, I— Hera's tits, what in Tartarus's name is *that*?"

A boat was approaching out of the dark, its prow cutting through the quiet stillness of the river. Its figurehead was a giant skull of bleached bone, and its empty eye sockets were fixed on the shoreline. Two rows of cracked teeth formed a misshapen grin. Twin shoulder blades arched down from the figurehead to form the bow, and enormous skeletal arms made up the hull, stretching back to the stern of interlocked fingers.

"How … how does it float?" Keres stammered, watching with mounting apprehension as the craft approached.

"Never mind that," Tychos said. "It shouldn't even be able to move! There are no sails! No tiller!"

"… and no captain," finished Helydices. He made the sign of Hera, almost dropping his obol. "It is Charon's ferry, come to take us to the Halls of Judgement."

"Then, where is Charon?" asked Keres.

The words had barely left his lips when two balls of flame burst into life in the skull's eye sockets. Its jaw cracked open, and a deep voice, as cold and as heavy as a tombstone, echoed from its tongueless mouth.

"Toll."

The legends had been wrong. Charon had never been the ferryman. He was the ferry *itself*, a fleshless automaton brought to life by the Gods.

Keres shivered, his shade feeling something for the first time since awakening on the shores of Tartarus. His obol quivered in his hand, and he unclenched his fist. With a grinding of bone, the huge skull turned towards him. The burning fires flared greedily.

"Embark."

Charon was less than ten feet away now. He drifted to a halt and waited, motionless. Either there was no current, waves, or wind … or the same magic that drove the boat forward countered any pitch or yaw, allowing him to remain perfectly still.

"What should we do?" Keres asked, eyeing the living craft with some trepidation.

"Surely you can't be contemplating staying on the shores of Tartarus for all eternity?" Tychos replied.

"I … I don't know. How can we be certain that Charon is taking us to the Halls of Judgement? He is proof that what we have been taught about the Underworld cannot be trusted. Who's to say there aren't other mistakes?"

"Maybe." Tychos didn't sound so sure. "I suppose if you decide to stay here, I will follow your lead. But eternity is a long time to spend with someone, Keres, even if it is you."

"You're both mad," Helydices said. "I'm going." He jumped into the water and began to wade towards the ferry.

"Well, what do you think, Keres? Maybe those vultures aren't that bad?"

"There's only one way to find out."

Helydices had reached one of Charon's log-sized humeri and was pulling himself over the side. The bottom of the boat was a mass of fused ribs, the keel a knotted line of vertebrae.

KERES.

The voice was like thunder. It erupted into his mind with such a detonating force that he cried out from the pain.

COME TO ME.

He screamed. Each syllable was a nail piercing his flesh. He dropped to his knees, the obol falling from his fingers.

"Keres?" Tychos's worried face hovered on the edge of his vision.

"Can you not hear it?"

"Hear what?"

COME. NOW.

It was too much. Keres tipped back his head and let out a terrible howl of agony. His eyes burned. He slammed his eyelids shut.

Athena, bless us with your wisdom. Artemis, guide our hand. Persephone, keep us from Charon's embrace. Hera, grant us your strength.

He recited the prayer over and over, clinging to it like a lifeline in a sea of pain.

Suddenly, it vanished.

He felt a cool wind on his cheeks.

"Ah, you are awake. Stubborn bastard, aren't you?"

It was the voice from his mind, although this time the words were spoken calmly, soothingly. Keres took a deep breath and opened one eye.

He was lying on his back in the mud, dressed in a blood-stained linothorax, his greaves pinching his calves, and a bandolier digging into his left armpit. A figure stood looking down at him, tall and muscular. In one hand it held a bronze aspis, its centre decorated with a hawk. Diving from the heavens to save him. Or damn him.

"Who …" Keres tried to say, but it came out as a weak croak. His tongue was stuck to the roof of his mouth. His neck was bruised and swollen. His legs refused to move. He could only lie there and stare at the man who had revived him. No, not the man.

At the God. At the Ruined God.

"Gather your strength, young Keres. And rejoice! For you have the honour of being chosen to stand in my phalanx. You will be the tip of the spear that pierces the Citrine Wastes and opens the path to Olympus. And then …"

Zeus let the shield drop to the ground.

"Then you will bear witness to the punishment enacted on those who dared to defy the greatest of all immortals."

32

GARRISON

"A soldier's work is never done. Even when all the wars have ended, the phalanx still remembers his name. As long as he can still stand. As long as he can still wield sword and shield in the defence of others. As long as he can still draw breath. The phalanx remembers his name."

CERBRIONES, 'ALALAGMOE'

"DEXIOS!" THE STRATEGOS was still on his knees, oblivious to Elena's enraged shouts. She scowled and stalked over to him. Rain plinked off his battered breastplate and darkened his crimson cloak.

"We have to do something!" she snapped. "The enemy are still in the city! Makar is grievously wounded. We need you!"

Dexios shook his head. "He has taken my son from me. I will never see him ag—"

"Malaka! You're worse than Crenate! I'm sick of all you selfish, self-centred men! Half of Thena has lost someone they loved. You are no different from them. What about the ephebes? *My* ephebes. Boys pretending to be men … Many have given their lives to try and keep this place safe." She wiped an angry tear from her cheek. "And Galleas, who helped me secure my position as sophistes, who had promised to take me riding. Needlessly butchered. Gods, Dexios, that man was probably the closest person I had to a father! Don't you understand? We all have people to grieve for. But the dead can wait. The living cannot."

"Look." Elena pointed at Makar. Graycea was trying to remove the fallen ephebe's thorakes, her tired fingers fumbling at the straps that held the battered armour closed.

"You can still help these people. You are a strategos. You know how to lead. So, *lead*. Tell us what to do. How can we survive this?"

Dexios tried to raise his right arm and winced. His gaze wandered to the blackened stain on the cobbles that was all that remained of Desha ... Hades, his ashes already washed away by the rain.

"The way I see it, we have two choices," he said slowly. "The main gate is ... was poorly guarded. We might be able to flee the city that way. Use the horses I left there to cross the border. The other option is to try and make it to the palace ... if it is still under Letho's control."

"Makar needs a physician," Elena said. "Half the flesh of his chest is charred meat."

"Boena is only a day's ride away."

Graycea cut in irritably. "He doesn't have a day. Frankly, it's a miracle he's still breathing. If we leave Thena, he'll die."

"I'm ... I'm not entirely sure about that."

"What do you mean?"

"Desha. Hades. Whatever you want to call him. He believed his death would help Makar live. Something about a God not being able to kill another God."

"And you trusted him? The Lord of the Underworld? A murderer?"

"He killed to protect his son," Elena countered. "To

protect me. And if I remember your story correctly … to protect you."

Graycea rubbed at her shoulder. "Perhaps you are right. But I would not bet this young man's life on it. I vote for the palace."

Dexios picked up his fallen xiphos, dried it as best he could with the edge of his cloak, and sheathed it carefully. The pain in his arm was subsiding to a dull throb. "My friends have gone to the palace. If my wife has any sense, she'll have fled there too. Elena?"

"The palace it is. Maybe the tauros will have done me a favour and killed Derka for me."

"The house slave? What …"

"A joke, Dexios. It was a stupid joke. How are we going to get Makar there?"

"This is Desha's workshop, right? There must be something inside that can be used as a stretcher."

It only took them a few minutes to find a couple of wooden poles and some large sheets. They lifted Makar as slowly as they dared. He had still not regained consciousness; his breathing was so shallow that Elena had to lean close to his mouth to listen for the ragged intake of air. Her eyes fell on the horrendous wound in his chest. Something gave her pause. Did it seem … smaller somehow? Ringed by a band of shiny pinkish skin that reminded her of Galleas's bald pate when he spent too long in the sun. Was it … healing?

"Praise Hera," she murmured, knowing deep down that Hera had nothing to do with it. This was the work of another God.

A Ruined God.

Dexios took his place at the front of the stretcher,

leaving Graycea and Elena to share the load at the opposite end. They entered the labyrinthian warren of backstreets once more, angling north-west towards Sisyphus Hill and the palace. The heavy rain slowed to a petulant drizzle, just enough to keep the cobbles damp and slippery. Elena cursed as her sandal splashed into a large puddle of rainwater.

A distant scream from somewhere back the way they had come reminded them that they were not alone.

"My old bones can't take much more of this," Graycea grumbled as they emerged by the temple of Hera.

"They won't have to," Dexios replied. "We're minutes away from the palace. Up the slope past the garrison."

The garrison! thought Elena. The survivors from the battle at the gatehouse had surely fled there. She looked towards the top of the hill for some sign of life but it was shrouded in a layer of thick smog; the result of the rain extinguishing the fires that had raged across the city.

"We were told to retreat to the garrison if the wall was breached," she said to Dexios.

The strategos glanced back over his shoulder. "That was foolish. It's a parade ground, not a fortress."

"But … if the main gates were closed …"

"The garrison gates? Impressive from a distance, but they're half-rotten and infested with all manner of termites. A donkey could kick those doors in. And on the other side … a wide, open space with no cover, no elevation, and no way out. A death trap."

Elena bit her lip so hard it hurt. *Gods!*

The sound of tearing fabric made her turn. The awning of one of the nearby stalls had given way under the weight of too much rainwater. Dirty brown liquid cascaded onto leather bracelets, tiny statues of Hera, and painted kylikes, sweeping them off their display stands and sending them clattering to the ground. A decorated cup rolled away from the debris, coming to a stop beside Elena's right foot. Two compellingly lifelike eyes had been worked into the horizontal handles. Persephone. The watcher. Offering her protection against the horrors of Tartarus.

Graycea caught sight of the kylix and gave a haggard smile. "May Persephone keep us from Charon's embrace."

"We should go," Elena said uneasily. "The sound may attract unwanted attention."

They started up the slope. The angle of their ascent meant that Elena was now supporting most of Makar's weight. The wooden pole rubbed painfully against her palms and banged against the top of her thighs. From the sound of Graycea's laboured breathing, she wasn't faring any better.

The garrison, Elena thought. *The garrison, then the palace, and safety.*

It was the smell that first alerted her to the fact that something was wrong. Indescribable yet strangely familiar. It pulled forth a memory from four or five years ago. A house slave had called her to the garrison kitchens; a rat had been discovered in one of the half-empty amphorae of grain. The rodent had managed to crawl inside but had then found itself trapped, unable to scale the smooth interior. It had panicked, fouling the grain with its droppings, and scouring the baked clay with its claws over and over again before perishing from fright and exhaustion. The stench that had assailed Elena's nostrils when she had entered the kitchens was the same as what she smelt now. A nose-wrinkling concoction of fear, faeces, panic, and death.

As they rounded another bend, the garrison gates came into view — or what was left of them. One of the doors had a huge cleaver embedded in the rotting wood while the second had been torn completely from its hinges and lay discarded on the path in front of them.

"Wait here," Dexios warned, carefully lowering his end of the stretcher.

"Surely you're not going inside?" Graycea asked.

"There may be people who need my help."

"Or tauros. Or Ruxians. We need you too."

Dexios hesitated. "I … I have to do this. I'm sorry. These are my men. My command. If I don't return, try and make it to the palace without me."

"I'm going with you," Elena said, pushing several loose strands of wet blonde hair back behind her ears.

"Sophistes …"

"It was my home for seven years, Dexios. I'm coming."

He stared at her. "Fine. But you stay behind me and do exactly as I say. Agreed?"

"Agreed."

They found two dead tauros lying before the broken gates. One had half a spear protruding from his snout, the other was missing his head. Dexios bent to touch the closest corpse.

"Nearly cold," he said quietly to Elena. "This isn't recent." He drew his xiphos and stepped gingerly over the mound of flesh. They passed through the gates and out onto the training field. The rank smell of the dead was overpowering.

"Gods," murmured Elena sadly. The ground was covered with fallen Theneans. Another senseless massacre. Another stunning defeat.

"They fought," Dexios said. "They tried."

The positions of the bodies told a sorry tale. A half-dozen unarmoured men close to the entrance with bloody wounds on their backs, caught unawares by the speed and ferocity of the tauran attack. Thirty feet away, there was evidence that a shield wall had been formed, bolstered by the arrival of hoplites from the Thenean phalanx, well-trained in the use of spear and aspis.

The wall appeared to have held, at least at first, then slowly the defenders had been pushed back. A trail of shattered weapons and trampled corpses led across the field past the statue of Cerbriones to the very far end where, with nowhere else to go, they had attempted some sort of last stand.

So many dead, Elena thought. *Soldiers who had survived the trip north to Ruxia or the tauran assault on the gates only to be forced to face the enemy again.*

"My father used to tell me that it takes courage to brave the unknown," Dexios said, sensing her thoughts. "He was right, but I have come to believe it takes even more courage to live through the terrible horrors that war can bring and yet still find the strength to stand in the ranks of the phalanx once more. These were honourable men. Brave men."

"Why is Ruxia doing this to us?" Elena demanded. "What have we ever done to them?"

"That's not how it works. There is no justice. No balance. Greed and arrogance are motives enough. Will you be all right to stay here while I check inside the buildings?"

She nodded absently. Dexios moved away, his sandals making a wet squishing sound. A door opened and closed. The door to her classroom, where only a month ago she was preparing the students for the ephebic trials. She could almost hear the ghostly echo of Keres's boyish laughter. Helydices's grunting expletives. Makar's constant apologies. Young, promising lives cut short by a Ruxian blade or a tauran axe.

A flicker on the edge of her vision, near one of the oak trees. Her heart beat a litany of hope. Then it happened again, and she realised it was only the wind ruffling the horsehair plume of a fallen lochagos helmet, protected from the rain by the tree's stretching branches.

The door banged, heralding Dexios's return. "Nothing," he said.

"More bodies?"

"No. Nothing at all. The place is empty."

"That's … strange. Letho said the garrison was to be used as an infirmary. Where are the wounded? Come to think of it, where is the rest of the phalanx? Several hundred men survived the battle in the north. There aren't that many here."

"Indeed," Dexios agreed, scratching at his beard. "Maybe they managed to escape somehow?"

"Or the tauros took them prisoner."

"It's a possibility. The palace should hold the answers we seek."

"We're just going to leave the fallen here?"

"A wise woman once told me that the dead can wait."

"If I was really that wise, I would have been on the first cart to Boena as soon as Polydius turned up on our doorstep begging for help."

The expression on Dexios's face told Elena that her words had caused him pain. "I'm sorry … I didn't mean to …"

"It's just … I thought I knew him," the strategos said with a disbelieving shake of his head. "I trusted him. He was always ambitious … but this?"

"No one could have predicted his betrayal, Dexios. Not even you. Do not torment yourself with past mistakes."

He smiled briefly. "More wise words?"

"I'm a good sophistes. Let's get back to Graycea."

They found the old priestess sitting on the remains of the wooden door, deep in conversation with Makar. He gave a tentative wave.

"You're awake!" Elena exclaimed happily.

"I don't understand it, either," Graycea agreed, prodding a bony finger at the boy's chest. "I could fit my entire fist into that wound. Now, look at it."

A pink circle of new skin covered most of Makar's torso, punctured in its centre by a small hole the size of an olive.

"It doesn't hurt," he said.

His voice has changed, Elena realised. He sounds more … confident. More in control. She studied him curiously. There was a firmness in his jaw that hadn't been there before. A fleck of iron in his eyes. Like his father. What exactly had Hades done?

"Can you walk?" Dexios asked.

"Aye. Um … Is it true, Strategos? Is my father … gone?"

"He is. I am sorry. He died protecting you."

"How? How did he die?"

"I …" Dexios trailed off helplessly. He shot a pleading look at Elena.

"It's complicated," she said. "Let's get to the palace first. I can't stand being in these soaked clothes for much longer."

Makar looked like he was going to say something else,

but then he shrugged and nodded. They walked the last few hundred feet to the top of Sisyphus Hill to stand before the basileus's fortified palace. The gates were firmly closed and the guards conspicuously absent.

"No dead bodies, at least," Dexios said. "A reassuring sign." He walked up to the door and hammered on the wood with the pommel of his xiphos.

"This is Strategos Dexios. Let me in, I have women and walking wounded with me."

Silence.

He tried again. "There are no marks on the gate. No tauran corpses. By all accounts, you are probably the last line of defence in this Gods-forsaken town."

A clinking of metal.

"I can hear you moving around in there! I am the basileus's son-in-law! Open the gates now, unless you wish to be the one who explains to Letho why you left his family outside to die!"

There was the sound of a heavy iron bar being levered from its supports. One of the doors creaked open, and Elena spied a familiar face framed in the sliver of light beyond.

Gods!

"Apologies," droned Derka. "We had to be sure it wasn't a trick. Praise Hera you are returned to us at last."

FREEDOM

"What Hera did for mankind was courageous, yes. But true sacrifice is not simply giving your life to save another. It is abandoning your dreams. It is turning away from everything you have been working towards. It is casting aside years of planning and hard work. True sacrifice is forgetting who you are so that you can become someone else. Someone the world needs."

GRAYCEA, PRIESTESS OF HERA

DEXIOS PUSHED PAST Derka into an empty courtyard. "Where are the palace guard? Where are Nambe and Krinne?"

The house slave straightened his chiton. "If you would follow me, Strategos. The basileus awaits you in the central gardens. He will explain."

They followed the dour-faced man to Letho's botanical haven. It had lost nothing of its beauty since Elena had last visited. Tasteful arrangements of late-blooming summer flowers filled her vision. Verdant leaves sparkled as the light reflected off pearl-like water droplets left from the recent rainfall. A pair of squabbling cuckoos flitted past, landing on the outstretched arm of a marble statue of Hera.

A paradise, Elena thought. *Oblivious to the world collapsing around it.*

Towards the rear of the garden, the basileus sat with his back to them.

"Letho," Dexios called, his sandals crunching up the gravel path. "What in Tartarus is going on here? Have you not heard? The main gate has fallen! The garrison is destroyed. We must regroup. Send scouts into the city. Organise the palace guard. Letho!"

The basileus turned, and Elena recoiled at the raw pain in his eyes. "I am sorry," he whispered. "I tried to stop them … I tried to resist … I wanted to warn you … but there is no escape. No escape for me." He raised his arms, and Elena gave an involuntary shriek. Both of Letho's hands had been severed at the wrists, the mutilated stumps crudely bound and covered in black sticky tar.

No no no no.

Elena felt the green walls of the garden close in on her. This was not a haven. It was a prison. She spun on her heel with a sob of despair.

I have to get out.

Polydius stood blocking the exit, surrounded by his fellow Ruxians and wearing a look of undisguised triumph.

"I just couldn't *stand* him fidgeting with his rings. Always twisting and twiddling. It was driving me insane, truly. The fingers had to go."

"What have you done?" Elena gasped. "Galleas … Letho … This is not war, Polydius. It is pure sadism. Unjustified *torture*. How can Xenokrates have sanctioned this?"

"Xenokrates? That old bag of bones? He only told me to take the city. Or tried to, anyway. Poor fool has lost most of his teeth, I can barely understand a word he says. The rest is all me."

"You … decapitated Galleas."

"He deserved it. He always treated me like piss, even when I became lochagos. I came second in all three of the ephebic trials, did you know that? Any other year and I would have had three laurels on my shield. I am a better soldier than Dexios will ever be, and yet, when the time came to choose a new strategos, Letho favoured the bastard who was sleeping with his daughter. The years of mockery and falsehoods I've been forced to endure with a smile on my face. Forced to leave my own city. *My city.* I prayed every night to Hera for vengeance, and now, at last, my prayers have been heard. I—"

"RUN!" yelled Dexios. He charged past Elena in a flurry of crimson and bronze and leapt at Polydius with his xiphos thrust before him like a spear. The other man's military reflexes saved his life. He was turning away as the blade came down, and the iron tip drilled into his armoured shoulder instead of his exposed neck. Dexios lent into the blow and with a squeal of protesting metal, the xiphos broke through the bronze and sank deep into the flesh beyond.

"MALAKA!" Polydius screamed. Dexios twisted and pulled. The weapon came free in a spray of bright red blood.

"TAKE HIM! TAKE HIM ALIVE!"

Polydius scrabbled madly backwards, clutching at his wounded shoulder. A dozen Ruxians drew their swords. Elena wanted to scream in frustration. Despite Dexios's diversion, the only way out was still blocked. There was nowhere to go.

"Sophistes," whispered Letho urgently. He beckoned at

her with a tar-blackened stump. "The medallion around my neck. Help me remove it, please. Quickly!" Elena saw a glint of silver and pulled hard at the fine chain. It was a simple trinket, one that could be found at any number of stalls in the agora. Two carved hands locked together.

"The sign of Hera. What good is this?"

There was a cry of pain from behind her as Dexios scored a hit on one of the Ruxians, forcing them back.

"Undo the hinge at the back and the fingers will form a key. Remember when I took you to the silo? The second door. The medallion will open it. From there, a tunnel will lead you out into the north-western hills."

"I … Letho you have to come with us."

The basileus raised his mutilated hands. "I would only slow you down. Besides, my daughter is still here. I couldn't reach her in time. The house slave and the misthios, too. I will stay and do what I can to help them. Maybe we can undermine Polydius from the inside. There is hope for Thena yet."

Another cry, this time from Dexios himself. Blood was trickling from a deep gash in his sword arm. The Ruxians were slowly attempting to encircle him.

"Graycea! Makar!" Elena shouted. "With me!" She turned back to Letho. "Thank you. We will not forget this."

He gave a derisive sniff. "I don't care about that. What I want is for you to carry word of what has happened here to every single one of our allies. Let them crush this ignorant bastard to a pulp. Oh, and Elena?"

"Yes?"

"My guest in the silo. He has suffered enough. The medallion will release him."

Elena nodded, leant forwards, and kissed him on the cheek.

"May Hera give you strength," she said and beckoned to Graycea and Makar who were hunkered down behind a marble bench.

"We're leaving. Through the tunnels."

"What about Dexios?" Makar asked with a nervous glance at the strategos who was bleeding from a dozen cuts. As they watched, he tore his cloak from his shoulders and threw it at one of the Ruxians, blinding him. The iron xiphos sang, and the man keeled over backwards, the cloak stained a brighter shade of red.

"He has made his choice," Elena said. "And given us a chance. Let's not waste it." She set off without waiting for a reply, pushing through the leaves at the end of the garden. She was surprised to find that she remembered the way to the silo with near-perfect clarity. In fact, everything had started to feel clearer recently. She looked down at her hands. Flat and steady. They had not been like that for a long time. Not since she had begun stupidly pissing her entire livelihood away on shoddy cups of wine that smelt like vinegar and tasted even worse.

"Are you sure this is the right way?" Graycea asked. "All these corridors look the same."

"Positive," Elena replied just as they reached the nondescript door that would lead them to their freedom. A distant cheer of triumph signalled Dexios's defeat.

"They'll be after us now! Come on!" She hurried to the top of the ladder and descended as fast as she dared, quickly followed by Graycea and the jeweller's son.

"Makar! There should be torches doused in pitch and

a flint around here somewhere. Give me some light. There is a … man in the room beyond. One of the assassins that your father prevented from killing the basileus. We are to set him free."

She steeled herself and opened the prison door. The disfigured occupant turned his head towards the sound and let out a pitiful mewling from between his stitched-up lips.

"You do not know me," Elena said, cursing inwardly as her voice warbled like a frightened child. "But I have come to set you free. Do not attempt to attack me. I am here with two … three armed guards. One word from me and they will cut you down. Nod if you understand."

The assassin's head bobbed frantically.

"Are you sure this is a good idea?" hissed Graycea.

"Probably not, but it's what the basileus wants. I think we owe him, for this at least."

"Hera protects," the priestess murmured, taking a cautious step back.

Elena undid the clasp holding the twin hands of the medallion closed, rearranging the fingers to form a key. She slipped it easily into the lock and with a click that resonated around the cramped confines of the cell, the manacles sprang open.

The assassin fell to the ground, salty tears leaking from beneath his sewn-up eyelids. He burbled something indecipherable.

Elena ignored him, retrieving the key, and hurrying to the closed door at the other end of the cell. She thrust the medallion into the lock, twisted sharply to the right, and let out a relieved sigh when the door swung open.

Derka was waiting for her on the other side, a thin-lipped

smile plastered on his cadaveric face. He slapped her hard across the face.

"Bitch."

His foot lashed out, whipping her off her feet.

"Did you really think I would let you leave?" he snarled in an uncharacteristic display of emotion. "My new benefactor would not be pleased." He kicked Elena in the ribs.

"Let ... us ... go."

"Thirty years of my life I gave to that slug. Thirty years of being treated like dirt. Thena would have collapsed into anarchy if it hadn't been for me. Balancing the books. Offering advice on lucrative investments. *I* was the one who made Letho rich. Yet still, he refused to release me. Thousands of drachmae in his pocket and he would not let me go. Well, now I am free."

A second kick connected with Elena's stomach, and she vomited noisily.

"Hidden passageways ... Pfff. How do you think he built these tunnels? Who ordered the doors? The locks? Who paid the workers? I found this place a day after he signed the contracts. Malaka."

Makar rushed in, hoping to blindside him. Derka sidestepped the boy's clumsy lunge and punched him hard in the gut.

"Ridiculous," he muttered with a shake of his head. "This is why I let Polydius and his allies into the palace. It is time for change. For Thena to have a strong leader, one who is not afraid to get his hands dirty. To cull the weak so that the strong will thrive. To—"

The assassin crashed into Derka with a nightmarish wail, knocking him to the ground. Skeletal fingers found the house slave's eyes and pressed down hard, eliciting an agonising scream.

Makar pulled Elena to her feet. "We have to go. *Now*."

She nodded numbly, head whirling. There was a horrendous squelching sound as Derka's eyeballs burst under the pressure. Gelatinous fluid ran down his cheeks. The house slave whimpered like a child.

"Into the tunnel," Makar insisted, shoving Elena through the door. She gave one last horrified look at Derka and fled, scraping her arm on the roughly-hewn rock. Makar followed, his torch spitting and crackling. Graycea slammed the door closed, and they heard the lock snap back into place.

"Charon's *balls*," she said with feeling. "I don't want to spend a moment more in this Gods-forsaken place. Feckless men and their feckless secrets. There is not enough room in Tartarus to house them all."

"It shouldn't be far," Elena said, peering into the darkness. Makar held his torch aloft, and they ventured deeper into the tunnel. It wasn't long before they could feel the faint caress of fresh air on their faces. A distant pinprick of light grew into the mouth of a small cave.

Elena was the first to emerge, blinking, into the daylight. Letho had spoken the truth: they were about a third of the way up one of the hills that bordered the north-western edge of the city. The thick grey clouds were dissipating, allowing a few meek rays to slip through the gaps.

"We are free," she said happily, turning her head skywards, relishing the warmth on her face.

Makar gave a bitter laugh. "Free? Perhaps *you* are, but

I am still shackled to my father's legacy. There will never be any escape from that."

Graycea frowned. "Do you not understand what he has gifted you? It is a great honour—"

"*Honour*? It is a burden. I can feel its weight even now, pressing me into the dirt."

"But ... you are to become a God!"

"You say that as if it was a blessing! What have the Gods ever done for us? What have they brought us apart from pain and suffering? The only two Gods I have seen in the flesh were arrogant, selfish bastards so focused on their own well-being that they were oblivious to the damage they caused. How many men did my father murder to protect his secret? Why didn't he help us against the tauros instead of hiding away like a coward? And what about Zeus? He could have saved Thena! Instead, he damned us all."

Graycea threw up her hands and stalked away, muttering angrily.

"You are right," Elena said quietly once she had gone. "The decision is yours, and yours alone. You stand at a fork in the road, Makar. To the left lies a path of freedom. You can abandon your legacy. Flee to one of the neighbouring poleis and return to your normal life. Be a jeweller. Be a soldier. Be whoever you want to be. Tartarus will remain unprotected. The Underworld will have no Lord. The shades will find no peace. But you, at least, will be content."

Her voice grew hard. "To the right lies the other path. The more difficult path. We find Tartarus. We brave the shores of the dead and the Halls of Judgement. We reunite you with your mother and complete your ascension. You will become a God, and the barrier will be restored. And yet ...

you don't have to be the God your father was. You can make your own rules based on your own values. You can be the one that brings change to the Pantheon. And to Tyrris."

Makar licked his lips. His newfound confidence had vanished, and he looked once again like the scared, wide-eyed ephebe who had fumbled his way through a year of Elena's teaching. He took a deep breath and gazed out over Thena.

"You … you said *we*," he said finally.

"What?"

"*We* find Tartarus … *We* reunite you …"

"Of course, Makar. You didn't think I was going to abandon you, did you? If you choose the harder path, we will walk it together."

He turned to her, fresh tears streaming down his cheeks. She went to him wordlessly and took him in her arms.

"Tartarus," he said. "I choose Tartarus. On one condition."

"Tell me."

"Once I become a God, once the shades of the dead can find the solace they deserve, then I will leave the Underworld. I will track down my bastard uncle, and I will make him pay. I will rip his heart from his chest and feed it to the vultures of my domain."

"Makar … you heard what your father told Dexios. A God cannot kill another God."

He pulled away from her. The innocent ephebe was gone, replaced by a man consumed by the fires of vengeance.

"That is why I will need you. Will you help me kill Zeus?"

She looked deep into his eyes.

Revenge is never the answer. It can only lead to more pain. A never-ending spiral of hate, each circle bloodier than the last.

Then she thought of Dexios. Of Keres. Of Helydices. But most of all, she thought of Galleas.

And how the Gods had stood aside and watched them die.

There was only one answer she could give.

"I will."

EPILOGUE

"We are told that the Gods are better than us in every way. That they exist on a higher plane of conscience, unburdened by the trivial mundanities that plague our everyday lives. Yet, they fight among themselves like children. They cheat and steal. They are consumed by anger and hate. They do not deserve our faith. Worship should be driven by admiration, not fear and pity."

GRAYCEA, PRIESTESS OF HERA

THE WOMAN RAN along the vaulted corridor, sandals flip-flopping on the polished marble stone. Golden columns twenty feet high flashed past as she accelerated, skirting a gaggle of servants before skidding sharply around a corner to enter another long hallway, this one decorated with lifelike paintings of birds. Hundreds upon hundreds of different species adorned its walls, from the majestic eagle to the iridescent kingfisher.

She barely spared them a second glance as she passed, banging through a door at the far end. The next corridor was in a state of disrepair. Faded tapestries hung tiredly from their frames, moth-eaten and bleached of colour. The gilded capitals were shedding their golden paint, flakes spiralling down from above like autumn leaves. Several became caught in the woman's long hair as she ran past, but she paid them no heed.

Time was of the essence.

A slight frown creased her near-perfect features as she saw that the way ahead was blocked. One of the columns had toppled over, creating a five-foot-high barrier of stone that filled the width of the corridor. The woman put on a burst of speed, vaulting over the obstacle, the tips of her fingers brushing against the marble as she passed.

Pushing through a set of carved double doors, she reached her destination. Spread out on the floor before her was a colossal three-dimensional map of Tyrris, from the scorching southern deserts to the Citrine Wastes far to the north. But it wasn't just a map. It was *moving*. Clouds hovered over the peaks of the Dorias Mountains. Waves crashed and rolled along the western shores. Minuscule triremes the size of twigs crossed the Straits, the wind in their sails.

And at the end of the room stood the map's owner, her stern gaze ever shifting, ever searching. The right part of her face was the epitome of beauty. Long curling locks fell gracefully to frame violet eyes and smooth alabaster skin. The other side was marred by a badly-healed scar that ran from cheek to chin, cutting along the edge of her bottom lip, and pulling it down into a permanent sneer. There was no hair to hide the scar: the entire left part of her head had been shaved down to stubble, leaving her scalp clearly visible.

"Report, Artemis."

"It is worse than we feared, my Queen. Persephone is clamouring for our aid. The barriers around Tartarus have fallen. Hades is dead."

The disfigured woman scowled, the scar heightening her

pout of disapproval. "Trivial. All of this is unfortunate, but not irreparable. What of the energies we have been sensing in Thena? Is it my husband?"

"My spies tell me that he has resurfaced."

"Excellent. It was only a matter of time before his arrogance would betray him. The fool. He should have stayed in whatever pit he crawled into after his catastrophic defeat. Send word to the others. Have the servants bring me my armour and saddle my steed. We ride."

"My Queen … I urge you to be cautious. The last time the Gods were loosed on Tyrris, we … we caused the Citrine Wastes. We were responsible for the deaths of thousands."

"Thousands of *humans*. Their lives are inconsequential. It is their *belief* that matters, and once they see me in the flesh, their faith in me will increase tenfold."

"But …"

"Do not overstep yourself, Daughter. It was not a request. We will not make the same mistake as we made two hundred years ago. They will not escape us. We will track the Ruined to the ends of Tyrris. We will show them no mercy. No respite. No redemption."

Hera, Queen of the Pantheon, reached up and traced her scar with one pale finger.

"And, if I must, I will tear the entire world apart to watch them burn."

End of Book One

THANK YOU

I F YOU ARE reading these words, then you have made it to the end of this book, and I cannot express how thankful I am that you decided to give my indie novel a chance! It's your support and investment that make it possible for writers like me to continue doing what we love. So again, thank you.

There is one more thing you can do before putting this book back on the shelf or deleting it from your e-reader ... and that is to consider leaving a rating and review on Amazon, or any of your other favourite review sites. Reviews are like precious gemstones to self-published authors. Without the humungous marketing budgets of traditional publishers, it is the only way for us to shine a little brighter in an industry where thousands upon thousands of books are published every single day.

Think of it as giving a little more light to my katasterismoi; my tiny constellation in a sea of uncountable stars.

Now, it's time for me to say goodbye and leave you in peace. We'll meet again soon, I promise. I have so many more stories to tell.

In gratitude,

Alex Robins

FREE STORY

SIGN UP TO THE NEWSLETTER FOR A FREE PREQUEL
NOVELLA!

CADUCEUS

SOME LIES CUT DEEPER THAN ANY SWORD

War has come to the fragile city-state of Carenos. A self-proclaimed 'King of the South' sows destruction among its outlying villages, cutting a bloody swathe towards the capital. As smoke from the burning wheat fields blackens the sky, Carenos beseeches its northern allies for aid.

Dexios, general of the Thenean phalanx, is one of those chosen to answer the call. After braving the tumultuous Sea of Scales, he arrives in Carenos at the head of three hundred hoplites, determined to put an end to the enemy incursion.

One threat, however, can often hide another. Something is stirring in the shadows of the sun-drenched lowlands, an age-old legend, abandoned and forgotten. Drawn from its den by the need to satiate its ravenous hunger.

And the enticing scent of blood.

https://warofthetwelve.com/newsletter

IF YOU ENJOYED PANACEA, THEN YOU'LL LOVE ...

THE WAR OF THE TWELVE QUARTET

Over 400 years ago, twelve great warriors united the beleaguered armies of men and scoured the war-torn lands of evil, pushing the enemy back into the underground pits and caverns from whence they came. To ensure their legacy, each of the Twelve founded fortress monasteries to impart their unique knowledge of war and politics to a select few, the Knights of the Twelve.

But now the last of the Twelve have long since passed from history to legend, and the Knights, their numbers dwindling, are harbouring a dark and terrible secret that must be protected at all costs.

The Complete Series is now available on Kindle and Kindle Unlimited

www.ingramcontent.com/pod-product-compliance
Ingram Content Group UK Ltd.
Pitfield, Milton Keynes, MK11 3LW, UK
UKHW040123131224
3629UKWH00022B/126